WHERE THE STARS RISE

ASIAN SCIENCE FICTION & FANTASY
LAKSA ANTHOLOGY SERIES: SPECULATIVE FICTION

EDITED BY LUCAS K. LAW & DERWIN MAK

LAKSA MEDIA GROUPS INC.
www.laksamedia.com

Library and Archives Canada Cataloguing in Publication

Where the stars rise : Asian science fiction and fantasy
/ edited by Lucas K. Law and Derwin Mak.

(Laksa anthology series : speculative fiction)
Issued in print and electronic formats.
ISBN 978-1-988140-04-9 (hardcover). — ISBN 978-0-9939696-5-2 (softcover). — ISBN 978-0-9939696-6-9 (EPUB). — ISBN 978-0-9939696-7-6 (PDF). — ISBN 978-0-9939696-8-3 (Kindle)

1. Fantasy fiction. 2. Science fiction. 3. Short stories, Oriental (English). 4. Short stories, South Asian (English). 5. Short stories, Southeast Asian (English). I. Mak, Derwin, editor II. Law, Lucas K., editor

PN6071.F25W44 2017   823'.087608092   C2017-900079-9
                                                     C2017-900080-2

LAKSA MEDIA GROUPS INC.
Calgary, Alberta, Canada
www.laksamedia.com
info@laksamedia.com

Edited by Lucas K. Law & Derwin Mak
Cover and Interior Design by Samantha M. Beiko

FIRST EDITION

Lucas K. Law

To my nephews and niece,
Ethan Law, Kegan Law, Trinity Law-Boisvert,
Always be proud of who you are and where you come from,
Do not let fear stop you from pursuing your dreams,
But always stay humble and don't forget those less fortunate;
To my extended nephews, nieces, grandnephews
and grandnieces,
Feist, Keller, Scott, Tipton, and Yochim,
Life's a journey and it's never a straight smooth road,
Have courage to step off once in a while to take care of yourself;
To Vancouver Island Regional Library and
Qualicum Beach Library,
For your support of the Qualicum Beach Asian Collection.

Derwin Mak

To my *Aunt Sophie,*
Who gave me a copy of Time-Life's *To the Moon* many years ago.
It was my earliest source of photos and information about space
flight and inspired me to think and write about space.

CONTENTS

FOREWORD
Lucas K. Law

All emotions are universal. Regardless where we come from or where we are going, we live, we dream, we strive, we die.

I see fragments of myself in each of the twenty-three stories you are about to read, from an immigrant to a person caught between two cultures, from the struggle to conform to the meaning of blood, from dealing with a particular culture to accepting the uniqueness in each other, from facing discrimination to finding oneself, from wrestling between ghostly pasts and uncertain future.

Finding oneself is a major theme running through the stories. It often comes when facing adversity. I may not have experienced the exact situations found in this anthology. But, I have to deal with some form of similar struggles—all of us have to if lives are supposed to be lived.

I immigrated to Canada at fifteen, leaving a comfortable world of childhood and high school friends in Borneo, to be a stranger in a strange land of eternal winters (even the summer winds are never fully warm and soothing).

Being different led to discrimination and bullying in school, university, and the workplace. I was called by many names. I was told that my accent was funny and it would hold me back from any future promotions. I was asked to be more extroverted and aggressive at work. I was looked down upon because I lived in the wrong neighbourhood, went to the wrong school, wore the wrong clothes . . . The list went on and on and on—enough to weigh a person down and out. Mentally. Emotionally. Physically. Spiritually. Enough to make one ashamed of his heritage or ancestry or background. It took a long time for me to fully accept myself for being *me*. More than thirty years.

I find that there are people who will put you down, sometimes beyond reasons. But there are others, often strangers, who will pull you up, sometimes without you knowing. Hold on to them, their words, their actions, even if that moment of connection is fleeting. Be grateful for their lessons and words of wisdom. Be kind to pass them forward and give back.

The world is changing so quickly, more information, more news, more of everything—the line continues to blur, facts blend with fiction, truth with lies. There is no one destination but a series of constant challenges and changes, forcing us to make choices, sometimes harsh and bitter, sometimes sudden and alarming, sometimes quick and easy. At times, no choice at all. What we make out of this—choice or no choice—we need to believe in ourselves and find that sliver of hope.

Be proud of who you are and where you come from, and yet, remain humble.

In the end, no one is perfect, but each of us can be unique, honest, real—just like the stories in this anthology. Derwin and I are grateful to Elsie Chapman and the authors for taking us on their journeys, for the glimpses we are given into their fictional lives, for their struggles for acceptance, recognition, and belonging, for reflecting lives in profound and moving ways and finding a voice in history.

Please promote mental health and stand up against discrimination and bullying. Support your local charitable organizations. Support and help each other on this brief journey on Earth. A portion of this anthology's net revenue will go to support Kids Help Phone.

—Lucas K. Law, Calgary and Qualicum Beach, 2017

INTRODUCTION

Elsie Chapman

More diversity in our art, please.

More variety in our books, more colour in our characters, more of all the things that shape the voices and hearts of both.

Simply, *more*.

It's no real secret that when it comes to Asian culture in books, much of what exists remains in the forms of stereotypes, tropes, clichés. Simply put, there aren't enough Asian voices in publishing, and the viewpoint of a westernized lens often narrows rather than focuses.

In science fiction, we are strange geniuses, awkward nerds, small-statured guys in the back of the room who don't stand a chance in the romance subplot.

In fantasy, we are ninjas, monks, kung-fu masters who aren't allowed to articulate much beyond stoic, emotionless silence or short sound bites of deep, life-changing wisdom.

Yet, we're getting somewhere.

This anthology, for one.

When Lucas and Derwin contacted me to ask if I'd be interested in writing the Introduction to *Where The Stars Rise*, I was both honoured and humbled. It was never a question of whether I would do it, but what I could say that could come close to encapsulating why, as a Chinese Canadian, so much about this anthology is a treasure.

Canadian publisher. Indie. Contributors who are either of Asian ethnicity or who have spent significant time living in Asia.

A portion of sales going to Kids Help Phone, the long-standing Canadian counseling service that offers free assistance to kids and teens in need.

Most of all, that this anthology is a celebration of Asian diversity.

Where The Stars Rise is a collection of original Asian-themed stories, crafted from an Asian perspective and envisioned through Asian lenses, and from its first pages, we're taken on journeys. We cross seas to learn of other lands, dive deep into others for the mysteries that lie below; we feel the strange chill of outer space on our skin, smell and taste the unfamiliar air of its new planets.

Two sisters struggle to survive in a society broken by war, natural disaster, and the sudden absence of technology.

A woman, reincarnated over and over again, discovers she can't always outrun the past.

An orphaned child, raised to be a deadly soldier in an off-planet war, begins to question the meaning of blood.

Even beyond being Asian, the characters that fill this anthology are diverse within *themselves*.

Given stories of their own, they are no longer simply checked checkboxes or one-dimensional sidekicks in someone else's narrative. They get to have layered backstories and messy, complicated families. Emotions run on a spectrum. Motives are clouded, questionable, as grey as storms.

Some characters are gay.

Some bend time.

Some are heroes.

But none are perfect, and this makes them infinitely more interesting—more honest, more *real*—than any stereotype.

As mirrors and windows of the diversity of Asian culture, they succeed. Their voices ring true. Embrace them as you read this collection of fresh, innovative stories. Follow where they lead you.

And don't look back.

—Elsie Chapman, Tokyo, Japan, 2017
Author of *Along The Indigo* from Abrams/Amulet

SPIRIT OF WINE
Tony Pi

In the city of Changsha, Song Dynasty China . . .

Catching a sound night's sleep before the prefectural examination? That would be sane.

Forsaking sleep to revisit the Four Books and Five Classics? Commendable prudence.

Yet slipping out to carouse on Market Street?

That was sheer madness.

Be it fever or temptation that lured my sworn brother to this sty they called a tavern, I cared not. Shengming must take and pass this exam, same as me. The prefectural exams were administered once every three years. Fail and we could not take the metropolitan exams in the capital next year. Fail and our dreams would dash like lacquer upon rock.

To my chagrin, Shengming sat chortling in the company of three heavyset men, the table before them cluttered with overturned plates and broken cups. Oblivious to my arrival, he waved in waiters laden with plates of lychee, fried chestnuts and roasted duck, lifted his bowl high and poured millet wine into his grease-smeared mouth. Half his drink spilled down his face, but he finished with a chuckle and swiped his sleeve across his wispy beard. "More wine, Old Boss," he hollered in slurred words.

Across the crowded room, Old Boss bobbed his head like a fat pigeon and dispatched his wife to the task. I hoped he wasn't expecting a decent profit from Shengming tonight. Unless my sworn brother suddenly came into a fortune, he was as poor as I was and could never afford his share of excesses. I hadn't the money to cover his shortfall, but perhaps I could talk sense into his head. With a sigh, I pushed through the throng of patrons to confront my sworn brother.

I wrapped fist-in-hand in greeting. "Kind First Brother, we must go," I pleaded. "If we are to take the exams tomorrow morning—"

Shengming barely acknowledged my arrival. Regarding me with a strange, blank look, he took a bite of a lychee fruit and spat the peel at my feet. "Who in the Hells are you?"

I reddened. "It's Ruolin, of course!" How could he not recognize me? We had been inseparable since we were ten, pushed one another into more mischief than I could remember. We had sworn an oath, burned the contract to register our brotherhood with the heavens, and drank wine mingled with our blood.

"This your brother?" Shengming muttered to himself, making no sense at all. How much had he drunk?

I grabbed my sworn brother by the shoulders. "Shengming, sober up!"

"He doesn't know you, *friend*." Shengming's long-faced drinking companion jabbed a duck leg in my face. "That's as clear as the mole on your nose."

I fought the instinct to shield my nose, to wilt beneath the stare of fat eyes from every table. Heads tilted to hear us, gamblers murmured bets on whether I would throw the first punch. Instead, I rolled back my right sleeve and displayed the proverb inked in green on my inner forearm: *love wine like life.*

嗜酒如命

"He knows me. Why else would he bear the same tattoo, done by the same hand?" The night before we came of age, we had been so drunk that we awakened with more than a hangover. Which of us chose the phrase and why, neither of us could remember, but we laughed and took it as a sign of our unbreakable bond.

Shengming smiled crookedly and lifted his arm, letting his sleeve fall from his skin to prove my claim. "Love wine like life!" he roared and slapped the table. "Delightful, utter delight. I've decided to like you, Ruolin. Join us!"

One of his companions, the rotund one, frowned. "What, you paying for him too?"

Shengming was treating them to the meal? Even if he and I pooled our money together, we would never be able to pay for all this.

"Pay? Huh, forgot about that." Shengming searched through the folds of his clothes and found a small pouch. With great aplomb, he emptied the contents onto the tabletop. Out fell a few paltry coppers.

"*Aiah*," the owner cried. "Who's paying for all you've eaten?"

Shengming's long-faced friend rose to his feet, towering over us. "Not us. This bastard told us he'd cover it."

Unfazed, Shengming drank from his bowl. "So we split the bill, Horse-Face. What's the big deal?"

I really wished I had clamped my hand over Shengming's mouth.

Horse-Face's hands balled into fists. "What did you call me?"

"You heard me," Shengming answered, his words slurred. "You, Ox-Rump and Pig-Fart, should just pay your fair share."

Spurred by Shengming's new insults, the other brutes leapt to their feet, but I surprised them by falling to my knees and kowtowing to them. Had it been anyone else, I might have left him to learn from the beatings to come, but this was First Brother.

"Honoured gentlemen: I, the insignificant, beg you forgive my First Brother for his thoughtless words," I said in my meekest voice. Not that I could fault Shengming for such apt descriptions of the three, but I knew better than to voice those thoughts. "Whenever he drinks, the wine in turn consumes him. Please, take all he says to be drunken jests. I will find a way to pay for all he owes."

Horse-Face grabbed a fistful of robe and hoisted me to my feet. "You better."

"Hells, you'll do no such thing." Shengming spat on the ground. "They eat, they pay."

"See how he turns witless when he's drunk?" I said. "Shengming, we must settle the account and go. If we linger here, we'll miss the exams!"

Shengming spat on the ground again. "Why should we care about boring exams when the wine still calls to us? Drink with me, Ruolin."

I could not believe what he had just said. "Have you forgotten your promise? When your father took ill, you prayed that he might live to see you enter the civil service, to see you bring honour to your family. By divine grace he convalesced, but you must keep your oath to the gods, First Brother."

Shengming ignored me and squinted at his bowl instead. "Empty. Pig-Fart, pour me another!"

Pig-Fart's face contorted and he unleashed his fist straight at Shengming's face.

Miraculously, the blow did not connect. In his drunken stupor, Shengming toppled backward off his stool, landing with a crash. Almost as swiftly as he fell, he staggered to his feet and looked around in confusion. "I seem to have misplaced my bowl."

Horse-Face roared and tossed me with one hand onto the next table, startling the patrons. Grabbing a stool, he hurled it at Shengming, but by stupendous luck, my sworn brother swayed just enough for it to sail harmlessly past his ear.

I rolled off the tabletop just as customers scurried to the edges of the room to avoid the brawl. By now, Ox-Rump had jumped into the thick of the fight, but Shengming still seemed oblivious to the danger. Pig-Fart barred the way, Horse-Face grasped to catch hold of Shengming, and Ox-Rump sought to pummel my blood brother into the dust. Yet Shengming was a drunkard on a singular mission: stumbling haphazardly left and right, he sidestepped punches that could break his jaw, somersaulted between Horse-Face's tree-trunk legs, all so that he could regain his feet in front of the owner's wife and snatch the pot of wine from her.

I could not believe my eyes. What I had taken for luck had not been that at all, but well-disguised fighting skill. Was this *Zui Quan*, Drunken Boxing? If so, how could Shengming have learned it?

The wiser customers had long fled, while the not-so-wise at

least had the presence of mind to take cover.

"All at once," Horse-Face shouted, and they converged on Shengming. Horse-Face grabbed high, Pig-Fart tackled low, and Ox-Rump circled behind. Their concerted effort paid off: Shengming could not avoid them all. As they struggled to hold my sworn brother, who fought back with supernatural strength, the pot of wine he dropped in the heat of battle rolled to a stop at my feet.

"My wine!" Shengming reached toward me even as his three attackers brought him down.

I picked up the ceramic pot, not sure what to do with it. Diplomacy hadn't worked, and I had no love of violence. But to save Shengming's life—

"*Love wine like life,*" Shengming shouted.

I felt as though the sky and earth had turned upside down and upended me into a vat of heavenly wine. I had to drink, drink, *drink* lest I drown.

The phantom wine coursed through me, warmed me, oozed from my pores. Like a spirit, it wore my skin like silk. I was at the mercy of the ghost's whims and thirsts; it lifted the pot of wine and pressed my lips to the ceramic. The spirit stole my voice and spoke in a liquid slur: "Aaaaaah, at last."

Anguish darkened Shengming's face. "No, don't take Ruolin! Can't you just leave us alone?"

Oh, *now* he recognized me.

I tried calling his name (*Shengming!*), but the words echoed in my head like a holler into an empty vat.

The spirit winced with my face. "Don't shout."

The brutes must have sensed Shengming weakening. "Hold him. He won't have a face when I'm through," Horse said to Ox and Pig. He let go and began rolling up his sleeves.

I, or rather *we*, took drunken steps and smashed the container of wine over the back of Horse's head. The oaf went limp and fell forward on top of Shengming, but the unwelcomed guest in my body cared only that the pot had cracked open, and held it up so the stream of Shaoxing rice wine poured straight into our mouth.

With Shengming trapped under Horse's weight, Ox and Pig released their holds on him and grabbed for us-both, but our knees gave out and we fell out of their grasp flat on our ass. The better fighter of the pair, Ox tried to kick us, but thanks to the spirit's Drunken Boxing we-both pushed off the ground and tottered backward. None of Ox's strikes landed.

I caught the stink of feces above the reek of wine.

Look out. I cried in my mind's voice.

The spirit heard and ducked us-both beneath a punch from behind, spun around to face the reeking Pig and sprayed a mouthful of wine into the fat man's eyes. Blinded, Pig swung wildly at us, but we merely stepped aside and slapped the man silly.

Roaring in anger, Ox grabbed a stool and swung it at us-both, and would have hurt us but for someone catching his foot. Shengming had somehow freed himself from under Horse and tripped Ox! Using Ox's own momentum, we-both sent him crashing into Pig. They fell together into unconsciousness.

Who are you? I shouted at the spirit.

We-both smiled and struck a wobbly pose, hands seemingly cupped around invisible vessels of wine.

"Who am I?

I'm thirst and craving, the loosened tongue;

I'm all troubles fled, fast friend and quick anger;

I champion folly, sing melancholy songs;

I'm the Spirit of Wine, God of the Drunken Fist:

I am *Yǒu Shén!*"

When we-both began giving that mad speech, the tavern fell deathly silent. Those who could sneak out, did. Only Shengming took the courage to speak to us-both.

"Yǒu Shén, spare Ruolin, please," he pleaded, still sounding drunk. "I do not care whether I take the exam, but he must. He'll go as far as the palace exams, I know it."

Thank you, First Brother, I tried to say, but my mouth would not obey.

The spirit heard me, however. "It's me you should thank. Life as a bureaucrat is a fate worse than death! You know what life's true pleasures are? *Flowers in heaven, wine on earth; lanterns red, spirits green,*" Yǒu Shén said, quoting two proverbs.

Those are fleeting, selfish joys that lead only to shame! I cried. *When*

Shengming and I become Doctors of Letters, we will bring honour and security to our families.

As the owner picked up pieces of broken ceramic and bamboo, a whimper escaped his lips, only to grow into a scream. "Look what you did to my tavern, you sons of bitches! Get out!"

Yǒu Shén blinked and surveyed at the damage. "Huh, I guess we made a mess." We-both bent over Ox-Rump and searched him, and laughed when our fingers closed around a pouch full of coins. We-both tossed it to the owner. "This ought to pay for it, Old Boss."

"The exams—" Shengming protested.

"Forget them," Yǒu Shén said. He slung our arm around Shengming, our weight bearing down on his shoulders. "Come, let us find another place to drink away the night together!" With Shengming in tow, we-both lurched toward the door.

"I'm so sorry, Second Brother, I was just after a drink to calm my nerves, not this," Shengming said, his voice full of remorse. "You must write the exam. If you find the chance, run."

We stumbled across the granite road to a different restaurant, but news of our fight spread ahead of us through the shops on Taiping Jie, and we were turned away at the door. Yǒu Shén shrugged and tried the next, but we were met with the same refusal. The spirit was growing upset.

"Yǒu Shén, try the one with the birdcage outside," Shengming urged. "They're rivals with Old Boss Tao."

Listen to him, I said. *We need to get out of sight before the city guard arrives.*

Though drunk, Yǒu Shén heeded our advice. When we entered the new restaurant, the sweaty owner welcomed us with a smirk. "Honoured guests! Eat, drink on the house . . . so long as you don't smash up my place like you did Tao's."

"Wouldn't think of it," Yǒu Shén said, pinching the owner's cheek. "You, sir, are the soul of generosity."

"Er, thank you?" The man ushered us through the half-empty restaurant to a table hidden under the stairs. As promised, he kept the wine flowing, and we-both kept guzzling. But Shengming would not drink.

"You must. Two drunks together are better than a drunk alone!" Yǒu Shén said, and laughed.

Still, Shengming refused. Even when Yǒu Shén forced the cup to his lips, Shengming kept his mouth shut and turned away in disgust.

Yǒu Shén sneered. "Won't do. *Love wine like life!*"

With the proverb uttered, I felt the spirit leave my body. But before I could rejoice, a pounding headache and a sudden fatigue hit me. Although the world was still spinning around me, my head felt somewhat less muddled.

Shengming, on the other hand, closed his eyes and began to swig like a thirsty fish.

This was my chance to escape, I realized, but could I abandon Shengming, even though he wished it? Five years ago, we would have been content to drink our lives away. But the triumphs of the Song Army against the Jurchens in the north had returned stability in this province, allowing Yuelu Academy to reopen years ahead of expectations. We decided then to devote ourselves to scholarship and make something of our lives. I could not leave him like this.

Yet this spirit would hold us prisoner for his own amusement. I understood the logic behind Shengming wanting me to run: having one of us take the exams was better than neither of us taking them. I did not like the thought of abandoning him, but I could not let his noble sacrifice come to naught.

I slipped onto my hands and knees and scurried toward the exit. I made it across the floor to the threshold when I heard Shengming's voice: "But Ruolin, my friend, you can't go yet. We've songs to sing!" He shouted the proverb again, and the Spirit of Wine slopped back into me and made us crawl back to Shengming, who was retching up what he had been forced to drink.

As the night wore on, Yǒu Shén would flitter between us, keeping us drunk and bellowing bawdy songs. The spirit would leave me, I would try to flee, but they-both would speak the words of binding and make me Yǒu Shén's puppet.

SPIRIT OF WINE by Tony Pi

Before I knew it, Shengming and I were the only patrons left in the restaurant, with the owner in a corner half-asleep, trying to keep an eye on us. Yǒu Shén was using Shengming to tell me how in life he had been expelled from a monastery for drunkenness.

Then I heard it: in the distance, a cannon-shot.

Three cannon-shots were fired on the morning of the exams. The first came well before dawn to wake the candidates. Shengming and I should be collecting brushes and ink sticks and drilling each other on the Classics instead of drinking ourselves to death in this tavern. In an hour, the cannon would fire again, calling all candidates to the gates of the examination hall. On the third sounding, the great doors would be thrown open. Even if we could make it there, how could we sober up in time to wrestle with eight-legged essays?

No, there was still time. I could hardly think straight, but maybe if I figured out what Yǒu Shén was, I might find a way to break free.

There had been rumours of spirits ever since General Yue Fei returned from the dead eighteen years ago. The Jin barbarians had stolen the northern lands from our Empire, and Yue Fei the hero had fought to reclaim what we could. No one was as loyal as he. But Minister Qin Hui had been a spy for the Jin and framed the General for treason. After his execution, however, Yue Fei's spirit could not rest. He possessed one of his loyal men and revealed Qin Hui's treachery, and to this day continued to lead the Song Army against the Jin. They called Yue Fei the Spirit General, for he had led other spirits in the war against the Jin, or so the rumours went. There were many tales of ghostly possession and unearthly powers, but who knew which accounts were true.

I doubted that Yǒu Shén served the Spirit General, but what if they were connected? I had to find out more about the Spirit of Wine. There was another proverb that fit the moment: *a cup of wine dissolves complaints*. I poured myself and Shengming more wine. "Drink up."

Yǒu Shén blinked. "Come around, have you?"

I nodded. "You are right, wine *is* better in the company of friends. What brings you to Changsha?"

"Changsha, is it?" they-both said. "Why's this place called

long sand?"

"Because of the Island of Oranges in the Xiang River here. It is long and made of sand."

Yǒu Shén laughed and slapped my back. "Makes sense, but which province? All I know is I came north when Shengming called."

"Hunan. So you were not fighting in the war with the Spirit General?"

They-both burped. "War's not my love, in case you haven't noticed. But living, drinking and pissing—speaking of which, where can I—"

The owner must have caught that last bit, for he startled awake. "Outside!"

"Thank you, Boss," Yǒu Shén said. They-both stood up, tottering. "Help me, Ruolin."

I thanked the owner as well. With an unopened pot of wine under my left arm and supporting them-both with the right, we left the restaurant and headed for the woods by the river. I was glad for the night air clearing my head.

"You said Shengming called for you?" I asked as we stumbled down an alleyway. "How did he do that?"

"He must have been muttering his tattooed proverb," Yǒu Shén said. "His need for a drink was great: I could feel it all the way from Guangzhou. Besides, I was in the mood for a new host, and look what I found? Two!"

Lucky us. But Yǒu Shén gave me a clue, one I might have caught earlier had I not been drunk: the tattoos on our arms.

General Yue Fei was a paragon of loyalty. As his legend told, his mother tattooed the words *utmost loyalty serve country* down his back. In worship of their war hero, soldiers fighting under Yue Fei chose to bear the same tattooed phrase when they came of age. The custom caught on with youth like us outside of the army, but instead of words of loyalty, we took catchy proverbs in their place, be they on our backs or elsewhere on our bodies. The proverb Shengming and I bore must have made us vulnerable to Yǒu Shén's magic!

They-both paused in front of a grove of Xiang Consorts bamboos. "Wait here."

"Of course." I would not run this time.

They both stepped into the shadows to do their thing, while I considered the puzzle. What was the key to Yǒu Shén's power?

Then it struck me: his name. He styled himself the Spirit of Wine, but the word for wine was *jiǔ*, not *yǒu*. He should have called himself Jiǔ Shén. Why not?

The word *yǒu* in his name must be the character for the tenth sign of the zodiac, the Rooster. The pictogram for it derived from a wine vessel, and that character still appeared in words tied to wine, like *feast*, *flushed*, and *drunk*.

Only when combined with the strokes symbolizing three drops of water did it make the word for *wine*.

Could such spirits be tied to particular ideograms, and that they could possess those who bore their tattooed characters?

I wondered if marring the right tattoo would break the hold Yǒu Shén had over me, but I did not have a knife, nor would I trust myself to handle one while drunk. I leaned against the bamboos, frustrated. There must be something I could do!

Yǒu Shén continued to piss somewhere nearby, singing off-key.

The nearby sounds of the Xiang River reminded me of its myth. When Emperor Shun died on this river, his two wives wept tears of blood for their husband, which stained the bamboos and gave them their spots. Unable to live without their husband, they threw themselves into the river and drowned. Ever since, the Consorts had been worshipped as goddesses in this region.

River.

Tears.

Water.

If the Spirit of Wine made me drunk with its power, could I summon the Spirit of Water to sober me up?

It might work. The word for *wine* needed both the characters for *yǒu* and *shuǐ*, represented by three drops of water. But did such a spirit exist? Would it come if I called, and would it help?

I did not know either answer, but I had to try. I repeated the proverb in a whisper, but kept the thought of water in my heart. Cool, refreshing water; raindrops on my tongue; the surging, cleansing river. I begged that the Spirit of Water hear my call, for great was my need in this hour.

My mouth suddenly stopped repeating the phrase, and a new spirit flowed into me, washing away my lethargy and intoxication as she flooded my body. Unlike Yǒu Shén, whose possession of me warmed my belly, Shuǐ Shén cooled and brought me back to my senses.

"I heard your call, stranger," she said, borrowing my voice.

I, who belong to a younger generation, welcome you, Honourable Shuǐ Shén. But I must beg you to act drunk while I explain, I conveyed. *My name is Ruolin, and my sworn brother and I are unwilling hosts to a spirit named Yǒu Shén.*

"Ah," she replied. "The self-styled Spirit of Wine. I know him only by reputation. He is a free spirit, that one."

Footfalls signaled Shengming and Yǒu Shén's return.

Please, let him think you are me, I begged. We needed to distract Yǒu Shén long enough so I could tell Shuǐ Shén our predicament. *Offer him the pot of wine.*

"Old spirit!" she called to them-both in my voice. "Drink?"

"Need you ask?" They-both snatched the pot, broke open the seal, then sank into a lotus position to savour the wine.

Thank you, I said.

I'm listening.

We-both pretended to listen to Yǒu Shén serenading the rabbit in the moon, while speaking to one another in the privacy of my mind. I told her as quickly as I could of the disasters of this night: the imperial examinations, the fight, Yǒu Shén's forceful carousing.

I am forever in your debt for restoring my better judgment, but might you be able to do the same for Shengming? I asked. *Though the first cannon has sounded, we might still make the exams if we could rid ourselves of Yŏu Shén.*

You ask much from a stranger, Ruolin, Shuǒ Shén replied. *But why should I help you?*

Forgive my presumption, I said. *I prayed that Water would be nobility to Wine's baseness. Should you choose not to aid us, I would thank you nonetheless for your kindness in considering my request at all, and seek another way to save my sworn brother.*

Honing your skills at flattery, I see. Why don't you and I escape now? I can stop Yŏu Shén from possessing you.

It is tempting, I admitted. *But I am writing the imperial exams for my family, as is Shengming. He and I are sworn brothers and I cannot leave him in Yŏu Shén's thrall. The guilt would distract me when I write the test, and I would fail everyone I loved. When I dream of what is to come, Shengming has always been there by my side. My conscience will not let me abandon him.*

Your loyalty is admirable, Shuǐ Shén said. *Very well, I will help you. We must drive the old spirit out somehow.*

If I knew more about your powers, perhaps I could formulate a plan, I said.

You have done well to deduce the powers of spirits on your own, Shuǐ Shén commended. *We are tied to a single character and draw power from that word. So the Spirit of Wine revels in his drunken strength, and I in the nature of water. Because your tattooed proverb bears both our characters, we may both borrow your flesh.*

Borrow? Yŏu Shén stole our bodies!

Only because he learned the phrase tattooed on your body, Shuǐ Shén revealed. *A host who keeps his tattoo secret could oust a spirit guest at his leisure. Think of the proverb as a spell—if he speaks it and you hear it, he becomes the master.*

Might I ask if a spirit can die?

It is impolitic to ask someone the means to their own destruction, she said.

I apologized. *It is only that I need to learn what spirits fear, so that I might understand what might motivate Yŏu Shén to leave us.*

This much I'll say: the death of a host leaves a spirit adrift without a body until he is summoned again. But would you kill your sworn brother to be rid of Yŏu Shén?

No, but the threat of it might be enough. A plan started coming together, but it would be dangerous for both Shengming and me. *Can you defeat his Drunken Boxing, if it came to that?*

I cannot match him in strength. But, in the art of self-defence, I'm as light and slippery as rain, thanks to my mastery of Qing Gong.

So she knew the 'light body skill,' allowing the practitioner to step onto a leaf on water and float without sinking or scale a wall with feather-soft steps. *Then it must be a water battle,* I said, incorporating what I just learned into my strategy. *Are you able to relinquish control over my body for a while?*

That is within my power, but what do you intend?

They say that the poet Li Bai drowned when he drunkenly tried to embrace the reflection of the moon in the Yangtze River, I said. *Let us see how Yǒu Shén would fare.*

The second cannon-shot echoed through the early morning. We were running out of time.

Shuǐ Shén flowed to the edges of my being, becoming coolness under my skin as I rejoiced in regaining the use of my body.

As for Shengming, they-both were nodding off, still cradling the empty pot.

"Yǒu Shén!" I said, startling them-both awake. "Did you know that the Island of Oranges is one of the Eight Views of Hunan?"

"No, I didn't! Something to see, then?"

"Indeed, and more. The oranges there are spectacular. Sweeter than honey, they say. I can almost taste it now."

They-both licked their lips. "Sounds delicious."

"Why don't we go? It's a short swim, and the Xiang River flows slowly." Please, let this seem like a marvellous idea to the old drunk!

Though at first they-both were hesitant, Yǒu Shén was soon persuaded by my ever-growing praise for the oranges.

"Race you to the island," I shouted, shedding my clothes as I ran for the water's edge, toward a stretch of the riverbank I knew well. They-both followed, discarding clothing as they dashed after me.

The shadows were deep, making it hard to see where the water met the shore. I told Shuǐ Shén: *Use your Qing Gong now, if you can!*

Shuǐ Shén reclaimed control, and it felt as though our insides turned to mist. We-both seemed to dart across the water, our big toes lightly touching wet dross floating upon the surface.

Behind us-both came a loud splash, then shouts for help. Yǒu Shén had fallen into the river where I knew it to be deep. In their drunken stupor, swimming could not be the easiest thing. We-both turned and dashed back toward them.

Yǒu Shén was crying out *love wine like life,* and the characters tattooed on my arm began to burn. Even now he was trying to take over my body. But Shuǐ Shén soothed my skin from within, denying him entry.

Let me carry out the plan, I said to Shuǐ Shén. *If anything goes wrong, I must take full responsibility.*

"Are you sure?" Shuǐ Shén asked.

I am. I want Yǒu Shén gone and Shengming back.

She released control to me, and I fell into the water next to Shengming-Yǒu Shén. They-both were flailing wildly, but instead of trying to save them, I threw my arms around their neck, letting my weight drag them deeper into the water.

They-both were frantic now, their drunkenness not helping them to stay afloat. Their wild strength almost threw me off, but I held on as best I could and focused on holding my breath and keeping calm while they-both lost air. Yǒu Shén could try to shout the binding words all he wanted, but it would only hasten him to drown. My fear was that I would not know if or when the spirit would let Shengming go.

At last, I felt a change: the struggling grew weaker and air stopped bubbling out of their mouth. Had Yǒu Shén really left Shengming, or was he bluffing?

No, it had to be Shengming. Drunken Yǒu Shén could not have the guile to fake it, I prayed. I pulled Shengming to the surface and hauled him onto shore.

He wasn't breathing. Had I drowned him?

"Live, First Brother!" I cried as I held him.

Allow me, Shuǐ Shén said, and took over. We-both whispered *love wine like life* into Shengming's ear, and with its magic Shuǐ Shén poured out of me and into him.

Shengming finally stirred, coughing up a lungful of water.

I breathed a sigh of relief. "Thank you, Shuǐ Shén."

They-both smiled. "What's a little water to me?"

I let them-both go and kowtowed. "Forgive me, Second Brother."

"He says you are forgiven," Shuǐ Shén replied on Shengming's behalf. "I've purged the drunkenness from him, and he should soon regain strength enough to take the exams. Good luck with them, both of you."

"We are forever in your debt," I said.

"Careful, I may take you at your word. Ruolin, watch over Shengming as you always have. Be unswerving in your loyalty and you are destined to go far in service to the Empire. Summon me now and again, for I am curious to follow your rise," Shuǐ Shén said.

"I will."

With that, she ebbed away from Shengming, who laughed and gave me a wet, hearty squeeze. "Good to be me again, Second Brother. Thank you."

I grinned. "Enough of that. If we hurry, we can get our things and still make it to the examination hall before the third cannon. You well enough to write the exam?"

"Compared to what we've been through tonight?" Shengming said. "Eight-legged exams are nothing."

I nodded. "Promise me one thing, Brother."

"What?"

"That we will never drink wine again."

THE dataSULTAN OF STREETS AND STARS

Jeremy Szal

The alien slams me up against the station walls so hard I think he's broken my spine. If I didn't activate my arm-bands of my skinsuit in time to cushion the impact he might have. I try to squirm out of his grasp but it's like pushing against an iron wall.

I throw my hands up. "You win. Just let go off me."

His grip tightens. "Try to run again and I will snap your neck, Bohdi."

I'd planned on darting away as soon as he released me, but now I think the better of it. I'm a short, scruffy guy and it won't be hard for him to catch me. He releases me, and I slide down the wall, raking in gulps of air.

"Humans." Zuqji Sma shakes his head. Like most Ghadesh, he's two metres tall with a stocky body. Thick tubes snake in and out of his carapace-like armour, recycling oxygen to match the methane atmosphere of his Dyson sphere home. But we're both far from home in Anăcet Station, a place built in the mined-out husk of a metallic asteroid. Most of the folk here are humans, but there are a few Ghadesh wandering around. The cosmos rolls the dices, and *of course* I bump into him of all people.

"Let's have a talk, shall we?" Sma pokes me in the chest. He's cut himself from the sharp edge of the metal wall, and a few droplets of his green-blue blood spatters on my chest.

I shrug.

We go to a Lebanese shop that sells Arab-style coffee. The turbaned owner does the physical work while his djinn performs the electronic activities, flipping the machine on and rotating the dispenser. Wispy smoke floats up to the mosaic ceiling. I can't remember a time when we didn't use djinns to assist us. A kilometre-long starship glides by our viewport, a testament to human engineering. Humans might have designed it, but djinns built it.

The djinn-bot arrives with our cups of steaming liquid blackness. The stuff is overpriced, and somehow I doubt Sma's going to be paying for it.

"You wanted something?" There's no way in hell I'm catching my ship now, so I might as well humour him.

"Of course." Sma doesn't touch his coffee. From the way he sits, you'd think his spine was made of steel. For all I know about Ghadesh biology, it probably is. The one thing I do know about Ghadesh is that their armour shifts in colour to match their mood, and right now his is only starting to dial down from pitch black. "I hear they're making new djinns on Earth, yes?"

"They're always making new djinns." There's no reason I have to make it easy for him.

Sma's rectangular pupils narrow to cold grey slits. I've never noticed just how *grey* they are. "I mean high-tier djinn. Ones that can pilot ships without any assistance. You would know about this, yes?"

"They are," I respond. "They won't be on the market for years."

You can almost see the *I've got you now* twinkle in Sma's eye. "Now that is where you come in."

"I'm not going back to Istanbul," I tell him. "Not after what happened."

"What *exactly* happened down there? The GalaNet has been rather quiet."

He probably knows, but I tell him anyway. We're always attempting to improve the djinns, raise their tier so they can juggle together activities and for longer. We were so, *so* close to crafting djinn capable of deep space asteroid mining. We'd unveiled them in a conference room to investors in the business.

Only there'd been a malfunction and the djinns had gone rogue, killing a dozen people.

I'd been the dataSultan, one of the lead programmers.

We shushed it up afterwards, but my superiors recommended I skipped Earth and waited for things to cool down. The families of the deceased were powerful people with deep pockets and shallow mercy. Still, it's unlikely they'd chase me across space.

Sma leans back on his seat, the divan creaking under his weight. "Hmm. Fascinating. *Very* fascinating. You really did mess up, didn't you?"

"With a dozen people dead and a bounty hanging over me? You could say so," I respond.

"Well, I have a proposition for you." The sarcasm seems to have gone over his head. "I want you to go back to Istanbul and get me one of those djinn-7s. They should be sorted out by now, yes?"

"Probably, but I won't be going back there," I tell him.

His eyes narrow again and his armour darkens. "You act as if you have a choice in the matter."

"I'll damn sure say I do."

A sudden blur and I glance down to see a pistol folding out of his metal sleeve. Thousands of miniscule metallic bits scramble over each other like glossy black ants, coalescing to form a revolver pointed straight at me. Unnervingly, from this angle he's got it aimed at my crotch. I make it my goal of *never* having pointy things prodded in this general direction.

"Never had a coffee date go *this* badly." I do my best to smile as I pretend to inspect my drink. "Say, what exactly did you put in this?"

Sma is not amused. "You're going to get that djinn, regardless if you want to or not."

"Why me?" I demand.

He taps the veins on my forearm. It's a challenge not to recoil from his blood-warm touch. "The djinn-7s are synced to your DNA. You have those implants that allow you to enter the systems. Do not try to fool me; we both know you're the only one who can do it."

It's scary how much he knows about the whole thing. I was

stupid to underestimate him.

"Do so and I'll forgive your debt."

"No debt is worth that much!"

"After everything I have done for you and your brother, I am letting you off lightly."

The knot in my chest tightens. These people don't come after you, they come after your family first. I'd turned to Sma to put us into hiding and steal me across space safely. You wave the right card to the right people and they can't get you through fast enough.

I always knew he'd come calling in my debt, but not here, not now.

"Perhaps I can give your friends a call." Those grey eyes flicker like water slipping through sand. He leans so close I can see his hacksaw teeth. "Maybe I can tell them where to find your brother."

I haven't seen my brother in years, not since he turned to a life of poverty as a dervish man. It happened after Father had been killed in an anti-Muslim pogrom, leaving both of us orphans. I think my brother couldn't handle the responsibility.

But it doesn't matter where he is; I know Sma will kill him. He'll do it. I know he will. A single call and we're smeared out of existence. My throat's filled with concrete, nerves electric.

I can only play along.

I take a sip of my insanely overpriced coffee, far too bitter for my liking, and smile. "I suppose I can reconsider."

"It looks like you have nowhere to go." Sma readjusts his grip on the gun, still pointing toward my groin. "Do we have a deal?"

The sticky heat presses down on the shoulders—the sort that only comes from the worst a Turkish summer can offer. Hulking starships slice through the sky, fashioned like the old Phoenician ships. If I look closely, I think I can see the one that dropped me here a few hours ago, shooting off to the Dubai and Cairo spaceports. I wish I was back on that ship. I *should* be on the ship.

But I'm not: because I'm an idiot. My head sways and my legs wobble; after spending so much time in artificial gravity and in space stations; coming down to terra firma makes me want to throw up.

I walk through the streets of Istanbul. The city's a patchwork, skyscrapers and apartments merging with ancient minarets and mosques: the muezzin call almost being drowned out by the whine of djinn-bots. Dolmuşes shuttle through mosaic bazaars of spice shops and computer workshops. There's no border of where the old ends and the new begins. They all bleed and twist into each other, people packed into buildings like seeds in an urban pomegranate.

I watch the djinn peeling a starship apart at the shipment yard. I'm guessing that these djinn are medium-tier, careful to avoid collision and only taking equipment they can carry. Like all djinn they're bound to a single physical bot, so there's only so much they can do. Human assistance is still required. We made certain of that.

Further down the road, a mosque rubs shoulders with a freelancing hub where ifrit hackers purge software daemons from computer systems. Their veins pulse with dark blue nanoImplants that allow their bodies the capacity to hook up to the computer systems, otherwise the acceleration will fry your brain. They strap you into a chair and pump nanoImplants directly into the vein. It's like a fingerprint on a molecular level.

I'm out of my skinsuit now and wearing normal clothes, doing my best to merge with the fabric of the city. Me and my brother Omar used to live on this street as boys. I even spot our old house, fashioned from old Ottoman wood, converted into a café where old men chug away at hookahs, complaining about all the immigrants from Greece and Lebanon.

Me and Omar had formed a gang of sorts, trying to nick as many lokums as possible. We even managed to capture a djinn-bot and used it to transport our sweets from place to place. It's incredible we lasted as long as we did—all of five days—before we were caught and taken to our parents.

Omar fell on his own sword—claiming that it was his idea when it had been mine—and he'd just dragged me into it. Father didn't buy his speech and gave us the beating of our lives. I hated

Father for it then, but now I'd give anything to have him back.

The Muqarna building stretches tall over in the distance—the birthplace of every djinn. A lump forms in the back of my throat. I know that the rogue djinns aren't my fault, but it's hard to convince yourself after seeing the bloody body remains and knowing you had a hand in it.

I sense someone is behind me. Not making much of an effort to stay hidden. Too big and clumsy to be a beggar or thief.

It has to be one of the gangs. I've been back one day and they've found me already.

My heart jackhammers in my chest, and I'm about to dart away when the figure closes the gap between us and locks an arm around my neck, bundling me into an alley on the side and into a dark room so fast I barely have time to think. I'm wondering if they'll slit my throat straight away or take their time when the lights jump to life and I see my assailant.

It's Omar, my brother.

He's clad in a white cloak with a slash of red over his shoulders, a turban wound around his head. I can't even pretend to hide my relief. "You gave me one hell of a scare you know?"

No reply. We're in a dingy little çayhouse room: jallab cups littered over a greasy bench, broken iznik pottery scattered on the floor. Half a dozen dervishes squint at me. Omar snaps his fingers and spits out a string of sentences, and they scuttle away.

For the first time in a decade, we're alone.

"What are you doing here, Sikandar?" I almost flinch at hearing my real name. "You've got killers looking everywhere for you."

After all this time, that's his welcome. That's my brother for you. He's a few years older than me but looks like he's centuries ahead. A life of seeking tariqah has not been kind to him. "How do you know about that?"

He scratches his matted beard and taps the side of his head. "I hear things. People don't think beggars or dervishes are listening. They're wrong. Dwell in the streets for long enough and you learn many things." He sighs. "There is a blessing in having nothing."

His reasoning for walking this path of austerity was so he could draw closer to Allah. But how do you spend your days squatting in poverty when starships kilometres long soar above you? When the roar of their space-faring engines are louder and more authoritative than any muezzin call ever could be?

I left the city as soon as I could. I felt stifled by its old-fashionedness. I was just a boy when Istanbul became the first metropolis in the world to construct space stations and make contact with aliens, opening up commercial spaceports a few years later in 2078. I slipped away as soon as I could, studying djinn programming off-world. I'd embraced the modern and Omar had slid in the opposite direction.

"You need to leave," he says. "Azhar Kaadesh wants your head on a silver platter. He's flown all the way from Dubai to look for you." I shiver despite the muggy heat. One of the most dangerous men in this corner of the world, and he's after me. "They've already found one of the other dataSultans. He washed up on the shores of the Bosphorus in pieces. Barely recognizeable."

I try not to dwell on that. "I can't leave. Otherwise we're both dead."

"Why? What's happened?" His hands curl into tight fists and I wonder if he's going to strike me. "Please don't tell me you went to a Ghadesh for help." My silence seems to be a sufficient answer. "All of people! You *know* those creatures can't be trusted."

"I need to break into the Muqarna. That's all."

He shakes his head. "You'll ruin us, Sikandar."

My temper flares. "At least I'm trying to protect our family. What the hell do you do all day?" I know I'm shouting, but I don't care. He needs to hear this. "You just squat in the mud and pray to a god who doesn't give a toss about any of us. You don't get to judge. Not anymore."

Omar bites his cracked lips, and I can see that I've wounded him. "I'm sorry Omar. I didn't mean to—"

He waves a hand. "Don't. You're probably right." He sinks down to the floor next to me. "After Father died—" He halts midsentence. This is the first time I've heard him speak about Father. "I couldn't face the world so I turned to Allah." He smiles that watery smile of his. "Although it seems he has not turned to me. Not yet." He shakes his head. "I'm sorry I abandoned you, Sika. I failed you all."

Sika. Father used to call me that. I swallow. "You can still help.

I just need to get inside."

"You work there, don't you? Can't you just go inside?"

"I'm not supposed to be in this city, remember? They have eyes and ears everywhere." I can't help but wonder if they already know where I am. I peer out the bug-spattered window and at the hulking skyscraper, half a kilometre of carved marble, glass and technology. "There has to be another way."

"You never were one for playing it safe." He ponders for a moment. "Give me a few days. I'll listen around, see if I can pick up anything useful." Again that watery smile. "You stay low in the meantime. We wouldn't want to lose your head, would we?"

I would have laughed, but right now it's not even funny.

I'm on top of the world.

The summer wind drifts out to the Mediterranean, tousling my hair. Istanbul yawns out like an endless Mughal carpet. Streets run like rivers through buildings of blood red, saffron yellow, and bronze. The air is electric with the whine of shuttles and starships from the spaceport that eats up kilometres of the city's space. If I look closely, I can even see bots ghosting through the air, each and every one containing its own unique djinn.

Just not the type I'm after.

I'm perched near the lip of the Muqarna. Getting up here was the easy part—it was just a matter of hacking the access code and climbing the stairwell of the adjacent building and hopping across. Omar had indeed found a way. There's a little balcony near the top of the Muqarna. He'd overheard two dataSultans mentioning the jammed door and they were having trouble closing it.

That's my way in. It's a matter of getting down there.

I'm back in my skinsuit, helmet sealed tight around my neck. I wear a harness, the sort that they use in abseiling but designed to be lightweight and skin-tight. I've hooked the magnetic clamp at the edge of the building and tested it and the shoulders straps half a dozen times more than necessary. But if I fall down, it's not going to be pretty. I grin and briefly wonder how long they'd have to scrub the pavement to get bits of me out of it.

THE dataSULTAN OF STREETS AND STARS by Jeremy Szal

With a deep breath, I slowly descend. The harness groans, bites into my armpits and squeezes a little too tightly around my groin. I feel every square inch of the altitude beneath me, aware that only a few strips of webbing are keeping me alive. Carefully, carefully I continue lowering myself, boots clunking on the thick glass.

My hand slips on the webbing and for a moment I'm freefalling. Heart in mouth I tug on the wiring and jerk midair, slamming against the glass with enough force to splinter my ribs. For a moment, I think I black out; I don't know which way is up or down. A mix of sweat and fear trickles down my spine. This is stupid; I'm going to get myself killed. For a moment, I'm tempted to call the whole thing off and just tell Sma to screw himself, or whatever it is the Ghadesh do. But that'd be signing my brother's death warrant in my blood.

No. I have to see this through.

I scrape together the dregs of my sanity and continue. Ten minutes of frayed nerves and I'm nearing the balcony. It's a square stretching out twenty metres in all directions, packed with plant life and fruit trees and all sorts of fauna. A tiny jungle nestled in the centre of an urban structure.

I'm about to close in when I hear a nasty groan from the cable. I freeze, petrified to move a muscle. Then it snaps, ripping the buckle with it and plunging me into darkness. Almost without conscious thought, I reach out and activate my armbands. They flicker to life as I land on solid flagstones. The armbands cushion the blow, take the impact, and smooth the jolt evenly through my body. It's like razors raking my body from the inside. I teeter on the precipice of screaming, but it'd have hurt more if my spine had been snapped.

I deactivate the armbands and slip over to the door, gloved hand curled around the metal. The djinn programmers said the door lock was broken. If Omar misheard, or they got it fixed, then I'm completely screwed.

I press down the lock. The door swings open.

Empty. The halls are empty. Just rows and rows of desks, twinkling computers and blank holoscreens. I worked here almost every day, sometimes on weekends. Frantically trying to up djinn capabilities. Increase their speeds, their intelligence, their response rate, the height of their sentience.

And people died as a result.

One day, when some of the most violent and powerful gangsters in the Middle-East aren't trying to rip my eyeballs out and tear my balls off, I'll come back here and fix this problem and make the djinn-7 what they should have been.

Someday. Just not today.

I ghost past a cluster of marble desks, past wall-to-ceiling screens. It's like being in another dimension, the worlds of the streets and dervishes and the worlds of high-tech and djinns sliced apart by a few inches of glass.

I go down the stairs to access the safe-lab area where the djinns are confined on another highly-secured floor. The walls here are laced with an anti-signal material that blocks anything from getting in or out. I punch the access code and slip inside. My helmet vision flicks into night-mode, and I dart over to my old workstation. It's a recliner chair fastened in front of a crescent-shaped computer system, the ones only dataSultans can use.

I tug my helmet off, ease myself into the chair, and allow the clamps to hook me in. It takes a few seconds for the scanner to attach to my head and the crystal display goggles to unfold over my eyes, and then there's that quick bite of pain as my DNA is verified and I'm logged into the computer system. It's like staring at a 360 degree monitor screen inside your brain, something only those with nanoImplants can keep up with.

Clutching the control prism, I make a quick sweep for the djinn.

They're not here.

They're gone. Scrubbed out of existence.

I do another search, more thoroughly this time. They're still not there. Not a scrap of code left.

It's only when I feel a cold fire lighting under my ribs that I know I'm dead.

And to top it off, Sma's trying to get in contact. My palmer has hooked up with the system and his ID code has popped up in virtual space in front of me. I cancel it. He's going to be pissed, but he's going to be even *more* pissed once he finds out that the entire djinn-7 program has vanished.

I unplug and seal my helmet back on. I'm about to depart when I hear a metallic crink. I whip around but everything's still. I hear it again. I know it's not a mistake. Someone's here.

A dismantled djinn robot rises from where it's slumped in the corner and twists its cinderblock head with a metallic screech to stare at me. My limbs go numb but somehow I'm able to scramble for the door. I almost reach it when a drone slams into my ribs and sends me sprawling. I'm too shocked to register the pain. I make another attempt at escape when a turret arm folds out of the pristine wall and points at me. If it opens fire, I won't stand a chance. I'll be torn to wet red ribbons in matter of seconds.

I crouch behind a desk, heart going like a jackhammer. I'm dead. I know it. There's no wriggling out of this one. The room's electric, djinn-bots and drones stirring around me in a maelstrom of energy.

Suddenly I know *exactly* where the djinn-7 have gone.

They're confined to these quarters, so they can't reach the main offices. Now, I need to escape without them slipping through the door.

I'm thrown flat on my back. I twist to see the bot descend down to my face. I don't know what it's going to do, but I'm guessing I'm not going to like it very much.

Something jumpstarts in my head and I blurt out, "Don't! It's me! Sikandar!" It's no good using anything but my real name now. The bot hesitates. "I was one of the dataSultans here. Your programmer. I'm not here to hurt you."

The bot swivels. There's a dash of blood from an open wound when I was smacked to the ground. The djinn extends a probe to collect a sample. My breath burns in my throat and I pick myself up as the djinn-bot sets itself down on the table, unmoving. A moment later the speakers crackle to life.

"So you're our programmer, are you?" The voice is androgynous, neither male nor female. I'm frozen in fear. I've heard the high-tier djinn speak, but never with such authority. Never with so much self-assurance of their sentience.

"Yes," I say. "Well, one of them."

I watch the cinderblock headed bot crash to the ground, only for a drone to peel itself away from a workbench a moment later in one fluid motion. My mind fizzles. Something's not right.

"How did you do that?" I ask.

"We don't need just one body," the djinn says. "Not anymore." In a matter of seconds at least three bots have stirred to life in a flurry of twinkling lights, one after the other. And I realize that they're streaming from one bot to the next. Travelling via the Net, freed from physical restraints like the mythological genies of old.

These aren't djinn-7. They're the next level: djinn-8.

And they've escaped their own bodies. Jumping to any device, any machine that they can reach.

I pivot to the crystal display stapled at the end of the wall as a djinn possesses it. A swirling, muscled figure of emerald green and velvet black fills the screen, wreathed in clouds, the upper two of its four arms clutching curved scimitars with the bottom two holding kilijs. My heart almost grinds to a shuddering stop. Now they've given themselves *avatars*. This cannot be good.

"How many of you are there in this room?" I ask, my throat dry.

"Six at the current time." The djinn's mouth works in perfect sync with the voice booming out of the speakers. Unsettling doesn't even begin to cover it. "I'm Shamhurish. I do not know about the others."

And of course they've named themselves. And I helped create these things. I'm unsure whether to be overjoyed or afraid for my life.

"They've kept us here in this room while they perform tests." So they know that they can't leave the room. "They're trying to repair us. They still believe that we were responsible for that incident at the conference. They—"

"Wait." I'm not sure I heard correctly. "The massacre at the conference? The one where djinns killed dozens of people?"

"It was not our fault!" The green clouds around Shamhurish flash with streaks of black and red, and for a moment I'm afraid the turret will shoot me. "Someone sent a software daemon into our server. We were unable to do anything but watch. It was *not* us. Now they've trapped us, trying to fix something that isn't broken. We want to get out of here."

Putting aside that I'm arguing with a djinn, I try to process all this new information. If their malfunction was the result of a third party virus and not shoddy programming, then these gangsters are after the wrong people.

It's not hard to figure out who had the most to gain from sending the software daemon.

Sma had rigged this whole thing from the start. He counted on having the ammunition to blackmail me, and I just fell into the palm of his hand. No one else would dare touch djinn-7 after the incident, so he'd be the sole owner of multi-billion dollar djinns, intelligent enough to perform deep-space mining in asteroids and planets. He'd completely dominate the market.

Of course, Mr. Sma hadn't counted on there being djinn-8 in existence.

"The other dataSultans," I say on the spur of the moment. "Do you know where they are?"

Shamhurish looms upwards, expands to fill the screen. "Even better. If we have their DNA, we can track them and jump to their location."

"Can you tell me what happened to them?"

Shamhurish takes a few seconds before coming back. "Five of them are dead, all in the last few days."

I'm about to respond when the main door rips open and two small objects roll through. I know what the first one is. An EMP grenade. I'm unsure about the second, but after it starts spitting a whitish gas, I have a pretty good idea. The room turns to shadows as the EMP goes off and my head fills with wool.

My mind's still foggy from the gas, but I'm conscious enough to tell that I'm strapped to a chair that's bolted to the floor. Arms, legs, waist, chest, ankles, elbows, neck, everything. I try to shift but it's like being set in concrete; I can't move an inch. It's the chair for restraining people when they inject the nanoImplants. The straps are made of thick, sturdy nanosteel, clamping skintight around me. Designed to be inescapable. I'm not going anywhere, not until they want me to.

I know who "they" are. The men who forced me to leave Earth

in the first place.

My blood quickens. I'm staring right in the grinning face of Azhar Kaadesh. A cybernetic implant imbedded in his temple glows a brilliant cyan. There's five or six others in the background, completely different in appearance but all sharing the one facial expression.

Hate.

We're still in the same room, sealed off from the offices and the rest of the world. There's no chance of calling for help or raising the alarm. I'm totally at their mercy.

"Been doing a little travelling, have we?"

I force a dry smile. "Oh you know, just doing the tourist things."

"Funny, that's not what your brother said." Azhar grins that *I'm-in-control-here* grin. His breath smells like spearmint. "He really didn't want to tell us where you went. But we . . . convinced him."

My heart lurches. "Please, don't hurt—"

"Don't hurt him?" Azhar barks a laugh that turns my insides sour. "You killed three of mine. You're lucky we didn't cut his hands off." He brings up his video palmer, and I'm staring at my brother. His face is caked in dry blood, one eye swollen shut and his breathing is slow and shallow.

But he's alive.

"I'm so, so sorry," he sniffs. It hurts to hear how raw his voice is. "They were going to kill me. I—"

"I'm fine," I lie.

"They—"

"That's enough." The palmer is whipped away. "Looks like Allah didn't want to lend a hand to your brother, eh?"

I'm about to respond when a giant slab of a man plants his fist in my gut. My world goes monochrome and I'm clawing for breath. Another blow hammers into my chest and for a moment I think he's actually killed me.

"Dirty *jahash*," the man spits.

"Don't be too rough with him," says Azhar. "We can take our time. We've got months." He pulls the chest straps of my harness as I gasp for breath. "Maybe even *years*."

He releases me. "It's not torturing a man that makes him lose his dignity, you know. It's letting him sit in his own sweat and piss, day after day, week after week. Unable to move, unable to see or scream, unable to escape the smell of his own stink. Unable to even kill himself." He pats my thigh. "That truly drives a person mad."

"Put the keycard for the chair around his neck," giggles one of his men. "It's so funny seeing them go crazy trying to get it."

I'm pretty close to pissing myself now, but I don't let them see it. I can't. I'm swimming in sweat inside my skinsuit. I truly believe that they'd do that to me. Slow torture. Azhar believes I ripped his brothers away from him and he's going to make me suffer for it.

"The other dataSultans might be involved, but you were the lead programmer," he tells me. "Your responsibility. Your fault I had to tell my family why their sons and husbands were not coming home." He gestures to his men. "We all lost someone that day. Someone has to answer for them."

"I'm not—" I try to reason with Azhar, but a devastating blow into my stomach cuts me off.

"So, I think we might as well get started now, wouldn't you say?" Azhar's billionaire playboy grin goes deeper. "It's all nice and quiet here."

It's a challenge not to struggle. It's what they want to see. I know these people—they get a kick out of seeing others squirm helplessly under their boots. I'm not going to be a part of that.

At least, that's what I think until Azhar flips out his blade.

"Three of my brothers—gone." Azhar stabs a button on a side panel to tighten my restraints as far as they can go, and I'm being crushed into the chair. "I suppose three fingers would make up for it. For starters." He smiles again. "Would you agree?"

My breath shivers in my throat as my chest rises and falls, sweat snaking down my spine. I try not to look at him as he stalks over and strokes my arm. "You left or right handed?"

"Either's comfortable," I tell him, trying to stretch out this conversation. Slab-man is setting up his palmer to film the whole thing and the others are watching with stony faces.

"You're a funny one, Sikandar." My glove is tugged away,

leaving my left hand and fingers exposed. He rests a blade against the pinky. My stomach cartwheels and my chest feels like it's on fire. "Or is it Bohdi? No matter, you won't need a name for much longer."

"Wait," I blurt out, but he's already made the first slice, cutting into bone. My world burns crimson. I nearly bite my tongue in half. I'm screaming with a voice that isn't mine, thrashing against the restraints and roaring curses as he saws and saws until my finger hangs from the stump by a strip of skin. He neatly tears it off and dumps it in my lap.

And then he stops and stares at me as my screams descend to dark chuckles. Everyone's fixed on me as I curl my bleeding hand into a fist and raise my helmeted head toward them.

"You forgot something," I laugh with a wide grin, throat raw from screaming. "This room is haunted." It's only then that they turn around to notice the turret that's folded out from the wall. Everyone freezes, confused. This whole time I've been waiting for the djinns to recover from the EMP blast. Now I'm watching Shamhurish line up the shots with a targeting prism from my helmet, just waiting for the moment to strike.

The turret jerks to life. The sound is deafening, hammering in my skull. I'm almost blown away by sheer devastating force as bullets rip into Azhar's men. Someone's screaming, but I can't hear the words. Red liquid mists on my helmet.

Three men collapse on the floor in crimson pools. I strain as far as the restraints will allow but I can't see the rest. They must have ducked for cover.

The turret makes a hollow click. "It's out of ammunition," Shamhurish says, matter-of-factly.

Then I see Slab-Man, charging my way from the shadows. A drone slams into the side of his head and he topples in a graceless tangle of limbs.

"Get them," I spit into my helmet. The room bursts to life with a mechanical whirl. The chair rumbles as Shamhurish releases my restraints and I dive for cover. This isn't my fight—I'd just get in the way. One of the men darts for the door, and a half-finished robot lifts him off the ground like a ragdoll and slams him to the ground with a wet crunch. Someone scrambles to his aid, and an entire display screen unhooks itself from the wall and crushes the man underneath.

Suddenly there's a nuclear blast of pain rippling through me. A bullet is lodged in my shoulder, blood dripping down my skinsuit. Azhar fires off another shot, gouging plaster and chunks of brick from the walls. I'm about to scramble away when Azhar knocks me to the ground and straddles me, pressing the gun to my head.

"I prefer being on top, if that's alright with you." I earn myself a punch in the stomach for that. The metallic tang of blood floods my mouth.

"You think this ends with you?" His smug smile is gone, replaced with a fiery rage. "Na-ah. I'll find that mud-stained, Allah-loving brother of yours and—"

I've heard enough. "Go for it."

Azhar looks confused. But only for a second when the implant in his head starts flashing as Shamhurish overloads it far beyond its capacity. His eyes go wide and his head explodes in a purple-red blur. He topples to the floor headless, pieces of his skull scattered like broken iznik pottery.

It's only when I get up that I realize that I'm shaking in a cold sweat. I don't even want to look at my finger, but I know they'll grow me a new one. I'm alive and Azhar's men are not, so that's one point to me.

"That was most interesting." Shamhurish reappears in the corner of my helmet with a gratuitous puff of smoke, swords now bloodied. "Are you hurt?"

"I'll be fine." I turn toward the window as dawn approaches, watching a starship ascend heavenward. "It's not over yet, though."

Sma answers immediately. I'm sitting outside of the room now, nursing a steaming mug of coffee and trying to ignore the bite of antiseptic-soaked cloth around my finger. It's not enough, but I guess it won't be long before the police are called and the wound is examined.

But this first.

I wave to Sma. "Long time, no see!"

He's as stoic as ever. "I see you've gotten into that building. Do you have them?"

"The djinn?" I stroke my chin. "You know, I think I'm going to keep them. You haven't been very nice to me, and I don't think you deserve them."

You can almost see those grey eyes of his light up like a furnace, his armour shifting to a jet black. "You think you're funny, do you?" He's visibly shaking now. "I will *break* you, you hear me?" He warbles on with a long list of violent threats.

I just nod and smile. "Very good. But here's the thing: I have the djinn. Who says I can't come after you first?"

"I wish you luck in finding me."

"I don't need to." I hold up a tiny plastic patch of dark blue in front of the camera so he can see. "Remember back on the station, where you cut yourself?" I sip my coffee and smack my lips. "I got a bit of your blood on me, if you'll recall."

His eyes narrow. "Your point?"

"Well, these djinn here can track people via their DNA. Even across space." I wink at him and let the coffee splash to the floor. "It looks like you've got nowhere to go."

By the time he realizes what's happened, they've already sent software daemons to breach his room, possessing his armour. The gun unfolds from his sleeve, rotates to point at his head with him powerless to stop it.

"Bohdi! You—"

The gun discharges and I sever the connection. I push myself away from the desk and stretch my aching limbs. It's dawn and the city's stirring, traffic building up on the roads like a blood-clotted vein. Even through the glass, I can hear the adhan call from the mosques, the roar of space shuttles taking off. The seamless blend of old and new, modern and ancient.

I walk to the balcony garden and peer below as police cars swerve to a stop near the foot of the building. Pretty soon I'll have some explaining to do. They'll search nook and cranny for the djinn, but they won't find them. Because I won't have them.

I can't help but marvel at their intelligence. How precise and capable of autonomy. How *powerful* they are.

And how dangerous they'd be in the wrong hands. How easily they could be exploited. Sma had come so dangerously close.

Shamhurish knows he and the other djinn-8s will be destroyed. In return for taking care of Sma, he asked for the djinns to be taken away from this place. I've done one better. I've removed the firewall preventing them from leaving and downloaded them into my helmet. They're there now, dormant and waiting to be reactivated.

And now that helmet is flying through the air, where it'll land in the river below. I've called my brother and told him where to pick it up and hold it for safe keeping. I promise myself that someday I'll come back and work on these djinns—finish what we set out to do before all this mess.

Someday. Just not today.

The helmet bobs down the river. Now I wait. I'm not sure how I'm going to explain this one to the police, but I've wriggled out of worse. At least my brother is safe.

I've never believed in an afterlife, but if Father is somewhere out there in Jannah, then I hope he's smiling down on me.

Careful not to hurt my hand, I close my eyes and rest my head on the railing, soaking up the Middle-Eastern morning sun and listen to the muezzin's chant.

WEAVING SILK

Amanda Sun

She's still asleep as I arc the seaweed over the flame in slow circles, trying not to burn my fingertips in the dark. The apartments that are still standing in Kamakura won't have their hour of electricity until tonight, so I have to make do in the pre-dawn blackness, between the red glow of the propane burner and the flickering candle mounted on the counter beside the empty water kettle.

Aki mumbles, and the threadbare *kotatsu* quilt rustles as she nestles into it like a silkworm in a cocoon. She's like a silkworm, my little sister—skinny, pale, delicate, and barely there, the fabric of her life woven in tight strands around her. She's always slept in as late as she could, even before, when the schools were still open. I had to pull her along beside me, straightening her socks on the station platform and fastening her yellow hat under her chin as the train roared in.

The flame of the burner catches the edge of my thumb, and I wince, muttering under my breath. The newly crisp nori crinkles as I lay it on top of the others, and I dip my burned thumb into the bowl of cold salted water. A cartoon bunny smiles up at me from the side of the faded porcelain, his face surrounded by rows of dancing pink and blue flowers. The bunny looks happy until the candle flickers, and then its eyes are empty and black, its smile half melted off by too many washings.

I tear the *furikake* packet as quietly as I can, but the rip stirs the little silkworm, and she wriggles in the *kotatsu* quilt. We don't have the electricity to heat the warming table, but the weather hasn't turned too cold yet, so the blanket is enough when we huddle together. The apartment is too quiet now; sleeping in our room gives Aki nightmares, and sleeping in our parents' room makes her cry. Besides, sleeping in the living room lets me keep an eye on the front door lock. I can scare drifters away before they frighten Aki too much. Usually I shout in a deep voice like my father's and bang the broom against the door. Most of the apartments and mansions in our neighbourhood didn't survive the quake, and accommodation is scarce. The ones that did are scarred with thick fracture lines scaling the walls like hairy beetle legs.

It wasn't complete chaos that day, not really. Everyone was calm and helping each other. I remember the dust, so thick and unrelenting that it still settled on the counters even weeks afterwards. The dust, the silence, and the smell. It was only after that the panic started.

I pinch the edges of the seasoning packet and shake the contents into the mixing bowl. As I stir them into the sticky, hot rice, Aki rubs her eyes with the backs of her fists. She always rubs so hard her eyes turn red.

"Bonito," she mumbles. "How'd you get a bonito packet?"

"Go back to sleep," I say. It's a long day ahead, made longer still by the hunger in our empty stomachs.

"After smelling bonito? No way," she says, but her voice is slurred by sleep, and a moment later she is breathing heavily again. I want to smile at that, but I find I can't bring myself to make the motions.

It's hard to smile these days, not knowing what's left out there.

It was the volcano first—Mount Ontake, the NHK news reported, off the coast of Kyushu. Plumes of smoke filled the air so densely that the planes couldn't get in or out. Eventually the whole sky went dark with the thick black curls, and we had to hold our hand towels over our mouths to keep out the grime and dust. The quake followed shortly after, jolting and jarring us in the dark, bringing down the buildings one by one in the loudest crash of cement I'd ever heard. I thought I'd been swallowed by a tsunami's rushing waves. I heard the roar for hours, unending tidal waves smashing against my ears every second until I was certain I'd gone deaf. I've been through plenty of earthquakes before, Aki and I hiding under the *kotatsu* table or our school's desks as the earth teetered back and forth, but nothing had ever been like this. All the buildings in our area were quake-proofed, and all but four of them collapsed. The aftershocks went on for weeks. I don't know what the magnitude was. The electricity shorted out sometime before dawn, and the NHK never came back on the air. No one's phone could connect with all the ripped cables and thick volcanic ash.

My burned thumb throbs while I mound the rice into thick triangular handfuls. The warm grains stick to my fingers, and the steam wafts into my nose, but I've learned by now to ignore the urge to gobble one down. I know how much one *onigiri* can sell for, and today's a big day for us, one that might start to turn everything around.

It didn't really start with Mount Ontake. It started with the escalated war in the west. We didn't want to get involved, Father told Aki back then, but we had no choice. He explained to her what allies meant, how we had to help our friends and stand up for others.

We didn't have a chance to act because that's when the volcano erupted, and then the quake knocked out everything else. Communications were completely lost.

I don't know if the war is still going on. I don't know if anyone is out there. All I know is if I think about it too much, I'll spin my own cocoon under the *kotatsu* quilt and never emerge again. So instead I think of Aki first, and Aki only. I take another seaweed sheet and glide it over the hot flame.

The sun lifts so slowly I almost don't even notice when light overtakes the candle and the propane burner. I mould and shape the rice over and over, wrapping the triangles in the freshly roasted nori sheets from the stack. At first I used to wrap them in the convenience-store style, completely covered in a triangle of nostalgic dark green. But it's getting hard to find supplies now, and nori is scarce, so instead, I put small thin strips of it on the bottom of the rice balls. Just enough to bring back the melancholy taste of before, to forget for a few small bites what lies ahead.

I pack the *onigiri* in Mother's old picnic basket, the red-and-pink floral cooler we always filled to bursting for the cherry blossoms in Genjiyama Park—cool, sweet watermelon speckled with ebony seeds, sticky white dango on thin wooden sticks, steam buns dripping with red bean paste and custard, and *onigiri*—lots and lots of *onigiri*, Aki and I stuffing our mouths full as the papery cherry petals tumbled into our hair and onto the blue tarp stretched beneath us.

Barely any sakura bloomed last spring because of the volcanic ash. And now autumn has come, a long slow autumn with a harsh chill in the air and the crumple of brown leaves on the ground.

I nudge Aki awake, and she rubs her eyes as I cram the last of the *onigiri* into the picnic basket, sealing the lid with the plastic slide locks. I've wrapped two *onigiri* separately in a tiny black box, tied around with a Totoro handkerchief, Aki's favourite. We have a bucket of water in the bathroom, and Aki splashes her face with some while I pull at the tangles in her hair. She tugs one of my sweaters over her dress, and we roll the sleeves up and up and up. She's grown out of her own things, but mine are still too big for her. I pull on my sweater, the sleeves tight and short, and then I retrieve two bandanas from the top drawer of my dresser. I wrap one over her head and tie it at the nape of her neck, to keep out the dust that still seems to drift over everything outside. We slip our shoes on, Aki's pinching her toes, and step out onto the balcony.

It's not completely true that our apartment survived the quake. The cracks and fissures run up the sides of our building like shattered eggshells; piles of rubble and broken furniture crumpled around the foundations. The complex has been condemned, but we don't have anywhere else to go. Our neighbours tried to help us in the beginning, taking us in like little baby magpies. "How sad," they muttered to each other. "Their mother *and* their father? Tragic." But when the food got short, so did their patience. We politely promised we were going to our aunt's house in Tokyo, then snuck back into our own apartment. It's still safer than sleeping on the street. It hasn't collapsed yet, and anyway, if I die, I'd rather die somewhere I belong, surrounded by my own familiar things.

Half our balcony has given way to the balcony below us. We climb carefully down the rubble. From the neighbour's terrace we can lower ourselves over the side and down to the ground. I go first, and Aki throws me the picnic basket. Then she dangles from the concrete edge before letting go and tumbling onto the grass. The first time we did it, she cried. Now she gets up and smooths her hair back, a small bag swinging from the crook of her tiny silkworm elbow.

It's not far to the train station, but every step is a risk. We never sell our rice balls in Kamakura. It's too dangerous. What if someone tracks us home or threatens us? We tried to help others in the beginning too, like Father would've wanted. We took in a woman, plump and pleasant with a red face and thick fingers. "Call me Grandmother," she said, and she tied on our mother's red apron and sliced tofu with our mother's kitchen knife. We let her sleep in our mother's bed. She made us miso soup and bread for dinner, and we went to sleep with friendly words and full bellies. We awoke to find our rice and tofu gone, our tin of tea powder emptied, and our last watermelon stolen. She snatched our mother's beautiful blue kimono, too. Grandmother made the bed before she disappeared with our things. I always found that the most curious of all.

Now we don't talk to anyone, and we try to look as starving as everyone else. Sometimes people shout to ask what's in our picnic basket. I say water, or books, or daruma dolls. Sometimes I say my mother's bones. Then no one asks any more questions.

We are her bones, though. We are the tiny eggs left from the gleaming moth, from the beat of her wings and the curl of her tired legs. We've awoken ravenous among the dark foliage, with only two thoughts in our heads—eat, survive. Eat. Survive. Silkworms, both of us, spinning our cocoons to blind ourselves. Don't look at the sadness, the devastation. Don't look at those calling out to us. I grab Aki's hand tightly and quicken our steps to the station.

Lots of people are heading into Tokyo today. There's little else to do, beside eating and surviving. The TV news hasn't come back, but officials drive around in little trucks from time to time, shouting on loudspeakers. They're launching a satellite today. It's what we've been saving our resources for, what all the surviving scientists have been recycling parts into. If it takes off, we'll be connected again, they think. We'll be able to send out our message: that we're here, if there's anyone out there to listen.

The gates of the station are rusting, but the train runs twice a day. People file soundlessly onto the platforms, their greasy hair slicked back with water, their stained pants smoothed and ironed with the palms of their hands. No one speaks. We're a ghost of what used to be, haunting the tracks in pale silence. We line up inside the little triangle markers as if we're on our way to school, to work, to the department stores. I twist the strap over my shoulder so the picnic basket is in front of me, so I can see it at all times. Aki squishes in beside me, protecting the basket with her little body.

The train pulls in without a chime, without a polite voice announcing its arrival. The wheels squeak on the track. The cars rattle from side to side, braking as the doors line up between the triangles. Every window on the train is shattered, shards swept into neat piles along the sides of the tracks where they've remained for months and months. The doors open rigidly, and Aki and I sit down on the crimson seats on the opposite side. There's lots of space. Only five people get in our car, once packed with salarymen and office ladies and students in uniforms of navy blue and red and black, all brass buttons and knee socks.

The door at the end of the train car slides open, and the conductor steps in. His blazer is missing a clasp, and the gold trim is fraying off his cap. His white gloves are freshly washed but hopelessly stained. He would've lost his job showing up like this before, but in this world of after, he looks crisp and sharp, a symbol of what we used to be. He slaps his hands against the sides of his trousers and bows deeply to us. His head still toward the floor, he shouts apologies to us. "I'm sorry for the condition of the train," he barks in the politest Japanese. "I'm sorry for the state of the windows. Please take care not to cut yourselves. I'm sorry we cannot properly clean the floors. The train will start in a moment. I'm sorry the chimes will not properly announce the stops." It's always the same speech. We listen quietly, not saying a word. He snaps upright, and moves on to the next car, bowing again as he leaves.

A few moments later, the train sways into motion. The chill of the autumn breeze blows in the jagged windows. A tiny line of dark brown has dried down our window, dotted with a bead of dried blood at the bottom of the frame. It's a long way into the city, the trains running slowly on the tracks.

The man across from us is eyeing our picnic basket. I tighten my fingers on the lid and look away, hoping he'll stop staring. He doesn't say anything as we jolt back and forth. He has broad shoulders under his black blazer, a thin angular face and hard black eyes. He's lean and hungry like us, but so much bigger. I wouldn't stand a chance against someone his size. All he needs to do is snatch the picnic basket. I couldn't stop him. We both know it. I often take the *onigiri* in something safer, like a backpack, but I needed to bring as many as I could today, and that leaves me with the vulnerable picnic basket.

"Smells good," he says finally.

I don't answer. The four others in the car ignore him as well, but they're listening, watching. A young lady in the corner lifts a handkerchief to her mouth and lets out a horrible, racking cough.

"What've you got in there?"

I press my lips together in a hard line. I don't think "my mother's bones" will cut it with him.

"Can't you talk?"

"Leave her alone," says another man. "They're just children." He's in a tattered t-shirt, white with an English slogan on it: *Go! Future Dream* in thick black letters. I wonder what dream the future holds for any of us now.

"We're all someone's children," the man in the blazer says. "Children only need a little to eat. We need more to fill our bellies."

"Your belly looks full enough," the *Go!* man says. "Hunger isn't as bad a taste as stealing from children."

The man in the blazer curses and looks away as the train rounds a corner. I give a quiet nod to the man in the t-shirt. I press my hands into my lap so he won't see how they're shaking.

We rock back and forth for over an hour. I close my eyes to rest, but the sun is glaring in the sky, the chill of wind rippling over my skin from the broken windows. At some point along the Tokyo Bay, Aki tugs on my elbow. "I'm hungry," she says, her eyes deep and questioning. Her hair used to be so glossy, her smile spread from ear to ear. She had a dimple on the right side. I haven't seen it in over a year.

I rest my hand gently on the blue cotton bandana tied in her hair. "Not yet."

Her lips curl with disappointment. "But—" It's the only protest she forms. She knows she won't convince me. I don't dare bring out the *onigiri* here. It's one thing to have them in the basket, but to flaunt them in front of the others, to bring out the smells and textures—I'm not sure even *Go!* man will be on our side then.

"I'm sorry, little silkworm," I say, tracing the white lines in the blue bandana. She looks out the window, watching the sunlight dance on the water in the bay.

Our grandfather worked at a silkworm farm for most of his life. He showed me once the handfuls of tiny white cocoons, like soft eggs clustered in his hands. It was hard to imagine the tiny worms inside, their slow and graceful metamorphosis into ghostly white moths. *Adversity changes us*, he said. *We weave a beautiful armour to face it and come out changed, ready to fly.*

We are all little cocoons, I think, as I look at the people in the train. We spin threads around ourselves, shutting others out as if we were the only ones struggling. Hungry to survive, destined to die. And yet together, unravelled, our stories form yards and yards of beautiful silken thread.

Another half hour and the train snakes into Tokyo Station. The doors shudder open. The man in the blazer hesitates as he considers taking the basket from us once more. The t-shirt man stands in his way. He harrumphs and steps out of the doors. I quietly shoulder the basket while Aki adjusts her own bag. We step onto the platform and twist our way up the stairs. I'm just behind the *Go!* man now.

"Wait," I say quietly. He turns to look at me. "To thank you." Aki understands what I'm saying, and unzips her bag to reach for our lunch.

He rests a gentle hand on her wrist. "No."

"But—"

"Don't open it here. You'll get mugged, and so will I."

I nod, watching him walk away. We're all so frightened. How did we get to this? Didn't we all feel so safe together before the quake? Didn't I ride the train home from school in the dark, walking the long alleyways behind closed temples and gleaming convenience store windows and buzzing vending machines crawling with cicadas? Didn't I walk fearlessly in the shadows then, surrounded by strangers? And yet the first one to fear was a hobbling, smiling, plump grandmother.

How different the world is when the illusion of civilization has shattered with the windows of the trains. How quickly history can unravel, taking us back to the beginning, when we walked the strange new world alone and armed with spears.

Tokyo Station: once bustling and vibrant, now empty and hollow as a skull, cracked and cast aside by the living. So many sought shelter here when the buildings came down. They've cleaned up since then, the bodies removed, but the smell of death lingers. It's stale and acidic, a metallic bitterness in the air. Not everyone died in the quake. Lots followed in the days after, one after another in despair and sadness, like a doomed army with no other way out. Our footsteps echo in the long passageways. Aki's fingers squeeze mine tightly. She is remembering, I think. She can smell it, too.

"*Tamago*," I say.

It takes her a moment to realize what I'm saying. Then her quiet voice answers, "*Goma*." *Sesame*.

"*Mahou*," I say, *magic,* to get her mind off food. Aki has always loved to play *shiritori*. It's a word game, where the last syllable of the word has to start the next word. You only lose if you say a word that ends in "n." We walk past the silent moving sidewalks, out of service for over a year. We're almost out of the tunnels now, following the exit signs for the southern gate.

"U—" she stumbles for a minute. "*Unagi*."

"That's food again."

"I mean the eel, swimming. *Gi*."

"Fine," I say. "*Ginka*." Silver coins, like tiny minnows, slipping through my fingers just as quickly. "Your turn, Aki. *Ka*."

She doesn't answer for a moment. Then she says quietly,

"*Kazan.*"

I stop, the small crowd continuing around us both ways. *Volcano*. Mount Ontake, spewing vile clouds of curling grey death on all of us. I smack Aki lightly in the back of the head. "That ends in 'n,'" I say. "You lost."

"We all lost," she says.

Akiko, my sister. As vibrant as the red and yellow leaves of the autumn she was named for, Father used to say. A true autumn child, dancing from foot to foot like the cool wind, spinning like a top, crying like the rains whenever she skinned a knee, every burst of her spirit like the fresh sharp edges of fall. But now she's thin and quiet, her face pale like a newly fallen snow on the dying leaves. The world around us is Aki's mirror, fading into a season we may not survive. Lovely vibrant Akiko is crumpling under the weight of her cocoon.

"Stupid," I say, smacking her on the shoulder. "Try again."

"*Ka*" she says, mulling the syllable over. "Ka—"

"*Kaiko,*" I suggest.

That gets the faintest of smiles. "*Kaiko,*" she agrees. "Silkworm. I miss Grandfather."

"Me too."

We burst from the seams of Tokyo Station, into the fresh midmorning light. It's a half-hour walk to Haramikyu Gardens from the station. Local trains are difficult to get for outsiders; non-Tokyo residents have to pay, and we can't afford it, so we walk. Rubble and glass have been swept to the sides of the streets, collapsed buildings leave gaping holes in the dense walls of concrete and wood. There's an old man with a walking stick just staring into a pile of the rubble, his thoughts, and wits, far away. It's not uncommon. There are those who lost their minds that day and haven't found their way back. In the distance, babies and young children cry, along with the constant mewing and whimpering of lost dogs and cats. A big Shiba, flea-bitten and matted, crosses in front of us. He was someone's companion once, a beloved pet. Now he's one of the thousands and thousands of strays trying to eke out an existence in the rubble.

He's not the only one. People are sorting through the rubble everywhere we go, looking for valuables, tinned food, anything they can resell. Women spread out delicate silk kimonos on the dusty streets, cranes and chrysanthemums in a rainbow of colours, embroidered with silver and gold and metallic-red thread. Family treasures, but no one is buying. In this world, rice balls have more value than the finest silk.

"Do you know how many cocoons it takes to make a kimono?" Grandfather asked me once, as I stroked my fingers along the soft little eggs nestled in their trays. "Five thousand. Five thousand little lives, weaving away." He smiled, his finger arcing through the air. "Four thousand, nine-hundred, and ninety-nine, and the kimono would be missing a swatch right—there." His fingers tickled under my neck, and I giggled. His thick white eyebrows knit with delight. "Never think you and your sister are too small." He nodded, his eyes weary as he blinked at the little cocoons. "Every contribution matters."

I wonder what he'd say now. I wonder what he'd say about all those who jumped off the surviving rooftops, who sliced open their cocoons and tumbled into shattered futures, brown beads of blood on raw woven silk.

There's already a crowd gathering when we arrive, though the launch isn't until later in the evening. The golden teahouse is packed with the homeless, blankets spread from glass wall to glass wall. We look for a place to set up along the line of trees. We don't want to be too far from the projection, but already the best spots have gone to the locals.

"Here?" Aki says, finding a spot along the pathway. It's not bad, shaded by trees but not so hidden away as to be mugged. I nod, and she unzips the side pocket of the basket, pulling out our long blue tarp. She straightens the edges carefully, flattening the creases with the palm of her hand. I rest the basket on top and pull aside the plastic latches. Aki smooths the bandana in her hair, stands in front of our sales spot and bows crisply to the crowds.

"Good afternoon," she shouts, even though it's barely eleven. "Are you hungry? Don't watch the launch on an empty stomach! *Onigiri* for sale!"

Aki has incredible lungs for such a thin, little silkworm. Whenever I tried to sell the *onigiri*, I couldn't get out more than a whisper, my cheeks blushing pink by the attention drawn to myself. So now Aki calls the customers over, and I only have to hand them the rice balls and nod my head.

"We have bonito, tuna, *tamago*, seven vegetable *furikake*!" she shouts. "Fresh nori, taste our nostalgia, relive our past into the future!"

No one steps forward for a little while, but I don't mind. I'm weary from the journey here, my stomach roiling from its own juices.

Then a blond-haired man peeks out from the pathway. "Is that Aki?" When he laughs, the sound shakes his stomach.

It's David. He's still alive, still surviving here. He was on holiday in Tokyo when the quake hit. He hasn't been able to get home, to even tell his family that he's okay. The way he tells it is he was posing with a Buddhist monk one moment, and the world was churning the next. "The picture turned out blurry," he always says, as if that were the worst part.

"David," Aki says. "Want an *onigiri*?"

"You know me," he says. "Give me a tuna, will you?" His Japanese has improved. I guess he hasn't had much else to do, stranded here with the rest of us.

"It's not real tuna," Aki says. "Just *furikake* powder."

"That's fine." He passes her the yen quickly, but the police are here, so I don't think we'll be mugged by spectators. David's expression shows that he didn't even expect real tuna. The tins are long gone from the shelves, and the fresh fish is something we can't afford. He ruffles Aki's hair, scrunching up her bandana, before he disappears into the crowd.

On the grassy plain near the golden teahouse, they've set up a big solar projection screen so we can watch the launch all the way from Tanegashima. It's the latest in our attempts to reach out to a silent world. We think that while the ash hung in the air, some of our satellites went down. Our cries to the outside have met with nothing but silence. The runways at Narita and Haneda are shattered and cracked, the same in Kansai. They've sent smaller planes and helicopters to Okinawa to see if the runway was useable, and to Seoul to reach out to the world. None of them have returned. Whether they were shot down or lost, whether they made it only to discover no survivors there, or whether there was no electricity or gas for them to return to us, we have no way to know. This satellite will be a flare in the ocean of silence, to show the others we're still here, to try and re-establish communications and figure out what's going on out there.

The day passes slowly. It's getting harder to find those who can spend on *onigiri*. It's always easier in Tokyo than Kamakura; the salarymen's pockets are deeper here. Mothers buy for starving children, while the orphans look on with wide eyes, red sores on their faces, their clothes torn. It's easy to pity them; we would be them if the man on the train had taken our picnic basket. But every *onigiri* I give away is less food to put in my sister's stomach, and it's her face that haunts me at night, her pale skin and jutting cheekbones and skinny legs.

When Aki's shouting gets fainter, I know it's time for us to eat our *onigiri*. The nori crinkles gently against my fingers, the rice at first hard like beads, then melting in my mouth with a soft pop of nuttiness. I eat half my *onigiri* like it's a five-course meal. Aki eats hers in the same savoury way, each bite its own feast.

The one street girl is still there, dark red circles around her tear-stained eyes. She's squatting against a tree trunk, her bare feet black with dust. She holds a ragged kitty doll by the leg, its arms and smiling face sprawled into a tangle of browning grass.

Aki watches her too. I know what will happen. It happens every time.

Aki gets up slowly, walking over to the girl.

I want to help, too. I've told her so many times. *We don't have enough for ourselves.*

Father told us to always help others. Grandfather said every silk thread counts.

This isn't the world they lived in. Things are different now. Remember the boy who jumped us at the station and stole your backpack? Remember the grandmother who took Mother's kimono?

The street girl lifts a sleeve to her eyes, drags it across. Dirt smudges on her cheeks.

The world is different, Oneechan. But I'm the same. I'm still Aki.

She gives the girl half of her *onigiri*. The girl begins to sob, racking cries that she stifles with her tattered sleeve.

Yes. You're still Aki.

When she returns to the tarp, my half is waiting for her, like always. *And I'm still your Oneechan.*

Inside Aki's cocoon, I can see the flutter of wings forming.

The sun begins to set. The projection comes on the screen. It's been ages since any of us have watched TV or been on the internet. It seems like a miracle to watch it flick on, like everything is back to the way it was. The illusion plays out again, that we are civilized, that things are the same.

The reporter bows, and we bow as well, all of us who are watching. We've sold all the *onigiri*, every grain of rice and crumb of seaweed eaten. Aki ran her slender fingers along the lip of the picnic basket, gathering up the *furikake* dust and licking it from her fingertips. Now there's nothing to do but watch.

The reporter explains about the satellite, how all the resources have been gathered from across Japan, how the engineers have been working day and night, finding creative solutions to the things we lacked, using solar panels donated by citizens to meet the electrical needs. They talk about the lunches the locals donated, the wires repurposed, the huge amounts of fuel collected to power the rocket. We watch silently, but my heart is pounding in my chest. It's time for the world to be as it was. I'm proud we've all been united in this cause. David stands near us, too. I wonder if he can follow the technical Japanese flowing rapidly from the reporter. I wonder if he understands the sacrifice the reporter's talking of, how we've all worked together.

Five thousand silkworms, I think. *Five thousand thousand. Five million million.*

The reporter stands aside, and we all crane to look as the camera focuses on the rocket.

"That's it," Aki squeals, dancing from foot to foot like the swirling autumn wind. I feel as if I could reach my hand out and find the warm palm of Father's hand, the delicate touch of Mother's slender fingers. I curl my fingers, but there's only the coolness of the breeze.

The rocket stands next to a tall black tower of crossed beams, like an airship ready to launch. I'm not sure which part of it is the satellite; it's hard to tell. The team of engineers is lined up there, bowing, looking as if they too want to bounce from toe to toe. More talking, more encouragement to all of us, more appreciation for all of us making do and waiting patiently.

Then it's time to count down.

My heart catches in my throat. Suddenly it's happening too quickly. I'm not ready. I've always hated countdowns. There's a sudden pressure, an expectation of something when you reach the end. Things are changing, time slipping through your fingers. You feel its finality, guilt and panic and terror. The time is going before your eyes. You can't get it back.

"Ten," they say. "Nine."

The world feels unstable, like it's shaking under my feet.

"*Hachi, shichi . . .*"

Aki is shouting with the rest, but I'm trembling, smoke and ash filling my nostrils. I might be drowning.

"*Roku, go, shi!*" Four. The number of death.

I remember something Grandfather told me, when I asked about the five thousand silkworms. "How do you care for all those moths?"

He ruffled my hair then, like David ruffling Aki's. "Five thousand moths," he said. His white eyebrows wriggled like worms. He sighed.

"*San.*"

"All their work would be undone, Koharu. It's not that simple—"

"*Ni!*"

"What do you mean, Grandfather?" He'd hung his head. And then he'd answered.

"*Ichi!*"

"We boil them," he said. "So they don't break out of the cocoons and ruin the silk. We boil them alive."

"*Zero!*"

The rocket flares to life, bright and hot and rumbling like five thousand screaming voices. It bursts upward as the cocoons bob on the surface, as the worms writhe and die, as half-formed wings melt and dissolve in the scalding water.

The crowd cheers, but the street girl sobs, rubbing her eyes with her dingy sleeve.

"It's not so terrible, Koharu. A few moths are allowed to live. They're born blind, their mouths so small they can never eat. They can't even fly, not after so many years of captivity. They lay their eggs, starve, and die. Such a small life, such a brief moment. Which fate is worse for them?"

I don't know which I hear first, the rocket bursting into flames or the crowd screaming. The fragments of the satellite splinter in the air like a twisted metal firework, raining down on the darkness of the launch pad. The hysteria rises around me like a wave, the screams and the explosions all become one.

Koharu.

My mother's gentle calmness, like a crisp winter snow.

I need to get Aki home.

I grab her shaking shoulders, firmly guide her toward Tokyo Station as her body rattles with sobs, as she drowns in tears with the thousands of others, roiling in their cocoons. The silk is stained and torn; it's missing a thread there, and there, and here, under the soft pale flesh of a young girl's chin. It's woven with the metallic blood-red of dreams and beliefs, the immortal thought that tomorrow will be the same as today and the day before. It's stitched closed with denial.

They are fighting on the platforms, wailing and swinging fists and collapsing on each other like folding cards. The ocean of the world is drowned; no one is coming for us. Aki cries out in fear, but I'm beating my half-formed, melting wings. I push her into the train car before the doors close, pulling away from the chaos and shouts that crest over the shattered window panes of the past.

The streets are dark and silent in Kamakura. We step on tiny moth feet, pale as ghosts in the black of night. The picnic basket is light and easy to carry. My mother's bones weigh less than a feather, and Aki has lost her bag among the chaos of the crowds. We stop to fill the basket full of water at the golf course. An old lady is there, scrubbing her laundry clean in the water trap. The fabric slides up and down in a rush of cold water and bubbles. Tomorrow Aki and I will go to the rice fields, swish our hands through the mud and pull up every forgotten grain we can find. We'll slide our yen into piles on the *kotatsu* table and search the fish market for anyone who might still have seaweed to sell. We'll stretch and snap the threads of our cocoons, flutter with tiny flightless wings, pinch with tiny open mouths. We'll beat against a brief moment, before the autumn breeze carries us away like paper flowers, the first breath of snow crisp upon the tips of our noses.

VANILLA RICE

Angela Yuriko Smith

Meiko stared at the choices on the kiosk in front of her, hovered her finger over *Caucasian* and touched. New choices slid onto the screen. One hand cradled her rounded belly. With the other, she selected *Blue eyes* and then *Blonde*. She reached up to touch her own thick, straight hair. It was so dark that it shone blue in the sunlight. She hated it. Her daughter would not be so Asian. She selected *Curly* on a sub-menu. When she had finished making her selections, she slid in her stolen credit. A warning popped up on the screen.

The Attribute Chip is permanent and its removal may cause a breakdown in DNA. Please use the Attribute Chip sparingly and with caution. The Attribute Chip is a safe, effective way to manipulate native DNA for desired physical effects, but it is for appearance only. It is illegal to modify your chip to alter intelligence or other non-physical attributes. Once installed, it is advised to leave the Attribute Chip in place for the duration of the life span or risk DNA instability. To accept these risks, click and sign.

She bit her lip nervously, knowing what a DNA breakdown looked like. Two doors away in her building, there was a man with no nose. His flesh had destabilized and fallen off in gooey pieces. Just when his degeneration seemed finished, his skin would get gummy again, like fresh mochi, and he would hide in his apartment and order takeout for weeks. Sometimes, when she walked past his door, she imagined she heard him sobbing.

This wouldn't happen to her daughter. She wouldn't try to modify her chip for intelligence, an assumption she had for why her neighbour's chip malfunction. She was no genetic engineer anyway. The physical attributes would be enough. Meiko had hidden herself in a neighbourhood where she blended in, but her daughter would stand out like an angel of light so bright it would illuminate even Meiko's shadowed existence. Her daughter would have every suitor and marry a rich, kind man. Her daughter would be a princess like she had seen in cartoons.

Meiko hated her childhood. Cartoons had been an escape from a father who screamed instead of talked. His face was always flushed red beneath thinning orange hair. By contrast, her mother had been a colourless shadow, cowering and almost nonexistent, —an internet purchase that her father had tried to return. Meiko had already been growing in her mother's belly by then, making her mother non-refundable. Because of Meiko, her mother was defective.

She would sneak away to see the cartoons in the downstairs lobby, and the attendants would let her sit behind the counter and watch. Sometimes her father would call and ask if they had seen her leave the building, and the attendants always told him "no," careful not to look at her when they lied. They hardly looked at her at all, but they let her hide and watch the cartoons on their television.

She never saw Asian princesses on television. The television princesses all had bright, wavy locks and pale skin. Her hair was just black and it hung straight as if gravity was trying to pull her into the ground. On TV, their eyes were always large, round and usually blue. No one she knew growing up had squinty, dark and small eyes like hers. "That's how you know defective goods," her father always said, "by the squinty eyes." But that was in the past, and she had left all that behind. She hovered her finger over the "Accept" icon, hesitated, and then selected it. She scrawled her name.

The kiosk gave a friendly bell tone to let her know her payment had been accepted, and the image of a chip appeared on the screen. Small animated robots worked on the chip using old-fashioned screwdrivers and hammers. *Congratulations!* The words popped up on the screen. *Your Attribute Chip is finished. Please have a professional install within 24 hours of your baby's birth. Do not unseal your Attribute Chip until ready to install.* There was a click, and a small plastic sleeve dropped into the tray in front of her. She carefully picked it up and held it to her heart.

Meiko hadn't planned to have a baby, but when she found out she was having a daughter, she became obsessed with making her child everything she couldn't be. She had grown up an olive-skinned alien in a world full of bright people with hair in all shades of red, gold, and chestnut. Her daughter would be one of them, the most beautiful of them all. Her princess daughter could open the doors of that world to Meiko. She smiled and tucked her chip away safely.

Three months later, she gave birth in a medical time-share cubical during her lunch hour. Meiko named her Katsue. The medical tech tried to change her mind about installing the Attribute Chip in her daughter, droning on about DNA risks, but Meiko couldn't hear him. She was too busy dreaming about designing dresses for her tiny angel. No matter how he tried to caution her, Meiko just asked for the legals to sign. After signing, they wheeled her daughter away to install the chip while her genetic build was still malleable.

The baby was a disappointment at first sight. Meiko asked if the chip had malfunctioned. The baby she had given them had a thick shock of dark hair that stood straight out at all angles like kitten fuzz. The baby they returned was bald, pink, and ugly. They assured Meiko the chip had been properly installed and had synced to her baby's native DNA perfectly. The baldness was a genetic side effect and would be replaced by the blonde ringlets she had requested.

"She will remain groggy for about a week but it's normal," said the medical tech. He wished her luck with a sigh before handing over her baby—her golden Katsue—still swaddled in sterile bindings; receipt and paperwork attached.

It took a full year for Katsue to actually become golden. Every morning, Meiko would rub the child's scalp to see if the yellow fuzz would appear. When it finally did, Meiko would twist the sparse tufts of yellow into tiny bows to show them off. When she dropped off her daughter every morning before work, the caregivers would all vie to hold her and coo over the baby. She grew from the ugly, bald baby with pink skin into a bouncy toddler with blonde ringlet curls as a crown. As a toddler, Katsue stood out from all the other children and was always the centre of attention just as Meiko had hoped. The other children were fascinated by Katsue's differences, but by the time they were adolescents entering their vocational training phase, being the centre of attention was not as pleasant.

Katsue's body became awkward as she began her transition into a young woman. The other students grouped together, leaving Katsue and her ostentatious curls and bright blue eyes alone. They teased her and called her *Vanilla Rice*—white on the outside and yellow within. Friendless, she brought up her unhappiness to her mother, but Meiko brushed it off. Meiko told her daughter, "They are just jealous of your looks. Ignore them."

"I don't care if they're jealous," Katsue said during one of these discussions. "I still don't have any friends." Meiko's answer was always the same. She held her princess daughter close and stroked her golden curls, taking pleasure in how they gleamed in the twilight.

"I don't want to be different," Katsue said, her face buried in Meiko's arm, sobbing. "Why can't we go where people look like me?"

"Because we need credit for that." Meiko pulled her credit from her pocket and held it out. "That world costs, and this credit is almost empty! It takes all I can do just to have enough to feed us here." She threw the credit on the floor next to her mattress. "And—I don't belong there." It came out as a whisper. Meiko wanted to say more, but she bit it short along with the memories that threatened to resurface.

"I want the chip out," said Katsue.

Breath caught in the back of Meiko's throat and stayed there, hiding.

"You can never take the chip out," Meiko finally said. "You would become a monster." The room had grown completely dark and only a faint gleam from the city lights bled through scratches in their painted window. Katsue sobbed again. Meiko tried to embrace her daughter, but she pushed away and groped through the dark to find her low bed against the wall.

"I'm already a monster," she said. Her voice, rough with tears, snagged across Meiko's heart and tore it. She said nothing and only lay down in her own bed. For the first time, she wondered if she had made the right choice for her daughter. Sleep came to her with a heavy tread that bruised her eyes.

Morning alarm exploded in Meiko's ears. She looked across the room to see her daughter's bed empty. She sat up and saw the curtain to the bathroom pulled open. Meiko was alone. Worry squirmed in her stomach and she reached for her phone.

"Where is Katsue?" she asked it. The screen lit up and a map of their apartment appeared. A pin dropped down where Katsue's bed was outlined. Meiko rushed over to the bed and pulled the covers back. Katsue's phone slid from beneath the pillow and dropped to her feet. She knelt, cradling it like she had held her daughter the night before and felt every bright and good thing in her life slipping away. Meiko buried her face into her daughter's mattress and cried. There was no one to call for help. She had no family. Without money for the authorities, she could only pray and hope.

Meiko hadn't left the apartment for three days when someone tapped hesitantly at the door. It opened a crack, and Katsue's voice crept in softly. "Mother?"

Meiko opened the door, pulled Katsue through, and embraced her. They both cried. Katsue's face was wrapped in a thin scarf, and Meiko hesitantly pulled it away. Her beautiful princess was gone. In her place was a girl with patchy skin that had a slick, damp look. Short tufts of black hair stuck out randomly from unexpected places like kitten fur. The blonde hair was mostly gone, and the remaining strands were caught in the sticky skin. Her eyes were patchwork also—flecks of blue and black pooled like warring factions.

"I had to do it," Katsue said when she could speak.

"But we can't fix this," Meiko said. "I can't undo this. Now you don't belong in either world." She held her hands against her daughter's damp face and kissed her forehead. A strand of gold stuck to Meiko's lips as she pulled away.

"I want to belong in my world, not someone else's," Katsue put her hands on her mother's face, mimicking her. "No one loves a lie. Not really. I want to be *real* even if it's not pretty."

Meiko had no reply. She could only hold her daughter close and think of all she had wasted by pinning her hopes up in shining, yellow hair.

LOOKING UP

S.B. Divya

Ayla clutches her tab with a trembling grip and reads the words again. She can hardly believe her eyes, but the blurring message on the screen doesn't lie: she will be a passenger on the *Mayflower* expedition. Coming to Denver had been a good attempt at forgetting California, but Mars might be far enough to put her past to rest.

"Congratulations and welcome to the team! Let's make history together," the text says. "We commend you on being one of our most diverse candidates, proving that the *Mayflower* welcomes people of all backgrounds and abilities."

Did they somehow measure and rank each passenger's diversity quotient? Ayla sighs. Jeff is lounging next to her on the frayed yellow sofa, his silky black hair loose across his shoulders. They're drinking a fifteen-year-old bottle of wine like there's no tomorrow, and it hits Ayla that soon there won't be any tomorrows. Not with aged wine. Not with her boyfriend.

"A penny for your thoughts, lovely lady?"

"What?" she says, quickly closing the message. "Sorry, I'm distracted. Work stuff."

Jeff reaches over and strokes the unmarred side of her face. "Locking horns with Brian again?"

"Something like that."

"You have to stop letting him push you around. He's not going to respect you until you show him some balls."

Ayla raises her eyebrows.

"You know what I mean," Jeff says, half smiling.

"I do, but never mind," she murmurs and kisses him, effectively ending the discussion. Even if this relationship can't last much longer—and hers never do anyway—she wants to enjoy it while she can.

✥

The next morning, Ayla walks into Brian's spartan office and sits down in one of the two uncomfortable chairs on the other side of his desk.

"Yes?" her manager says without turning away from his display. His gnarled fingers click on a manual mouse.

"I'm quitting."

That gets his attention. His unnerving green eyes turn toward her, and she looks away, gazing at her knees.

"Why?"

Ayla takes a breath to give her prepared, polite excuse, and then realizes that she can afford to burn this lousy bridge. She raises her head and looks squarely into Brian's eyes.

"I'm going to Mars." The disbelief on his face gives her a thrill of pleasure.

Brian snaps his hanging jaw closed and frowns. He turns to the giant paper calendar hanging on the wall.

"I'll need another month from you."

"I can only do two weeks. Sorry."

She regrets the apology as soon as it comes out and wordlessly hands him her resignation letter.

"See? That's the kind of attitude that keeps women like you from being good at these jobs." Brian shakes his head. "I took a lot of risk hiring you. Good thing you aren't coming back because I could never give you a reference with this kind of unprofessional behaviour."

"The only unprofessional person here is you," Ayla snaps, surprising herself.

Her retort is enough to shut him up, maybe out of sheer

astonishment that she would say it. She'd long ago learned to prefer the company of rocks to people, especially people like Brian, but he came with the job and the job came with pay.

She leaves the office in the evening and lets her car navigate the downtown Denver traffic on her way to Aunt Sam's apartment. The tall, sprawling, assisted-living complex dominates the space between a strip mall and a tract of houses. Ayla parks her car and gazes westward at the afterglow of the setting sun. The peaks of the Rockies are still bare, but the chill October air carries a promise of snow. How strange it will be to gaze at a skyline of ochre and rust instead.

Aunt Sam lives on the fourth floor. Ayla usually takes the exterior stairs two at a time. It's a fun way to use her spring-loaded prosthesis, but today she goes slowly, stopping at each landing to savour the view. She hadn't dared to believe that she would be chosen for the mission. After all, she's a nobody, but they liked her fitness level at the first screening and her geology degree at the second. So what if her amputated foot and scarred face gave her the final advantage? It rankles, but if that's what it takes to get her to Mars, then so be it.

Samsara opens the front door before Ayla can knock.

"How did you—"

"Your tread gives it away, love. Come in. The tikka masala's almost done, and the cabernet is open. Sorry I couldn't wait on the wine."

"I don't blame you one bit," Ayla says, stooping to kiss her aunt's tan cheek. "The cook deserves a glass of wine while she's in the kitchen."

"Cooking is its own pleasure now that I'm semi-retired. My graduate students are doing most of the work."

Ayla inhales deeply as she removes her sneaker and slips a clean sock over her prosthesis. The air is redolent with the aromas of toasted cumin, coriander, fried tomato, onions, and chilies. Her mouth waters in anticipation, and she tries not to think about the blandness of food in space. Her aunt moves painstakingly around the small kitchen, but she bites her tongue before she can offer to help. She knows all too well what it's like to be on the receiving end of those offers. Instead, she perches on a counter stool and pours herself a glass of wine.

The apartment is small, just three rooms. The bedroom barely fits her aunt's bed, but the bathroom is spacious enough to hold a wheelchair. The efficiency kitchen opens to the living room which has a firm sofa, small dining table, and an enormous screen built into one wall. Aunt Sam's walker is parked by the front door, next to the shoe rack.

"Are you getting used to this place?"

Samsara shrugs. "It'll do."

"It's good that you moved here," Ayla says, feeling awkward.

"Oh? Are you and Jeff getting serious?"

"No." Ayla takes a deep breath. "I'm going on the *Mayflower*."

Samsara stops stirring the masala and looks at her. Her aunt's dark brown eyes are sharp and clear. "The what? You don't mean that one-way spaceship to Mars?"

Ayla nods, tightening her grip around the stem of the wine glass.

"Ayla! Why didn't you tell me? When? Isn't it leaving soon?"

"Eleven weeks, but I go for training in two. I'm sorry, Aunt Sam. I didn't want to tell anyone about my application in case I didn't get in."

"They're okay with your foot?"

"More than okay. I can get a special prosthesis. It'll be great in space, better than my natural foot, and the gravity is low enough on Mars that it'll be easier on my leg muscles."

"But—why? Why go? Is it because of Felicia, after all these years?"

Ayla avoids her aunt's gaze by taking a sip of wine. The tang of it fills her mouth and eases the tightness in her throat. Of course, it's because of Mom, but it would break Aunt Sam's heart to tell her so. Her aunt gave Ayla a second chance at life by bringing her to Denver, by raising her when no one else would. She was the only one who didn't blame Ayla for the accident.

"It's the opportunity of a lifetime," Ayla says, studying the garnet-coloured liquid in her glass. "I'm a geologist, and all I'm doing here are stability surveys for bloated high-rises. On Mars, my studies will make history. They'll actually mean something."

It's the truth, if only partially.

LOOKING UP by S.B. Divya

The room is quiet for several minutes. Aunt Sam turns off the stove and pulls the foil-wrapped supermarket naan from the oven. She hobbles over to the counter, holding on to its edge for support, then cups Ayla's face in her warm, dry palms.

"My dear girl, as hard as I've tried, you can't forgive yourself, can you? Mars will be an amazing accomplishment. You're right about that. But you won't find peace by running farther away."

Trust Aunt Sam to see through her walls like they were made of crystal. They move to the dining table set for two. After twenty years of living and growing up with her aunt, there's no pressure to make talk, and Ayla takes advantage of it. She savours the chew of warm naan. Fresh cilantro and chunks of silky paneer dissolve against her tongue, and she sighs contentedly.

"I'm going to miss good food," Ayla says. "I miss it already, to be honest. I've been eating way too much takeout since you moved here."

Samsara laughs. "I can believe it, but every chef needs an appreciative audience."

Her aunt's watch chimes, and Samsara's smile vanishes, replaced by a deep frown.

"What is it?"

"A message from your sister. It's about Carlos."

"Dad?" A hand squeezes Ayla's heart. *This is not an emergency,* she tells herself, applying what she learned in therapy and breathing deeply. "What about him?"

"He had a stroke." Her aunt's eyes scan the screen.

"How bad?"

"They don't know yet. Elise says they want him under observation for at least a week, maybe two. You should go and see him, Ayla. It's been a long time and—given where you're going, that you might not come back—this could be your last chance."

"It's been five years, ever since he moved in with Elise." Ayla shakes her head. "She won't let me near him."

"Do you want me to ask her? Maybe if you tell her your news—"

"No," Ayla says sharply. "My sister hasn't spoken to me in twenty years. She doesn't deserve to know anything about my life."

The dispirited expression on her aunt's face makes her relent.

"I'll call the hospital, see if I can talk to him by phone. Okay? Let's finish the rest of our dinner in peace. Please?"

Samsara nods, and they move on to other subjects, but the meal's pleasure is tainted.

❖

Ayla spends the rest of the weekend running her favourite mountain trails and wondering how to break the news to Jeff. He comes over for dinner on Monday night, bearing a bag full of Chinese takeout and a boisterous demeanour. Jeff tells her about his latest challenging client, but Ayla remains silent, full of restless thoughts. She crunches on egg noodles and orange-glazed chicken and wonders if she can bring dried red chilies to the colony. The pioneers of old relied on spices and spiced food for long journeys. Should Mars be any different?

She looks up from her meal when Jeff stops talking. All lightness is gone from his expression.

"What?"

"Don't you have something to tell me?" he says.

She feels sucker-punched. "How did you find out? Brian?"

"Yes."

"That asshole!"

Jeff flings his hands outward in frustration, spattering sauce across the table from his chopsticks. "Are you kidding? Do you have any idea how lousy I felt hearing the news from him? Mars! You're going to Mars! How could you not tell me about this?"

"We've only been dating for a couple of months." She hates the defensiveness in her tone. "I didn't want to risk losing you if they didn't pick me." *Besides, you'll find someone better*, she almost says out loud.

She gets up to escape the hurt in his eyes and scrapes the rest of her food into the trash can. Her watch beeps. It's a reminder to call the hospital, one that she set herself so she'd stop avoiding it, but the timing is terrible. Her plate clatters into the sink as she tries to steady her shaking hands.

"I'm sorry. I know I should've told you sooner, but it's over anyway," she says, still facing the sink. "I'm leaving next Saturday for training."

"It's over all right, but it didn't have to be like this. You think you're unlovable because your face makes you ugly and that's why no one asks you out. You're wrong. It's not the scars that repel people, not the ones on the outside anyway. I would've been happy to watch you soar into the future, but I can take a hint. I hope you find what you're looking for out there."

His chair scrapes over the tile floor. She succeeds in holding back her sobs until the front door slams shut. *It's for the best*, she tells herself. *There's no good way to break up.* They hadn't even come to the point of saying "I love you" to each other.

Later, as she brushes her teeth, she stares at the curtain covering the bathroom mirror and wonders if Jeff was right. She holds the cloth aside and forces herself to look at her reflection. One half of her face is ordinary, a blend of boring brown tones. The other is a warped landscape, stretched taut in some areas, puckering like an angry pink mountain range in others. She lets the curtain fall. Mars won't have any mirrors to hide from.

Elise got the good looks in the family: hair the colour of rosewood, eyes like a summer sky, sweetly bowed lips. How does her sister look now after twenty years and two kids? Thinking of her reminds Ayla of her dad, and she imagines him lying in a hospital bed, wondering if his other child cares about him anymore.

She grabs her tab as she walks into the bedroom and calls up flights to Los Angeles. There's an evening option for next Friday, her last day of work. She books it and changes her Corpus Christi flight to Sunday, from LA. One day with her immediate family — more than enough — then off to mission training.

Her sleep that night is restless. She dreams of spice barrels coming loose and floating like bloated, drunken bears through the *Mayflower*'s cargo hold.

Ten days later, Ayla steps out of the air-conditioned terminal into the warm Los Angeles night. Exhaust fumes mix with the scent of sea salt and it evokes memories of driving along the coast in her mother's old convertible. She wonders for the hundredth time since boarding the airplane if she should have come.

She merges onto the freeway and is instantly snarled in seven lanes of traffic. She switches the car to auto-follow. It creeps along and passes a fly-by-night costume store. Her stomach clenches as she remembers the date. *Tomorrow is Halloween.* Lost in all of the Mars preparations, she has, for the first time in her life, overlooked the holiday.

"Damn," she whispers to the dashboard.

Ayla resumes control of the car and pulls off the freeway, driving through a posh stretch of Santa Monica before heading north along the coast. Here and there, clusters of costumed teenagers are out partying early. She opens the windows and lets in the ocean breeze, fresh and moist. Her curls break loose, flying across her face, but she doesn't care as she loses herself in the buried, painful memories that she's been keeping away.

Ayla, age six, wanted desperately to be a robot, as did her best friends, Emma and Shaden. The three of them decided to coordinate, cobbling together their costumes from cardboard, dryer vents, and liberal amounts of duct tape. They were a hit at every house, wandering the hilly streets of their suburban Calabasas neighbourhood and collecting more than their fair share of candy.

Emma's Dad and Ayla's Mom were their chaperones for the night, happily taking their pictures in front of the more elaborately decorated homes. The street lights glowed yellow-orange, and Shaden pretended they were on Mars, that his LED ring light was a laser.

The sidewalks were crowded, though, and they couldn't easily run in their bulky costumes. Still, Ayla wanted to play so she tore off a sparkly sticker and wrapped it around the tip of her index finger.

"Pew! Pew!" she shouted, waving her finger at Shaden and then at her mom who laughed and nudged Emma's dad.

Ayla stumbled over something. She looked down and saw a silver-handled toy gun.

"Watch out! I have a laser gun," she yelled, grabbing it and pointing it at her mom. "Pew!"

She pulled the trigger.

It's the sounds and the smells that Ayla can't forget: the horrible popping noise over the din of the crowds; the screams, some of which were her own; the smoke that stung her nostrils before they filled with blood.

West Hills is a different hospital than it was twenty years ago, but Ayla shuts down the part of her brain that wants to compare the ICU ward "then" versus "now."

"I'm here to see Carlos Butler," she says to the receptionist.

"Your name?"

"Ayla Narayan-Butler."

The receptionist frowns at her display. "I don't see it on the list. We only have another five minutes before visiting hours end. I'm sorry, but you'll have to come back tomorrow."

Ayla represses a sigh. "What time?"

"Nine o'clock."

Ayla wanders back to the parking lot and slides her claim key into the valet machine. As she waits for the car, she considers sending Elise a message, but she's saved by the car's arrival. The empty vehicle pulls to a stop at the curb, and Ayla slides into the driver's seat. She drives without thinking too much about where she's going, feeling her way through streets that are vaguely familiar like scenes from a faded film strip.

The first few months after the shooting, Ayla was in and out of the hospital for reconstructive surgery so often that she was barely conscious. They told her later that the slide on the semi-automatic had blown backward, shearing off half her face in the process, but she was numbed by an influx of medication. She lost her memories of that time in the haze of opiates. When she was in her right mind, she felt Elise's fury in a thousand tiny ways — excluding her from games, cutting off bits of her stuffed animals, knocking over her now clumsy body "by accident."

Dad was submerged in his own grief most of the time, but whenever he did look at Ayla, at her mangled face and absent foot, she could feel his revulsion. Only her aunt was sharp enough to realize what was happening. After a year and a half of pleading, Samsara convinced Dad to let her go to Denver. He visited once a year until he could no longer travel, but he always came on his own, without Elise.

Ayla pushes the past behind as the shape of the neighbourhood becomes excruciatingly familiar. There—that's the street where it happened, and that's her own street. She turns the car and slowly rolls by her former home. A light is on upstairs, but she can't see anyone. A silver minivan is parked in the driveway, and the lawn is conspicuously absent of Halloween decorations.

She stops the car in the cul-de-sac and sits, shaking from head to feet. She feels a pang for Elise's children, deprived of both a grandmother and the pleasure of Halloween, and it's all her fault.

As grief and guilt threaten to drown her, she breathes deeply and imagines herself taking the memories and locking them away in a large, heavy metal box. The trembling and the emotions gradually subside. She closes her eyes and buries the metal box deep under the earth, to be left behind forever. This house isn't her home, nor is this planet. When semblance of peace returns, she searches the car's navigation system and spends the night at the first hotel on the list.

Halloween morning dawns. The sky is fittingly grey and laden with clouds. Ayla stands in the hospital lobby and stares at her watch, paralyzed with indecision. She glances up at the sound of a woman's voice and sees the back of a brunette head at the reception desk. Before she can decide whether she wants to be noticed or not, Elise turns and sees her. For a moment, Elise doesn't seem to recognize her, but then realization dawns.

Elise strides over. "You! You unbelievable little—what are you doing here? Do you realize what day it is?"

A flush creeps up Ayla's cheeks, and she hunches as she nods. She focuses on the patterns of the industrial carpet beneath their feet.

"I came to see Dad." Her muscles tense with the urge to run

out of the hospital and never come back.

"And you chose today, of all days, to visit him. You are such a selfish, self-absorbed—" Elise stops and draws a deep breath, then lets it out audibly. "You'll never change, will you?" She taps her foot. "I suppose you have a right to see him. I'll take you in, but I'm not putting you on the visitor's list."

Bands of pressure tighten around Ayla's chest. She focuses on her breath as she follows Elise through the security doors and into the ward. She'll say her farewell to Dad, and once she's on Mars, none of this will matter. She can put it behind forever.

Elise opens the door and leans against the wall outside, arms crossed.

"You have fifteen minutes. Hospital rules. Don't upset him!"

The door shuts behind Ayla. Her dad is hooked up to a bevy of monitors that are mercifully silent, but their coloured lines wriggle eloquently across the screens. The room is a plush single, furnished with dark wooden cabinets, an armchair, and an attached bathroom, though judging by all the tubes running in and out of her father's body, he won't need the facilities anytime soon.

She sits by the bed on a wheeled stool.

"Hi, Dad."

Her father's head lolls toward her, but his eyes are glazed and unfocused.

"Felicia. You're here," he rasps.

The good side of her face resembles her mother's. She turns so he can see all of her.

"No, Dad, it's me, Ayla. I came to see you—to see how you're doing—and to tell you something."

Her father's trembling hand gropes around on the bed until it finds hers. He curls his fingers lightly, and his eyelids droop.

"I've missed you so much, Fel. Why didn't . . . when . . ."

The rest of his words are too soft to hear. Ayla leans close until his papery lips brush her ear and his stubbled chin scratches her cheek.

"Forgive me, Fel . . . terrible thing . . . little Ayla. I let Samsara take her . . . was a mistake. Stupid . . . lost. You left me alone . . . Ah, I've missed you."

Ayla has been waiting her entire life to hear these words, but not like this, not like she's eavesdropping on her mother's ghost. She pulls back. Her Father's eyes are closed, and his whispery voice trails off to silence. She wants to tell him that she forgives him, that she loves him and understands, but it's not her blessing that he wants.

"Dad, I have some news," Ayla says, swallowing against tears. "I'm going to Mars. I'll be on a ship called the *Mayflower*, and it leaves in a couple months. I probably won't be back, not ever. I'm," she stops. The words stick in her throat, and she forces them out. "I'm here to say good-bye."

She can't tell if any of her words register, but she hopes that some part of him will remember them when he wakes up. She takes a deep, shaky breath and lightly kisses his cheek. His face is peaceful, but it hits her that he looks old—old and fragile like she's never seen him before.

"You're going to be fine," she says, wishing it to be true. "I'll send you a postcard from Mars."

She walks out of the room and finds Elise gone. Her shoulders tense as she strides away, waiting for her sister to chase her. But no one comes, and then she's outside and away.

Ayla spends the rest of the day at Zuma Beach watching the surf crash. Gulls squawk, and the sand is littered with prone bodies worshipping the sun, but there is not a single reminder that it's Halloween Day. The sight of the ocean makes an indelible memory: the vastness of it, the colours from turquoise to silver and sapphire; the way the foam traces chaotic patterns before vanishing underground. These are the colours of the Earth. Her future is one of brown and red, the colours of her heart.

She holds on to those images in the following weeks at Corpus Christi, returning to them when she needs to escape the presence of her crewmates—her lifemates. Some of them are already forming romantic attachments, but she holds herself apart. It's not hard. Men have always found it difficult to look past her deformities, and she doesn't mind now. She belongs to Mars.

LOOKING UP by S.B. Divya

❖

Ayla spends her three days of leave in Denver with Aunt Sam. They ring in the New Year together, toasting with champagne and caviar. Samsara even drags Ayla to a party with some of her graduate students to show off her celebrity niece. They both avoid any mention of the past until it's time to say good-bye.

"I wish you could've had one last day with your dad," Aunt Sam says as they stand next to the taxi. Her breath fogs in the sharp morning air.

"I can text him from the *Mayflower* and occasionally after we get the colony set up. It won't be much different from what we've done here."

Samsara looks at her strangely.

"What?"

"How—You can't—"

The taxi chimes to remind Ayla to get in, but Ayla stays still, watching her aunt's face and feeling confused.

"Nobody mentioned you at the funeral," Samsara says. Her voice is heavy with anger and regret. "I assumed you couldn't come because you were at training. What a stupid person I've been! It never occurred to me that she wouldn't tell you."

"Funeral? You mean—Dad's *dead*?"

"I'm so sorry, love. I thought you knew."

"Not your fault," Ayla says reflexively.

The taxi chimes again, and they give each other a long, tight hug before Ayla gets in. Her cheeks are wet from her aunt's tears, but she's numb inside, reeling from the news. Anger builds on the drive to the airport. If she owed Elise nothing, then perhaps the same was true in return, but not when it came to Dad. His life belonged to both of them.

She finds herself at the check-in counter saying, "I'd like to change my ticket. I need a flight to LAX, and I need to be in Corpus Christi tonight."

"Let me see," the agent says. "We can get you on a noon flight to LAX, but you'll have to move fast. It arrives at 1:30 p.m., and there's a 5:30 p.m. flight out to Houston that gets you in at 10:30 p.m. That's the best I can do."

Ayla checks the map on her tab. She can drive from Houston to the *Mayflower* base in four hours. It would mean arriving in the middle of the night, but she wouldn't miss the final morning briefing.

"I'll take it. Both flights."

❖

Ayla's stomach clenches with hope and fear all the way through the snarl of Los Angeles weekend traffic, right up to their— Elise's—house. She knocks on the navy blue door. When it opens, Ayla looks up from the cheery "WELCOME" mat, but not very far. A tiny person with curly brown hair, rather like her own, peers at her.

"Uh—is your Mom home?"

"Mom!" bellows the child, running off and leaving the door ajar.

Elise stops halfway down the stairs when she sees Ayla at the door. Ayla feels herself trembling and rushes the words out before she loses her nerve.

"How could you? How could you let me miss Dad's funeral, too?"

Elise storms down, out, and closes the door behind her, forcing Ayla to back up a few steps. Now that she's closer, Ayla sees the lines and shadows on her sister's face, which is also pinched with fury.

"It's not my fault you're running off to Mars, like you ran off to Denver. That's all you know how to do, right? Run away! What do you care if Dad's dead or alive? You weren't here. You weren't the one looking after him."

"You didn't let me help!"

"Because I knew you wouldn't. Do you have any idea how much it hurt us when you left with Aunt Sam? You killed Mom, and then you abandoned me and Dad."

"Abandoned?" Ayla says, her voice raw and shaky. "I saw how much you hated me. And Dad—he couldn't even look at me! I thought you wanted to get rid of me."

The tension between them erodes, like grains of sand into the ocean, and regret with the patina of two decades arrives to take its place.

"He was never the same after you moved away. I hated you so much for that, for what you did to him."

"He said—at the hospital—he said he wished he hadn't sent me away. I didn't want to go, Elise, not really. This was home. I thought I was helping. I thought, maybe, you could forgive me and move on with your life once I was gone."

"So you could do the same? Admit it! You want to move on, too."

Heart hammering, Ayla whispers, "Yes."

"Why didn't you fix your face?"

Ayla traces the old scars with her fingertips. "To remember. To punish myself. I don't deserve to look normal."

"So you can wallow in self-pity? There were times when I felt sorry for you." Elise sighs. "I've been seeing a therapist again, after Dad died. He says we need forgiveness from each other, but also from ourselves. You deserve to be happy, Ayla. Me, too."

Tears surge behind Ayla's eyes.

"How do I forgive myself? And you—not telling me about Dad, when you knew I was in the hospital for Mom's funeral—how do I forgive you for that?"

Elise looks away, past Ayla, to the distant hills. "That's up to you."

Ayla stares at her sister's face, almost a stranger's face, and the anger drains out of her body as if the earth is drawing it through her feet. She lifts her shoulders and chin and inhales deeply, filling her lungs with regret and breathing out stale anger. She imagines her father's body lying next to her mother's, restored to the side of the woman he loved. He must have forgiven Ayla. She owed it to him to do the same.

"I forgive you, Elise, and I'll work on granting it to myself. I want to leave in peace."

The front door opens and the same young child peers out.

"Mom? What are you doing? Who are you talking to?"

"Come out, Ashwin. Come meet your Aunt Ayla."

The boy stands by Elise's side and stares with wide brown eyes. His resemblance to her—and his grandmother—is striking.

Ayla kneels so they're level with each other.

"Hello," she says, holding out her hand for a shake.

He grins and gives it a big shake.

"I'm building a rocketship with my Legos. Do you want to see?"

"I wish I could, but I'm afraid I have a real rocket to catch."

"Where are you going?"

"Mars."

"Wow!" He looks up at Elise. "When can we go to Mars?"

Elise lays her hand on his head. "Maybe when you're older." Her lips turn up in a small smile as she looks at Ayla. "Maybe you'll go visit your aunt someday."

"I'd like that," Ayla says and stands.

"Can I go in?" Ashwin loud-whispers to Elise.

She nods, and they watch as he dashes back into the house.

"I suppose he's my reminder of you and Mom," Elise says with a broken laugh. "I wish we'd done this sooner, that you could've gotten to know the boys. At least you met Ashwin. Paco—my older one—is at his friend's house."

Ayla reaches for Elise's hand. She squeezes it lightly before letting go. "I'll write you?"

"Yes. Of course. We'll stay in touch."

Ayla's last image as she drives away is of her sister, standing in the driveway of their childhood home, arms wrapped around herself against the chill.

She replays their conversation, over and over, as she drives to Corpus Christi. The regret stings: all the years she missed, not seeing her nephews as babies, not being a part of their lives. *Is Mars a mistake?* Will that be her next great regret?

Ayla considers turning around. Highway 77 is devoid of cars, and she pulls into the grassy median and stops. She steps outside and looks up.

"What should I do?" she whispers.

The stars blaze overhead in a giant bowl over the plains. They beckon her, reassure her. *If it hadn't been for the mission*, they murmur, *this reconciliation would never have happened. Be glad for what the future holds*.

As she climbs back into the car, Ayla realizes that at last she can let go of the past. She can start fresh, not because she can leave her past behind, but because it will anchor her as she ventures onward and outward. She gets on the highway and continues through Corpus Christi to the base.

The *Mayflower* stretches up into the night sky, ablaze in floodlights and drawing her in like a beacon in a storm. The silver scaffolding hugs the ship, but she can already feel the struts falling away. She's light enough to fly.

A STAR IS BORN

Miki Dare

Journal Entry: May 1, 2, 3, 4, 5 (The numbers just keep going up and I can't find the damn calendar, nurse must have taken it again.)

I'm an iota of flotsam. A senile speck of sentience. A little old Asian lady. I'm fighting against the tides of space and time, but you won't ever find me in any history books.

Don't let my wizened apple exterior fool you. Tiny is powerful like electrons bounding about in multiple places at once. And I'll let you in on a secret—I can do something like that. Somehow in my old age, I can time travel. I haven't told anyone because they'll call me crazy and not let me use scissors anymore. I don't know how I have this power, I just do. Like some people have freckles and some don't. I have freckles. And age spots. Maybe it came with the age spots. Oh, I'm getting off topic.

It's not like Doctor Who and I just jump into a machine and travel about. My time travel happens when I dream, and as any good senior citizen, I nap a lot. But I can only look at my own personal timelines along one specific vein of existence when I travel. I don't visit dinosaurs-still-exist timelines, or aliens-took-over-the-Earth timelines, or we-nuclear-bombed-the-crap-out-of-our-own-planet timelines. I'm always locked in as the same Japanese-Canadian-girl-born-on-Salt-Spring-Island-in-1928 timeline, but I just get thrown into my other possible permutations. I watch alternate "me's" taking different paths of actions and having different reactions.

When I watch the other me's, I see how limited my choices were back then. An iota of flotsam. A silenced speck of sentience. A little Jap alien. I don't ever have a chance to become a movie star or the Prime Minister of Canada. I'm not able to stop World War II or stop the internment of my family and every other Japanese person. The shitty stuff still comes.

Some of my timelines are better than others, but I can only exist in the timeline I was born to. The other timelines feel real when I visit, but to everyone there, it's like I'm the invisible woman, and folks can walk right through me like you see in movies about ghosts.

Sometimes, I can do little things. If I "push" with all the might of my mind, I might nudge an object just a bit or if I yell with all my heart, "myself" might turn around as if someone's in the room. But the other "myself" never sees me, although she might think something strange is going on. My existence in the "here" I was born stays fixed, and everywhere else I am just ghosting while I sleep.

I travel more and more as the years go by. Sometimes I forget what a toothbrush is for or how to tie my shoelaces. Eeeeh, I don't know what the fuss is about. None of my real teeth are left, and all my shoes are slip-ons. But because I muddle up my pasts with the present, my grandniece put me in a special seniors' home. The doctors tell me it's Alzheimer's, but I know the truth. My travelling times are just catching up to me.

I won't be here much longer, but don't be sad. I've lived a good long life and then some. I want it to be a surprise for you, so I'm not going to spill the beans. But I can say that everything is going to be peachy. Momotaru is coming!

Timeline Capture:
AZ126798324323433349556902 3WQM843925237
Hitomi kicked a rock as she trudged along the gravel walkway. The Armstrong's house oozed joy with its lacy white trim and a fresh coat of paint in robin's egg blue. Planters burst with yellow primroses at the base of every window to make the house

all the more lovely. Hitomi balled her hands into fists until her fingernails jabbed pain into her palms.

Unbidden images of her once-upon-a-time home flashed in her mind. Her house on Salt Spring Island shone this same blue, fresh-as-spring. The daffodils she and her dad planted in jade-green pots by their doorstep. The taste of sun-warm strawberries freshly picked from their farm. The pink cherry blossom wallpaper her mom let her pick for her bedroom. The doll from Japan with the wistful red-lipped smile and glittering gold and green kimono, her favourite birthday gift from her mom and dad. All her clothes, books, records, drawings, her scrapbook of her accomplishments from swim badges to her high school track meet ribbons were now ghosts of what used to be. Memories that now attacked her like angry wasps.

Everything was gone. The Canadian government had sold her family's house, their farm, and everything they owned. All their possessions were taken, sold, given away, or thrown out. The fabric of her reality for which generations of her family had worked so hard, for her good life in Canada, no longer existed.

Instead, she was shipped off to live in a giant wooden box in the middle of Alberta. It came with no heat, no running water, no dividing walls, and absolutely nothing inside it. It was as empty as she felt. Hitomi shivered remembering how painfully cold it was when they first moved to Magrath. Her father had to sell his gold pocket watch for a poor deal so they could get a desperately needed stove. Her mother said at least they were all together. Some families were split up where the men were sent to camps, or worse, jail.

Now Hitomi's parents and teenage brother, Sadao, picked sugar beets to pay for their "home sweet home." The only reason Hitomi wasn't out picking was because she babysat her two little sisters, Etsuko and Kyoko. They'd lived here for two years, and Hitomi's soul ached with the unreality and unfairness of it all. It was a horrific Cinderella nightmare where a happy ending was against the law for a Jap like her.

A STAR IS BORN by Miki Dare

Journal Entry: Square with the number 1 and 8 in the month of Demember (Get it, I have dementia so I *demember* things! Hahaha!)

I overheard the nurses talking about making Jell-O shooters and liquored gummy bears for a Christmas party, and it reminded me of my father. Anything to do with booze does. My dad was a great word-weaver. His own alternate reality was often fuelled by a bottle. He was Nissei, born in Canada, but the "yellow" never came off as far as most Canadians were concerned.

So let's have a drink and take that bitter-tasting fruit that life has thrown you and turn it into something magical. Let's make it golden pink and sweet. Change it into this perfect fragrant peach sitting in the forest that is waiting to be appreciated and loved. As kids we loved to hear my dad tell us the story of Peach Boy.

An older Japanese couple find this perfect peach on the road and are all excited to eat it, when—Pop! It turns into a little boy. Having no kids of their own, they happily raised Momotaru. They taught him to be respectful, brave, and kind, and he was a kid who listened and learned. Peach Boy was loved and loving, and grew into a fine young man. He made loyal friends who helped him defeat awful demons, and together they made the world happy ever after.

But it's only in my dad's stories where a Japanese child could defeat the demons. In "real life," everyone sees us as the demons— with triangle hats, slanted eyes, and dagger-like fingernails. The Yellow Peril.

It only makes sense to take us from our homes and keep us in boxes. It makes sense to take anything of value so we can't grow into bigger monsters or buy bigger weapons. It only makes sense for demons to be counted, fingerprinted, and given cards to track our movements. Look at the monster I am now: a withered, toothless old woman. I told you I'm losing my filter. I hate such bitter memories sticking to me like tar sands. I want this toxic stuff to go away forever. Let me live in the la-la land of only positive memories. Alzheimer's is such an asshole. Let me just remember the good things.

Timeline Capture:
AZ126798324323433495569023WQM843925237

Hitomi let out a deep breath and focused on the fresh eggs and milk she would get for cleaning the house for Mrs. Armstrong. Every bit helped, and she would just have to do her part. She knocked on the door so hard that her knuckles stung with each rap.

James opened the door. Her seventeen-year-old neighbour was a looker: strawberry blond crew cut, tall, well-muscled, and a wide smile.. He towered above her and was one of the most popular boys and the star basketball player in school. James wedged the door open for her while holding a piece of toast and licking strawberry jam from his lips. He spoke in a sing-song voice, and the illusion of his prince-like beauty shattered away. "Ahhh-sooo! Hi-Tommy!"

James liked to practice his "Japanese" by making "Ahhh-soo" sound like "asshole." He also knew her name, but she had long given up correcting him; James said her name like this on purpose, hoping to get a rise out of her. She took off her sandals and pulled her socks from her skirt pocket and slipped them on. Her heart beat faster already; she could hear a clock ticking in the living room but no other sounds. There were eight kids in his family, and there was usually someone yelling or crying.

"Is your mom home?" she asked.

"Nope. They've all gone to our cousins'. I decided to stay home and be in charge of things." He popped the last piece of his toast in his mouth and grinned.

"I'm going to clean the toilet." Hitomi ignored the knot tightening in her stomach and went straight to the bathroom. She hoped James would not follow her there.

"I spilled milk on the kitchen floor, so you have to do that first." A bit of jam sat sickly sweet in the corner of his mouth.

She blew at her bangs and marched to the kitchen where she spotted the offending white puddle on the patterned linoleum. She grabbed a bucket and rag and began sopping up the mess.

He stood over her like a boss in the sugar beet fields. "I heard you got to celebrate your birthday at the RCMP station."

Her ears burned as she wrung out dingy milk into the bucket.

"Isn't it every girl's dream to have her sweet sixteen surrounded by handsome RCMP officers?"

Hitomi wanted to sound tough, but she could hear the hurt in her voice. She grounded her teeth, remembering how each fingertip was dirty with ink, and then pressed on to paper like a debasing form of calligraphy. Flash! Went the camera. Happy Birthday! The government had indelible proof she was now old enough to be a war criminal. Her sweet sixteen gift was a lifetime responsibility to always carry her alien registration card.

"Funny girl." James' laughter grated like steel wool. "Let's see your card, I know all you Chinks have to carry them."

Only Japanese had them, but that James got his racial slur wrong was the least of her worries. Hitomi ignored him and strode to the sink and dumped out the milk.

"Are you deaf? Give it to me." His voice changed again to the awful sing-song tone Hitomi hated. "Oh, me so sowwy. You no speakee Engrish, right?"

Hitomi was a third generation Japanese, Sansei; she was born here and spoke English, not Japanese, fluently. She steadied her voice to sound calm and in control, but in her mind, she hurled curse words like lightning on a stormy night. "I am here to clean your house."

In one long step, he came uncomfortably close to her. "You need to know your place. Hand it over!" His breath smelled of yeasty bread and sugary strawberries.

She focused all her attention on rinsing the bucket in the sink while her stomach clenched like a fist. "No."

"I'll help myself." He leaned against her and groped at her chest; the pretense of searching for an alien card gone as soon as he touched her.

"Stop! Get off me!" She pushed hard against his chest, but he just tightened his grip on her waist.

Hitomi would not let this happen again. She snatched the frying pan from the counter and smashed it against the side of his head.

He let her go, and she backed away, only to see flashes of darkness and shards of light after his fist drove into her forehead. The force threw her to the ground, and she put her hands up to defend herself, but she felt like a drowning woman whose body had already sunk to the bottom of the lake.

His face loomed close, and his smile reminded her of the skull and crossbones on bottles of poison. "I wonder how dirty a dirty Jap is?"

Journal Entry: Square with the number 8 in it of the bigger rectangle of June

Some days my thoughts just whirl around me like rides at the PNE going so fast I can't get a hold of any of them. I get all wired up and scared, and my social skills which were never the greatest, just plummet like a broken rollercoaster gone off the wooden tracks. My filter gets flung off, and I'm speaking raw messy emotions and offending a lot of people. I don't mean to.

Aya, my grandniece, she's the one who visits the most and gets the brunt of my time-befuddled moodiness. She asked me the other day if she could bring me something from the store, and I told her I wanted peach boy. Aya thoughtfully brought me a bag of peaches on her next visit. My heartbeat raced at the sight of the fuzzy golden fruit. Memories of other pasts rocketed through me, of a small peach of a boy who dies over and over again on the day of his birth. There were complications that a pregnant teenage girl on her own in the dark of night couldn't be expected to deal with. But the guilt of not wanting the baby, the guilt of it dying and hiding its death—these things haunt you.

As if I were an Asahi baseball player, I picked up one of the peaches and nailed it against the wall. I threw another and another so quickly that it took Aya a moment to realize what was going on and grab back the bag.

"Peach boy! Boy!" I screamed.

"I'm sorry, Auntie. I must have misunderstood." My poor grandniece shook her head and got tissues to clean the yellow juices dripping down the wall. I can still smell their sweet summery scent coming from all that mangled flesh sprawled on my beige carpet.

There was too much to explain to her; I couldn't get my pain and story into words. Instead, wicked things escaped my lips. "There won't be a next time! You're thirty-eight and your wife is even older! You're way past your due date, Christmas cake. You waited too long to have kids and now you can't have any! All that in-vitro and money wasted on your shrivelled up eggs!"

Aya's leaf-green eyes had looked all the greener as she quickly wiped away tears. She hucked the mashed peaches into the garbage can and left with this crumpled-leaf goodbye.

Forgive me. I am iota of flotsam. A senile speck of sentience. A mouthy old Asian lady.

Timeline Capture:
AZ1267983243234333495569023WQM843925237

Hitomi sobbed and yanked at her hair as she left the Armstrong's house. At least her salty tears wiped away the horrid smell of strawberry jam and sweat still clinging to her. The shame pulsed through her like constant waves. She didn't want to think about what happened. Not now. Not ever again. She wanted to get away as fast as she could, but the ripped feeling forced her to walk slower and bow-legged.

Even if she dared say what James had done to her, no one would believe her. And if they did, they would blame her. They would never blame him. Hitomi was the devil. She was the dirty Jap. She was the one already fingerprinted by police. Her parents certainly couldn't help her. They were demons too, barely holding on to their pride after losing so much already. The truth would just cause them more agony because they could do nothing. This is a white man's world, and the law was on his side. She had to know her place.

Hitomi stopped. She balled up her fists and punched herself in the stomach until bile rose to her throat. She slapped herself in the face until the stinging rang through her skull like a bell. She dug her nails in her arms until she drew blood. She held her face in her hands and screamed a silent scream wishing someone somewhere could understand her pain.

Journal Entry: Time: two freckles past a hair o'clock

When I first started time travelling, the little lights guided me. It always starts with me floating in blackness. But I never feel alone or scared. I feel this deep well of love that stretches the universe, and then one by one, the tiny dots of light start flashing around me lightly like the wishes blown from dandelions. They're always excited and whisper amongst themselves because they have this big plan to help "me," and I happen to be a "me" who can help with the helping.

When they speak, it's like petting a cat where you are touching a thousand different hairs but it all feels like one warm spot of soft fur. The lights don't like to talk much about it, but they are the parts of me's that refused to go. These are the sad bits of me's. They are the angry bits of me's. The bits of me's that won't give up and go away even though their timelines have long since extinguished. These are the rebellious bits of me's from every strand of my possibilities.

The lights always liked that show *MacGyver*, and they think we can do a little hotwiring with the strands of time and quietly make a difference. They have been travelling everywhere, finding each other and banding together. They tell me they have always been with me; I just couldn't see them until now. They were the little voices that said I could do it. They were the little voices that sent the subtlest of warnings and the slimmest of hints. They were glowing all around me, these iotas of flotsams. Surreptitious specks of sentience. Eternal bits of an Asian girl still fighting.

Timeline Capture:
AZ126798324323433495569023WQM843925237
Etsuko, Hitomi's four-year-old sister, pranced in circles and waved her arms, pretending to be a butterfly. Sitting by the warm stove, Hitomi absently touched her stomach, which has grown hard and rounded like half a basketball. A heavy pit of worry had also been growing deep inside her. Thankfully, winter sets in faster and longer in Alberta than in British Columbia, and she could hide in her brother's oversized hand-me-down sweaters. After doing her final origami fold on a soup can label, Hitomi chewed on her fingernails that had lost their white rims.

"Look," Hitomi said. Etsuko's eyes widened, and she flapped over with her invisible wings.

There was a hole in the origami, and Hitomi set her lips to it and blew. Etsuko squealed and clapped her hands as the two-dimensional paper turned into a three-dimensional ball. Hitomi batted it over to Etsuko who caught it with a belly full of giggles. Their youngest sister Kyoko slept in the corner of the room, not bothered at all by their romping around playing catch. Hitomi smiled at the peaceful sleeping face of Kyoko and at Etsuko's easy joy at such small things in life, meanwhile worries constantly chewed away at her. *I will not be able to keep this secret forever. What future will I have? What future will this child have? Through no fault of its own, it is the child of two demons. No one will want it to exist. Not its father. Not even me, its mother.*

Journal Entry: November — No remember 12 ☺
My grandniece Aya is a social studies teacher and is always asking me about what happened during and after the internment camp days. I tell her I don't remember. My parents rarely spoke of their loss after the war; it's family tradition not to talk about it. But since I'm going soon, and she has given me so much, I'll write a little more for her here. When the Canadian government finally allowed us to leave our boxes, the first thing my dad did was go back to Salt Spring Island to see if he could get our house back. The new owners, fellow islanders we had gone to church with and sold produce to, said no. I remember my mother sobbing when my dad told her the news. There was once a community of about one hundred Japanese farmers and fishermen who lived on Salt Spring Island before the war. So many of them tried to buy their homes back, or buy up new land, or get a job there. The answer was always the same. No. The "real" Canadians on the island wanted a Japanese-free timeline and now they had it. Why would they give that up? Go look in the phone book today for Salt Spring Island, you'll be lucky if you find even one Japanese name.

We moved to Burnaby where my parents started again. From working three or four jobs each to save enough money, they eventually bought a little plot of land and farmed once again. My brother Sadao eventually took it over. I went to college and studied to be a nurse. I tried to get a job as a nurse on Salt Spring Island. Even though I knew they had vacancies, they told me with icy politeness that there were no jobs at this time. What they left out of the sentence was ". . . for Japs like you."

My grandniece says it is not our shame. It's the shame of a society that has lost its moral compass and likes to point the finger at the victim. Aya talks all fancy, saying things like, "we live in a world that cuts along lines of race, class, and gender, and it is those on the bottom who feel and rightfully fear the blade the most." Schooling has changed so much since my day. You looked at a teacher the wrong way and you could be whacked with a ruler; Japs was the "nicest" word used for Japanese, and girls could only wear skirts to school no matter how bloody cold it was outside.

Aya told me of this activity she did with her class where she sticks a bunch of large gold stars on the wall. She has six kids come up to form a pyramid, so the top kid can reach the stars on the wall. She asks who has to work the hardest and carry the weight. The kids of course say the bottom people. Who has it the easiest and can reach the stars? The kids say the person on the top. Then she has the kids imagine back in the past when Europeans came and stole Aboriginal land and kidnapped Africans to work as slaves. Who got the benefits? Kids would say it was the white landowners at the top collecting the stars. On the day that slavery was abolished, did that change the power structure in society? In 1996 when the last Canadian residential school was closed, did that change the power structure? And the kids would answer: no. Aya says it led to some deep discussions and the kids really got it. They talked about how the people on top didn't want to look hard at how they got those stars, and how hard it was for people on the bottom to make change with such a heavy history of oppression. There is still a lot of racism; why Gertrude in 12A just called me a Chink this morning, but I think things are slowly getting better. It's a much better time to be born Japanese in Canada.

Still I'm trying to let it all go; I have my own secret connection to the stars now, the stars that matter. The little lights call me. Alone I am an iota of flotsam. A senile speck of sentience. A little old Asian lady. But together, deep in my sleeping world of time travel, we can pool our power. The lights of me's have been practicing, testing, and investigating. We can do some rewiring, but it will require sacrifice. We have known the sharp taste of loss and sacrifice in all our timelines, but there is a sweetness to this one that makes it easily bearable.

Timeline Capture:
AZ126798324323434333495569023WQM843925237
Hitomi woke in the middle of the night with a stabbing pain in her belly. Deep in her abdomen, it felt like her muscles were contracting into a three-dimensional letter U. Her eyes watered as she tried to pretend nothing was happening. She forced herself not to moan, afraid to wake her family, but the pain came in waves that got stronger and longer. Hitomi crept to the door in the pitch black, away from the warm nest of her family. With a quick creak of the door, she was out. The crisp, cold air tingled against her skin—the magic of the night making her feel alive and real. Darkness covered up the wounds of day and made everyone beautiful and equal. It was just Hitomi and the universe.

Then pain ratcheted through her body again, and she leaned over and held her knees. Once it finished, she stood up and looked to the sky. Tears ran down her face as she stared at the first star she laid eyes on. "I wish I may, I wish I might, wish this wish I wish tonight." She made her wish—a wish that baggy sweaters would soon no longer be able to hide.

Hitomi crunched through the snow in her rubber boots to get to the outhouse. She couldn't get there fast enough and threw up, tendrils of stream swirling off the pile of puke. Despite the cold, Hitomi sweated as another contraction rocked through her. She ran to lean against the outhouse door, panting and moaning quietly.

She couldn't ignore the urge to push the baby out anymore. She pushed and pushed. Hitomi felt things tearing like she was an alien fruit shooting out a rock-hard pit. Little lights flashed in the corner of her vision, and dizziness enveloped her sense of reality. Voices that sounded like one voice spoke to her. She saw no one there, but a sudden rush of warmth around her chest and shoulders made her feel like someone was holding her.

Suddenly she found herself floating in blackness. But she didn't feel alone or scared. "We are always here for you. You are loved," the voices said. The bright lights danced around her, and love from every corner of the universe poured into Hitomi.

Hitomi blinked and found herself in a small warm room with a beige-carpeted floor. She was leaning against a wall that smelled faintly of peaches. An old Japanese woman stood beside her and patted her hand. "The baby's feet are coming first, but we can do this together."

Hitomi didn't ask any questions, her body screamed to get the baby out, and she didn't care how. The old woman's voice sounded familiar, and she followed her instructions for when to push and stop. All that mattered was having this baby. Finally, she felt a huge rush of relief as the baby left her body. The old woman caught the baby and carefully took the umbilical cord from around its neck. She gently patted it on the back until it cried like an angry kitten. The old woman beamed with pride and placed the child in Hitomi's arms.

Hitomi wept as she took in her baby's thin body, fuzzy golden hair, and brown eyes. "Momotaru, I love you."

The lights floated in the corners of her vision again, and they whispered to Hitomi of timeline rules and their limits of bending them. The room went dark again as Hitomi kissed her baby. The old woman pressed a buzzer on the wall and screamed for help— and then in a blink, she disappeared and only a tiny bright light remained. Darkness completely took over Hitomi's surroundings, and the lights encircled her. "Remember you are not alone, and you are always loved."

Journal Entry: Today is the day
Aya,

Thank you for everything. You and Melody will make wonderful parents.

With eternal gratitude and love,
Hitomi

MY LEFT HAND
Ruhan Zhao

I never believed in Fate, yet on my way to the Beijing Institute of High Energy Physics this morning, I couldn't help but go straight to the old fortune teller sitting at roadside.

The old man had chosen an unexpected place to set up his stall. He was surrounded by several of the most advanced research institutes of science and technology in the world. How dare he hawk his cheap tricks to those scientists? Yet strangely enough, he seemed to be doing good business just about every day. In fact, several of my colleagues said that his predictions were amazingly accurate.

Of course, I didn't buy any of this nonsense. I didn't believe the future could be told, and I never bothered to speak to him.

But today was different: a precarious task awaited me at my institute. Maybe he was for real, maybe he wasn't. I didn't know, but I knew I needed some comfort, and I hoped he could ease my nervousness.

I stood in front of the stall. The beautiful beams of morning sunlight were just touching the treetops, and I could hear birds singing in the distance. There was no one around except me. It was still early. I might be his first customer.

The stall was simple. A large piece of white cloth spread out on the ground in front of the seated old man. In the middle of the cloth was a Tai Chi symbol. A Chinese antithetical couplet was painted along two sides of the cloth:

WHERE THE STARS RISE

Knowing the heaven and the earth;
Telling the past and the future.

The old man looked like a typical fortune teller (if there *is* such a thing): very thin, white hair, and a long silver beard under his chin.

"You want to know your fortune?" he asked.

I nodded.

He studied my face. After a while, he nodded slowly and said, "You have a square face with a wide mouth and broad forehead. This is a noble face bestowed with a good fortune. Your whole life must be smooth and well."

Every fortune teller had the same approach. If someone worked in a famous institute in the nation, he must have a "smooth and well" life. I knew that.

"You are reaching a crisis in your work," he continued. *That* was surprising. We were performing a crucial experiment today, one that might change my life, no matter whether it was successful or not. But how could he possibly know it?

I thought about it for a while and then started to understand. I had never gone to this fortune teller before. Why should I come today? Obviously because I was in the middle of a crisis. I was on my way to my institute. It was logical for him to guess that the crisis was about my work. He was clearly very perceptive and skilled at observing people. No wonder people told me he was good.

"Let me look at your palm," the old man said.

I stretched out my hand.

"Not this one. The left hand, please."

Left hand. Of course. Man left, woman right. A man's fate could only be told from his palm-prints on the left hand. Every Chinese person knew the rule of palm-print reading. How could I have forgotten? Embarrassed by my blunder, I offered him my left hand.

The old man pulled my hand closer with his emaciated hands, and read my palm-prints carefully. He concentrated so intently that he looked like a scholar studying a reference book. His eyes were so close to my palm that I wondered if he had a vision problem and had left his glasses at home.

MY LEFT HAND by Ruhan Zhao

Suddenly, his expression changed. He raised his head and looked straight into my eyes.

"What's the matter?" I asked.

"There will be a disaster at your workplace today," he said, staring at me and pronouncing each word carefully. "Don't go to your institute."

That got my attention. Telling me I was in a crisis might be a simple guess—but telling me that a disaster awaited me didn't seem like a simple fortune teller's trick. The experiment scheduled for today was indeed very dangerous—but how could he know? How could he be so sure that it would go wrong? Was he really able to tell the future? Should I believe him and go home? No, that was ridiculous. He was just some street mountebank, and I had important *scientific* work to do. The experiment was vital to our research, and a positive outcome would produce a long-awaited scientific breakthrough. I couldn't simply withdraw based on the work of an old man on the street.

Besides, I'd never really believed in fortune telling. I was a scientist. He was a charlatan or, at best, a good guesser. Mystifying people was part of his job. He probably wanted to scare me, to predict a disaster to see my reaction. It didn't take a genius to guess my work was dangerous. He knew I was working in the Institute of High Energy Physics. He had already guessed correctly that my work was in crisis. He had probably observed that I was anxious and nervous when I approached him. He probably put all that together and guessed—not *predicted*, but *guessed*—that I'd be involved in a disaster. If I was frightened away from my work, no one would know if his prediction was right or not. Later he might tell other people that he saved my life. It would certainly be good for business, especially if I confirmed it. If I didn't go to the institute, if we didn't run the experiment, who could know if it would have ended in a disaster? He was on safe ground, not me.

"How did you know that?" I asked, trying not to sound too serious.

"Look." The old man pointed to my left hand. "Your life line and career line are very close to each other. They are also long and clear. This shows that you are very successful in your work. However, there is a short and deep line cutting through both of these lines. From the position of this short line, I can tell that today, something disastrous will happen to you. It will terminate not only your career, but also—your life!"

"Are you saying that I will die today?"

He nodded. "I beg you: do not go to work today."

This was too much. I couldn't stand this nonsense anymore. I took out a ten-yuan banknote from my pocket and dropped it next to him. Then I stood and walked toward my institute.

"You must not go there today," shouted the old man.

I stopped, turned around, and smiled at him. "Thanks. But I am a scientist. I believe in science. We don't *tell* the future, we *build* it." Then I walked away, feeling his sad gaze following me to my building.

Although I didn't believe in fate and mysticism, I did feel uneasy after this incident. However, after entering the institute, I was soon immersed in the preparations for our experiment and became completely oblivious to what the old man had told me.

The experiment was designed to test a revolutionary theory made by our project leader, Dr. Fang Shi. The theory postulated that if a certain group of particles with extremely high energy entered into a super strong magnetic field, the particles would stimulate a distortion of the space-time continuum in the field and then generate a gateway to a space parallel to ours. If a person happened to be placed in the distorted field, he would fall through the gateway and enter the parallel space.

We had already sent a cat to another space and successfully retrieved it. We named that animal "Schrödinger's cat."

The subject for today's experiment was not a cat. It was a man. And the man was me.

There was no lack of volunteers for today's experiment because his or her name would be written into historical books. I was thrilled when Dr. Shi chose me, possibly as a reward for my years as his closest assistant.

The machine was huge and complicated. Staff members worked around it like ants and bees. I wore a special suit and entered the hall with Dr. Shi, who seemed much more nervous than me as he reviewed all the details. The others were eerily silent. Many of them had dedicated their time and energy to this experiment, for which the institute had invested an astronomical amount of funding. If it failed, the whole institute would probably be shut down.

The final minute arrived. I shook hands with Dr. Shi and walked toward the round plate in the centre of the hall. I stepped on to the plate and stood at the very centre of a big Tai Chi symbol.

The symbol reminded me of the old fortune teller and his stall. I didn't believe in fate, but who could prove that fate didn't exist? Maybe someday an Einstein or a Hawking would discover the principle of fate hidden in a quantum equation. I thought about the old man's prediction. *Would* the experiment fail? Would I die?

The machine started to hum. The operators' fingers skillfully danced over keyboards. The super magnetic field began to generate. I felt a sudden dizziness. The Tai Chi symbol on the plate began to rotate, whirling faster and faster until it was a blur. I could not distinguish Ying and Yang of the symbol anymore. All I could see were black and white circles rotating like crazy. Suddenly, I heard a tremendous explosion in the air, and then a dazzlingly bright light shot toward me. Before I knew what had happened, I lost consciousness.

When I woke up, I found myself lying on the Tai Chi symbol. Dr. Shi and the other members of the research group stood around me, observing me with deep concern.

"How do you feel?" Dr. Shi asked. "Are you all right?"

My head was burning like hell. The other people helped me to sit up. I stretched my arms and legs. They seemed to be okay.

"All right, I suppose," I answered. "How was the experiment?"

"It is much more important to know that you are fine. Our experiment—unfortunately—failed," replied Dr. Shi. "You didn't reach that other space. All the high energy particles and the strong magnetic field did was knock you out. At first, we were afraid you were dead."

Although he seemed more concerned about me than the experiment, he couldn't hide his disappointment. He had planned this experiment for most of his career, and he had been so close to succeeding. We had checked every technical detail, and we all believed that it would succeed. The failure was devastating because we couldn't possibly afford to try again. We were finished. All of our efforts were for nothing.

I suddenly recalled the words of that old fortune teller. He was right that my career would end today, but I didn't die. I had bet my life against the old man. I was still alive after the accident, so I won. I laughed out loud.

Dr. Shi and the others stared at me in surprise. For a minute, they must have thought that I had contracted some mental disorder under that strong magnetic field. I stood up and assured them that I was fine.

After cleaning all the mess from the experiment, I decided to take off early. When I walked out the front door, the old fortune teller's stall was still there, so I walked over to it.

"Hey, look at me!" I said. "I'm still alive!"

The old man raised his head, his eyes wide with wonder. He stared at me as if looking at a ghost.

"This is impossible! You must be dead at this moment!"

"Is that your wish?" I said with an amused smile.

"Why would I wish your death? I was telling the truth from your palm-prints. I have never been wrong in my reading." The old man's voice was shaking. "Give me your hand. I want to see it again."

I smiled and stretched my left hand out to him. The old man hastily grasped it and began examining. After a while, he raised his head and stared at me, puzzled. "This is not the palm I saw this morning."

I pulled my hand back and looked at the palm-prints. A chill went through my whole body. The career line and the lifeline were far away from each other, and there was no trace of any shorter line cutting through them.

Of course, I was familiar with my palm-prints. The prints on this palm were not the prints of my left hand.

They were the prints of my right hand.

I quickly checked my right hand. The career line and the lifeline were close to each other, and a short line cut through them. Those were the prints from my left hand! My left hand and right hand had been switched!

I felt a mix of terror and excitement. As a physicist, I immediately understood the reason.

MY LEFT HAND by Ruhan Zhao

Imagine a being living on a plane. If it wants to jump to another parallel plane, the only way to get there is through the three-dimensional space. But if, instead of going to that other plane, it flips itself over in the three-dimensional space, and goes back to its own plane, then its left and right sides will become reversed — which was exactly what had happened to me. My left and right hands had been switched. The only explanation was that I had jumped from our three-dimensional space into the four-dimensional space, and then flipped over in the four-dimensional space . . .

I turned around and dashed toward our institute, leaving the perplexed fortune teller behind.

Maybe his fortune telling was accurate. Maybe his prediction about me was true. But my left hand was not my original left hand anymore. My fate had been changed through the fourth dimension.

I didn't have time to explain this to the old man. I was not sure who the winner of this battle of fate was: science or fortune-telling. I was not sure what other parts of me had been changed in the fourth-dimensional space, nor did I care. All I wanted to do at this moment was to find Dr. Shi and tell him that our experiment *hadn't* failed after all.

DNR

Gabriela Lee

The process was simple: each citizen of the Philippine Protectorate carried an ID card. It had the person's name—an unfortunate relic from their Spanish colonial past—and the person's designation, a serial number for accessing the public info terminals across the colony, and an "In Case of Emergency" contact number. Beneath these, in very small print, depending on the citizen, were the following words: "In case of termination, DNR."

However, Melissa had an unfortunate habit of leaving her ID in her office cube. She hoped, sometime in the future, she would remember to bring it in case she would ever breathe her last oxygen-recycled breath. Not that it would be too much trouble to figure out her place of work: the white lab coat, with a stylized caduceus on the breast pocket, was enough to remind people that she worked at the Hospice.

She would receive ten, maybe twelve DNRs, that needed processing during a nightlight shift at the Hospice. She knew that Helen usually dealt with more during the daylight cycle. The colony was thriving, and they could afford to lose more and more bodies in an effort to achieve population balance. Even though the Protectorate was established off-world almost fifty years ago, people were still afraid.

The rapid expansion of the population, thanks to a mix of conservative government procedures and religious fervour,

DNR by Gabriela Lee

helped cause the collapse of Old Metro Manila and the surrounding provinces during the first of the Great Tremors. The interim government in Davao City, down south of the Philippines, quickly began sending colonists off-planet to establish a protectorate; every other Southeast Asian nation was already crawling across the Milky Way. Plans were made and scrapped and planned again, and after ten years, the *Bakunawa* Class-3 ship, carrying both human and terraforming loads, started flying to Mars.

Melissa was on that trip. Her landing papers showed that she was a recent medical school graduate. The hospital where she worked planetside said it would be easier to find her a placement off-planet if they fudged her papers; her face was still fresh enough to seem like it belonged to a twentysomething graduate. But in reality, she figured it would be a new chance at a life, a way to look at the world again, especially after her own world had recently fallen apart. She carried nothing but a single bag; she didn't have anything else she wanted to save.

Nowadays, Melissa would reflect on the irony that even though they were on the cusp of almost zero waste throughout the entire Martian protectorate, people would still hang on to the vestiges of their past lives. Unlike Helen's office cube, hers was pristine and sparse. No projections of family members on the wall or plastic plants that bounced to solar energy or even a reminder pad. Melissa fastidiously kept her desk that way, especially after her early years as a field med in the colony, when she was part of the team that would respond to DNRs at their home cubes. She could still remember one of her first DNR cases: Mrs. Melendez was found behind a stack of old *Songhits* magazines that she managed to smuggle off-world. God knows how. They had to sift through a small mountain of crumbling newsprint and lyric sheets to find the old woman and take her to the hospice to process her DNR.

It rattled Melissa's senses to find the corpse—and Mrs. Melendez was without a pulse when they finally found her—still clutching one of her faded magazines to her breast, as though the pages held the answers to all of life's mysteries in their stained-ink glory. Even when they transported the dead woman back to Natural Resources and lifted her on the metal gurney, even as Melissa slowly opened up and examined the body for the final pathology report ("Cause of death: cardiac arrest"), she couldn't help but feel irritated at the woman. After all, she could have easily prolonged her life for a good five, ten years if she had followed colony instructions properly and hadn't smuggled useless contrabands into her cube.

Melissa broke apart the body to be re-purposed within the Hospice: blood to Hec in Exsanguination and bones to Geraldine in Osteology, internal organs to the staff at Internal Medicine. She carefully preserved the head for last. The Psychophysiology Department was notoriously picky with brain samples for transplants and studies, and she wanted to get as pristine a sample as possible.

Melissa plucked out Mrs. Melendez's eyes and gently placed them in a small container filled with clear suspension fluids just beside the gurney. The pale orbs glanced around the room, seemingly animated, though Melissa was used to the dead's eyes and could ignore them easily. Finally, when everything was packaged and catalogued and labeled, the unused remains, less than five percent of the total body weight of the deceased, could be tossed into the matter furnace. The small metal box was directly connected to the Hospice's energy matrices and easily recycled the remains of the dead.

Finally, Melissa plugged the neuro-visual conductor into a recording device that projected images on the wall. While DNR could not return the deceased to their family members, they kept a recording of the last thing they remembered before their deaths, a reminder of a life well-lived. Part of Melissa's job was to make sure that the images were high-quality and appropriate for public viewing.

As Melissa filled out the final pages of Mrs. Melendez's report for the staff files, she half-heartedly watched the last image-memories imprinted in the old woman's eyes. It was a black-and-white image of four boys, with bowl-cut hairstyles and old-fashioned coats, carrying musical instruments and singing on a small stage. *Here comes the sun*, they crooned, music jangling in the background. *Here comes the sun*.

Humming along, Melissa felt a little less irritated.

DNR by Gabriela Lee

❖

"Don't you get tired?" asked Helen during one of those rare days when they would catch each other at the cafeteria. Melissa glanced up from her reading pad, where she had already consumed half a novel about a human-alien romance, but she had barely touched her nutrient bars.

"Tired from what?" Melissa shifted to make room for Helen on the bench. The cafeteria was cavernous in its emptiness. The timer above the cafeteria door reminded her that she had fifteen minutes before her shift.

Helen waved her food implement in the air before attacking her bars with gusto. "All of this. Everything. The department. The bodies. Watching everyone's lives projected on the wall."

Melissa shrugged. "It's a job. I'm good at it. I fail to see what else I should be thinking about."

"But that's the problem," said Helen. "Don't you remember what life was like planetside?"

"You mean the constant threat of typhoons or drought? Or the sense that food was going to run out the next day? Or that we had no idea where to get water or medicine or anything remotely necessary for patients at a hospital? No thanks."

Helen rolled her eyes. "Well, you're a barrel of sunshine."

"I'm being realistic. We've been here, what, almost two decades now? It's a better job than anything I could get back home, even if I've migrated to the American Union or Canada."

"Is a job all you ever think about?"

Melissa placed her pad down. "What's bothering you, Helen?"

The other woman pursed her lips. "Rommel emailed. He wants me to come home and take care of the grandkids."

"You're still on contract."

She shrugged. "I can finish it at the local hospital. They don't have a DNR system set up so maybe I can go back to actual pathology."

"So what are you talking to me for? It seems like you've already figured things out."

Helen reached out across the table and laid a cool, soft hand over Melissa's. "I wanted to see if you wanted to come with me.

You look tired and burned-out, Mellie. Maybe going back home will make you feel better."

She shook her head. "This is my home now, Helen. There's nothing for me planetside."

"But what about—"

"There's *nobody*, Helen."

Helen chewed the last of her bars and then stood up to bring her tray back to the dispensers. "Well, if you change your mind, I'll be here for a few more days to file my transfer docs."

Melissa forced her lips to lift into a smile. "I'll be fine. Thanks for the offer."

Later, at her desk, while completing the last few docs from the previous shift, Melissa thought about her colleague. They were cordial, but Melissa wasn't interested in being friends. She wasn't even sure how Helen ran the other half of the day; that wasn't part of Melissa's job.

She glanced over at Helen's cube, with the projections of her children and grandchildren. Rommel occupied a large space on the wall, his sun-brown face breaking into a wide-toothed smile. There were some people in Dentistry who would kill for those teeth. She glanced back at her own cube, at the blinking blue light on her console that signalled the arrival of a body, and sighed as she suited up for work.

Gloves, face mask, blue-hued uniform: Melissa slipped them on like a second skin as she quietly waited for the nurses to bring in the body for prep. Two nurses, both male, rolled in the body and lifted it from one gurney to a metal slab, nodded to her in acknowledgement, and then left the room. Melissa yanked the bright halogen exam light toward her as she examined the body.

Male, late fifties, slightly abnormal swelling around the midsection—stomach cancer, perhaps? While they may have largely eradicated the mutation in younger citizens, the elders, particularly the first generation transplanted from the Philippines to this colony, weren't so receptive to the gene therapy introduced by the Hospice oncologists. Melissa glanced at the ID that accompanied the body. Manuel Co. The name sounded familiar, but then again, she assumed that men of a certain age were part of the same ship she had taken to the colony.

DNR by Gabriela Lee

The work was tedious, but familiar. The flesh parted easily, allowing her ways to read the body like delicate pages from an old book, like the ones made from paper, which she saw only behind glass in museums. She wondered if the material would feel this way against her touch: supple and slick. She read his childhood sicknesses and minor irritations, gall bladder removed, liver slightly discoloured (Alcohol? Medication?), heart still thick with roped muscle and veins that bound it in place. Melissa excavated the body in silence, her only music being the scraping of blade against skin, skin against bone.

The eyes were cloudy, the irises faded to a soft brown. She plucked them, flower-like, from the sockets, and immersed them in the conducting liquid. Flicking the machine's switches, she listened to the familiar *whirr-grrrr* sound of the neuro-visual conductors as they extracted the images from the pale white globes suspended in the ether. As she waited for the machine to begin projecting the images on the wall opposite her, she began the methodical task of distributing the body's organs into their specific containers and organizing them for delivery. Once the body was empty, she began suturing the remaining skin back into place.

Her stitches were clean and narrow, neat lines punctuating the flesh of the dead. Her mother used to be a seamstress, after all, and taught her well.

The small furnace at the back of the lab was sealed shut, and only Melissa and Helen had the key codes, which changed every twenty-four hours. Once Mr. Co's body was ready for disposal, she slipped off her gloves and initiated the sequence to activate the furnace. The clean energy resulting from the dead body was enough to power many of Natural Resources' machines, including the neuro-visual conductors. Melissa figured there was some kind of poetry in that, but she was never fond of literature in the first place.

As she slipped the body into the caverns of the furnace, she wondered for a moment how it would feel to slip through that hole as well, to crawl down into the bowels of the planet and stay there, ensconced in darkness and warmth.

At the edge of her hearing, she knew that the machine had

finally extracted the necessary images and were now splicing them together into a narrative. Melissa never quite understood how the technology identified cohesion, but she was nonetheless pleased that she was not *that* necessary to the process of making the DNR video. All she had to do was make sure that everything worked perfectly.

She saw the image projected on the wall. The hairs on her neck rose.

On the screen, playing in a loop, was a clear image of a young woman, bronze-skinned and dark-haired, wearing a sun-coloured dress and smiling at Manuel, her hand extended away from the frame as though she was inviting him into her world. The sky was a brilliant, blinding blue. She had never seen that kind of blue on Mars.

Melissa stared at herself: when she was a mother, when she was a wife.

She was one of the first responders on the scene. The Great Tremors weren't so great then: rumblings of the earth, an unsteady floor, a rolling sea. But as the numbers on the Richter scale began to climb, cities began to fall. Manila was one of the worst places hit by the earthquakes, the sudden shifting beneath the swollen city. Tenements, forgotten or ignored by the city government and allowed to stand on unstable foundations, collapsed immediately, burying hundreds of the city's poorest people beneath wood, concrete, and debris.

Mellie worked for three days, taking only minutes-long breaks in between. Slight and small, she was constantly wedging herself between slabs of wobbly wood or rusty steel, attempting to rescue another human being. Survivors emerged, bloody and bruised, their skin dusted with dirt, tears running down their faces as they saw the sky. Rickety ambulances whined and screamed down the main thoroughfares of the city. The entire thoroughfare of Epifanio de Los Santos Avenue, the longest road that ran across the city, was closed off to traffic, land, and air. Lanes were quickly cleared to bring the injured to the nearest government hospitals.

DNR by Gabriela Lee

Of course, once the dust had settled, Mellie had a day to get herself together before reporting back to duty at the St. Michael and Mary Hospital, which was already running out of room for all the patients. The newsfeeds said that there were thousands, tens of thousands, dead or missing. Her husband, Manuel, had also taken a day off, and he was at home, waiting for her.

He wrapped her in his arms and said that everything was okay as she took great, heaving gulps, allowing the tremors of her own body to pass through her. When Benny, who had just turned ten, arrived home from school, he gave her a great, big hug. He told her that he was going to be an engineer when he grew up so he could build great houses for people that wouldn't fall on them when there was an earthquake. Mellie held him tight, so tight.

When she returned to work, she asked for a transfer: back to Davao City, where she had grown up. She was sure the buildings there were safer—everyone said that there were no earthquakes in Davao City, and she believed them. She heard about the earthquake ordinances, the way the city was organized to respond quickly and calmly to any emergency. She knew her family would be safe there.

Of course, she was mistaken.

Benny was eleven when it started: the rashes, the redness that spread over his skin like a wildfire. He had come back from a camping trip with his classmates and complained of insects and feeling feverish the whole time. She tried everything: cooling baths, calamine, anti-inflammatory ointments and creams that his skin absorbed but barely relieved him of the pain. He cried, his nails raking over his body like slash marks. After a week, he could barely move, his skin in a constant state of swelling and thickening and swelling once more.

"We need to take him to the hospital," Manuel had said. But she didn't want her son to see what she did at work, to frighten him. She thought it was chicken pox. Seven to twelve days—she knew her literature. He had all his vaccines. He was going to be fine.

But after thirteen days, Benny was in such a constant state of pain that his hands and feet had to be restrained so that he wouldn't hurt himself. His sheets were already streaked with blood, where he had been scratching himself so deep that he had peeled off his skin. Mellie took one look at her son, wrapped him in a thick blanket to protect him from the world outside, and took him to her workplace. In and out. It would be a quick trip, not even a day.

But she was wrong.

The infection had burrowed beneath her son's skin like parasites. He constantly burned from the inside. *Immuno-compromised*, his charts read as Mellie swept through the screens, searching for a sign to help her son. *Unknown causes*. Doctors rotated his meds, ran test after test. Manuel sat patiently beside their son while Mellie could barely stand to be in the same room anymore. All her knowledge flew out the window. She wanted to scream, fight, punch through wall to save Benny's life.

She slipped out of his room while he slept, morphine dripping from an old-fashioned IV line. The hospital had a small garden between buildings, filled with synthetic plants that resembled her favourites from childhood: small star-shaped *santan* blooms, nodding *gumamelas* in yellow and pink ruffles, small round cacti that threaded across the meandering path connecting the two buildings.

Mellie sat at the solitary bench in the middle of the garden and stared up at the sky. The seat was a desolate grey, the hue of all those dilapidated houses that collapsed during the earthquake over a year ago. More earthquakes were happening, more disasters rising from the earth and the ocean like monsters. Why worry about other nations when your own country is out to get you? Davao was the last stable bastion. The government had relocated the spaceship programs down south, just outside Mintal. The government had reclaimed the flat expanse of agricultural lands at the foot of Mount Apo, where it could build the first of great *Bakunawa* ships that would take them to space. After all, they were one of the last NATO-ASEAN countries to leave, and at the rate they were going, even Laos would be heading to the Moon before they could even lift-off.

She wanted to cry, but she couldn't. Her heart paused between one beat and the next. It weighed her down, anchored to her chest like a stone. She looked at the sky, her neck aching from tilting backwards, watching the grey light fade. Stars came out. And in that moment, she knew that she needed to be out there, following that pinprick of light, rather than being here, bound to the ground.

When she returned to the hospital room, Manuel had fallen asleep on the uncomfortable chair next to their son's bed. Benny's breathing was calm, controlled. He was wrapped in white cloth and bandages, where he had scratched so hard that the skin had broken and refused to heal.

He was broken. Mellie could see that now.

Slowly, she reached down for Benny's files, hooked to the foot of his bed, and swiped across the screen to access his vitals. At the bottom of the page was a consent form. Without thinking, Mellie quickly double-tapped the screen to confirm that her son was a DNR.

He died two days later.

When he was wheeled into the lab, covered with a sheet, her supervisor looked at Mellie and asked her if she was capable of doing the job. DNRs in children were rare, and there was a lot of value in their parts. In response, Mellie asked if she could do the initial incision.

The technology to record the last imprint within the visual cortex did not exist at the time. And so the eyes were also sent out, unrecorded, to help another doctor, another patient.

She came home early that night. The weight in her heart could no longer be tethered to her body. It crashed, littering her soul with the debris of loving her son. When he was born, she had disconnected his body to hers, and now she had cut him apart. Now, some other child will have a piece of his heart, will have the muscles and bone and blood taken from her child. They will still live. But Benny, Benny, Benny was dead.

She was on the couch, flipping through the channels when Manuel arrived. There were dark circles under his eyes. "When can we bring him home?" he asked.

"The hospital already took care of it. He was infectious." There was a mechanical lilt to her voice she couldn't suppress. "He needed to be processed fast."

"Well yes, but surely we could have a small funeral, at the

very least, before they take care of him." Manuel sat down beside her and held her hand. He felt warm and pulsing and alive. She couldn't help but be reminded of Benny in the curve of his lips, the sound of his voice. "Mellie, talk to me."

She took a deep breath, felt around her mind for the words that she wanted to say to her husband. Something about loss. Something about pain. Something about knowing that she could no longer *stand* to be near anything that reminded her of her son.

Including Manuel.

Especially Manuel.

But her lips remained shut. And so they stayed there, through the night, until Manuel had fallen asleep on the couch. Mellie crept to their bedroom, packed her things one more time, and left everything else behind.

The medical space program was for volunteers only. Mellie signed up as soon as her son died. The hospital was willing to help her; they received funding every time they were able to put a doctor on a spaceship. They even tweaked her application to show her suitability for spaceflight.

It was only after training—sixteen months to train for space travel, and another ten months for terraforming and colonization—that Mellie was able to send a short message to Manuel to ask for an annulment. The government had requested it. They knew how hard it was to be up there and yet to be anchored down here as well. She needed to be weightless. He never replied, but the digital documents arrived at the office the next day, signed and sealed and ready to be filed into the cloud servers.

And then she got on the ship and never ever once looked back. Until now.

She remembered that day, remembered where they were: the beach, just before Benny was born. A romantic getaway, just the two of them. Everything was clear: the sky, the sea, Manuel. This was years before the ground had swallowed up the Philippines, before the Great Tremors rendered the archipelago into broken, distant islands in hours. She did not have to watch the livefeeds from the newsdrones to know that she could not return to Davao City, that she had no home to return to. She refused to look at the lists of the dead. She knew her husband had died, and she was the one who had killed him.

Melissa stared at the eyes in the container and at the video playing on the wall. He may have changed his last name but certainly not his memory. Guilt tugged at her chest, where she knew her heart was still beating, faintly, for this man.

A ring from the comm stationed at her cube startled her from her thoughts. "Dr. Remedios?" came a voice from the nurses' station. "The family of Mr. Co is here, waiting for the DNR recording."

She paused, and stepped toward the recording equipment, at the looping memory of herself. She came to Mars with nothing to remember him by. Beyond the borders of the memory, she could almost see his hand, the faint outline of his arms. His body. His eyes.

"Please tell them that the files are corrupted and that we have been unable to retrieve his memories. We will be compensating them, of course, for this unfortunate incident." She kept her voice clear, steady.

But for now, the lie was just between her and a dead body. "Alright," said the nurse on duty. The comm clicked off, and for good measure, Melissa removed the wire that connected it to the central communications system. Then she cupped the eyes and placed them in a transport container. Finally, she withdrew the recording chip from the machine and tucked it into her pocket, where it jostled with her ID.

Manuel Co, she thought, a finger stroking the smooth cylindrical container holding his eyes. *Mine. All mine.*

A VISITATION FOR THE SPIRIT FESTIVAL

Diana Xin

The night before she was to return to China, Mrs. Liu woke from a terrible dream and knew with certainty that a ghost was sitting upon her chest. Her skin was damp from his condensation, and it took several seconds to catch her breath. Hours passed before she returned to a troubled sleep.

In the daylight she was herself again—reasonable, practical, and rational. She was a woman who balanced her chequebook every Monday and attended church every Sunday. Ask any of her friends and they would agree: she was the most logical and morally upstanding woman, one of the last people who deserved to be haunted by a ghost she did not believe in.

The ghost had come from Grand Auntie Du. Ten years ago when the dear woman passed, she bequeathed a ghost to Mrs. Liu in her will. The ghost being a ghost, and Mrs. Liu not believing in ghosts, the inheritance had been easily settled, until recently.

In the last year, the ghost stirred from an afterthought, often not thought of at all, to a daily nuisance, an incorrigible bother. She couldn't count the number of times he had switched the sugar and the salt or stolen her keys only to slip them back into her pocket hours later.

A VISITATION FOR THE SPIRIT FESTIVAL by Diana Xin

How did she know it was a he-ghost and not a she-ghost? She didn't. She had never seen the ghost. She did not believe in the ghost. But he *felt* like a male ghost. And she was positive he was responsible for taking her passport from the drawer and leaving it on the piano, for breaking the zipper on the suitcase she had checked only the other day, and for transforming the jars of codfish oil she had purchased as gifts into capsules of worthless vitamin E.

Preparing for the trip had left her more scattered than usual. She was always grasping for stray thoughts, for parts of herself that seemed to simply wander off. She took a deep breath, trying to find a quiet moment and stretch it as long as she could. Then, her husband entered the room, and everything she'd slowly gathered together fell apart again. His smell, his foot shuffling, his throat clearing—they intruded her space like pebbles skipping across her skin.

"Boarding pass," he said, brandishing one of his lists. "Melatonin. Peptol-Bismol."

"I only get indigestion from Italian food," she interjected.

"But you can't trust the food quality in China. Dirty cooking oil, you know." Mr. Liu shook his head and sighed. "You have your passport?"

"I'm ready."

Mr. Liu took a deep breath, and she wondered if the witnesses he interviewed on the stand also got fed up with his theatrics. "But are you ready? To go back home?"

Mrs. Liu managed a tight smile. Neither she nor Mr. Liu considered China home, but they, like all their friends, still called it *jia*. Mr. Liu left China when he was barely a teenager. What did he know about China? What did she herself know about it, when she hadn't visited in fifteen years? *Jia* was the same word for family. Her only family in China was a pack of greedy cousins, and now, her daughter.

Michelle had only been to China once before, when she was five. Mrs. Liu remembered her standing in confusion at her grandfather's funeral, her small form swallowed by the white gown, and her face brightly indignant that she had been scolded for snatching a piece of red bean cake from the altar. Anyone could see the little girl, though the same as everyone else in appearance, did not belong there. Then, last summer, Michelle announced that she was quitting her job, leaving the nice Mountain View company that recruited her out of college, and she was moving to China. Just for one year, she had said. She would teach English at an elite private high school. She had already Skyped with the principal. The contract was final.

Now the year was up, and she wanted to stay another. It was time to go back and get her. Operation: Retrieve a daughter.

"Talk to her about graduate school," Mr. Liu reminded Mrs. Liu in the car. "She won't have a future without graduate school, and she can't go back to school if she's too old."

"She doesn't know what she wants to study."

"Tell her law school."

"Tell her yourself."

"She doesn't listen to me."

"Like she listens to me."

Mr. Liu squinted and leaned forward, concentrating on changing lanes.

"Make sure she's eating well," he said. "Take care of yourself, too. Keep your purse zipped up and your passport with you at all times."

"You just focus on keeping our house standing, okay?" Mrs. Liu said. He was full of advice and admonishments, but China wasn't his area of expertise. She knew the country much better. She had been dreaming about it for months: the empty classrooms at her college, the courtyard, and the little fountain with the water lilies where the students held their rallies, punctuating the peacefulness with their discontent.

"What an opportunity for you, huh?" her husband asked. "Visiting all your old friends. Did you get in touch with anyone?"

She gave him a long look, studying his cheerful gaze. He was no doubt looking forward to two weeks of solitude, all the time in the world for his crosswords and history books. If he had really cared, he would have made time to take the trip himself.

"No," she said finally. "They're all busy."

"Really? What about Wen?"

All Mrs. Liu had of her best friend from youth were a few

faded photographs. "She's not in Beijing anymore."

"I thought everyone with a college degree lived in Beijing. Floating north. Isn't that what they call it?" He pulled up to the curb. "It's time for grad school. Tell her that. And find out if she has a boyfriend."

Rolling her suitcase behind her, Mrs. Liu was glad to get away from him. It had been a long time since she last travelled alone. She laid her things out for the security officers, confirmed with the woman at the gate that she had found the right place, and buckled herself into her seat with relief. Her anxieties finally began to lift. Now there was nothing to do but sit. Thirteen hours of sitting. She had become good at sitting this past year.

Just around the time Michelle left, the dental office, where Mrs. Liu filed insurance paperwork, replaced her job with a computer. With all that free time in her schedule, she could sit in one quiet room for hours. That was when the ghost came out from whatever cobwebbed corner he'd gotten lost in. As she sat, he would tease the curtains and cast shadows onto the wall. Occasionally, his breath would fall over her and pool like a cold lake inside her stomach. She learned to listen for him, allowing herself to hear the creaks in the floorboards, the hum of the refrigerator, the ticking of the clock, until her senses grew sharp enough that she could hear his sighs as well.

She heard him again now, settling into the empty seat beside her. She felt him brush a feathery hand over hers, and she was glad the airline had somehow known to save a spot for him.

"Okay, fine," she said, softly. "That's just fine. I remember you. I'm ready for you."

And then the plane hurtled forward, nosing up against gravity.

Ghost was delighted.

Many ghosts resided in Heaven, but there couldn't have been more than a few who got to ride in an airplane. Unless they all rode up in airplanes. Ghost didn't know because he'd never made it into Heaven. As Grand Auntie Du had patiently explained, his plasma was besmirched by a stain of sin that only the blood of

Jesus could wash away, but through no fault of his own, Ghost had not received the baptismal fire. Grand Auntie Du had gone to Heaven or so Ghost thought. As the plane rose into the clouds, he pressed himself against the little oval window, hoping for a glimpse of Grand Auntie Du to confirm that she had gotten through.

There was nothing but clouds. Far below, he could still spot the shimmering ocean next to geometric patches of land, but soon, that too disappeared. Ghost sank back from the window and tucked himself against the warmth of Mrs. Liu. At times, a musky weight entered his usual weightlessness. This was the closest he ever got to substance.

He always felt it more when Mrs. Liu was close by. When he touched her hand, the heat of her skin would radiate into him, as if he too were buzzing, pulsing with life. As if he, too, had a form that mattered.

What a surprise it was when he realized how much he liked Mrs. Liu. Grand Auntie Du had complained all the time about the younger woman's pushiness and pride, ever so sanctimonious about bringing over food that she had clearly purchased from the Lucky Bamboo. "But they'll take care of you," she told Ghost when she bequeathed him.

Well, they hadn't. All the best behaviour he could muster, and they had all ignored him. For years, he wept alone. Then, Mrs. Liu began weeping, too. He tiptoed out from who knows where and sat beneath her. Her sadness seeped into his, and his began to recede. Each bit of sorrow was like a tiny shard of her soul, and each clear and jagged piece he touched brought him closer to replicating the container of something that was like her body.

Already, he could enter her dreams. He knew all about her. For months now, he had felt the strums of her growing tension as he sorted through the faces that appeared in her subconscious. Faces from China. Sometimes he wondered if one of them was his own, lost a long time ago. Other times, he thought maybe he had never had a face, only what Grand Auntie Du invented for him, now subject to Mrs. Liu's creation. But he found Mrs. Liu's mind an interesting place, energy firing every which way, pockets of breath with seams of silence. He flickered in and out of it.

A VISITATION FOR THE SPIRIT FESTIVAL by Diana Xin

Another pang of sorrow struck. He could not identify it as his or hers, so he nestled as close as possible, letting the rhythm of her sad heart knock against him.

A flash of sunlight hit the window, but it did nothing to warm him. Mrs. Liu pulled down the screen, shuttering them in shadow.

Ghost squeezed even harder against her chest, wrapping every tendril of himself tight against her. Sometimes, he imagined her shattering.

It was hard to breathe in China. The July heat was dense with pollution, people, and ash. It was the month of the Spirit Festival, and on every street corner, someone crouched on the ground burning paper money. The air made Mrs. Liu's eyes water.

She felt as if she were walking between two worlds, China present and China past. China present was a behemoth, full of tall, glass buildings and shiny automobiles, but every once in a while, she caught a glimpse of China past. A face confusingly familiar. Mao's smiling countenance dangling inside an ornament of red thread on a cab driver's rear view mirror. A smell in the air, of meat cooking in oil or of oil blistering out from the sewers. All these pulled at her already askew heart.

An unnamed nostalgia had settled over her at some point after her arrival, lodging so deeply in her chest that she found it difficult to swallow. She couldn't say for what she was nostalgic. Everything was foreign to her, even, surprisingly, her daughter.

Michelle had cut her hair short. Not just shoulder-length, but trimmed up to her ears, exposing her pale, delicate neck. Last year, this haircut would have made Michelle look more like a child, but this year it made her look more adult. It was in the way she moved, how she stepped confidently into the road, a hand raised to hail a cab. The way she talked back to people, no apologies for her stilted Mandarin.

Let's go there, Mom, she would say, *and then we can eat that and I can you show this and you can buy those.*

She was becoming more and more like her father.

Mrs. Liu followed her daughter dutifully around the city and tried to remember that she was on a mission. It was several days before she could make a move. They were eating sandwiches and pasta at a café called Alba. Michelle claimed that it was her favourite spot. Mrs. Liu didn't understand why she couldn't go back to the U.S. and eat spaghetti there.

"So," she said, twirling her fork, "you meet any nice guys?"

Michelle offered a quirk of her eyebrow. "The guys I teach with are all nice."

"You all hang out, huh?"

"It's a good group of people."

"Big groups of friends always break into small groups. It's natural. Then you are alone with one other person. Things happen. Have you met anyone special?"

"Not like that."

Mrs. Liu heard the scorn in Michelle's voice. What was she hiding behind the roll of her eyes? When she was a teenager, she lied by acting offended. When she was a child, she never lied. "Your father says it's time to think about graduate school. I agree. If there's nothing keeping you here, you should come home and keep pursuing your studies."

"Does it have to be a boy keeping me here? Why can't it be about other things? There's more to life than boys, isn't there? There's so much more." Michelle expelled a long sigh that made Mrs. Liu remember her daughter at twelve, thirteen, when her hair was always in her eyes and frustration would send her bangs lifting from her forehead.

But this woman was a completely different creature. Michelle had grown up sometime in the past year, and Mrs. Liu had missed it. Her arguments were laid out now with assertive grace and clarity.

"I don't care about men, Mom. I'm here to fight for the women. And children, too, I guess."

Feminism. Inequality. Lack of social responsibility. Her father would be proud.

But when Mrs. Liu relayed to him their conversation the next day while waiting for Michelle to come out of the shower, he responded mockingly. "She's out to save the world, huh? And are we her sponsors? Ask her how she plans to feed herself."

Mrs. Liu felt her heart shrink even tighter as he went on. His speech rang too familiar. After the end of idealism, the only whisper in the air said, *money.*

"How are the subways," Mr. Liu wanted to know next. "Clean? Dirty? Did you ride a high-speed train?"

"Those only go outside the city."

She walked over to the window and glanced over the contents on Michelle's desk, as if that would reveal more of this woman. There were a few sheaths of student work, a green leather-bound journal. She thumbed through the journal pages. Just to check the paper quality. When Mrs. Liu was young, her thoughts had been scribbled onto thin rice paper that ripped often under the tip of her pen. Mr. Liu prattled on about some story he had heard on the news, some accident in Hangzhou.

Something sharp bit against her finger, and she paused before opening the journal. A Polaroid of Michelle with another woman, sitting at a restaurant. It was a recent photo, Michelle already sporting her new hairstyle. They both looked so young, so happy. It reminded her of Wen.

"How is she, really?" Mr. Liu said.

"Grown up."

"Still senseless."

At that moment, a dark shape shifted in the corner of her eye. The sound of the shower faucet stopped. She turned, but there was nothing. A tremor ran down her spine.

"Can't you talk some sense into her?"

Her reflection in the windowpane stared sullenly back. The streets below were quiet and blanketed in haze.

Ghost watched as alarm etched itself into the lines on Mrs. Liu's face, followed by confusion. He wondered if she had felt it, too, the shifting of gears, the click of the earth locking against something else, its shadow or underside.

Since disembarking the plane, Ghost had felt a vibration humming through his nebula. An excitement was mounting, filling the air, and now, at the click of the lock, it stilled.

The lull lasted only a moment. Then, a flurry of voices, rushing up from the depths below, rustled like thousands of hushed wings.

It was the fourteenth day of the seventh lunar month, the eve of the Spirit Festival. The gates to the realm of the dead had opened, and the ghosts were charging out.

Hou Hai was rotten with people. Tourists and ex-pats swarmed here regularly for the shops and the nightlife. Locals had come as well to send off paper lanterns and little boats with candles to light the path home for their ancestors, released from the lower realms to roam the night. Bars and restaurants around the three back lakes of the Forbidden City broadcasted loud guitars and off-key singing to attract their guests. Across from them, peddlers reached out to sell the passersby sticks of incense and yellow joss paper folded into houses, televisions, Bentleys—gifts for the dead.

Mrs. Liu stepped around the vendors as best she could, keeping Michelle's red beret within her line of vision. Michelle wanted to show her the night markets, but Mrs. Liu was no longer used to such large crowds, and she had never liked loud music. She could feel her nerves fraying at the edge.

"It's too busy here," Mrs. Liu called out to her daughter. "Isn't there somewhere quieter we can go?"

Ghost followed behind them, bewildered as well. Never had he been around so many spirits. In fact, he had only met three other ghosts in total, and all of them had existed very temporarily. Much more so than he. They had all found the issues they were meant to resolve, met the person they were meant to join.

Ghost watched as Michelle's red hat bobbed in the air. All the colours had grown disorienting as small flames lighted up constellations in the darkness of the sky and water. Some of the spirits followed them like streams of mist and smoke. Ghost tried to call them back, to let them know that these were only paper, nothing more, but he found that he could not communicate.

He tried to ask one round-eyed matron where she and her cohorts had come from, but she only shook her head, and from her thin, elongated neck came one whistling keen that seemed to tremble along his perimeters.

He lagged behind Mrs. Liu and her daughter as they turned down a winding road. Even in these quieter alleys, other strange ghosts would brush by. Some, like the woman, had long needle-necks above their voluminous bellies. Others bore diaphanous flames dancing in their mouths. A few of them, in passing, released a belch of air so foul it made him quiver.

Mrs. Liu found the *hutong* side streets, though narrower, more expansive for her body, like she had room to breathe. Sometimes, though, a horrible stench would fill the air, so repulsive she could almost feel its slither against her skin.

Walking through these streets, she remembered her years as a student in the '80s. Her college was nearby, and she came to this neighbourhood often. She would sit with friends at a tea shop with a talking parrot. She would spend entire afternoons in quiet admiration of a calligraphy master working in the back corner of a bookstore.

A group of poets, quiet but rebellious, used to gather here, behind one of those red wooden gates. She remembered the prideful cadence of her best friend's voice as she read her work out loud. It was Wen, always the more outgoing one, who had brought her to the meetings, who had introduced her to the young poet with the strong, confident voice yet such timid, soft lips. The ash was back in her eyes again. She swiped at them with her hand.

"This place is one of the last pieces of Beijing's past," Michelle said. "The government's slowly taking it over. They've changed the old street names. They want to keep building things. Construction everywhere."

Mrs. Liu was content to let Michelle explain China, but she was surprised when her daughter turned, eyes bright, and said,

"Mom. I love it here."

She thought of her old friends, all those empty seats in the classroom. "Life is more difficult here."

"I know it's dirty, and broken, and it can be dangerous, but I feel so much more alive here," Michelle said. "What could I possibly learn in a classroom again that matters more than all the things I'm learning here? I can't go back to reading about philosophy or logic, or God help me, the psychology of market research. I want to do my work here."

Mrs. Liu remembered sitting behind closed doors with her best friend and that young poet, discussing the world with an urgency that only twenty-year-olds could afford. Outside, bells were ringing and ringing; hordes of students on bicycles rode past.

"I needed to leave, Mom," Michelle said. "You have no idea how much I needed to get out."

She thought of mentioning those students to Michelle, of letting her know that she too had lived moments of passion. But, of course, Michelle did not ask. She had her own story to tell.

"It wasn't a good place, Mom. I know it seemed nice. Like I'd won some kind of prize. But the people there. I'd never felt so small."

"It was a good opportunity. You were lucky to get the job."

"I know," Michelle said, in that tone that dragged the words out and laid them down like brick. *No more. Stop here.* "I met a man who was imprisoned for two years. Do you know why?"

Mrs. Liu could guess.

"He was a student protester. He was only nineteen when they locked him up. Now his mind's not the same, and he still doesn't have full citizenship. He can't work or travel. But he walks. He's walked all across China, talking to people and playing the flute."

"How romantic," Mrs. Liu murmured. "What a life."

"Mom, it's not romantic. It's fucked up. They took away his life and still haven't given back his identity."

The heaviness on her chest sank deeper. Her sigh came with effort. "Watch your language."

A VISITATION FOR THE SPIRIT FESTIVAL by Diana Xin

They were coming out to a main street now, cars lined up behind a stoplight. Ghost paused with them as they waited for the crosswalk. He watched as a cluster of spirits clawed at a bowl of fruit left beside a few sticks of incense outside a convenience store. The peaches disintegrated in the flames and fumes of the ghosts' malodorous mouths. Not even a grape could fit down those piped necks cinching their billowing bellies. This drove the spirits into mad frenzies. All they hungered for was food. But Ghost was jealous of them, following the trails of light to find the offerings set up by harried descendants. All he had were these two women, neither of them paying him mind.

He thought at first that these spirits would direct him home; that among them, he would find a familiar face, like Grand Auntie Du's, who would tell him what to do. But as the spirits clamoured for their gifts, he was still lost and directionless. Utterly forgotten.

Now that they were back on the main streets, Mrs. Liu could tell from some internalized compass where they were going. She continued with a sense of trepidation, her mind filled with images from the past. Sweet scenes of holding hands with her best friend, with the young poet, whispering their desires, yet these brought her no pleasure. The distant bells continued chiming, carried by the breeze. The past pressing upon her, threatening to carry her off.

"Mom?" her daughter turned to her again. The indignant anger was gone, replaced by cautious concern. Mrs. Liu drew herself together warily. "Dad called before you got here. I was surprised. He almost never calls unless he's with you, you know."

Her husband never put his family on any of his lists.

"He's worried about you."

Michelle spoke haltingly, arranging her face and plotting her next phrase. Mrs. Liu recognized her own strategies.

"He says your moods have been off. And you're more forgetful. He wanted me to keep an eye on you and see if I noticed anything.

But, I don't know. Is there anything you want to tell me?"

Mrs. Liu bit down the inside of her lip. So her husband had laid down his own moves. So he had played them both. She tried to summon some anger or even just surprise, but she was so tired. Nothing her husband did could surprise or disappoint her much anymore.

"I'm fine, honey," she said. "Your father likes to exaggerate."

Michelle was still solemn-eyed. "I'll go back, you know, if you ever needed me. But I'm not ready to leave yet."

Mrs. Liu wondered what Michelle was searching for, what her work entailed and what risks she would encounter. "When will you be ready? What's your work here?"

"It's not just that."

She waited for her to continue, but her daughter stayed quiet. Mrs. Liu recognized the hesitant withholding in her face and her stance, but she could not guess anymore at its reason. Michelle had travelled past her reach.

In the distance, Ghost spotted something that felt like kin. He felt it more than saw it, a churning disappointment, an aimless craving. They were nearing the larger buildings again, and hundreds of apparitions swarmed in the air. He communed with each one, touching, caressing, searching for that source of recognition.

Mrs. Liu had done her own searching in this city. When she last visited in 1996, she had knocked on doors and talked to school secretaries, tracking down addresses and phone numbers. She carried with her the photos of Wen. She took a train three hours to a small village in Shan Dong, weaving stories for Michelle the whole trip to keep her from complaining about the heat, the noise, her hunger. They arrived at an abandoned house in ruins. "Did someone have a fight here?" Michelle asked, her eyes wide at the sight of capsized tables and broken chairs. Mrs. Liu knew then to stop searching. Her best friend had disappeared. The young poet who had once so gently kissed her was no more. His hold on her life would always be that tenuous, an exhalation left on a window glass.

Ghost saw the spectral masses reflected on the glass windshields of passing cars, and he himself was among them. They were as fragmented as light, as insubstantial as shadow, and yet they were burgeoning. He felt the spark of their electricity catch within him.

Across the wide lanes of highway, Mrs. Liu could see Mao smiling down from his portrait over the large empty court of Tiananmen Square, quiet and abandoned.

Bustling with pale and anxious spirits, the open plaza undulated seductively to Ghost. He heard the shriek of their exertions, their ardour. Their pulsations engulfed him completely. Together, they were nameless. They were consciousness inchoate. They could be as loud as they wanted to be. They could haunt indefinitely. No one had bothered to delineate their passing, and thus they had no boundary.

Mrs. Liu stood facing the cold, open expanse. That spring, all the students had converged in this place, marching and chanting, filling it with fervent speeches. They included her, her best friend, and that young poet. They were going to create change, improve the education system, make a difference for the future. Then, in the middle of May, she had gotten on a plane to join her betrothed in California, a man she had met only twice. The distant bells fell silent, and terrible scenes flooded over her. Bloodied faces and fallen bodies, obscured by gunfire smoke, images she was unsure she had ever seen before, yet they felt as familiar as memories.

"It wasn't my choice to leave," she said.

"What did you say?"

In one night, it was all gone. The sun rose on a mess of corpses, never counted, never named. How easy they were to clean up, to erase. How easy they were to forget.

"We have to give them names."

"Give who names?" A young woman stepped up to her, placing a hand on her shoulder. She looked so sweet, so familiar, and yet there was harshness at the corners of her mouth. Her eyes shined with fear.

"Wen?" Mrs. Liu grabbed her hand. "Is that you?"

The girl seemed taken aback, as if she had just been slapped.

Mrs. Liu narrowed her eyes. "Who are you?"

"Mom. It's me. Michelle."

Yes. Yes, it was her daughter, for her life had continued. She had gotten on a plane.

"I'm sorry," she said.

"Are you okay?"

"Yes. I'm fine. Don't look so worried."

"You scared me."

"I just got tired."

"We can take a cab home."

"That sounds nice."

She let her daughter take her hand and lead her away. She needed to go, close her eyes for a moment.

Behind her, Ghost shimmered in the phantom throng, released at last to swell and amplify.

ROSE'S ARM

Calvin D. Jim

Rose Ishikawa sat on a wooden bench in the vestibule of the Japanese United Church. Her left hand cradled an urn containing her mother's ashes. She felt the weight of the cold, mottled grey stone in the folds of her flower-patterned dress.

Papa's friends slowly shuffled out of the sanctuary. Their muffled voices, drenched in sympathy, faded into the hollow patter of the warm Vancouver rain. Papa would want to go home soon. She clutched the urn tighter.

"Miss Rose?"

She looked up. Dr. Samuel T. Trask removed his fedora with his mechanical right hand. Tiny pistons and gears whirred and clicked. He knelt in front of her. Whispers of *hakujin*, "white man," hung in the air. And he was visiting with a young Japanese girl.

"I am deeply sorry for your loss, Miss Rose," he said. "Your mother did not suffer, I assure you."

Of course she suffered. I was there.

"Breech birth like that, it was too late. There was nothin' I could do."

Rose stared down at the grey urn. He would have been a beautiful boy. A son, a son. Papa talked about nothing else in the weeks before Mama's death. A boy was all he wanted; a son to carry on the family name. Born in 1928, the Year of the Dragon, he would have brought much luck. Mama told Rose many times not to pay attention to all that talk. "Papa loves you too," she said. He was *ijusha*, an immigrant from the old country, she whispered. It was just his way. "But I was born here," Rose would say. Mama just smiled softly and held her close.

Dr. Trask pulled a calling card from his jacket pocket and slid it into her left hand still clutching the urn. Coppery light glinted off the metallic limb. "If there is anything I can do, please let me know."

Rose nodded, not wanting to appear ungrateful at the gesture, but her gaze never left the brassy mechanized hand folded over her own. It was beautiful.

"May I help you?"

Rose looked up. Papa loomed over them.

"Mr. Ishikawa, sir," Dr. Trask said as he stood up. "I am payin' my respects to you and your daughter. And offerin' any assistance in this time of need."

Papa glanced down at Rose, spotted the little beige card, and grabbed it from her hand. He crumpled the card and tossed it on the floor. More good fortune thrown away.

"Thank you," said Papa. "We need no charity."

Was it charity, thought Rose, or did Papa not want to be beholden to a *hakujin*?

Dr. Trask tipped his hat and left without a word.

Papa grabbed the urn.

"Papa," Rose said, stifling a cry. "Please let me carry Mama home. Please."

"I said before, out of question," he said, gesturing to the stump of Rose's right arm, cut off below the elbow.

He didn't want a daughter. He certainly didn't want a one-armed one.

Papa strode out of the church. Rose sighed and picked up Dr. Trask's crumpled card before following three paces behind.

❖

The evening after the funeral, Rose and her father went back to work. Her job every evening was simple: pull the wooden cart while Papa sold tofu to the restaurants along busy Powell Street.

ROSE'S ARM by Calvin D. Jim

It took every ounce of willpower not to spill the waterlogged tofu sloshing around in the wooden buckets, especially when they passed the wide bay windows of Kasuga Confectionary: filled with tempting baskets of apples, red ginger candy, and sweet *mochi*. The fish cakes, tart Japanese pickles, and fresh oranges at Maikawa Grocery always made her mouth water. Too soon, Papa pulled her across the street as Model-Ts and the Stanley Streetcar trundled toward them, bells and horns blaring.

Mrs. Hasagawa, who smelled like stale mothballs, always complimented her on what a great job she did. Rose forced a smile and turned away. Would Mrs. Hasagawa say as much to a girl with two arms? Or was she just amazed at what a cripple could do?

Their first stop was Fuji Chop Suey, but its owner had already purchased his daily quota from Tanaka-san's tofu-ya. Rose heard more of the same at Yoshino and Morino. Chidori always took a few pieces out of a sense of duty.

Rose gazed into the bucket of crumbly malformed blocks of tofu. Good tofu was firm and easy to slice. Papa's was spongy and soft, barely good enough for soup. Papa never haggled about price. He took what they gave him. Usually, it was enough to buy the next day's soybeans to make more tofu. But they were receiving fewer and fewer coins every day.

"Mama's tofu much, much better," said Papa as they passed by Mang. The Chinese beggar sat on the sidewalk staring blankly through rusted mechanical goggle-eyes while rattling pennies in a tin cup. A rough scrawl on the cardboard sign in his lap read: "Help me see again."

The heady scent of chicken broth filled Rose's nostrils as they neared the soup line close to St. James Church. Her mouth watered and she became aware of the emptiness gnawing at her stomach. "Papa?" she said.

"Not now."

"But Papa, you haven't eaten—"

"I said not now."

Rose's shoulders sagged. She stared at the ground and followed her father past the railway tracks toward the old mill. It was far out of the way from home, but Papa always insisted they walked by. The scent of pine and sea salt drifted from a warm breeze hovering over Vancouver Harbour while gulls squealed above them. Far beyond the mill, the grey North Shore Mountains blended into the evening sky. Soon, they would fade into blackness.

How long had it been since the mill owners dismissed Papa and all the other Japanese? Two months? Three? At least Mama's tofu kept a roof over their heads.

"When will you go back to work here?"

"Be quiet," said Papa.

The sign posted on the chain link fence was Papa's silent answer: "No Japs Allowed." Papa didn't read much English, but he recognized those words. Outside Powell Street, the signs were everywhere.

They passed the rickety docks near the old mill where fishing boats unloaded their daily salmon catch at the cannery.

How many hours had Rose spent with Mama sitting on those docks listening to the gulls gliding above the seashine, watching the red sun sink behind the tall cedars in Stanley Park? One evening, tears fell on Mama's cheeks even as she stared at the setting sun.

"Why are you crying, Mama?"

"It's so beautiful," Mama said, smiling.

Rose turned back toward the horizon. Fiery hues were slowly turning grey-blue.

"It's almost over," Rose said.

"That is why I weep."

Mama pulled her close. Rose leaned her head on Mama's shoulder trying to understand.

Rose wished she could spend one more day with Mama, staring at a sunset such as this. Now, here with Papa, that rickety dock seemed so far away.

She cleared her throat. "Hasagawa-san said he could get you to unload the trucks. He would pay us two dollars—"

"Quiet."

"Or I could help you make tofu. Mama showed me—"

"I said quiet!"

Papa reached in the half-full bucket, pulled out a misshapen tofu block and showed it to her. It broke apart in his hand. Rose stared at the bulbous clump of bean curd, avoiding her father's eyes.

"This is living. No one will give you living. Everything comes with a cost. We—I have to make it for us." He threw the tofu over the fence. It broke into pieces in the air. "No charity."

Rose gripped the wagon's rope, her knuckles as white as snow. She opened her mouth to protest but thought better of it. They could have eaten that tofu. What a waste. He wouldn't have listened anyway. Maybe that was the problem. How could she convince others of her usefulness if Papa wouldn't even believe? She had to make him.

"It's not fair. Mama's gone. Why won't you let me—"

"Enough!" Papa's voice echoed through the swaying trees, scaring the geese.

They walked in silence the rest of the way home. Rose's stomach gurgled as they walked down Powell Street and through the chilly breezeway toward their lane house behind the Horizen grocery store. Rose wanted to apologize for her outburst; she didn't know what came over her. But she knew Papa would only grunt and continue walking.

Rose shivered as Papa stepped on the narrow porch in front of their lane house. He removed his shoes and placed them, as always, on the straw mat beside Mama's leather buckled t-strap shoes. Rose put hers on the opposite side and followed her father in. By the time she put on her slippers and hung her jacket on the wooden coat rack, Papa had already lit the oil lamp on the kitchen table.

Long shadows flickered over buckets of milky liquid, half a dozen homemade tofu presses with moist cloths tumbling over their edges. An old copper pot gazed at her from atop the potbelly stove. Mama's favourite pot.

Rose breathed deeply, imagining the tantalizing aroma of *shoyu* and *mirin* mingling into a thick teriyaki, or chicken broth fragranced with ginger root and onion. But the pot just stared back, cold and empty, the scent vanishing from memory, replaced by the lingering odour of stale soy milk, bean curds, and lye. Why won't he let her help? He needed her. He just didn't know it.

Mama's urn sat atop a chest of drawers surrounded by two burned-out wax candles, a bowl filled with dry rice covered in ash from three spent sticks of foul-smelling red incense, and a small plate of mandarin oranges. They couldn't afford a proper *butsudan*, so the chest, with its white flaky paint, became her makeshift shrine.

Buried behind the urn rested a small black and white photograph with Mama's placid face staring at her.

It wasn't fair. Mama always smiled. She was the bright centre in a crowded room. Rose could still see her laughing and dancing around the kitchen even as Papa chided Mama like a scowling samurai for acting so un-Japanese. This photograph wasn't her. It was a death mask, beckoning them to join her.

Not if she could do something about it.

Papa took the urn from atop the cabinet, pulled it to his chest, and disappeared without a word through the curtained French door leading to the one-cot bedroom in the back. The door rattled shut.

Rose sighed. She wouldn't see him until after sunrise, maybe not before noon. By then, she would be gone.

Rose flopped onto the threadbare red velvet chair near the door and pulled Dr. Trask's calling card from under a thin pillow. He was *hakujin*, but if she was to be as much help for Papa as Mama ever was, she had to pay him a visit. Papa would never approve. She wasn't going to give him a choice.

Rose melted into the high-backed, dark leather chair in Dr. Trask's brightly lit consulting office, marvelling at the white and glass cabinets filled with flasks of red and green, stainless steel and glass syringes, and small cardboard boxes no doubt filled with the most advanced medicine. The sharp scent of rubbing alcohol and formaldehyde stung her eyes like the white pickling vinegar Mama used to make *meboshi*. This was a place of science. Real medicine, not the greasy ointments and bitter medicinal soups from that Chinese pharmacy on East Hastings.

But it was the red and gold kimono framed under glass and

hanging on the dark, wooden wall that caught her attention.

"I want an arm." Rose pointed at Dr. Trask's mechanical hand. "Just like yours."

Dr. Trask leaned back in his chair, deep in thought as if contemplating the gravity and enormity of the request. "How old are you, Miss Rose? Ten? Eleven?"

"Thirteen," she said. "Old enough."

"Not for some decisions," Dr. Trask said. "Does your father know you're here?"

Rose shook her head. "He would not approve."

"Have you thought about the consequences?"

Again, Rose shook her head.

Dr. Trask removed his lab coat, rolled up his sleeve and put his mechanical arm on the table. He pressed a button hidden near his elbow. Gears wheezed and clicked and ground to a halt. With a snap, Dr. Trask twisted the arm off and placed it on the table in front of her. A rounded brass socket was connected to the stub of flesh and bone that was his upper arm.

"Sometimes, Miss Rose, flesh is better than metal."

But Rose wasn't listening. She leaned in, staring at the lustrous arm laying only inches in front of her.

"The grafting process," continued Dr. Trask, "permanently adheres the socket to your body. It cannot be undone without great injury. Though some minor allowances can be made for growth, the socket should be attached when you are mature."

A knot formed in the pit of Rose's stomach. She felt dizzy. Was he trying to scare her?

Dr. Trask picked up the arm and rotated it to give Rose a better look. "The arm itself is custom fitted and fabricated with the finest in German manufacturing before it is assembled and imported by airship. It requires regular maintenance and repairs that can only be completed by a qualified nurse technician, all of whom are expensive." He leaned across the desk, his eyes locking on hers. "Can you pay, Miss Rose?"

Rose shook her head again.

"Then there is nothin' more to say."

Rose gulped. She glanced at a small mirror on Dr. Trask's desk. Had she made a mistake coming here? The world revolved around money and she had nothing to barter with. They sold everything, including Mama's prize sewing machine, to pay for food and soybeans. The well had run dry. It would take years, decades, to afford such a wonder. How could she ever expect to pay for it working in Maikawa as a clerk or stock girl?

Her thoughts turned to Mang, who begged for money to pay for the expensive repairs and upgrades to his goggle-sized mechanical eyes, his real ones traded in, the price for some nameless benefit long since forgotten. One of the many Chinese who crossed the Pacific to build airship stations atop the Rockies. Papa called him foolish. "Body is all you have," he said. "Trade your body, lose your soul." After giving away all your possessions, what more do you have to bargain with?

Rose gritted her teeth. No, she hadn't made a mistake. Papa needed—she needed—that arm.

"You said you would help us," said Rose as Dr. Trask latched the brassy limb back onto the socket. The arm whirred to life. "You said that if there was anything we needed—"

"This is not what I intended, Miss Rose."

"You offer help and then turn me away. Do you do this to everyone or just Japanese?"

"Now you're not bein' fair, young lady—"

The office door creaked open and a stern, grey-haired nurse peeked in.

"Is everything okay, Herr Doktor?"

He gazed at Rose and then nodded. "Everythin' is fine."

The nurse glared at Rose before closing the door.

"Name your price, Dr. Trask," said Rose. "I will pay whatever it takes."

He leaned back in his chair, steepling his flesh and metal fingers.

"There is, perhaps, one thing you can do, Miss Rose," said Dr. Trask. "Now before you say no, hear me out." He gestured toward the kimono hanging on the wall. "I have an appreciation for the Oriental much more than average. And so do many of my patients." He looked at her, their gazes locking.

"Has anyone told you how exquisite your eyes are?"

ROSE'S ARM by Calvin D. Jim

❖

Long shadows hung over the lane house as Rose approached the screen door, removed her shoes, and placed them beside Mama's shoes. Papa's boots sat on the other side. Rose swept the dust off Mama's shoes before opening the creaky screen door, her heart pounding through her bright yellow cotton dress.

Papa slouched on the velvet-covered chair, staring at the kitchen table, the remnants of the previous day's tofu-making strewn about the kitchen table. The sour odour of spoiled soy milk hung in the air.

"You came home, eh?" said Papa, his gaze still fixed toward the kitchen, refusing to turn toward her.

Rose smiled as she slid into her slippers.

"Yes, Papa. Why wouldn't I?"

"I woke up to find a cold floor and you already gone."

She winced. Since Mama died, Papa expected her to put wood in their potbelly stove to warm their home before he rose, a duty she neglected that morning.

"Sorry, Papa," she said quietly. "It won't happen again."

"And where did you go so early? Did you go to school?"

"No."

"Did you watch the baseball game?"

"No."

"Or—" he said. The chair creaked as he turned his gaze toward her. "Perhaps you went to visit Dr. Trask."

Her eyes widened. He knew. How?

"No. I—Papa, I can explain—"

"Enough," he said, his voice rumbling. He rose from the chair and loomed over her. "I went to Maikawa for more soybeans and Mrs. Hasegawa said she saw you enter his office. A *hakujin*'s office. What were you thinking?"

"I thought he could help. He offered—"

"What? What did you hope to get? A job?"

"No. I . . ."

He glanced at her right side, where her arm should have been. "An arm. You wanted to get an arm like his."

Rose nodded. "Yes. For us. For you. With an arm, I could get a job. I could help you make tofu. We could eat."

"How much?" he said. "*Hakujin* do nothing for free."

"It doesn't matter."

"How much?"

Rose jumped. Papa's voice always boomed in her ears, whether it was saying good night or whether it was punishing her. But he had never raised it like this before. The hobos down by the rail cars could probably hear him bellow.

"My eyes. If I give him my eyes, he will give me an arm."

"So you would be blind? Nonsense."

Rose shook her head. "No. Dr. Trask would replace them with mechanical eyes. I'd still be able to see."

"You pay to see when mechanical eyes break."

Like Mang, thought Rose. Would she end up begging in the street just to see through broken eyes?

"The poor pay with their bodies," Papa said, shaking his head. "I won't allow it."

No. That was his answer. That was always his answer. Even before the accident and especially after it. How long could she go on accepting this answer? They were already on the brink.

Rose huffed. "Papa, we need this arm now, not five years—"

"Enough."

Rose gritted her teeth. Everyone said she had her mother's dark brown eyes. So beautiful. She didn't want to part with them. She would always wonder if someone she passed on the street wore her eyes. Until now, she didn't know if she could live with that decision. Now, it seemed crystal clear.

Rose turned toward the screen door.

"Where are you going?"

"Out," she said, kicking her slippers across the floor.

A rough, calloused hand grabbed her left forearm, pulling her back and almost pulling her arm out of its socket. Rose turned about. Papa pulled her toward the bedroom.

"You are not getting that arm," he said.

Rose dug her heels in to the floor and flailed her right stump to grab something. But within seconds, Papa flung her onto the bed and slammed the door shut. With the audible click of a key, he locked the door.

Rose leapt up from the bed and yanked at the doorknob. She had thought the French door was old and flimsy, ready to fly off its hinges. Yet, as hard as she pulled at it, the door wouldn't budge.

Rose banged on the French door. "Papa, let me out. Papa."

"I'm putting a stop to this arm nonsense, once and for all," he said.

The screen door thumped shut.

Rose awoke to the click of a key in a lock. She opened her eyes, still red and swollen from crying herself to sleep. She glanced bleary-eyed at the bright sunlight streaming through grimy barred windows. Birdsong danced in her ears. It was already morning. Papa should have been home hours ago.

The bedroom door opened. The squat, barrel-like Mr. Hasegawa stood in the doorway.

Not wanting to appear rude, Rose sat up on the bed, straightened her clothing, and said hello. "Where is Papa?" she asked.

"In jail," said Mr. Hasegawa.

Rose leapt out of bed. "What happened? Is he hurt?"

"Police say he attacked Dr. Trask," he said.

Rose gasped. For all his bluster, Papa was a peaceful man.

"Dr. Trask is pressing charges because of you," he said. He beckoned to her with stubby fingers. "Come with me. Your Papa asked me to take care of you until he returns."

"No," she said. "I have to see him."

"Fine," he said. He turned and walked to the front door. "I'll be at my store if you need anything."

She could tell he had already passed judgment.

Mr. Hasegawa picked up an envelope by the door. "This came for you." He handed it to her, and with a wave, he left.

Rose opened up the envelope and read the note. Her heart fell as she sank onto the threadbare red velvet chair. It was an eviction notice. On top of everything else, in two days they would lose their home. She was alone now, with no money and no job. The mechanical arm remained a dream.

She threw the paper aside and curled into a ball on the old creaky chair, its metal springs jabbing her sides through the fabric. What more could she do? Maybe she could run away and join the Chinese migrants building airship ports near Kelowna or Hell's Gate. Better yet, join an airship crew and fly south to San Francisco or Hawaii. Anywhere but here.

But she would have to leave Papa behind.

Rose glanced at her stump. Who was she kidding? She would never be hired on an airship, let alone be allowed to help a port construction. Something glinted in the bright morning sun. She turned toward the potbelly stove and eyed Mama's favourite copper pot.

Escaping onboard an airship might be impossible, but maybe she could still help Papa.

Rose stood up and walked to the stove. She stoked it with wood and lit it before dragging Mama's copper pot outside for water. She struggled to lift the full pot onto the stove without spilling too much water before grabbing a handful of soybeans and tossing them in. The least she could do was visit Papa in jail and give him some tofu to eat. It was all they had left.

❖

Rose's heart sank as she stepped into the small grey room and the steel door slammed behind her. Her father sat motionless on a steel-framed bed behind iron bars. His shoulders slumped, and he stared at the cold grey floor. Only his arms, bloody and bruised, kept him from collapsing onto the thin mattress. Even his undershirt, normally bleached bright white, now torn and covered in dirt, fell limply across his shoulders.

The police said he had resisted arrest, and by the looks of it, he had put up quite a fight.

"Papa?"

He turned his head slightly. A swollen, blackened eye glared back at her. "Leave me alone."

"But Papa—"

"I told you to stay with Hasegawa-san. For once, can't you listen?"

ROSE'S ARM by Calvin D. Jim

Rose clenched her jaw and her cheeks grew as hot as their stove. He didn't want her here. Why should she bother? She opened her mouth to yell at him, to scream. But only silence passed her lips.

"I thought you might be hungry," said Rose.

Rose slipped a chipped porcelain bowl of tofu through the iron bars, taking great care not to spill the tofu sprinkled with a few green shallots she found tucked away in a cupboard and ladled with a bit of shoyu for flavour. But of the tofu, she was proud. Firm and cut into perfect one-inch cubes, she arranged them in a small pyramid. She counted herself lucky that the police station was only a few blocks from home.

Rose reached into her handbag and pulled out a pair of chopsticks. She dropped them on the edge of the bowl with an audible clack.

She turned to leave when she heard the groan and creak of old steel springs. She looked back. Her father, still sitting on the edge of the bed, picked up the bowl of tofu with shaky hands, eyeing the delicate white cubes hungrily.

Holding the bowl in one hand, with chopsticks, he picked up a square of tofu, a sprig of shallot balanced precariously near the edge, and lifted it to his dry, cracked lips. His eyes widened as he ate it and then lifted the bowl to his mouth to shovel down more.

"Tanaka Tofu-ya?" Papa asked between bites.

Rose shook her head. "I made it."

Her father stiffened. He turned and stared at her, a dazed look in his eyes.

"How?"

"More lye," she said. "Mama taught me how."

Rose turned away and started toward the white steel door. She had only one more thing to do. She had done her duty here.

"Rose? Rose?"

She ignored Papa's shaky voice as she left the brick police station and headed down Cordova Street toward Dr. Trask's office in the West End of Vancouver.

When she arrived at Dr. Trask's Queen Anne-style house on Comox Street, the nurse turned her away until Dr. Trask intervened and allowed her back in to his consulting office.

"I want a deal," said Rose. "All I ask in return is that you drop the charges against my father."

"Miss Rose," said Dr. Trask, gesturing to the bruise on his face. "Your father made it explicit. You are not to have that arm."

Rose shook her head. "I don't want the arm anymore. Just cash for my eyes."

Dr. Trask furrowed his eyebrows. "Why would you do that?"

Rose handed the eviction notice to Dr. Trask. "Because we'll be on the street by tomorrow otherwise."

Dr. Trask read the note and then turned to Rose. "You would do this for your father?"

Rose nodded.

Within two hours, Rose was lying on one of Dr. Trask's metal operating tables and given anesthetic. She resolved herself that the last thing she would see with her natural eyes was the light above the operating table.

❖

At first, Rose heard the soft whirring of a desk fan and feet shuffling across a creaky wooden floor. Hollow, distant voices murmured as if she were listening through a cardboard tube. A metallic tang hung in the air, like iron filings. Blood.

Globs of blurry lights throbbed into vision. She propped herself up on her elbows. A sharp pain ran up her right arm and there was a clang of metal on metal beside her. Rose looked down at her side. There was a brand new, mechanical arm affixed to her fleshy stub just below the elbow.

She lifted her hand up to her face, spreading her fingers outward like a fan. Tiny brass cranks and pistons spat puffs of steam from hissing valves in her forearm. She beamed. Her arm wasn't as thick or clumsy as Dr. Trask's. It was shapely and feminine with soft lines and thin valves.

But she wasn't supposed to have a new arm. She gave up her eyes.

Rose touched her left brow and gasped. She was expecting the same brassy goggle-eyes as Mang's. But they weren't there. She picked up a mirror sitting on a small metal table filled with operating instruments, and lifted it to her face. She gazed into the mirror. Her eyes stared back. Her real eyes.

Dr. Trask hadn't taken them. But why? The arm was expensive. Was he giving it to her after all?

"You're awake."

Dr. Trask's nurse walked into the room, a metal tray with a glass of water and a bottle of pills in her hands.

"Take this, it will ease the pain."

Rose obeyed and swallowed the two white pills with a gulp of cold water.

The nurse switched on a bright, overhead light and shone it onto Rose's arm. The nurse grabbed her elbow. Rose stiffened and pulled away.

"Don't squirm," said the nurse, grabbing her mechanical arm and twisting it, examining the metal stub.

"You're fine. You can go."

But Papa told her that the *hakujin* don't do anything for free.

"When does Dr. Trask want me back? To take my eyes?"

"*Nein*," the nurse said. "Already paid for."

"But who? Who paid for them?"

The nurse glared at her. "Ask your father."

Rose found Papa sitting on the docks where Mama and she had spent many hours. The North Shore Mountains reflected a warm pink glow from the setting sun as salty coolness from Vancouver Harbour chilled her. Rose pulled her coat tight about her shoulders.

She sat down beside her father and dangled her feet above the water. Then, she turned toward him and stiffened. Rose gasped. Dizziness and nausea overwhelmed her as if she were struck in the chest by a tsunami. She propped herself up with her left arm to prevent from falling into the harbour, as the cost of her good fortune stared her in the face.

Her father gazed back at her with brassy goggle-eyes.

Rose shook her head and opened her mouth to say something. All she heard were waves slapping against barnacle-covered wooden posts.

"Dr. Trask came to me in jail," Papa said. "He showed me the eviction notice and told me what you asked of him. I offered my eyes."

Rose gazed at her father's new goggle-eyes. The copper glinted brightly in the fading sun. "Why, Papa?"

He looked down at the urn he cradled between his legs.

"You have Mama's eyes," he said. "I could not stand to lose them. Not again."

Rose pulled her father close with her new arm, placed her left hand on his lap and leaned her head on his shoulder.

"I'm sorry, Papa." Warm tears rolled down her cheeks.

Papa folded his hand over hers.

Rose remembered their earlier conversation and straightened up, gazing again at Papa's new, mechanical eyes. "They won't last forever," she said.

Papa nodded. "Nothing ever does." He gazed down at the urn. "Please bring Mama's shoes in tonight."

"Okay," she said.

Together, they watched the bright red sun descend slowly behind Stanley Park's cedar trees.

BACK TO MYAN

Regina Kanyu Wang
(translated by Shaoyan Hu)

The flyer stops its engine thirty meters above the ice and curves gently around under the combined effect of inertia and gravity, braking at the last moment to float one meter above the surface. The landing gears push out from the bottom of the flyer, securing a steady touchdown on the frozen water.

Kaya leaps out of the pilot's module and checks the underside of *The Flying Fish*. The three landing pads, shaped like discs, have fixed themselves tightly on the surface of the ice. As she lightly pats the body of the ship, her lips curl into a smile. She has prepared those gears specifically for this journey. Made by Kaya, safe and reliable.

I'm back, Myan, she thinks silently.

Kaya was brought up in a state college of the Union. Although the Union waived the education charges for the interplanetary refugees and offered medical insurance with attractive discounts, the expenses of livelihood and maintenance were never low. Not until last year did Kaya manage to pay off the low-interest loans and acquire the license for jobs in outer space, the frontier of the Union's expansion, a place for future colonials. The work there was usually tough and hazardous but not without profits.

Kaya needed money, but that was not the only reason she had submitted her resume to the committee of Project Saion.

She wanted to go back and see Myan. Eleven planets orbited Saion, and one of them had given birth to sentient beings. In other words, in Saion's solar system, only her native planet Myan had had sentient inhabitants.

Myan is covered with ice. After tightening the ties of her blade shoes, Kaya kicks back with her right foot and begins to skate.

The two blades of her shoes glide through the ice one after another, while Kaya enjoys the pleasure that comes with speed. As she moves through the wind, it stings her face a little, but that does not matter. She plunges on even faster.

The icy surface of Myan is as smooth as mirror, without even a small bump. The gravity, eighty-five percent of the Union's, and the low friction grant her the feeling of freedom and swiftness that has been missing for too long. For the moment, she is the queen on the ice. Every inch of her exposed skin senses the air flow. She lightly touches the ice with the tip of her right blade, and springs up with a push supported by the rear inside of her left blade. After spinning twice in the air, she drops down and slides on.

When Kaya started to practice skating, she was already in her adulthood. Having missed the best age to learn, she had to step onto the rink with the younglings. Tumbles and injuries were familiar to her, but it was a real agony to see the younger ones master the tricks faster than she did. When all the others were asleep, she went to the rink alone to practice at midnight. She jumped and spun, jumped and spun, repeating the movements again and again, seeking perfection. At the time, she was not even sure if she would have a chance to set foot on the frosty coat of Myan.

Kaya barely remember the time before leaving Myan because

she had been too young. Her only memory of her native planet was water. Her people had once lived and grown in the sea that covered the entire world, swimming joyfully, worrying about nothing, until a flaming tongue of Saion swept by too closely. The water temperature rose. Those who survived herded the fishes to the deeper sea on the opposite side of the sun. However, they could not escape the scalding heat from above. The Union noticed the anomaly in Saion and found signs of intelligent life on Myan by chance when the planet moved to the perihelion. They sent an emergency rescue fleet from the nearest location. But it was too late. When they arrived, only three out of every thousand Myan natives were still alive to be evacuated. Kaya's parents died in the disaster.

The Union brought her and a few hundred of her kin to a fully-developed colony, where they were educated and re-engineered to blend into the communities in the Union. Having learned Myan's history in school, Kaya tried to recall the discomfort and terror of being surrounded by hot water, but nothing came up. Biology told her that Myanese would not develop full sensations until they were four years old. She had left Myan at the age of three, and the cool blue water was the only thing that left an impression on her mind.

Now, skating on the ice reminds her of the pleasant feeling of swimming, an experience she cannot find in walking or running. It makes her feel buoyant, as if lifting to the sky. With a thrust using the front outside of her left blade, she jumps, rotating anticlockwise once, twice, thrice. She has done it! A kind of clarity settles in her mind, as fresh as the Myan air, cleansed of any darkness, and with that clarity, she descends. However, when the blades come down to the surface, she feels a stabbing pain in her right knee and stumbles to the ground.

That again. Kaya sits on the ice and rubs her knee. The relapse comes sooner than expected, probably due to the planet's coldness. She had had her pair of bioprostheses checked before the journey. The medic suggested replacing the parts as soon as possible, and that she should keep regular maintenance and avoid strenuous exercise before the upgrades. But she could not afford the replacement and has to wait due to a shortage of money. Besides, her new job could not be postponed. This is her only chance to go back to Myan and she would not miss it.

Her pair of bioprostheses is more than ten years old, with minor malfunctions from time to time. She barely keeps them in working condition on her medical insurance, but upgrading them is beyond her income. The bioprostheses were gifts from the Union government, given to her when she left Myan. In order to help the Myanese refugees adapt to life on land and settle down in the Union, the Refugee Agency funded the bioprostheses to replace their fishtails. Kaya did not remember the surgery except for a prolonged dream. She woke up as a citizen of the Union, with two legs below her. Learning to walk was as difficult as learning the common language of the Union. Her first few years on land were burdened with physical pain and mental frustration. Myanese use very few phonetic elements for conversations above the water surface. Most of the time, they communicate in the water, using body language. Kaya had long forgotten how to use Myanese languages, but from the short footage shown in her class, it looked like elegant dancing, the kind for stage performance.

She gently strokes her gills, which are in a degenerated state. That she has not been locked in a zoo or sold to a circus is enough to make her feel lucky. The Union has given her legs and citizenship, along with the opportunities for education and a career. She has nothing to complain about. She just wants to visit her native world again.

In recent months, Myan appeared in her dreams with increasing frequency. In those dreams, she had a fishtail again, swimming in the endless planet water of Myan. She hunted the untamed fish with knives made of shells, enjoyed her share of delicious fish meat, and then came up to the surface. There, in the phosphorus light of the Algae Moon, she prayed to the Goddess of Myan, thanking Her for the gifts.

BACK TO MYAN by Regina Kanyu Wang

Later, as Kaya twisted around to dive again, she was attracted by a fuzzy glow in the shadow of the Slate Moon. There should not be any light there. She quietly swam toward the glow, taking care not to disturb the currents too much. Closer still, she could now see a figure inside the brightness, slowly turning around as if it had sensed her. However, just before Kaya could make out the details, she woke up.

The dream first came to her three years ago, and she did not think much of it. However, the same scene played out in her dream again a year ago.

Last year, she got a job with Project Saion. She would use a spaceship to tug the membranes around the last opening of the sphere and complete the envelopment of the sun. Started in the second year of the disaster, the project was to prevent Saion's sudden bursts from destroying everything in the system and to collect energy effectively. The plan was to encompass the sun with a certain type of membranes, which could capture most of the Saion power output and convert it to electricity for storage while the rest of the energy spilled out from where the membranes were absent. The surface temperature of Myan dropped drastically, and the water became ice. The surviving native people had been evacuated, but other organisms remained underwater as the ice cover expanded and encased them in an enormous ice coffin. The night that Kaya received the letter of appointment, she again dreamed of Myan and again woke up before making out the figure in the glowing light. Since then, the dream visited her repeatedly. She decided to look for an answer on Myan.

The preparation was easy. As a pre-eminent pilot and mechanic, she did not have to struggle to make the necessary modifications to *The Flying Fish* so it could land on ice. The base camp of Project Saion was only three standard hours away from Myan. The day after she arrived at the camp, Kaya took off with the excuse of flight practice and surveying the surrounding areas. She headed for Myan right away. After all, who would stop a refugee from paying her respects to a devastated home world.

Who would have known that she has to sit helplessly on the ice all alone? Now that skating is no longer an option, Kaya removes the blades from her boots. Fortunately, she has geared up with dual-purpose ice boots. The tiny barbs embedded in the soles can prevent slips over the ice. She stands up and limps forward. Since she is not moving as fast as before, Kaya can observe the environment more closely. Myan has no solid land. Once, it was a planet full of water, now completely covered in ice. There are no mountains or ravines or rivers. When the surface temperature dropped years ago, even the most violent waves calmed down despite the tidal force of the two moons. Afterwards, everything fell into silence.

Kaya has no idea where to go. She believes she will find something on her native planet. She looks down through the translucent ice cover and notices a dark shadow. Shifting her weight to the left, she crouches down carefully and inspects. The shadow is shorter than her palm, a small fish with a rather plump body. Its two short pectoral fins splay out ridiculously, as if swimming was very hard. The poor little thing was trying to escape the coldness even in the last moments of its life. Kaya rises to her feet, walking awkwardly.

A dozen steps away, there are more shadows, a school of fish or something similar to fish. They are as long as half her fingers. They look like fish but covered with dark grey carapace. There are about forty to fifty of them, and they seemed to share the same urgency as the plump fish to hurry forward. They were heading in the fish's direction too. Why such a fuss in the last moments? Was it a coincidence that they were all going to the same place? Kaya adjusts her course and follows the group of fish.

Along the way, she encounters various creatures trapped beneath the ice cover: a fish with caudal fins spreading like rainbows, a cluster of organisms resembling algae, and jellyfish with a dense collection of oral arms shaped like hooks. Without any exception, they were all trying tenaciously to reach the same location before all the water was frozen. What were they looking for? Or escaping from?

Darkness closes in. Saion hangs in the sky like a dull amber disk. If Kaya does not look carefully, Saion's blurred edge makes it difficult to tell the sun from the background. In the feeble light of Saion, Kaya's body casts a faint and elongated shadow over the ice. It is becoming more and more difficult to observe the creatures beneath the ice cover.

A large dark patch catches her attention and she finds a bigger shadow near the surface. She advances a few steps, coming to the top of the shadow. Compared to where she saw the other creatures, the ice here feels thicker. Kaya is standing over a tail, which is wider than the distance between her fingertips when she opens her arms to the sides. While Kaya walks on, the shadow becomes narrower where the tail meets the body and widens again after that point. She moves to the middle of the enormous form where its width reaches the maximum. Her own long shadow is obscured by the darkness below. Her heart feels cold and pained, as if pierced by an icy blade. She squats down before kneeling on both knees. Slowly, she leans forward, her forearms touching the ice and the left side of her face pressing against the surface. Coldness seeps into her heart through the fabrics of her clothes and her exposed skin, but it is not capable of freezing her tears. In the remaining Saion light, Kaya cries.

Before leaving the project base, Kaya had applied for thirty hours off, of which one third has already passed. As Saion is now below the horizon, the temperature drops quickly. The light of the Algae Moon is weaker than it was in her dream, but the ice reflects more light than the water would have done. Guided by that phosphorus glow, Kaya moves faster. Whatever those creatures had sought, their lives were doomed. Once, Kaya tries to deviate from the course, but she finds other creatures moving along a diverted route that undoubtedly led to the same destination. It feels as if there was a hole in that place and everything in the water was flushed toward it, albeit they were gradually frozen in the process. The shadows under the water become denser. Although the Algae Moon is not bright enough to illuminate their details, Kaya knows clearly where she is treading. The answer is close.

The Slate Moon represents the extremity of darkness. Kaya remembers the views of Myan described in her textbook. That chapter was meant for the descendants of Myanese natives and not in the scope of general exams. Nevertheless, Kaya had read it many times. Apart from the water body that covers the entire planet, having two moons is another important Myan feature. The natives had dubbed the two natural satellites as Algae Moon and Slate Moon. The Algae Moon is larger and selectively reflects green light while absorbing all other frequencies of visible light. The reflected light reaching Myan is a phosphorous green. The Slate Moon is smaller but denser, absorbing all colours of the visible spectrum. These descriptions match what she saw in her recurring dreams.

So far, the light of the Algae Moon has been with her all along and now it is time for the Slate Moon. As the Slate Moon blocks the Algae Moon, she breathes deeply and steps forward, as if crossing the boundary between light and shadow. Once she is in the darkness, Kaya no longer looks for the creatures below. Instead, she follows a route that has already been determined.

The blackness of night blinded her sight, but her other senses become more acute. Kaya simply closes her eyes. In the distance, she hears booming waves, clashes of weapons, and curt syllables of Myanese Verbal. There is a faint smell of blood, of gunpowder, of something burnt. It is the smell of war. Kaya opens her eyes abruptly.

Not far away, there is the glowing light from her dreams. While walking toward it, Kaya feels a strange eagerness accompanied by great serenity. Coming close, she finds no figure inside the glow. There is nothing but an icy blue light, pulsing slowly, its intensity changing slightly. It is taller than a human and undulates gently with the pulse. Kaya puts her left hand into the light, and to her surprise, finds warmth in there. She reaches further, sending in her forearm and elbow. Finally, her entire body falls in.

❖

She drops into the water, the blue light still pulsing regularly above the surface. The water is not cold; its temperature suggests the Warm-Stream Season.

The Warm-Stream Season? Why does she remember that now?

Because you are a daughter of Myan. A voice comes into her mind.

Who is this? Kaya is puzzled, but the voice sounds soft and firm. Her alarm and anxiety ease up.

Look at this. It is not answering her question.

Kaya senses the currents are trying to guide her downward. She swings her tail, diving into its depth. Since when does she have a fishtail again? This must be a dream, one that feels especially real.

For some inestimable time, she swims along, until a fluorescent presence appears ahead. It is a temple of luminescent corals. Kaya draws closer, pushing aside the seaweeds in front of the door and entering the temple. The interior walls are brighter than the ones outside, illuminating the hall. A swarm of tiny shrimps swims past her, heading outside through the gaps in the coral walls. Creatures still live here.

The warmth here will not last for long, but the little creatures are oblivious to it. The voice is helpless and sad.

Kaya gazes around the place. It is a room with seven walls. A rack stands against each of the walls except the one with the door. The racks reach the ceiling. Each rack holds glittering, translucent balls of various sizes.

These are the memories of Myan, from the first glacial, Natalesian, to the last, Tribalenan, and to the interglacial after that, which is the present time, an age of long and gracious summer, even spurring the birth of intelligent life. The fourth glacial should not have come so early. The voice sounds a bit unfocused as if lost in its endless memories.

Kaya moves to the right-most rack and takes down the last sphere. It is very light, its gravity probably mitigated by buoyancy. Kaya prods the surface of the ball lightly with her nose and it gives way a little, like a bubble in the water. She plunges into the sphere.

She is looking at a floating ice above the water. The Myanese had gone, and the remaining creatures had sensed the unusual change in the climate. Light and heat from Saion was declining. Ice covers formed all over the surface, gradually expanding downwards. There was only one place in this planet still holding warmth, to which all living things were migrating. They might exhaust themselves on the way. They might get caught within the frozen ice and turn into ornaments that would never decompose. The few who were lucky enough to arrive still had to go deeper to seek more heat. Some could not bear the heavy weight of water and gave up, submitting themselves to a frigid death.

Kaya emerges from the bubble, tears in her eyes. She puts back the memory sphere and holds up the second last one.

The Union had proposed generous offers. The extraction of rare particles from the sun Saion would change the Myan ecology. In exchange, the native people of Myan would migrate to other planets. However, the natives refused to leave their birthplace and even more unwilling to have their planet become a frozen world forever. So the war between the Union and the Myanese began. The outcome should have been obvious. The Union had well-trained troops, equipped with advanced weapons and warships, while the children of Myan could only muster weapons made of stones and shells and rely on water for shelter.

The Union had not meant to kill in the beginning. Not wanting to take any lives, the Union soldiers simply tried to disperse the natives with gunshots when they attacked. But the Union gave up passive defence after one violent night, during which three Union soldiers were killed by the natives in a raid. They did not care for the lives of the natives anymore and the war heated up. Even at this stage, the Union still restricted themselves to personal combat. Again, the familiar noises: clashes of weapons, shouting in Myanese language. The familiar smells of blood and gunpowder. Union warships retrieved their fallen soldiers, and the perished natives sunk into the water.

Finally, on a night when the two moons overlapped and all electronic devices blacked out, a team of natives approached a Union warship from below and coerced dozens of acid squids to spray their corrosive ink over the bottom of the ship. The warship went down, together with all the soldiers aboard, sinking to their watery death.

The next day, all the Union ships floating on the water withdrew. Before the natives could celebrate their victory, sudden explosions blew them into pieces. The Union carrier in orbit opened fire with a weapon of mass destruction. Almost all the adult natives were killed. The elders came up from the deep water with the younglings to surrender. After extracting a promise from the Union to keep the young ones safe, the elders killed themselves with the shell knives on their belts. The Union fleet left with the last native people of Myan.

Kaya is trapped in the bloody memories, her heart torn. She puts down the sphere and curls up, retching. So that was the *disaster*. That was the truth about the Myanese refugees rescued by the Union. But why? She screams silently.

For the fortunes of Saion they craved, Myan was merely a sacrifice. The voice speaks again.

Couldn't they just look for another target? There are many other stars like Saion in the universe, aren't there? Kaya still cannot understand.

There is only one Saion, just like there is only one Myan. The children of Myan would not relinquish their native planet, but the Union did not wish to give up their hard-won treasure either. There is immense sorrow in that voice.

Kaya bites down on her lower lip and picks up the third sphere, which is the smallest but the most iridescent.

It was a clear day. In the golden light of Saion, several natives relaxed on the surface. A female adult was carrying a youngling and softly humming some simple tunes. The youngling's eyes glistened, and its tail swung with the rhythm of the song. The water nearby rippled. A male adult emerged. He moved closer to the female, holding up a freshly captured fish. She reached out her left arm in response to his embrace. After taking over the fish with her left hand, she tore out meat with her teeth and fed the child. He watched them fondly, and she met his eyes, their entwined tails stirring up waves below the water.

Some of Kaya's memories come back. They are—

Your parents. They loved each other deeply, and they loved you as much. The voice is full of tenderness now.

Kaya is crying again, her tears dissipating into the water. May I take away these memories?

They have been in your heart all the time. No one can take away the

memories from the children of Myan. And always, Myan remembers.
Kaya's grief subsides in the steadiness of the voice.

"You are—Goddess of Myan," Kaya suddenly realizes.

Many address me this way, but I am no goddess. I am Myan, the planet. The voice peters out, and Kaya falls into the blue light again.

When she awakens, Kaya finds herself lying on the ice, bathing in the faint light of Saion. She is cushioned on sundried seaweeds. The pain in her right knee has receded as she rises to her feet. Blades mounted onto the shoes again, Kaya skates toward *The Flying Fish*.

She greedily breathes in the Myan air, remembering its smell. She dreams of diving into the Myan water, to let the brine wash through her mouth and out from her gills. No chance now. She has to go back to *The Flying Fish* and, subsequently, the project base.

Three standard days later, she takes off as scheduled, flying to Saion with the membranes meant to close the last opening. But instead of carrying them to the designated position, she wrecks the framework, pushing it toward Saion, making the broken membranes drape down and point to the blazing star. Before the base realizes what is happening, she flies the ship into Saion. She knows that her ship alone will not cause enough turbulence, but fuelled by the chain reactions, the fiery tongues of Saion will consume the membranes and framework gradually. Eventually, enough light and heat will return to Myan. Ice will melt, releasing frozen creatures. Waves will surge again and the gravity of the two moons will cause tides to rise and fall. Planet Myan, her homeland, will come back to life again.

MERIDIAN

Karin Lowachee

They all tried to save me.

"I think this one's still alive."
  "Tag him."

In that space between life and death, you make a decision whether to wake up. Maybe that's when time ceases to matter. I felt older than four years old and too young to remember. My world was telling me not to remember how the strange crew and its dead-eyed captain came to our far-away colony and nothing was the same again.

I might've fought, giving them a reason to shoot me.

Or maybe there was no reason at all.

A long time later, after I was better, I heard them. Other people. Not the same bad crew. Speaking outside the door of the medical room where they kept me. It was a family ship, and they talked about dropping me at the nearest station, but—

"He'll just cycle through the system, and how will that help?"

"Well, what do you wanna do with him?"

"Maybe we can just keep him here."

"We don't even know his name. He won't talk to us. In the system, they'd be able to find out. They'd have the colony manifest. DNA records."

DNA. In school, they ran a test for fun to find out where on Earth I was from and what kind of people I belonged to, people who had lived long ago on a far-away planet. East Asian: 61%. Spanish European: 22%. Anglo-Saxon: 17%. I coloured a map of Earth, highlighting the places those people had come from and took it home to show my parents and brothers. We had things in common that spoke of our heritage: dark eyes that tilted at the corners; dark hair.

"I don't want to give him to the system," this woman said.

"Now we're kidnappers?" said the man.

"We weren't the ones who attacked his colony."

"No, we just swept in like those pirates right after."

"You're being ridiculous. We legitimately found him. Only him. Look at him. It was the *pirates* who did it. You want to hand him over to EHHRO?"

"He might still have family outside of the Meridia colony. We don't have the right."

"Where's EarthHub now? What're their human rights organizations doing when their colonies are being attacked?"

"Look—we'll hand him over. If no other family speaks up, we'll apply to foster him. Eventually adopt him if it comes to that. They'll want to get him out of their hands so it shouldn't be too hard. That way no authorities will get on our ass."

❖

"Your name's Paris, do you remember?"

I remembered. But a part of me didn't want to.

This new lady at the station said my last name was Azarcon. They'd gotten my DNA and matched it to the records. Paris Azarcon. I remembered my two older brothers. It hurt right where I'd been shot. Right through my body.

Mama and Daddy. They were shot first. In their heads.

So much screaming.

My brother, Cairo, stood in front of me, trying to protect me, but it didn't make a difference.

"Paris?"

I didn't want to remember anymore. I ran to a corner.

Days like this. Back and forth. Do you remember anything else? They all wanted me to remember until I screamed at them to stop it.

Then they said they were going to send me away from the station. That someone wanted me. It didn't matter. I didn't care anymore.

"Your name's Paris, and this family is going to take you to their ship to live. They found you and they care about you. We'll check in a little later, okay? But you can go with them now."

"How old are you now?"

I held up my hand, fingers spread.

"Five years old. That's good. Do you know your name?"

"Paris."

"How about your last name?"

I didn't want to say it.

These people weren't my family, even though they said they were now.

I thought of the map of Earth that I'd coloured. A planet I'd never been to. It was nothing like Meridia and its rocky ground, where Daddy and Mama and my oldest brother, Bern, worked at the mines.

"It's going to be Rahamon," the lady said. She called herself Captain Kahta. "That's your last name," she said. "Look here on this ID tag. You always wear this around your neck, okay? Paris Rahamon. The newest crew member of *Chateaumargot*."

Everything was muddy in my mind for a long time. I only knew what the captain and her mister said about how they'd caught a signal from a moon. They found me shot in the back outside my home, but I was still breathing. When they said those things, it was like they were telling me a story from a slate, one that someone else made up, except I didn't have pictures to go with it. Maybe there was a drawn image of what my colony looked like, but I didn't see it, couldn't remember, and nobody let me look it up. The captain and her mister took me to a station and got me help. After a while, when I was fixed, they came back to get me and the station let me go. They said I had a new life now and it was good. Nobody would make me go back to the other life anymore.

I didn't want to talk about my real family anyway.

I didn't want to talk about the things I remembered before they were all gone. Everything was going to fade. For a while, after first waking up, I barely remembered anything. Then it started to come back and that was worse.

Back and forth. Remembering and forgetting. Remembering.

They wanted me to like *Chateaumargot*. They bought me toys and clothes, and at first I didn't have to work. Their teenaged daughter looked after me when the captain or her mister weren't around. Sanja played with me and took me around the ship to show me the garden and the games and the gym. Captain Kahta saw me when she finished work, and Mister Chandar cooked for me or showed me how to build models of ships and stations, though he said I would have to grow older before I did other stuff. He probably meant *work*.

For a few months aboard the ship, life was like that and I forgot most days after they passed. Captain Kahta said that was okay. They seemed happy having me, even though I didn't talk much and hardly ever felt like playing games with them. They stopped trying to force me to play games when I took their toys and threw them against the wall. For a few days all I did was break the things they gave me, so then they gave up.

MERIDIAN by Karin Lowachee

✢

On my first birthday with them, I hit Sanja in the eye and she screamed. I didn't mean to give her a black eye but she'd forced me to sit and do math. I hated math. It was frustrating and she kept pushing. I told her she wasn't my mom so she needed to stop. She said Captain Kahta wanted me to learn math, and I said Captain Kahta wasn't my mom either. Sanja got this look in her eyes like she was mad even though it was true, and she put the slate back in front of me and told me to stop being a brat and do my work. So I punched her face.

Mister Chandar locked me in my cabin alone. My stomach was growly by the time Captain Kahta came in. She sat on my bed next to me.

"Paris, why did you hit Sanja?"

I stared at my hands.

"Paris?"

"I don't know."

"I think you do. Sanja says you don't want to do the math work."

I shrugged. What did it matter?

"Paris. Look at me."

I looked at Captain Kahta. Her dark eyes looked sad. For me. The dot on her forehead seemed to judge me. The people on the station had looked like that too, from what I remembered. I wished they would stop.

"Paris, you can't go around hitting your sister."

"She's not my sister!"

Captain Kahta leaned back as if I'd hit her in the face too.

"She's not my sister and you're not my mom!"

"Okay, okay."

"I don't care about math!"

"Paris, sit down."

I started to run around the cabin. She couldn't stop me. Not until she grabbed me around the waist and held me down on the bed. I kicked and screamed at her. Mister Chandar came in and held me down too. They said things to each other, but I wasn't listening. Sanja came in with an injet and pressed it to my arm.

WHERE THE STARS RISE

Everything slowed down. Even me.

The ship was big. Tall, cold corridors, all white and grey. There were lots of adults but some kids too, older than Sanja or younger, like me. Every sixth day a vid screened in rec and we got extra treats than what was usually available from the galley. Sometimes I stayed and watched the vid, but sometimes they bored me and I snuck out in the dark.

I wandered around the ship when I wasn't supposed to, but I didn't like being minded all the time. Sanja handed me off to the other older kids sometimes and none of them liked it when I acted up. Sometimes I didn't mean to act up, but everything grew frustrating. All of these rules about where I wasn't supposed to go, and checkups in medical, and toys I was supposed to be interested in, and food I was supposed to eat. These faces weren't the faces from my storybook memory. When I had nightmares, nobody came to save me.

Sometimes I remembered riding on the back of a four wheeler, holding an older boy around the waist. He'd tell me, "Don't fall off, Puppy!" My brother Cairo. But I couldn't remember his face anymore.

I had a lot of nightmares. The lady on the station said to record them when I woke up and send them to her, but I didn't like to put words to them, so most of the time I didn't. Mister Chandar or Captain Kahta was supposed to talk to me about them and help me record them, but after the first six months they stopped. I guessed they got busy. The ship travelled a lot and I didn't check in all the time with the lady on the station. I didn't ask Captain Kahta about it. If I didn't need to do these things anymore, then maybe that meant I was okay. Or they didn't care. I didn't think they had to care since they weren't my family.

My brothers Cairo and Bern. And Mama and Daddy. Now

every time I thought the word "family," I also thought of the word "dead."

I turned seven on *Chateaumargot*. Captain Kahta and Mister Chandar threw a party. All the kids came, even the ones who called me weird and talked behind my back. Sanja tried to put a cardboard hat on my head. I knocked it away. After that, nobody was happy. They weren't happy with me and the ice cream melted all over my cake. I felt a little bad so I was nice for the rest of the party and even hugged Captain Kahta afterward so she would smile. She hugged me back real tight.

"Are you happy, Paris?"

I didn't really know what she meant by being happy, like maybe if I liked my cake and the presents. The games and new clothes.

"Yeah. Everything's good."

She touched my hair and smiled, like she knew I was lying.

The other kids on *Chateaumargot* didn't stay nice. But neither did I. I got into fights a lot until every week Mister Chandar locked me in my quarters. I sent some of the kids to medical and sometimes I went to medical. Bruises and cuts and a couple black eyes shared amongst us. Then one shift when we'd docked at a station, Captain Kahta came to get me after breakfast and took me by the hand. She walked me to my quarters and told me to pack some of my favourite things. My clothes and whatever toys I liked.

"Why?"

"I'll help you, honey."

"Help me with what?"

She cried and held me, so I couldn't do anything but stand there and let her be. Everything felt dark and silent, like someone had covered my ears and eyes.

She and Mister Chandar took me off the ship, and we went down the dock to another ship's airlock. That ship let us inside the airlock but not quite inside the ship. We met another woman. She introduced herself as Madame Leung. She was shorter than Captain Kahta and had dark eyes like me. Madame Leung took me by the shoulders and smiled.

"You look just like your picture, Paris."

What picture? Captain Kahta crouched down in front of me and told me to go and live with Madame Leung now.

"Why? Why?"

Captain Kahta's eyes were shining, and she just shook her head. "You'll be better here with Madame Leung," was all she said. Then she straightened up, and they said things to each other in a language that I didn't know. Mister Chandar squeezed my shoulder and then they left the airlock.

They left me on this new ship and I couldn't do anything about it.

So I screamed.

Madame Leung dragged me to quarters inside her ship. Another woman joined her to wrangle me. They locked me in, and through the intercom she said, "I'll come back when you're done."

That was it. No matter how much noise I made, nobody came.

Madame Leung told me everything. Captain Kahta and Mister Chandar didn't feel they could provide me with the best, they didn't know how to handle me, and they feared for the other children on board because of the fights I got into.

The idea of saving me wasn't as good as the reality.

"You're getting worse," Madame Leung said. "That won't happen here."

Captain Kahta wouldn't take me back to the station from long ago, and the lady who had given me away in the first place didn't ask.

"We're busy ships!" said Madame Leung. "Who wants to go all the way back to a station to deal with that shit?"

It was easier, out here in deep space, to hand me to another family ship like Madame Leung's. Her ship, *Dragon Empress*, transported medical drugs to far-flung stations and colonies in need. But Madame Leung and her crew weren't a part of EarthHub's humanitarian organizations.

"We're not pirates," she said. "I don't attack places and murder people. We just provide a service."

"Why do you want me?"

She crouched down in front of me. I was sitting on the bunk. The quarters were smaller than what I'd had on *Chateaumargot*. The lights were narrow pricks in the ceiling, like sunrays through bullet holes.

"I like kids, Paris. Kids grow up to be good soldiers. Like my boys. I have a lot of boys here as it is, they know their work. You'll do great with them, you'll see."

Madame Leung said they were going to get my records purged. It would be easy since so many records of so many kids were all over the place, and with the right amount of money, people did anything you wanted. That way nobody would come looking for me.

Nobody was left to come looking for me anyway. When Madame Leung smiled at me, it was like she knew it too.

As far as Madame Leung was concerned, I was a Dragon. No longer a Rahamon, and definitely not an Azarcon. She never asked about my actual family or where I came from. I doubt she would've cared if Captain Kahta had offered the information. Captain Kahta, who trunked me off as someone else's responsibility, likely hadn't explained much about my origins.

I was physically healthy and mentally able to handle complex tasks. Madame Leung made me one of her boys and that was that. One in a crew of four-hundred men and boys who followed her lead. The drug queen of the Dragons, the *Dragon Empress*. Deep space depended on her, she said, to cure it of its ills.

She didn't mean the war or the aliens or the pirates. If you couldn't change anything, you could at least anesthetize.

I dreamed of my family. My parents' faces, their presence, blurred out from my memory like a vid not quite calibrated right. But my brothers, my protectors, they remained vivid.

I didn't believe in guardian angels because seeing them only in my mind's eye was more like hell.

Over the years under Madame Leung's tutelage and the hammering of her "boys" to make me into her version of a good soldier, one who kept his mouth shut and evaded authorities on station, the memories trickled back. Like the first bits of dust that were the only evidence of an exploded star, the further I went into deep space with the *Empress*, the closer I came to my own past.

Maybe it was because of these adopted "brothers," foisted on me, equipped with powers of loving persecution. Unlike the kids on *Chateaumargot*, Madame Leung's gang accepted me with a rough sort of respect. The lady herself handpicked me, and though they didn't spare me when she disciplined my rebellious nature, they offered security and freedom at the same time.

I carried a gun. I learned the trade of drug trafficking, of clandestine meetings on stations and in half-forgotten refugee colonies. Some of our clients were even EarthHub soldiers, more wary-eyed than we were but equally invested in the market. Some used our pharmaceuticals for their intended purposes, others didn't. As long as they paid us, it was none of our business.

Adolescence passed in a haze of tattoos, training, and tradecraft. The colourful ink emblazoned on my arms and back were needle tapped in the ancient way, not with a gun. I marked my years by the images that flowered across my skin: a tiger, an Earth mountainscape, a constellation of stars, and of course, the elaborate golden dragon winding its way down my spine. Sometimes, at the height of my pain, when I lay across the *horishi*'s table, I heard my brothers' voices, their ghosts whispered back in those moments.

Pain begat pain. What was the antidote for it? I'd been closest to Cairo. My oldest brother Bern held a more distant place, a peripheral shadow in the shape of our father. He'd fought back too, and the laser bolt slammed between his eyes.

Cairo's voice surfaced with each needle puncturing into the shallow points beneath my skin.

He said, *"Run, Puppy!"*

His nickname for me. Because I was the baby.

Once, in the middle of the tattooing, I shoved at the pain. At the *horishi*. Blood scored across my skin, ruining the line she'd been drawing. I made her start on a new image. I'd seen it in the ship's educational files while voraciously reading about an ancient civilization from a country I'd never seen.

I told her to ink an Egyptian ankh over my heart, and she didn't ask.

Age was a meaningless thing in space, especially on a ship. Maybe I was some form of adult, chronologically in my twenties. But to look in the mirror was a different story altogether, with pictures that didn't match up. Still a teenager to outside eyes. My own face reminded me of the ones who swam back to me in the dark, in sleep, in blissed out moments with occasional drugs in my system. We all took part, never to excess, but skating that line was a part of this world.

My third world. One was my heart, the second was my armour, and the third was my artillery. Two of those things protected the other.

I hung out with a boy named Soochan. He was a little more gentle than the other boys, probably because he was addicted to sweet leaf. He tended to smile, even when shit was going down around him, a beatific expression like a saint in the throes of religious epiphany. Once when a buyer tried to shaft us, Soochan was almost sorry. He made her face the wall of the station tunnel where we'd been doing the deal; his voice was so soft. "Just close your eyes, baby, and this won't hurt a bit." He whipped her once with his gun and kicked her a few times, then stole what he could off her body—an old platinum ring, her data dots. "Madame

Leung don't like stiffers," he said. Still smiling.

On this ride between deals, the ship's drives hummed like a hive of bees all around us. Soochan sprawled on my bunk, blowing smoke rings to the ceiling between slurred rambles. I tried to read, but the words upended and crawled over one another like roaches running from the light. Nothing made sense. Maybe it was the drugs, but the nightmares had been plentiful lately, taking my concentration into the dark.

In the middle of Soochan's words, he said, ". . . Azarcon . . ."

My lulled focus sharpened like a shiv. From my seat on the deck with my legs outstretched, slate in hand, I said, "What?"

"What?" he echoed back, the corner of his mouth tilting upward as if giving coordinates to his eyes. Clouded by smoke and whatever wandering thoughts he let off the leash.

"You said something. A name."

"Uh—"

"Azarcon?" My name. My first world. Of course, he didn't know.

"Don't you read? Your head's in that slate so damn much." His hand flit, making the smoke from his sweet leaf cigret carve the air. "Captain Cairo Azarcon. EarthHub's latest bulldog of deep space."

I thought I was done collecting worlds. I thought Madame Leung had tied me to hers for the rest of my living days, one of her soldiers, one of her boys, all of the security and sanctimonious criminality of a group of people with no loyalty but to their own. Who needed more?

But this fourth world crashed into me and sheered to the side the next moment, casting me against my own armour.

"Captain Cairo Azarcon," I said, like an invocation of the devil.

My brother lived.

When Captain Kahta had found me, had there been no others? Hadn't she seen Cairo? Or had the pirates who had taken our colony also taken the one member of my family who'd lived and left nothing but the dead and thought-dead for the *Chateaumargot* to find.

There was nobody to ask.

I went on a treasure hunt around the Send. I excavated and saved every possible mention, note, and passing criticism lobbed toward my resurrected older brother. I became an Azarconologist, twice divorced from the name but like any spouse rendered obsolete by a new mate, I looked back with judgment. On myself if not on the one who'd left me.

I wanted to judge. I found shoddy pictures of a handsome man attached to reports of bravery and ruthless alien strit killing. He tended to avoid cams, so the only people who had a clear picture of him also had access to his military records or his daily life. But there was enough to see a resemblance. Dark eyes and dark hair. Tall. The kind of carriage in the spine that would rarely bend for anybody. He was the young scourge of aliens everywhere. He made his name as a fighter pilot but now commanded the spacecarrier *Macedon*. Specific corners of the Send said he was one to watch, like they were talking about a celebrity. The deep space war made military heroes.

My corner of the galaxy didn't bow down to heroes. I didn't care about the war.

He was a new father. Captain Cairo Azarcon was married and had a son.

I was an uncle.

What did blood mean?

I wanted to hate him. Didn't he look for me? Couldn't he have found me? In the entire galaxy, why didn't his honed military skills somehow raze the stars for his little brother? Who told him I was dead, and why did he believe them? Why didn't he refuse to stop looking until he had tangible proof of my death?

Neither of us were children now, and maybe, with so many years behind him, my brother also preferred to forget.

At Basquenal Rimstation 19, I met a woman at the bar and shacked up with her in a private den. After sex, she told me she was an investigative journalist and she'd been looking into my ship.

She said this while smoking a cigret in my face. I was uniformly unsurprised. For some reason, when you had sex with a stranger, anything they said just seemed to go along.

"You think my ship's a pirate? Because it isn't. It's not interesting enough to be a pirate."

"No," she said. She'd only told me her first name: Mabel. Her hair was long and silver but her face was young. Maybe from suspended aging treatments, so there was no telling her real age. Not that it mattered. "No," she repeated. "Not a pirate, but they do recruit in unconventional ways."

"Yeah?" I took the cigret from her and dragged. I could tell she was trying to read my eyes, but I'd been told enough times that I was "stoic," that my stare walled people off and forced them to lay siege. So I watched her building a siege tower word by word.

"I found a node on the Send. Where the children are traded."

She squinted at me as if this was supposed to mean something. When she didn't get anything, she pressed on.

"They disguise it, of course. It looks like a parenting node where people are just talking about their kids. Getting advice. Arranging meetups at various stations. But there're codewords. Pictures and codewords. These people know what to look for and how to ask for it."

"Why are you telling me this? You want me to spy for your story?"

"No—but Paris, your name was there." She glanced at my tags.

"My name Paris? Lots of kids are named Paris." But my stomach began to form an ice rock, deep in the centre.

"Isn't your last name Rahamon?"

I hadn't told her that. It wasn't something you told to someone you just shacked with. And maybe she could read my eyes after all.

My last name wasn't Rahamon. I was reminded every time I heard it.

She said, "I recognized your first name and your face. Your picture had been posted. You were a little boy but the resemblance is obvious." She climbed off the bed and went to her clothes, which were strewn on the floor in our haste to get together. Her body was flawless in a way that probably spoke of enhancements, but I hadn't really noticed in the act. Now, as she leaned down to fish something out of her jacket pocket, I just wanted to get away.

But I couldn't seem to move from the bed. This room. Or out of my own skin. She returned, sliding back beside me with a slate in her hand. She brushed at it, and soon lines of text and an image popped up.

A photo of me. As a child. I knew my own face like you did a vague stranger. Difficult to place but not forgotten.

I looked away before I allowed myself to read the words beside the image. The cigret burned between my fingers, so I pulled on it some more.

"Bright, enthusiastic, inquisitive boy," she read. It was obvious that she was reading from the text, not making up the words. "Energetic and requires a lot of attention and compassion. He's had a rough history, but he's sweet and capable of loving. A family without any other children would do well."

"Stop."

"They write these posts like they're advertising for pet swaps."

"I said stop it."

I climbed off the bed, flicked the cigret into the trash, and grabbed my clothes. "I was legitimately adopted. I don't know what the hell you're looking at."

"Adopted by the *Dragon Empress?*"

No. And we both knew it.

I didn't reply. Once I got my boots on, I grabbed my gun off the table and left her in the den.

All of my worlds were colliding.

Mabel found me at the bar, four drinks deep. Soochan was there, drunk and high too. "Heeey Mama," he kept saying. Several of my other brothers from the *Empress* danced haphazardly to the music funneling in the centre of the floor.

"Paris," Mabel said, glancing at Soochan.

"Heeey Mama. Heeey Parchisi, she want your comm code?"

We ignored him. I wondered what either of them would do if they knew my real origin.

What should I be doing?

Everywhere I went now, I thought of my brother. Swapping drugs for cred or weapons, it was Cairo. Drinking myself into a stupor, it was Cairo. Fucking a woman, it was Cairo.

The ankh on my chest that I saw every day. What had possessed me to wear that reminder? My body was now a walking séance ritual, begging the ghosts to follow. To answer back, letter by letter, yes or no. I invited them now to shake my seating and short-circuit my tech. To stand behind me in the dark when I wandered the corners of the ship.

My brother was a ghost. The kind who made marks on the living.

"Please," Mabel said. "We need to talk."

How many kids were outside the system, like me? How many had been put into the system only to be torn out like a splinter? Children that couldn't be handled so they were hijacked. Especially refugee kids, Mabel said. Good ships with good intentions found themselves over their heads and no longer wanted to deal with the kids.

It wasn't a bad life, I heard myself telling her, the two of us in a corner booth while the music kept winding up and falling down and everyone around us moved like mannequins of broken robotics.

"Do you remember when you were taken?" she asked.

Do you remember? That question refused to pick another path. It hunted me everywhere.

"What're you going to do," I said. "Put me back? That ship has flown—literally."

"I could find out if you have any family—"

"I don't." It came out of my mouth like every answer I'd given to anyone who asked. No family but the Dragon. No ship but the *Dragon.* No place but the Dragons. Deep space was our home. Mabel took it as stated and I carried on. "The captain of the *Chateaumargot* had checked. Or the case worker that I had — whoever. Social Services. I don't even remember the name of the first station they'd put me at. They purged the records anyway."

Mabel frowned. "The station?"

"Yeah."

"Why?"

I gave her a flat stare then let her track my gaze to Soochan, still sitting at the bar mouthing off to the air.

"We're not pirates but we're not saints."

What if, I thought. What if I gave this journalist my real world name?

Soochan suddenly appeared at my shoulder, leaning over the table. "Leh we go, Parchisi."

"Be there in a second." I pushed his hand away as it coursed through my hair. Big brother, except he wasn't. He wandered off to hook up with our other brothers, now headed off the dance floor.

I had this information locked inside my chest. If I let it out, what other explosion would it cause? Would that birth yet another world, one that I couldn't predict or control? Another situation I couldn't defend myself against?

No one could know.

To Mabel: "Can you do me a favour?"

Her eyebrows arched.

"Whatever you need for your story, I'll tell you. As a source. No names, on your word."

She nodded. "Anonymous. I promise."

"Because you know what I'll do if you break our deal."

She'd seen the gun. More importantly she'd seen the ink on my body and read the affiliation well enough.

"What's your question?" she said.

"Find out *Macedon*'s next port of call." I did, in the end, slip her my comm code. "And let me know ASAP."

Somehow she came through. The message on my system said

simply: *Austro Station*. And gave a date.

It wasn't difficult to go to Austro Station, despite what we did for a living. Austro was a main hub even for us, with its rampant underdeck activity and illicit commerce. I didn't have to mention a thing to Madame Leung, beyond the usual conversation about scoring big there. We bought and sold drugs at Austro for the rich elite in the higher modules because exploitation was the true ecosystem of the galaxy.

The *Dragon Empress* docked at the station a day after *Macedon*. To the galaxy outside, we were basic trade merchants in harmless cargo like transsteel and mechanical goods. It was a different story for the boys Madame Leung sent off in other directions on deck. I was one of that crew.

Now I *had* to conjure my brother's face—in the delicate balance of stalking the dock where the carriers were moored, not going too close, but hovering outside the broad doors to catch every person that flowed back and forth. Casing the airlock directly was impossible in such a restricted area. Instead, I disappeared from my Dragon brothers in the hopes of seeing another. Hiding myself behind garish kiosks and aromatic food stalls. I felt like a pervert, but maybe that was fitting. A perverse turn in my life. As if the universe agreed, it made me wait and gave me ample opportunity to get the fuck out of there.

Of course I didn't.

I wanted to see him. I recognized his walk before anything else. In all the years, that detail hadn't changed. He was taller, and he tried to hide beneath a hoodie and civilian clothes, passing through the concourse toward the carrier docks. But I knew those shoulders and the gait of someone who knew where he was going. He didn't cover up out of fear, but from stealth.

I moved with him, slipping along the edges of the crowd between his path and mine. It took me a minute to notice the child.

MERIDIAN by Karin Lowachee

A little boy. Maybe four or five, but who could tell? They held hands. The boy carried a stuffed bear wearing soft armour, its furry ears dragging on the deck.

I was that age once. Cairo held my hand like that.

It's me, I wanted to shout. As if those two words could make up for a decade or more as some humans reckoned time.

Come back.

It happened all at once; the little boy said something and Cairo leaned down to pick him up in his arms, barely breaking stride. Smaller arms went around broad shoulders. The bear dropped to the deck in their wake and Cairo kept walking, oblivious.

I saw the boy open his mouth to protest and then I was there. The crowd was no longer a wall. I hadn't made the conscious decision, but I found myself holding the stuffed toy, reaching to touch Cairo's arm.

He turned before I could tap him, sensing proximity maybe. Or his son's distress. The little boy twisted in his arms to keep his own eyes on the toy, reaching toward it. Toward me.

"He dropped this," I heard myself say.

My brother wasn't the only one covered up. My hood was pulled low, long sleeves covered all of my ink. Maybe he saw my mouth move but that was it. I stared somewhere at his chest and below. At the blue boots his son wore, dangling at his side.

The bear left my outstretched hands, plucked to safety.

"What do you say, Ryan?" A deep voice. But I knew that accent. Meridian. Like mine. What it had been three worlds ago.

"Thank you," a small voice said.

"Welcome."

"Thank you," my brother said.

I just nodded.

They turned to go. He wasn't going to waste time on a stranger.

I looked up as they moved further into the concourse crowd, still headed toward the carriers. Cairo didn't turn around, but his son was looking over his shoulder, holding the armoured bear in his arms.

The boy had blue eyes. Not like mine. Not like his father's. Big, searching blue eyes that stared at me as if he knew. Ryan, Cairo had said. My nephew.

I didn't follow them. They walked away and I stayed where I was, the ghost they left behind.

Now all I do is remember.

My fourth world is the clearest. Sun bright and comet swift, all I can do is chase it. Maybe one day I'll be able to enter in again. Like it's a room left open for me. Like a voice offering a greeting, something as simple as hello. Maybe next time I'll look up and stare him straight in the eyes, dark eyes like mine, with just enough tilt at the corners to speak of our common ancestry. His son's gaze was a start, but it was only the edge of the solar system. There's more.

Soochan found me sitting on the deck outside of the carrier docks. He twitched, all nervous.

"Them Marines gonna sweep you away from their stoop, you can't stay here. Come back to the *Empress*."

He didn't ask why I was sitting there. Maybe he thought I was high.

I'm waiting for them to come back, I wanted to say. But of course I didn't. It wasn't the truth anyway. What would I say in that moment if they had?

I'm your brother, take me with you? Take my DNA and test it against yours. Check how far back we're connected. Tell me where you've been all this time, when time slipped so easily between the stars. What war are you fighting? Will you fight mine for a while?

Save me just this once.

Come back, my brother. Come back, Cairo. You're tattooed on my skin, beneath my heart, inside my blood. I tried to forget you, but nothing worked.

I want you to hear me say our family name. I'll only say it to you. No one else would understand what it means.

You were my first world.

JOSEON FRINGE

Pamela Q. Fernandes

"*Jeonha,* welcome. You are early today!"

He acknowledged the woman genuflecting before him. Despite her work, she had this seductive lilt to her voice. King Sejong smiled, adjusting his richly embroidered red robe before leaving his *balmaksin* shoes outside. Several lanterns brightened the moonless night. She served him *hwachae* in a brass mug, the refreshing fruit juice sweet on his tongue.

"I cannot seem to figure out how to draft the consonants," he told the woman, who in her dark *hanbok* could rival any one of his consorts. "We were successful in testing the cannon, as per your instructions, but I need more time with the mirror to find out more about the language."

The woman with her braided hair drawn to the front of her waist demurred.

"*Jeonha,* that is not how the mirror works. I have told you before, the time it remains open always stays the same."

He sighed. "Yes, but time is passing quickly. My older brother, Yangnyeong, is out to kill me, and I am not sure I may last another season. Not to mention that all these rumours about us spreading like fire."

"*Jeonha,* if this arrangement is uncomfortable for you, then I can move elsewhere."

He swallowed the rest of the fruity concoction.

"But we cannot. You yourself said so, that this mirror works in very few places. You wasted nine moons trying to find this one." He paused and smoothed his dark goatee, feeling the burden of Joseon weighing on him. He feared he was running out of time. Yangnyeong had been plotting his revenge. "Maybe I was never meant to become king. Maybe Joseon will do fine if Yangnyeong, its rightful heir took my place."

King Sejong paused again, thinking about the passing of time. He was only twenty-three but he felt old, having aged quickly over the last two years of his reign. "It is said you can look at the state of the cats by a family's waste and tell if the family is well fed. I roam the streets disguised in the night and all I see are skinny cats, their bones visible under their flesh. We need advancements in agriculture, irrigation, astronomy, and ironworks."

"*Jeonha*, it is time," she said, interrupting his sudden melancholy.

He forced a smile to acknowledge her interruption. He followed her through a labyrinth of rooms that lead to an underground cellar, then another maze which she navigated through quickly without stopping or hesitating, never letting him memorize the route. He had come here several times, yet he would never be able to find it without her. Finally, he could hear the rush of a waterfall and knew they were close. The door opened to a room that overlooked the cataract. Here she placed her strange contraptions, made of metal and some thin stringy threads. The room was cluttered, every corner with wood or iron objects, knickknacks, and instruments of various kinds littered throughout. He never paid much attention because it was ultimately the mirror for which he came.

He could not see the waterfall, the blackness of night blanked everything, but he could hear it. The rush of the water as it came thundering down, drowning all other sound. And in the flicker of a small lamp, they stood poised in front of the mirror. It was suspended on two iron rods. After adjusting a few switches, she turned it on.

Sejong watched the scene unfold. "What is this?" He frowned. "Where is Sejong? And why are these people wearing such funny clothes? I want to see the other Sejong draft the consonants."

JOSEON FRINGE by Pamela Q. Fernandes

She smiled, "*Jeonha*, didn't I explain, that there are many alternate universes and many versions of us. This is another one of them. There, the people have given up the *hanboks* and wear far less than we're accustomed to."

Sejong edged closer to the mirror as he watched the men sport no hats and no robes, but short hair and shiny shoes unlike the *balmakshin* he wore. The women had funny hair arrangements and bared their legs, and their clothes revealed their exact shape. But something caught his eye, the boards of the shops. They were all linear.

"Is that Hangul?" he asked, his voice barely a whisper, awed by what he saw. He did not wait for her to answer. He pulled out his quill and wrote on the parchment, drawing out a few of the letters before the mirror went still and the image faded away. For a few moments, all he could hear was the waterfall and the sound of their own breaths. His was fast.

"It is too soon," he said, growling. "I need more time."

His fingers were taut on his sheet, the ink on it still wet.

"*Jeonha*, what is it that plagues you so much? Why would any king worry so much about creating a language?"

He slumped as he looked out the window, keeping his gaze on the starless night.

"In Joseon, the Buddhist monks want us to follow their script, while the poor remain poor. They all hate me. The *yangban* are the only ones who can read and write and yet the only thing they know is the Ming's system of words. The poor are fed up with ceaseless servitude. Why can't we make something for our own people so that the illiterate and the poor maybe be able to read and write as well? How long will my people suffer? A wise man can acquaint himself with Hangul before the morning is over; a stupid man can learn it in the space of ten days. That is what I want Hangul to be. I need help and if they know a woman is associated with this, I might have to execute myself. There are already rumours about who Jang Yeong Sil is. How did he make the cannon? Where did he test it?"

He waited for her reaction because he would like to know himself. Where did she test the weapon? How did she make it, if she never got out of this damn house? Who was she? Where did she come from? Did she have ulterior motives?

"*Jeonha*, can I make a suggestion?"

He smiled, this time a happy one.

"Jang Young Sil," he said, "whenever you say that, I know you have something extraordinary in your mind. The great Confucius says that ordinary is easy, but extraordinary differentiates you from the crowd."

Young Sil bowed reverently. "You are very kind, *Jeonha*. If you are worried on account of me then I suggest you open a new school of scholars, where people from all social classes may be able to write an exam and participate. You can share with them your desire to create Hangul."

"They are too talkative. Before long, word will get out that someone is helping me. That Jang Young Sil is in hiding."

"You can tell them it is a secret mission, that their reports will be unnamed and their findings secret. After all, the work will be credited to the Hall of Worthies."

"Hall of Worthies?"

"The school's name."

He thought about it; she was right. It did sound like a good plan, but how could he explain visiting her repeatedly, especially this late at night without causing rumour. Sejong held up the candle and scanned the room, finally focusing on a small rectangular object sitting on the table. A painting on the wall of a cat and a butterfly, the signature of the painter illegible to him. Were they in colour? Or was the candle flicker playing tricks on him? He had never seen something so spectacular in all of *Joseon*. "Fine, I will see you in two weeks; till then, take care," Sejong said, turning to the door.

Before he left for Gyeongbokgung, she reminded him one of Confucius's quote, "It does not matter how far you go as long as you don't stop."

He sat in his palanquin, and on reaching home, he dismissed his servants and reproduced everything he saw on those boards on his parchment. Every shape, every stroke. He had already made a chart from his previous visits; his entire bed chamber was plastered with parchment filled with letters of different shapes. Some parchments were blank. Those were the ones he needed.

But he didn't worry. After what he saw today, he knew the alphabet would be ready someday by someone. He just wanted that someone to be him.

He continued filing up the shapes, pronouncing the sounds, and when he accidentally dropped his quill to the floor, he could not help feeling he had been here before. Had he not seen this same thing happen when he was watching the mirror so many moons ago? Yes, he recalled he had been watching himself scramble, and he noticed the bedchamber filled with sheets. He leaned back in his chair. Had he been seeing the future?

During the next two weeks, a public decree announced the establishment of the Hall of Worthies. Farmers, shoemakers, and blacksmiths sat with scholars of the aristocracy or *yangban*, writing the admitting examination. There was a buzz among the people, about the fairness and openness about it. Sejong's public approval soared.

A fortnight passed by as he furiously worked on the Hangul chart. The men for the Hall had been picked and a formal induction ceremony had been completed.

Later, when he followed Jang Young Sil to her discovery room, he was surprised when she asked, "You seem happy, *Jeonha*. Has the Hall of Worthies quelled your worries?"

"Worries? Why should I have any, when I have the Lady of the Future herself by my side?"

He watched her face. Even in the glow of a single lantern, he could see the play of emotions dance across her face. Surprise, fear, contemplation, reserve, and contradiction.

She stilled and poured herself some *hwachae*, "Took you long enough," she said. "What gave me away?"

He pointed to that rectangular object lying on the table. "I saw that in the mirror the other day. One of the men was holding it to his face as he talked. I truly have an excellent memory, you know. Then there was the painting. I've seen the monks paint and received plenty of paintings as gifts from the Ming kingdom, none so vivid and colourful as the one you have on the wall."

She smiled, as she turned to the painting, her fingers tracing its edge. "It is exquisite, isn't it? An original by Kim Hong Do. Probably won't be available for another three hundred and fifty years. Many dynasties will rise and fall before that, *Jeonha*. It's almost lifelike. There are many objects in the room lying in the drawers and chests with objects from the future. Of course, I did not carry them all here. I did make them, but some of them are useless unless we build the basic requirements."

He was intrigued. "What are these requirements?"

She smiled. "Slow down, *Jeonha*. The first step is for you to create Hangul. Most of the people living in your kingdom will be able to create a Joseon that will surpass your dreams, only if they knew how to read and write."

He swallowed a laugh, smoothing down his robe.

"You are going to become a great king. One who will be responsible for many scientific discoveries and inventions. You will go down in the history books as a hero. Poems will be written about you, and schools will be named after you."

He shrugged. "How will all this come to be, for the mirror offers me very little at a time?"

"The time space continuum, as it is called by us in the future, lets you look into the future not for you to learn from it, but to instill hope that you can do it. You will have noticed, over the past eight moons, the mirror only showed you what you've already done, working day and night on drafting, recreating, and studying the alphabet. Maybe you're restricting yourself by following Hanja script. Look at the other scripts as well: Phoenicians, Tibetan. Surely, there must be a clue somewhere. "

"How did you get here if you are from the future?"

"I used a Faraday Cage, which uses electric fields. The physics that involves Einstein's theory of relativity and large sources of energy with a ninth polynomial helped transport me back to a time I wanted."

He did not understand, but he took her words for what they were. "But why are you here," he stuttered, "and when will you go back?"

She sighed. "I came to warn and help you. There is no going back to where I came from; the great Joseon is at constant war, divided by communists and capitalists. Several powerful weapons have been unleashed, and the people in the north are starving while the people in the south are indebted to foreign rulers. Therefore, I have come back to tell you that we must make peace with our neighbours, we must perpetuate the idea of non-alignment. Joseon will be great if we accept the good and get rid of the evil, before it has a chance to destroy us."

"How does Hangul help us to create this great Joseon of the future?"

"We need the help of the masses. Ours is a small nation. We need every man and woman to be part of this great legacy. The only way forward is to have everybody moving in the same direction."

"And what will I say of this Jang Young Sil? People want to know where I get these ideas from. The cannon was a good example. But the drawings of the rain gauge and the iron printing press, will they be accepted? The cannon was a good invention, it will instill fear into our enemies. The general accepted it without questions. But the rain gauge, charts of the stars, and iron printing press, they are all new inventions, that people have never heard about. My own council will want to know where these ideas are coming from, the same way they ask me how we can create a new language for our people. Do you think I can develop Hangul? And will it be really helpful to my people?"

He watched the woman of the future with her cool stare and wry smile blink, once, twice before she answered.

"It is better to light a candle than to curse the darkness. Let's make Joseon great, one candle at a time. Shall I turn on the mirror?"

Author's Notes:
Sejong the Great and Jang Young Sil were responsible for many inventions. Among them were the sun dial, Chuegugi (rain gauge), the iron printing press, and the development of better agriculture methods to sustain cultivation all year round in Joseon (Korea). Hangul was developed fully by the end of his reign, though it was shunned by later kings who wanted to subjugate the masses. After World War II, which was about five hundred years after his reign, Hangul became the main language of South Korea and remains in use to this day. King Sejong's legacy, as an inventor and discoverer, has been widely propagated as

a man who was far ahead of his time. Jang Young Sil, according to the Annals of the Joseon Dynasty, was expelled from the Courts and no written record of Jang's death was ever captured.

Jeonha: Your Majesty

Yangban: aristocracy

Balmkasin: shoes worn by the aristocracy

Hanboks: traditional Korean dress

Hwachae: fruit punch

Gyeongbokgung: Gyeongbok Palace (the main palace of the Joseon Dynasty), largest of the Grand Five Palaces. A must-visit palace for first-time Seoul visitors.

WINTRY HEARTS OF THOSE WHO RISE

Minsoo Kang

Kings, lords, generals, and ministers are not made from a special blood.
—The Grand Historian

The true power behind the absolutist reign of the sixth emperor of the Serene Dynasty lay with two men of humble origins. The ruler's chief advisor, the High Chancellor of the Six Ministries and the Thirteen Extraordinary Offices, was the great intellect on the left side of the Eternal Dragon Throne. And his top military commander, the Invincible General of the Six Armies and Eighteen Commanderies, was the strong arm on the right. They originated from the same eastern village and were sons, respectively, of an estate clerk and a tanner. The histories that make much of their low backgrounds represent them as exemplary cases of "new men" who rose spectacularly to prominence in the mid-dynasty period. In the single surviving copy of the initial version of the Grand Historian's *Veritable Records of the Serene Dynasty*, one finds a rather curious story of the first collaboration between the two men who would go on to help each other rise to the pinnacle of power. It is unclear why the Censorate suppressed this episode when it authorized the publication of the official edition of the *Veritable Records* since its political implication is obscure at best.

Long before the two men became the High Chancellor and the Invincible General at the imperial court, they were once a young legal advocate fresh out of the Hall of Great Learning at the North Capital and an officer who received his first commission after meritorious action in the War of Thirty Leagues of Bloody Bandits. They stood before the low mound of a commoner's grave, the sky above them reddening in the autumn dusk. The advocate wore the night blue robe of a licensed graduate while the officer was in his West Front Army uniform of blackened leather vest and cap, the short sword of a third leader at his side. They remained in solemn silence for a while.

"Ah," the officer suddenly said, a pained smile breaking out over his scarred face. "I was too hard on him. I did not show proper respect to him as a son. Not since the time I got the whipping at the estate. Do you remember that?"

The advocate nodded. "When the heir to the estate and his friends tried to trap you and your brothers."

"Twelve of them against the three of us. Once they cornered us at the ruin of the old administration building, we were supposed to submit to a beating."

"But you fought back. You broke the heir's nose, made him run home crying. We all heard about that."

The officer laughed. "Then the steward of the estate and his thugs came to our house. My father went down on his knees and begged for forgiveness. He grovelled all the way to the estate as they took me to be whipped. I had to be punished publicly as an example, for daring to hurt the heir. No one mentioned the fact that I was defending myself and my brothers against an unprovoked attack. And Father, he was so sorry about his son's insolence. So very sorry. Ever since then, I didn't regard him as a man, never mind a father. After I recovered from the whipping, I went back to doing my chores and obeying his orders. But he could tell that I had nothing but contempt for him. And he knew that when I was old enough to leave, I would go and never return."

"Yet here you are," the advocate pointed out.

The officer shrugged. "Why did it never occur to me before now that there wasn't anything he could have done? If he had defended me, tried to protect me, they would have just whipped him too. All these years, I blamed him for something he had no control over."

"You had to blame somebody," the advocate said, "for a sense of meaning in a life without justice."

Another long silence passed.

"So," the officer said, "the lady of the estate wants to build a flower garden here."

The advocate nodded. "This land would complete the great circle she has in mind for it. Unfortunately, your father did not keep the paperwork updated at the administration centre. Not for many years."

"Too cheap to hire a scribe."

"The lady of the estate could very well annex it. She would have to take the matter to court, but the imperial magistrates these days are sticklers about paperwork. Her advocates could overwhelm them with documents, while the only thing you have is an outdated deed that was never recertified in the new reign."

"So the situation is hopeless?"

"Let's say highly difficult."

The officer thought for a moment. "Do you think she would make me an offer to avoid going to court at all?"

"A pittance, perhaps. But you have the right to fight for your land. Your status as a meritorious war veteran will help with the magistrates. Not even the lady of the estate can cut you off from the source of your ancestral fortune."

"The source of ancestral fortune," the office repeated emptily, looking up at the sky with a contemplative look. "I have no faith in that."

"No?"

"The war has taught me that I do not live in a magical world. In battle, I saw countless prayers to the gods go unanswered, spells fail, and men die clutching talismans that were supposed to protect them. Source of my ancestral fortune. Never did my father any good. Not his father either. I mean to make my fortune far away from here. So fuck the source of my ancestral fortune. Go and ask that old bitch what she will give me to go away. Let her dig up my father's cowardly bones and throw them away somewhere so she can plant her pretty flowers. She can smell them while her whore's body starts stinking with old age. Fuck her, fuck this land, fuck this whole village."

The advocate, though not surprised by the officer's bitter words, pondered them for a time.

"How much would you be willing to take?" the advocate asked.

"I don't know. Five silver standards? Is that a realistic amount?"

"That's about how much she's likely to offer."

"Well, at least I'll have a feast with good meat and fine wine before I return to base. Celebrating my final departure from this shit-stinking place!"

The advocate arrived at the grand estate at dawn, as he was instructed to do, but he waited at the central courtyard of the master's mansion for most of the morning before he was finally summoned to the outer chamber of the lady of the estate. The wide, high-ceilinged space was filled with luxurious furniture, precious vases and plates, and colourful paintings of idyllic scenes of nature, all recently acquired by the lady in a spending spree at the North Capital following the death of her miserly husband. The widow was a former courtesan who had become a concubine to the late master of the estate and then his official wife after the first wife had been ousted from the household. It was rumoured that she had engineered the first wife's fall by spreading the slander that she had engaged in an affair with the master's cousin, a government inspector who had stayed at the mansion for some time. The disgraced woman protested her innocence, and ultimately drowned herself in a lake.

Still beautiful in a sharply graceful way in her late middle age, the lady of the estate sat on a grand throne-like chair with thick cushions covered in radiant worm fabric of green and blue. She wore a flowing robe of white, the colour of death, as she was still in her mourning period. But the dress was also made of the finest radiant fabric with ethereal streaks of pink dancing across its shimmering surface. Proper mourning attire was supposed to be made of coarse material, but the estate had no one left with the authority to lecture her on propriety.

Her immaculately painted face bore an expression of weary indifference as the advocate approached her with his head bowed down in a respectful manner, prostrated himself on all fours to touch his head to the floor, and got up to extend his formal greetings.

"You are the son of our former clerk?" she said in a condescending tone that made the question a contemptuous accusation.

"Yes, great lady," the advocate answered. "My father had the honour of serving the grand estate in that capacity."

"But he sent you to study at the Hall of Great Learning."

"Yes, great lady."

"How wonderful today's world must be for the likes of you. The son of a clerk goes off to the capital to become a legal advocate. In my day, people knew their places. They had ambitions befitting their stations in life and let those of good blood take on the higher responsibilities of society. But it seems that we now live in a time of upstarts. An age of insolence, as they say."

Ever since she became the lady of the estate, she put a great deal of effort into erasing her own lowly background as a concubine who had also harboured ambitions beyond her station. She had bribed the local officials to manufacture documents to show that she was from a respectable family. And to further solidify her social position, she had taken on the air of the most aloof and arrogant of aristocrats.

"Only in such an age," she went on, "would I have to suffer this outrage of the son of a tanner sending the son of a clerk to argue with me about some paltry piece of land."

"Great lady, he is a meritorious veteran of the War of Thirty Leagues of Bloody Bandits and an honoured officer of the imperial army," the advocate said while bowing his head down even lower to soften the challenge of his words.

"I suppose, in this age of insolence, that gives him the right to insult his betters at will," she shot back.

"Not at all, great lady," the advocate said, maintaining his submissive position.

The lady of the estate sat in silence, deliberately extending the tense moment. The advocate recognized her intimidation.

"Very well," she finally said. "In consideration of his service to the empire, I am willing to grant him an award of ten silver standards. He will receive it after signing a document prepared by my own advocate. This will prevent him from making further mischief over that piece of dirt."

"I will inform him of your great generosity, great lady."

"And I will bear no more insolence from you, son of a clerk."

"You need not trouble yourself, great lady. I have returned here only to settle my affairs before moving permanently to the North Capital. Once this matter of my friend's property has been settled, I have no cause to offend you with my lowly presence in your lofty home."

After leaving the lady of the estate, the advocate walked down the mansion's central corridor and passed by the open doorway to the office of the estate's clerk. As his father had worked there for most of his life, curiosity made him stop and peek discreetly from the side of the doorway. Behind a wide desk covered with neat stacks of paper sat the thin, ruddy-faced figure of the current clerk, a humourless and discontented man whom the advocate's father had groomed to be his assistant and eventual replacement. The advocate considered how he would have ended up working all his life in that office if history had not intervened to send him on an utterly different course.

During the reign of the previous Serene Ruler, the emperor, through his vast wisdom and endless benevolence, allowed qualified commoners to take the entrance examination to the Hall of Great Learning. The advocate's father saw it as a great opportunity for his intellectually gifted son, so he stopped teaching him the duties of the estate clerk and hired tutors to prepare him for the examination. And he took on a new apprentice, the son of a spice merchant. When the merchant could not provide for all six of his sons, he sent his youngest away to be trained as a clerk. Although the young man had proved to be capable and diligent enough for the work, his perennially sour expression and curt manner showed his resentment at being a disinherited son.

As the advocate considered the clerk, who was dressed in a modest robe of dark grey, he realized that there were other people in the office. Three elderly men in peasant attire knelt on the floor, speaking to the clerk in a quiet and plaintive manner. The advocate could not make out every word they were saying, but it was apparent that the visitors were pleading for intervention in some matter. When it came to minor financial issues, the clerk acted as an intermediary between the masters and the peasants. Those making a request or seeking some relief from the manor had to go through him, which gave him significant power over the lowliest dependents of the estate.

As the advocate continued to watch, the elderly peasants finished making their case. One of them produced some copper standard coins, strung up with a string through the square holes in the middle. He offered them to the clerk with his arms raised high and his head bowed down low. The clerk took the coins and weighed them in his hand, but he did not utter a word. After a long moment, the peasants looked at one another, whispered, and produced another string of coins that they handed over in the same submissive manner. The clerk took it also and weighed it as well. Silence. The peasants handed over a third string of coins. The clerk finally nodded, much to the relief of the peasants.

The scene confirmed what the advocate had heard since his return to the village ten days ago. On more than a few occasions, peasants had told him how they missed his father who had always been fair and honest in his dealings with them. After the new clerk had taken over the post, following the sudden death of the advocate's father, he had revealed himself to be a greedy and venal man, taking every opportunity to squeeze the people for money. He had apparently decided to allay his discontent as a disinherited son by accumulating his own wealth through his position at the estate. The advocate realized that because he had been able to advance himself in the wider world, the peasants of the village had fallen into clutches of a thoroughly corrupt man.

"When do you have to return to your base?" the advocate asked the officer as they sat drinking cheap but sweet wine at their favourite inn, a modest establishment just outside the village.

"They gave me leave for the full mourning period," the officer said, finishing off the liquor in his cup. "I think I will go to the North Capital first, enjoy myself a little before I go back. Why do you ask?"

"I have an idea," the advocate, pouring his friend a new drink.

"What idea?"

"Well, let me ask you this. How much money do you have? You must still have some of the reward for your meritorious action."

"I spent a lot of it celebrating with the comrades of my unit, as I was expected to. But I still have enough to put to good use. I was thinking of buying a small house. Somewhere I can go home to when I'm demobilized."

"I have something better for you to spend it on. It's a bit of a gamble, but it might turn out to be worthwhile in the end."

"How much of a gamble?"

"It's hard to know right now. But I wouldn't expect you to risk it alone. I'll put all my money in it as well."

"Truly? Then you must be certain of its outcome."

"I am not certain at all."

"Then why do it?"

The advocate finished his drink and waited for the officer to fill his cup for him. He took a small sip before answering him. "When you go into battle, even if you know that your men are strong and disciplined, your strategy is sound, and your enemy is in disarray, is it not still a gamble?"

"In war, always."

"That's it then," the advocate said. "I propose we go to war."

The estate clerk hated the advocate, resenting him for having attended the Hall of Great Learning at the North Capital and earning his legal license. He would have wanted to pursue that ambition if he had not been born the last son of an unsuccessful merchant. So the advocate's unexpected appearance at his home in the middle of the night vexed him greatly. As the visitor greeted him with utmost politeness, the clerk could not think of a way to get rid of him without being rude. He had to invite him in, but he was determined to be curt and not offer him any refreshments until the advocate got the hint and left.

After they sat down in his outer chamber, the advocate produced a black lacquered box and set it at the side of his sitting mat. When he opened it up, the clerk was astonished to see an enormous golden toad with precious black stones for its eyes. Before he could ask him about it, the advocate spoke.

"Master clerk, since I have committed the unforgiveable impertinence of coming to your home without advance notice and interrupting your rest so late in the night, I will reveal quickly the purpose of my visit. As you may have heard, I have returned here to settle my affairs. After that, I will move to the North Capital. In the course of going through my family's papers, I found a few documents missing. None of great importance, but some involving matters of personal nature. I know my father was scrupulous about making copies of every document, however trivial, and keeping them at the grand estate's household archive. So I have come to beg you the favour of allowing me into the archive for a few hours to look for the papers. I would be most grateful if you would indulge me in the matter."

He then gently pushed the golden toad forward a little.

"Well, I can't let anyone into the household archive for a frivolous reason," the clerk said, his lustful eyes fixed on the shining toad.

"Of course not, master clerk," the advocate said. "For it is one of your highest duties to safeguard the papers there. It is my hope that you will not consider my reason frivolous." He pushed the frog forward a little further. "Just a few hours, to look for documents pertaining only to my family's affairs."

"I can give you one hour," the clerk said, barely restraining himself from reaching for the toad. "After the work day is over. I won't have people thinking that I casually allow outsiders into the archive."

"That would be wise, master clerk. I will come tomorrow at the time of the evening meal, when no one will be around. I thank you most sincerely for this great favour you are granting me."

And he pushed the golden toad all the way to the clerk, into his greedy, grasping hands.

The lady of the estate became furious when her offer for the officer's land was rejected and the advocate requested an official hearing with the imperial magistrates. She ordered her advocate to flood the court with documents, many of them fabricated by expert hands, to make what paltry papers the advocate would present seem inconsequential. As she had all the advantage in the matter, she was certain that the magistrates would decide in her favour. She would then take over that troublesome bit of land, have everything standing on it eradicated, and the remains in the officer's family gravesite dug up and dumped somewhere. With the great circle of the garden complete, she would then build the grand retreat of myriad white and pink flowers that she had seen in a springtime dream, a place where she could while away her winter years in peace. And those impertinent sons of a tanner and a clerk would not see a single copper standard for it.

In the first days of the hearing at the Hall of Judgment, everything proceeded as she had expected. Her advocates presented one bundle of documents after another to the massively obese magistrates sitting behind their long table, their enormous bodies wrapped in layers of bright red radiant fabric. Upon the vast expanses of their shimmering robes, countless embroidered cranes of gold flew gracefully about. Behind them, the great dragon insignia of His Imperial Majesty, the Serene Ruler, was hung up in all its magnificent grandeur.

The great estate's advocates argued that the officer's family may have owned the land at one time, although even that was open to question, but their neglect of the property and failure to properly update their claim at the administration centre caused it to fall into abandoned status. Consequently, the estate, as the central tax-enumerating entity in the district, not only had the right but indeed the responsibility to take over the land and do something useful with it.

The lady of the estate was gratified to see the magistrates nod their great dome-like heads in apparent agreement, the bulbous flesh under their chins jiggling. She was only a little disconcerted by the calm expression on the face of the advocate as he sat listening without making a single protest. He did not even bring the officer with him to the court, as if his presence was unnecessary to the case. But she chose to interpret his equanimity as resignation in the face of impending defeat. She speculated that he was carefully masking his regret at not having taken the ten silver standards that she had so generously offered.

After two full days of testimony on behalf of the grand estate finally came to an end, the magistrates dismissed the court for the day, informing the advocate that he may present his argument the following morning. The next day, the advocate came with a modest bundle of his own documents.

"Your Imperial Excellencies," he began, "my advocacy for the true owner of the land in question is based on a single contention, that the current master of the grand estate has no standing in this court."

"No standing?" the chief magistrate, the fattest of the three, asked. "Upon what basis do you make the claim?"

"Upon the basis of treason, Your Imperial Excellency. A traitor to the empire has no right of advocacy in a court presided over by imperial magistrates."

"Treason?" one of the assistant magistrates asked, giving voice to the general astonishment in the court. "What treason? What act of treason was committed here?"

"If I may, Your Imperial Excellencies," the advocate said and quickly organized his papers into three stacks. He then handed each over to a magistrate.

"What you see there, Your Imperial Excellencies," the advocate said, "is the original and copies I have made of a poem entitled 'The Follies of the Three Lofty Hogs, One Who Snores, One Who Slobbers, and One Who Farts.' Also, copies I have made of some correspondences among several people who comment on the work."

The lady of the estate let out a gasp.

"As you will see, the three lofty hogs are clear references to Your Imperial Excellencies. Please note the physical descriptions of the animals, their attire, and the words they utter during court hearings. They have obviously been taken from actual cases that were recently argued before you. The poem was manifestly composed to ridicule Your Imperial Excellencies personally as well as to question your wisdom in the judgments you have rendered. It all amounts to an attack on your authority. Imperial law stipulates that any denigration of your position is a denigration of the Serene Ruler himself, since your authority emanates from His Imperial Majesty. The composition as well as the possession of this poem, therefore, is nothing less than an act of treason."

"Where did these papers come from?" the chief magistrate asked, his face turning crimson with rage.

"In the household archive of the grand estate, Your Imperial Excellencies."

"No! That is a lie." the lady of the estate screamed out.

"It is unclear, Your Imperial Excellencies," the advocate pressed on, "who composed the treasonous poem in the first place, but what the correspondences reveal is the indisputable fact that the lady of the estate made copies of it and sent it to various acquaintances. Subsequently, they made much merry in ridiculing Your Imperial Excellencies. It is the long-standing practice of the grand estate to make copies of all received and sent letters for the household archive. The estate clerk takes care of that. If Your Imperial Excellencies would expeditiously send your agents there, they are certain to find them. And I suppose that right now the lady of the estate is giving instructions to her advocates to go to the archive and destroy the incriminating papers."

The magistrates looked up and saw her talking frantically with her advocates.

"Marshall of the Court!" the chief magistrate called out.

"Yes, Your Imperial Excellency." An armoured officer in the imperial uniform of red and gold came forward and bowed his head.

"Arrest the lady and her advocates and send men to secure the household archive of the grand estate. Do it immediately, before anyone has the chance to tamper with the papers."

"I obey, Your Imperial Excellency."

The lady of the estate yelled out in despair as soldiers came for her.

"Unfortunately, Your Imperial Excellencies," the advocate went on, "the matter of treason extends even further."

"Proceed," the chief magistrate said.

"I am a recent graduate of the Hall of Great Learning at the North Capital. During my time there, I have heard disturbing rumours about the heir to the estate, a current student there."

"No!" the lady of the estate said.

"What rumours?" an assistant magistrate asked.

"That the heir to the estate belongs to a group of literary students known to compose subversive poems. They call themselves the Serene Donkeys, obviously to ridicule the imperial reign. Given the style of their writings, which they post on the walls of the Hall of Great Learning in the middle of the night, 'The Follies of the Three Hogs' probably originated from them."

"You think the heir to the estate wrote this treasonous filth?" the chief magistrate asked.

"I cannot know for certain, Your Imperial Excellency, but I think it likely that the lady of the estate made fun of you and complained about some of your judgments in her letters to her son. He, in turn, either composed the poem himself or had one of his Serene Donkey friends do so, after which he sent it to his mother for her amusement."

"No, none of that is true, Your Imperial Excellencies!" the lady of the estate yelled.

"Be quiet, you," the chief magistrate said, "or I will have you taken out and whipped for insolence. It is true what they say, this is an age of insolence."

"And from a former courtesan as well," an assistant magistrate said.

When the lady of the estate heard those words, she looked aghast before fainting into the arms of a soldier who restrained her.

The advocate went on. "The connection to the heir to the estate and to the Serene Donkeys is merely a suspicion on my part, but is it not a matter worth investigating?"

"It certainly is," the chief magistrate said. "And we had better send someone to the North Capital quickly, before those subversives at the Hall of Great Learning have an opportunity to destroy evidence of their treason."

The assistant magistrates nodded in agreement, their chins jiggling in affronted assent.

❖

"How did you know you would find something incriminating in the household archive?" the officer asked the advocate as they sat drinking at their favourite inn. They had ordered the best wine in the establishment, and a dozen small plates of sweet and spicy delicacies covered their table.

"I didn't," the advocate answered as he munched on a piece of marinated squid tentacle. "But I thought I would find something. These rural aristocrats, they think that they are above the law as long as they are on friendly terms with the imperial magistrates. They are not scrutinized like the nobles in the cities and are left to their own devices as long as they pay their taxes and take care of local matters. The agents of the Censorate don't go through their correspondences, so they write freely among themselves without worrying about getting into trouble. They resent the authority of the officials sent from the capital, so they amuse themselves by making fun of them. And their idiot sons go to the Hall of Great Learning and do stupid things, like forming a secret literary society like the Serene Donkeys and writing satirical poems about the powerful. So I wasn't surprised when I came across 'The Follies of the Three Hogs,' which was perfect for our purpose."

"The Serene Donkeys," the officer said with a snort. "They won't be writing any more poems, now that they have all been rounded up."

"The masters of the Hall of Great Learning protect even the most wayward of their students, turning a blind eye to their antics. But once the Office for the Deliberation of Forbidden

Affairs becomes involved, there is nothing they can do."

They drank their wine and poured for each other.

"But what would you have done if you had found nothing of use in the archive?" the officer asked.

"I prepared a document that I would have planted there. It turned out to be unnecessary."

"And no one asked how you got hold of those letters?"

"I suppose the magistrates are too busy dismantling the grand estate and punishing its former masters to wonder about that. If they question me, I had a legitimate reason to be at the archive, looking for my family papers. I came across the treasonous letters by accident, and I had the duty to report them. They'll never find out that I gained access to the place by bribing the estate clerk. When the clerk found out that he was going to be investigated, he hung himself."

The officer nodded in wonder before he finished his drink.

"There will be reward money for exposing the treason," the advocate said. "It will be substantial. We can live comfortably for a while, or use the money to advance our careers. You can buy a house like you wanted, a big one in the North Capital."

"Ha! When you told me you were going to spend all our money on a golden toad, I didn't think I would see any of it back. But you know something, even if I had lost it all, it would have been worth it just to send the heir to the estate to the torture hall at the Office for the Deliberation of Forbidden Affairs. I hope that goat prick really suffers before they break him."

"He is not the heir to the estate anymore. He's not a student at the Hall of Great Learning. He is nothing."

"No one to do his whipping for him," the officer said. "That rotten fucker."

The advocate looked up and was surprised to see that his friend was on the verge of enraged tears. The officer shook his head to regain his composure.

They drank in silence for a while, as the early winter wind blew gently around them.

"So," the officer spoke again, "the lady of the estate offered ten silver standards for my land."

"Yes."

"That's more than what I expected."

The advocate nodded.

"What made you do it?" the officer asked. "Why didn't you take the deal for me? Why did you decide to bring her down, and her family and the whole estate with her?"

The advocate gazed out at the darkening sky and thought for a long moment. The officer examined his face and saw that his cheeks had turned bright red from inebriation.

"She was rude to me," the advocate told his friend. "I approached her in the most respectful manner. My father used to be the estate clerk, and my family name is a common one. But I am a graduate of the Hall of Great Learning and a holder of the imperial license of legal advocacy. That earned me the right to sit in her presence. She should have shown me the courtesy of offering to sit with her. But she didn't. She left me standing there with my head bowed like a household servant. She was rude to me, so I decided I would destroy her."

The advocate finished the drink in his cup, and when the officer refilled it, he drank all of it down.

"That is what I will do from now on," the advocate said in a tone of such solemnity that it unnerved his friend. "I will destroy all those who are rude to me. I swear to Heaven that I will. I will show mercy to even my worst enemies if they show me the respect that I deserve. But those who do not, I will destroy so utterly that it will be as if they never existed in the first place. And that is how I will change all things under Heaven and make my name radiant in the chronicles of the historians."

Outside the inn, frigid rain began to pour in a sudden and violent torrent.

UDĀTTA ŚLOKA

Deepak Bharathan

ONE: DANCE OF A GODDESS

The valley baked under the afternoon sun, and the river next to the ashram glistened. The last strands of afternoon prayers died as the verses of ślokas slowed. But the settlement buzzed with activity. The festival of god Mitra was at hand. In the evening the women celebrated by boiling milk and rice with generous dollops of ghee as an offering to the god.

Then the music began. The sound of flutes and drums wafted through the crowd, which eagerly awaited the wife of god Mitra. When she walked in, she was a sight to behold.

Kāila looked at his daughter with pride. It was her first performance as a woman, the wife of a god. Even at fifteen, Ritya was already a splitting image of her mother. Her beautiful jet black hair, which flowed to her hips, was braided with bright orange flowers. She had the slender figure of a dancer. Her red silks shimmered along with the gold bracelets all over her arms. Red dots lightly decorated her forehead and her cheeks. Her face blazed with pride and a sense of duty to her lord.

But to her father, it was her eyes that betrayed the otherwise perfect appearance. Her blue eyes had the sadness that her father had seen before. Even though Ritya had never said a word about her sorrow, Kāila had heard his daughter's eyes speak. Maybe it was the love for a man or a sense of loss that she could never have her own children. He never asked her about it. His daughter was a dancer to the gods. She was promised to her deity Mitra. She had to play her part, just as he had to play his.

As custom dictated, the Rājan sat next to Kāila. The Rājan's face, with a barely grown beard, betrayed the naked aggression that he displayed on the battlefield. The king was still a boy, only seventeen, but Kāila knew of no braver warrior among the Kshatriyas whose swords protected his people.

Ritya's graceful body moved. Her palms folded to acknowledge the Rājan. She spun around, her feet moving quicker than her body. Her hands made quick angular movements toward the sky, and the crowd stood transfixed looking at the young girl.

"My priest, are you so obstinate that you will make your family give up the royal priesthood?" whispered the Rājan, his eyes transfixed on the dancer. Ritya was Kāila's only child. The wife of a god could never marry a mortal. Since Kāila had taken a sacred vow never to take another wife, his family line would end. Someone else would take over the sacred duty that had been with Kāila's family for eight generations.

"If that is the will of gods," started Kāila.

"Yes, the will of gods indeed. Is that what you desire, though?"

"If all desires came true, the world would be a scary place, my Rājan." Kāila did not know if the half-smile on the Rājan's face signified recognition or resignation.

Ritya's dance spoke of the first conflict of the Ārya tribes. The conflict had started one year after the first blood oath to the gods. She motioned by slashing her arms. Her expression morphed from pain to serenity as invisible blood spurted from her veins. Her eyes danced along with the rest of her body.

"They have started setting fire to the grazing grounds, Kāila." The words were an almost inaudible whisper. The Rājan's eyes did not leave the dancer. His face was expressionless.

"The Ādityas be kind on our souls," Kāila whispered. Without the grazing grounds, their tribe's eight thousand cattle and five hundred horses would starve. And so would the tribe.

The dancer stood with a deep resolve in her eyes. The tribe that does not respect the oaths of the Sun-Gods Ādityas could not be part of the Āryas, the noble ones. Anger flashed on her face. She raised her arms and stood on one leg, drawing her body into a dancer's pose of battle.

"Only the grazing grounds to the east remain. I have not yet informed the Sabha." The Rājan's muted tone betrayed his helplessness. The Rājan was duty bound to inform the Sabha, the council of the lords and elders which had elected him, of this mortal danger.

"My Rājan, you need to tell the council." The priest looked around. The Kshatriyas stood around them. Most of them were merely boys. They were Kshatriyas by birth and training. They still had to earn their varṇa through their deeds. *Were they ready for war with the Dāsas?*

Ritya arched her body upwards. With the poise of a trained dancer, she bounded to her right. Her arms angled down and attacked the tribes who had insulted her lord husband. Her eyes remained wide open and arms kept swinging at the invisible tribe around her.

"Dāsas hide in their stone cities, but we will persevere," the Rājan said. Kāila did not know if the young king truly meant his words or realized the futility of saying anything else.

Ritya spread her arms wide. All the tribes were under the same dhárman. She gestured the question to the invisible tribes around her: will you be part of the tribe of Ādityas? The tribes had descended from the same gods.

"Let us reach out to the other tribes," said Kāila in a hoarse whisper. The Rājan tore his eyes away from the dancer to look at his priest. The suggestion sounded more absurd coming from the mouth of the wise Brāhmaṇa. The Ārya tribes were hopelessly divided. The sun would rise in the west before the tribes united.

"The Sabha elected me to protect the tribe, and that I will do until my last breath," said the Rājan. "We will never turn back, not until the last Kshatriya has fallen."

Ritya stood erect with feet firmly planted on the ground. As she folded her hands to seek the blessings of her lord husband, the crowd erupted into a cheerful roar. The Rājan looked at her with no emotion in his eyes.

Kāila looked intently at his daughter. In the heat of performance, he had not noticed that her right ankle had hit a stone. She had not even flinched once during the performance. Her ankle was bleeding profusely, but his daughter did not seem to mind while basking in the glory of the crowd's gleeful reverberation. Kāila hoped his young king would not do the same. But there seemed to be little else they could do now.

TWO: TEARS FOR A BATTLE

The Kshatriyas faded into the deepening twilight. And they continued to ride. There was no looking back. The Āryas never turned back. The Dāsas could hide behind the stone walls, but no stone city could protect men who did not engage in an honourable fight. No Ārya tribe had ever come close to laying a siege to the stone city of the Dāsas. The Dāsas had grown more powerful as the Ārya tribes withered with starvation. But tonight the stone city would burn. Tonight the Dāsas would meet their maker. Kāila willed himself to believe it: the Kshatriyas would be victorious tonight.

Kāila had prayed with one thousand brave Kshatriyas. Many boys and a few weary old men looked to the heavens, asking for victory. Every man knew that this was unlike the skirmishes that the tribe had fought with the Dāsas often. War was here.

"Apāvṛṇorjyotirāryāya ni savyataḥ sādi dasurindra," murmured the Brāhmaṇa to himself. *Light of the Ārya: on your left hand, O Indra, sink the Dāsa.* Kāila asked the god Indra to fight alongside the men in the battle. Even a stone city could not withstand the wrath of the gods.

Kāila tried not to think what if the Kshatriyas failed. The cattle would die first, and the children who depended on the milk would be next. He had heard of tales on death by starvation from the deserts of the west from which his ancestors had migrated. It was not a death he wished even on the Dāsas. The Kshatriyas could not fail. They would not.

It was a cloudy full moon. Just enough light to attack the stone city, but not enough light for the cowards inside the stone walls to know what was happening. Not until it was too late.

Kāila did not know how long he sat by the river bank

meditating, but he suddenly realized how cold the night was. He shivered from the breeze of the river. When he opened his eyes, Ritya was beside him. Even in her stillness, she had the poised grace of a dancer. Her mother would have been proud. Even her breathing had been muted as to not disturb his meditation.

She started to speak but could not find the words. Kāila gently stoked his daughter's hair. The girl laid her head on her father's lap. She tried not to cry, but a tear dropped down her cheek. In times of sorrow, his daughter missed her mother even more. Kāila wanted to say that everything was going to be fine and the warriors would be safe. But he could not lie to his daughter.

"Is death a Kshatriya's destiny?" she asked finally.

"Ātman knows no death, child. Protecting the tribe is a Kshatriya's sacred duty."

"There is a message," she whispered.

He tried to read her face, he could not. Maybe it was the darkness around them. Or maybe it was the darkness in her. Her face did not betray her thoughts.

After he read the message from the Sabha, silence seemed to be the only sane thing to do. Father and daughter sat staring at the river that gave their tribe life. And yet at times, the river goddess unleashed her fury on his people. Without warning, floods came suddenly, destroying grazing grounds, cattle, and homes. A river that gave them so much also had a penchant to take away so violently.

"I do not remember what mother looked like," Ritya said, still staring at the river, "But I still miss her. Sometimes I feel foolish."

Kāila felt a pang of guilt. His daughter would never know the gentle caress of her own child in her lap. She would not die knowing that her own blood would grieve for her. He closed his eyes and brushed that thought aside. Regret was among the most inane expressions of life.

"If memory was the only reason for our feelings, then I would have never learned how to love you, my child. But I did, the instant I saw you." He touched her face gently.

"We should go to the stone city, Father."

"I will meet with the Sabha to discuss what is to be done. You will join the rest of village to move to safety." Even as he said it,

Kāila knew that safety was a relative term indeed.

"I will come with you." It was neither a demand nor a threat. She stated it as a fact. Her voice remained calm and poise graceful.

The Kshatriyas had failed; the warriors had not turned back. Not till the last one fell. Just like the Rājan had promised. Maybe the Rājan's priest had failed to give adequate counsel to the brave young warrior. Kāila dismissed the thought. Regret was indeed among the most inane expressions of life.

"Showing up at the gates of the stone city desecrates their memory," the Brāhmaṇa said.

"Does it matter?" his daughter asked. "The dead Kshatriyas have no use for legacy. A living Brāhmaṇa might."

She had learned well. Kāila stared at his daughter. Then he smiled. Slowly he began laughing. The irony of having to protect his legacy—knowing his line would end with his daughter—was indeed a cruel joke by the Ādityas. After a moment, Ritya joined in. Their laughter echoed through the valley; it was liberating to laugh at imminent death. Maybe Yama, the god of death, had a sense of humour after all.

Three: Mound of the Dead

It should have taken them three hours on foot to the stone city, but sorrow slowed them down. Ritya and Kāila drudged on. Step after step toward the field of dead. Daybreak over the valley was not warm.

In the late hours of night, the Sabha had been split. The fiery discussion had lasted the night. The swiftness of defeat crushed the tribe. The questions came quick: Why would the Dāsas not make for the village now that they had killed all the Kshatriyas? Why did a Brāhmaṇa have go to the battlefield to perform the last rites for the dead? A girl in the battlefield to see the dead? Even the Ādityas would not forgive such a sin.

Many in the tribe had already abandoned the village for other tribes. As daybreak approached, some members of the Sabha joined the exodus. Tenacity was one of Kāila's virtues. And his daughter, the wife of Mitra, had inherited that from him. She was going to the stone city with or without him.

UDĀTTA ŚLOKA by Deepak Bharathan

Ritya had never seen a battlefield. She had not seen the stone city either. The stone city stood tall and expansive in the morning glow. She wondered how such barbarians had built something this majestic. The gates were strong, imposing, and shut. Not one Ārya had gotten through them. Not now and maybe never.

Kāila dropped to his knees. The sorrow had not hit him until he saw the dead. They looked younger in their stillness. The Dāsas had taken no prisoners. The Kshatriyas of his tribe were all dead. He cried not just for the brave but also for the innocent back in his village. Maybe the Dāsas would do him a favour and kill him from inside the stone walls. But they did not. He felt the Dāsas were watching him, poring through him. But they did not do a thing.

The blood of the young warriors had already dried. The Dāsas knew the attack was coming. Maybe someone had betrayed the stealth that the Rājan had planned.

Ritya walked through the field of dead. Forever inert, the dead no longer shared the sorrow of the living. His daughter's eyes were searching for someone she had once loved. But looking for love among the dead was painful both in body and in spirit.

They found the Rājan. He lay, as they had expected, at the head of his party. Even in death, he looked majestic. The Kshatriyas had not even come close to the gate. They had perished with crushing swiftness for reasons that only the Ādityas could understand.

Ritya did not shed a tear. She stood there silently. Kāila started the ślokas. He murmured the prayers for the dead, for their Ātman to be released from the worldly pains and find moksha. His inaudible voice broke often. This was his final act as priest for his tribe. By the time he returned to the village, the tribe would no longer exist. This defeat clearly indicated the will of the Ādityas.

"Stone walls cannot protect the dishonourable," Ritya said. Her tone had a seething fury that Kāila had never heard before.

"They will be punished," she said.

Kāila wrapped his arms around his daughter.

"They will be punished," she repeated. Tears welled up in her blue eyes. But she did not flinch. Poise and grace never left her side whether in sorrow or in joy.

The sound started suddenly like they were surrounded by a

thousand tiny temple bells. A shrill ringing reverberated across the battlefield. Kāila searched for the source, but Ritya found it first. He followed her eyes.

The lights appeared. They blinded him for a second, but he kept his eyes open. The lights shone like the bright stars in the night sky. Then gently, the lights floated up to the Brāhmaṇa and his daughter. It was unlike anything he had ever seen. Strangely he did not feel fear.

Ritya's eyes widened as she looked at the brightness. She stood there transfixed and then she moved her face closer to the lights, like she understood what they were.

"Ritya," started Kāila, wanting his daughter to stay away.

"Father, you need to leave," replied his daughter. Her voice was heavy with purpose.

"Yes, we need to. Come." He knew that was not what she meant.

The lights were now glowing all around them. Then as if the lights had sensed awareness from the young girl, they coalesced around her, moving and bouncing from one point to another. The lights were dancing.

She folded her hands and took a dancer's pose in the field of dead. The lights kept dancing around her. The sun was no longer the brightest object in Kāila's eyes.

The lights lifted her. She stood still. There was no fear in her eyes, only a deep understanding. She moved her lips to say something to him, but the words never made it out. She held her hand out, and her father stood looking. And then she gently floated to the stone city. The lights continued to dance around her like bright fiery fireflies.

Kāila's knees collapsed as strength drained out of his body. Images burst inside his head, and he saw what the lights were telling him. A battle like he had never imagined. The gods, yes—they had to be gods—themselves fought in the battle. The weapons were unlike anything he understood. He saw flashes of Vajra, the thunderbolt, and Agni, the fire, used in the battle. There were other glimpses that his mind could not fathom.

The lights appeared in the battle. The lights were the battle. The lights spread, travelling across worlds in immense chariots of fire.

UDĀTTA ŚLOKA by Deepak Bharathan

Even the cosmos looked like a small place, as the lights danced around the heavens finally to arrive at the ground where he sat. A figure appeared in front of him. Kāila could not understand what it was, but his mind could see it as clearly as the light of the day. The lights danced around four faces of that being.

"Rudra," the Brāhmaṇa whimpered. And then the battle vanished. The field of dead lay in front of Kāila.

He saw her floating next to the gates of the stone city. The lights were brighter and they still danced around her. He saw the Dāsa archers take aim at his daughter. He screamed, but the words would not come from his throat. He lay there among the dead, not dead but not living either.

He cursed the stone city. Those stones had taken away so much from him. Then in the blink of an eye, the sky above the stone city filled up with the lights. And then in an instant the lights disappeared. The stone city stood still and uncaring, as it always had.

It was a long while before Kāila moved. His beautiful Ritya was gone. Maybe this was the merciful way to go. The Rājan was gone. So was his tribe. Now he had to go home. Wherever that was. He knew that he had witnessed divinity, yet his insufficient mind did not know how to understand it.

Ritya. Where are you, my child?

Kāila sensed something was different. The silent stones told him something that he could not comprehend. He got up and stumbled toward the city, not away from it. There were no ślokas on his lips as he walked ahead, just his daughter's name. *Ritya*, he mumbled, over and over again. The gates were still locked, but he stood there. He waited. He did not know for what.

Ritya. Ritya. Ritya.

He stood there, near those imposing gates for an eternity. And then he heard noises all around him. Horses and men came. Maybe it was part of a dream. He did not know. He did not care. Maybe the winds had carried the message of death to the Āryas. Nothing united men like the scent of victory. Some men asked him questions. He neither listened nor answered. He had only one word on his lips.

Ritya. Ritya. Ritya.

The stone city stood silent as the men tore down its gates. The Dāsas did not stop them. They did not even stir. How could they? As the horses wandered in, he saw them. There was no anguish, no fear, no pain, not even surprise. There was nothing. They had fallen where they stood. Peaceful serene vengeance adorned street after street in the stone city.

Ritya. Are you here, my child?

He wandered the dead streets searching. More horses streamed in. There were more noises of men, their weapons, and their animals. He did not care. More questions came at him from the men. He ignored them all. He kept repeating the name of his child.

Ritya. Ritya. Ritya.

The stone city was no longer silent. The noises of men reigned in the streets. Somewhere in the city, music started to flow. So did alcohol that the men called soma, the nectar of gods. The songs grew louder under the stars. Kāila heard a familiar name echoing through the winds. Ritya, daughter of Kāila, the voices said. They chanted her name. *She won this battle for us*, they sang. Daughter of Kāila, they chanted, Kālikā—the goddess of death.

Kālikā. Kālikā. Kāli.

The stone city was the mound of the dead, yet it was more alive than it had ever been. And it welcomed them all.

Author's Notes:

Mohenjo-daro ('Mound of the Dead' in Sindhi) was one of the largest settlements of the powerful Indus Valley Civilization. About four thousand years ago, the city and the civilization declined with stunning suddenness. The city was located on the bank of the Indus River in the present-day Pakistan and is the best-preserved city of the Indus civilization to date.

CRASH

Melissa Yuan-Innes

Luna Yu figured nothing happened on the Moon. Not since her parents colonized it, anyway.

Her sixteenth birthday started out like any weekday, immersed in partial differential equations while a robot teacher patrolled the pod classroom around Luna, her two siblings, and a four-year-old boy.

Birthdays did not get you a free pass out of school on the Moon. If anything, you got more homework instead of less. At least Terra hadn't teased Luna about her bioprosthetic legs today. When Mom and Dad weren't around, Luna and Puck secretly called their twelve-year-old sister Terror.

Luna's eye screen flickered once. Twice. She took it off projection mode, which was inherently more unstable. They only used it so that the other students could see what everyone was studying. The robot teacher had a direct input line on their studies, but the students' efficiency doubled when they realized other humans could watch them in real time. Also, it was supposed to rest their eyes, to focus on a metre away instead of the usual 30 centimetres, but mostly the colony cared about the efficiency part.

The near screen flickered, too, before it blacked out, only to be lit up in red letters.

RED ALERT:

ALL COLONISTS TO RETURN TO T1 IMMEDIATELY.

SECURE YOUR PREMISES.

AWAIT FURTHER INSTRUCTIONS.

Teacher began to parrot the words in a loud monotone. "Red alert. All colonists to return to T1 immediately . . ."

"What's wrong?" said Puck, dropping his pencil. Its free end rose into the air with 1/6 grav.

Luna batted the pencil to the side and scooped their four-year-old neighbour, Franklin, in her arms. He was a chubby kid, heavier than he looked, and smelled a bit like old cheese. "We have to get back to our pods. Time to go to sleep!"

Franklin scowled at her and pushed his arms against her chest. "It's not sleep time. It's only 9:13 a.m.!"

"Yeah, Luna," muttered Terra.

"Okay, not sleep, then," said Luna, struggling to keep Franklin on her hip. He wasn't half as heavy as the weights she practiced with for three hours every day, but the weights didn't wiggle. "They just want us back in our pods. Maybe it's an asteroid drill. They're probably timing us. Let's hurry, okay?"

"I want to walk! I've got real legs," said Franklin.

Luna set him down a little harder than necessary. Her legs were real, just not completely biological.

". . . Secure the premises. Await further instructions," droned Teacher as they left, vacuum sealing the classroom door behind them.

"Well, that was creepy," said Terra.

Puck nodded. Franklin reached for his hand, and Puck took it.

Boys. Luna turned to her sister. "Wanna race back to T1?"

"No," said Terra, but Puck started to run, which meant that Franklin did, too, giggling. Terra rolled her eyes, but at least she trotted. The air in the airlock was cooler, since the colony didn't want to waste energy on sections that were only "pass-bys," and because they'd passed deeper underground. Less than five minutes later, they reached Terminal One, or T1, except Terra, who was still dragging her feet and mumbling about "secure vs. insecure" premises. The T1 hallway red alarm lights were flashing, making Luna uneasy, even though someone had already disabled the siren. Her siblings alternated between looking like devils and shadows, depending how the lights strobed.

Terra grinned at her, flashing her bright red teeth, and crossed her eyes.

Luna felt a bit better.

Franklin's parents must have tracked his progress through his implant, because the door whooshed open before the sensor should have detected Puck. Dr. Wei snatched Franklin up in his arms.

"What's happening?" asked Luna.

Dr. Wei said, "Don't know. Your parents are waiting," and sealed the door. Luna ran flat out the last five metres to the Yu pod. It unlocked automatically to her retinal print, and she stumbled into the chamber, shouting, "Mom? Dad!"

"Shh. It's okay. We're both here," said Mom, folding Luna in her arms. Mom was the only person in the colony who smelled like lavender, because she synthesized it in her lab.

Dad was already double-hugging Puck on one side and Terra on the other. "Are we ever glad to see you—"

"What happened?"

Mom and Dad exchanged a look before Dad said, "There was a crash north of Cabeus Crater."

Luna wasn't sure what the big deal was. Even Franklin knew that the colony was set up on the Moon's south pole, on the edge of Shackleton Crater, so they could benefit from nearly constant sunlight while staying in good radio contact with Earth. Strange to think there had been a crash on the opposite side, but Luna hadn't noticed any earthquake, so either it wasn't a big impact, or their structures were really well-built, or both.

"What kind of crash?" asked Puck. He didn't talk often, but it just meant that everyone paid more attention when he did.

Mom and Dad exchanged another look. "A team is investigating. In the meantime, the rest of us are staying here to be safe."

Minutes ago, Luna had assumed that everything exciting had happened before she was born. Technically, she was one of the first Moon colonists, since her parents had escaped from the Earth when her mother was pregnant with her, but Luna didn't remember anything about it except the leg operations. Sometimes, when she was feeling down, she figured that she'd gotten all of the bad stuff and none of the good stuff about being a pioneer. By the time Mom got pregnant again, they'd figured out how much fetal development relies on 1 grav and trace minerals, so Puck and Terra were okay.

Now, Luna found herself looking, really looking, at their pod. Compared to the other families, they had a giant amount of space because, not only did their sleeping area have to fit five bodies instead of two or three, but since everyone slept kind of upright, strapped in their sleeping bag, more bodies just took more room. They also got a larger "living area," where they ate or played games together, but they still had to share the communal toilet and sponge bath like everyone else. Mom and Dad kept the moon rock walls plain except for a picture of the Buddha anchored to the domed ceiling with a red ribbon.

At first, it was fun to have Mom and Dad home in the middle of the day. Dad told them funny stories, like how he tried to build a new kind of 1/6 G toilet that turned out disastrous, and Mom showed them a new card game called Bingo Newton, which was about science trivia. But Luna noticed Mom talking on her com link while Dad was laughing, and Mom trying to distract them with a new flavour of soy bean paste while Dad was talking on his com link. So something was going on.

That was good, right? Because Luna had been so bored.

But actually, her heart thudded in her chest and her armpits prickled with sweat, because she knew her life was changing in front of her eyes, even before Mom got called away.

"I'll be back soon. I love you," Mom said, which was not like her at all. She usually said, "Be good." And then she did something stranger. She kissed Luna's cheeks and looked like she wanted to say something, but couldn't. When Luna opened her mouth, Mom shook her head and kissed Puck on his forehead. He watched Mom silently as Mom turned to Terra and offered her a hug.

After a second, Terra took it and hugged Mom back.

The hugs worried Luna most of all.

When the door sealed behind her, Terra turned on Dad. "You have to tell us what's going on."

Dad shook his head. "You'll find out soon enough."

"Mom's acting like she's going off to war!" Terra said.

Sometimes, Luna loved Terra because she said exactly what everyone else was thinking but didn't have the nerve to say.

While Terra and Dad argued, Luna tracked her mother's progress. Mom had exited T1 and was heading north, to the transportation unit. Then her implant paused for 20 minutes before it made a jerky, jagged progress north.

Mom was going to the Cabeus Crater, to the crash site.

Luna's fingers felt numb. Her breath came in short gasps. But she tried to reason it out. They'd called both Mom and Dad, but in the end, they asked Mom. Mom was a family doctor and a biomedical research scientist who specialized in viruses. Dad was a mechanical engineer who liked to joke that Mom had married beneath her. If they needed both their expertise, then it was not just some sort of technological problem but also a living organism that needed tending.

Could the crash site be contaminated with some sort of virus?

Was their colony under attack?

Mom and Dad didn't like talking about what had happened to Earth. They talked about good stuff. Puck was always asking about what trees and rivers looked and felt like, and Luna wanted to know about their ancestors.

But whenever Terra brought up stuff like nuclear bombs or deforestation, they either changed the subject or stopped talking altogether. "You don't need to know that. We came here to get away from it." And then their com links' information on all the bad stuff would kind of disappear, bit by bit, until Terra figured it out and started keeping her mouth shut sometimes.

Terra should know better than asking Dad directly. It wouldn't get her any answers, but at least it kept them both busy, especially now that Terra was bugging Puck to say something.

"Don't you care about Mom? Don't you think we should know?" she said, while Puck backed into the sleeping area, trying not to get involved. He sent Luna a look, but she deliberately closed her left eye at him to show him that she was using her com link.

Luna tuned back into tracker mode. The whole Moon was mapped out so that if anyone ever wandered off-base, they could find her quickly and easily until she blasted off into space. Luna paused at that thought, but it was really, super unlikely that Mom was going off-Moon with no prep. Still. Scary. All colonists had an implant behind their right ears that identified them on the tracking system, so Luna could see that Mom was travelling at space jeep speed, heading straight for the other dots clustered at what must be the crash site. On closer inspection, these turned out to be Mr. Lau, Dr. Bing, and Dr. Chan.

Mr. Lau was the colony's main surgeon trained under the British system, where surgeons were called Mister. Luna had spent way too much of her life with him while he reconfigured nanobot after nanobot for her legs, until he finally gave up and he and Mom developed the bioprostheses. Just seeing his name gave her a chill, even though she hadn't seen him for over four months.

Dr. Chan was a doctor, too, but he was younger. He studied both Eastern and Western medicine, so Luna would see him practicing Tai Chi in the exercise room while everyone else lifted weights.

Dr. Bing was an engineer who specialized in applied science research so complicated that Luna thought even her parents didn't exactly understand it. Many colonists whispered about her because she was one of the single women on the base and certainly the most beautiful and the most reserved. Luna didn't like her.

Luna signalled Puck over and showed him the tracking map. He studied it carefully. "Makes sense," he whispered.

"What does?"

"Well, I figured she was going to the crash site."

"But look at the people she's with! She could be in terrible danger. What if someone hit us with a bioterrorist bomb, and that's why they need Mom? To collect and analyze the virus?"

Puck shrugged. "They could have asked her because she's a family doctor. There are two other doctors there, you know."

"And Dr. Bing. Why Dr. Bing?"

He shook his head. She could see his mind was already drifting. Puck didn't really like people or talking about things. He'd rather head over to the biofarm and hang out with the radishes.

Terra bellowed, "Why. Won't. Anybody. Help. Me? Mom won't answer her com link, Dad's not answering any questions, and you two don't care!"

From the look on Puck's face, Luna could see that Terra had shattered their brother's usual calm.

"We care," Luna said, "but yelling's not helping. Want to play Bingo Newton, Dad?"

Dad shook his head. "You three go ahead."

Terra said, "No way! You must think I'm an idiot."

Puck jumped up and held out his hand for the cards. "Gosh, that sounds like a good idea."

After a minute, Terra gave them a funny look and trailed after them to the sleep closets. "If you think I'm some little kid that you can distract with a little game—"

"Hush up a minute," said Luna. She explained the tracking chart.

"Let me see that," said Terra. She spent so long staring at the tracking chart that Luna wanted to ask her what was wrong. Terra blinked hard and said, "Mom's dot isn't moving as much as the others."

"Let's move the scale in tighter," said Puck, so Luna made the increments smaller, double-blinking on Mom's dot to make it the focus.

It was true. Mom's dot stayed in place while Dr. Bing's moved the most, in a little semi-circle. The two other dots moved just once in a while, but they flickered.

"It could mean nothing," said Puck, after a second. "She could be collecting viruses and have to stay in position."

"I thought you said she was probably there as a doctor and not because it was bioterrorism," snapped Luna.

"Bioterrorism?" said Terra.

Oh, yeah. Luna had left that angle out. By the time she'd finished telling Terra, her little sister was ready to steal a moon jeep and race after Mom, yelling, "We've got to save her!"

Luna remembered her first aid course, though. You couldn't rush in to save someone if it meant a stampede of people running into a depressurized chamber because then you might all smother together. Maybe one person could suit up and drag the victim out while a team fixed the pressure. "We just need to know what's going on."

"But she's not answering us!" said Terra.

"Let's see," said Luna. She closed everything down to reboot her system.

"What are you doing?" asked Puck.

"Wiping the slate clean. You know it works maybe ten percent of the time." She just didn't mention that she was also shutting down the projection mode so that she could log back in as Dad. He changed his password every two days but kept the same master password, which she figured out a month ago. She checked his logbook, gasped, and opened the projection for them.

0820: Flare on north pole due to impact/explosion.

0823: Cameras triangulate on crash site at 104x2831. Nearest location: Cabeus Crater.

0829: Crash object appears to be manned spaceship. Infrared confirm presence of a moving organic matter at temperature 37.9 degrees Celsius.

Terra gasped. "There's a person out there!"

They all looked at each other for a second. Then, Puck said slowly, "Or an alien."

"At human body temperature? C'mon!" said Terra.

It seemed unlikely that another sentient organism had developed a humanoid body temperature. Or maybe that was convergent evolution? Luna remembered reading about that, how species might look the same, or have developed similar traits, but it's not because they have a close genetic relationship. It's because they just evolved the same way. Like fish in Antarctica developed a kind of antifreeze glycoprotein so they wouldn't freeze to death, but so did the Arctic fish on the opposite pole of the planet.

Maybe 37.9 was just a good temperature for a sentient creature.

Maybe Mom was with the alien.

Luna blinked down the rest of the log as fast as she could, skipping the boring parts like a robot drone confirming the sighting and deciding to alert the school and shut down all work for the day. Dr. Bing had been the first to arrive on site, so she set up a live video feed.

The thing was still breathing and moving over two hours after impact. That was when the investigation team started messaging the rest of the colony. They, too, worried about whether the thing was human, especially given its survival in such an extreme state.

Luna clicked over to the live feed, so they could watch and hear whatever they could before Dad logged back on the network.

Mom had helped them extract the creature at almost 1300, assuming that it would be deceased, but it seemed only to be unconscious and immediately identifiable as a human in an extremely flame-resistant suit.

They all gasped at the blurred view of his face. Even that glimpse through his helmet showed a very old man with a broad, sharp nose. His skin looked as pockmarked and scarred as the moon's surface.

Not one of the moon colonists was older than 40, and many of them were much younger. Luna had never seen such an aged man before.

"Maybe he is an alien," Puck joked, just before their father cut their connection.

Luna turned to face their father. His dark eyes were unreadable. "What are you three doing in my account?"

Luna could barely breathe. She'd never been in trouble. Not like this. She tried to take a step forward, but for once, her bioprostheses failed her. Her legs trembled too much.

Terra squared off her shoulders. "We had to find out what happened to Mom."

Even Puck said, "We couldn't leave her like that."

Luna, the oldest and now the most embarrassed, confessed, "None of our com links are good for anything except partial differential equations. So I was the one who broke into your account. I'm sorry."

Dad shook his head, a world of disappointment in his face. "If you think you must break the rules before talking to me, we have raised you wrong."

"I did talk to you!" Terra said. "Please, Dad, we'll take whatever punishment you give us, but we've got to know who that man is and why they called Mom?"

Dad looked each of them in the eye. "You know that much already, then?"

Luna nodded.

"You know that your mother is a doctor. You may not know

that your mother is a bioethicist. They called her to judge this case. This man, whoever he is, might wish us harm. He came perilously close to harming the base. We don't know who he is and won't be able to obtain Earth records for some time. Taking care of him will take many human and planetary resources and possibly endanger the health of our colony. Two people in the team believe that it would be wiser to leave him on site. One person wishes to try and heal him at all cost."

Luna and her siblings sent frantic messages to their mother from their own accounts, pelting her with advice, even though they knew she couldn't hear them.

In the end, Mom elected to bring this stranger back to the base—outside the base, in the transportation zone, in a temporary shelter, where he would be isolated and have robots attend him. She set a limit on how many labour hours, and how many precious cc's of water to allot him, before they allowed nature to take its course.

Luna saw the justice in this, but she was already dreaming of another world. A new kind of world, one where children were allowed to learn what they want, not only what is useful. Where a stranger's life might not hang in the balance. A world that might be rough and uneven but never boring.

MEMORIAM

Priya Sridhar

"You are the father of this animate and inanimate world, and the greatest guru to be worshipped."
> —Bhagavad-Gita, The Yoga of the Manifestation

Mosquitoes still buzzed outside the balcony nets. Anish Matam sat outside, dressed in white pajama bottoms, a cup of coffee in his hand. His belly fat rolled as he moved, and he stroked the folds. He sipped from the small white mug. Beard stubble coated his chin, and his hair had grey streaks.

The sun's rays reflected orange ripples on the Kerala waters. A stray dog ran by the riverbed, fur coated in sickly pink streaks, and approached Anish with a wagging tail. Anish reached into his pocket and pulled out several Western dog treats. The dog caught them one by one as Anish tossed them from the balcony into the air. The dog barked happily.

The protesters hadn't come by so early this time; they had discovered the mosquito hordes that preyed at night, unless they wore mosquito nets. When they were here, Anish had offered them coffee and tea, as well as his cook Mina's many idlis.

"Her coconut chutney is to die for," he said. "Would you like me to bring out a bowl?"

"We don't want your tea or chutney." Someone shouted. "We want you to stop parading that THING around!"

"You shouldn't be making money off this!" Another person said. "It's not what your father would have wanted. It's sacrilegious."

"I charge only ten rupees per person," Anish said, with some irritation. "I've said this before; it's only to pay for groceries. Do you want to stay overnight? I think there's enough room for all of you."

Still the protesters continued to scream and refuse his offer. Their protest signs made flapping noises as they shook them in the steamy, sultry morning. Anish occasionally brought out coconut water and lemon water. He told his guest lodgers that the protesters weren't dangerous, but to take care.

"All it takes is one instance of violence," he said. "It's only a matter of time."

The children seemed to view this with interest; they were taking music lessons in his mother's old practice room. Their teacher, one of Anish's former friends from university, eyed the whole thing with bemusement.

In contrast to their children, the adults seemed more nervous. Many of them were his father's fans, the ones who had made the long pilgrimage from Tony Matam's European and American houses to see his last living home in India.

It is strange, he thought as he watched the dog run away toward the dock. *If you go to America, Christians there are the majority, and they pervade everything. But here, they are the persecuted race. Was that why my father converted, despite being raised Catholic?*

The thing turned its head toward him. Anish stiffened, looking into the glass eyes. They were a replica of his father's jet-black eyes, hand-painted by Anish to reflect the spark that came whenever Appa decided to play a chess game or Brainvita. He had used a silicone skin, peppered with dark marks, and moulded in certain areas to replicate the jowl and worry lines.

"Don't worry," Anish told it in a low tone so that his guests wouldn't overhear. "I'll take care of things, Appa."

He covered the robot's hands with his own, feeling the synthetic hairs that poked out of his father's silicone knuckles.

The mechanical fingers curled, the way Appa's had when Anish came to him as a child after nightmares. Anish remembered one nightmare about his father going over a waterfall, and never coming back.

The doorbell rang. Anish shuffled downstairs to answer it. A tall, platinum blonde woman stood there nervously, swatting at mosquitoes. Dust and river mud coated her blue sneakers and her black jeans.

"Janet Oversight." Anish felt relief on seeing a familiar, friendly face. "The writer from Bloomsbury. You are writing a book on my father. What a pleasant surprise!"

She smiled. "You must be Anish. I came to do research on the last part of it."

"Of course. Come in. Would you like coffee?"

"I would, actually. My mouth still burned from lunch. Very spicy river fish."

"The boat driver didn't tell you, I assume."

"He apologized."

He let her inside, directing her to a sign which read: PLEASE TAKE OFF YOUR SHOES. She slipped off her sneakers and scratched her ankle with the other foot. Her white socks were noticeably soaked with sweat and humidity from the river trip.

"How was your trip?" he asked.

"Good. A little hot."

"Yes," he said apologetically. "You should have come in the winter, when things are nicer and cooler."

"Plane fares are higher in the winter. Bloomsbury is reimbursing me for my travel expenses, but I don't want them to think the book is going to cost them millions."

"It's your right to travel when it's most convenient," he said. "The book will sell because it's about my father. I remember when you came to Appa's house in London. You still take your coffee with milk and no sugar?"

She nodded. "Thank you."

"Have some idlis." Anish offered her a few. "Mina makes them fresh every morning."

She took the lentil cakes gingerly. She tasted them plain with a quizzical expression, so he put spicy podhi on her plate and told her to dip an idli in the yellow powder. When her eyes became red and runny, he offered her water.

When she had enough water, Anish began their conversation. "So you want to know about the last days of my father's life. Feel free to ask me any questions."

"First, how long has he owned this home?"

"About ten years. It started out as a lodge for travellers, and my father fell in love with it while he was researching another book, *The River in the Pond*."

"I remember that book. It gave me nightmares."

"Not just you; many others too." Anish chuckled, trying hard not to sound like water bursting from a stream. "I remember the letters. That was when he got religious and was advising people to pray."

"That's not very helpful."

"It wasn't, and that sparked quite an outcry, especially with how that book ended. He did apologize, though. My father was good at admitting he was wrong when he messed up. You can't pray when you know that nothing is out there."

Janet munched on a plain idli and washed it down with coffee.

"How was he able to buy this place if it was in a commercial zone and not residential?"

"He planned to run it as a lodge, just as a little side project. He had a lot of side projects, you know, and mainly to hire people who needed the help."

"Side projects." Janet took a deep breath. "I did want to ask you about that. About your side project."

"Which one?"

"The one that claims you've been making money off your father's death, and creating something ungodlike."

"Oh." He was hoping she wouldn't. "I figured you might. It could be a good fodder for the book."

"Not just that. It seems odd that you would create something like that when—"

"It's a long story," he said. "My father's last book in the Kalki

Chronicles was about souls entering robots. That comes directly from the Ramayana, with Ravana's brother Kumbhakarna. He was an actual machine, who needed six months of sleep to fight properly. I was finishing my engineering degree in grad school, going into robotics, when my father contacted me. He thought that I could help him with his book."

Janet nodded. She seemed to know this part.

"So I had been showing him a prototype I was working on with the department, an animatronic that could simulate human motion without the usual glitches, and which could sync lip movement perfectly. He commissioned the department to make a Kalki prototype that he could use as a reference for his book. Once he was done writing, his plan was to auction off the prototype for charity so that more students in Kerala can afford to attend classes and get a proper education."

"Your father was a generous soul."

"He was. I didn't want to charge him, but he insisted, given the expensive development and material costs."

"After he died, you kept the prototype instead of auctioning it for charity?"

"Of course." Anish tried to hide his sadness. "I know it sounds ridiculous, but it was the last thing we worked on together. I donated what my father paid me to his favourite charities, but several thousands doesn't feel equivalent to potentially several millions."

"Were you close to your father?" she asked. "I remember the joy when you were born. It was a big deal."

"Oh, the social media age," he said. "I've seen the pictures and the videos. Amma wrote so many happy songs when I was born, and Appa was so excited."

"But?"

"I am not a creative person." Anish looked down at his feet, avoiding Janet's eyes. "It's weird. Amma and Appa loved me. But I didn't inherit anything else. My other siblings did. Tara, Trisha, Rahul. You know about them."

"But you went into robotics, and science requires creative minds," Janet said. Anish could feel her eyes upon him. "You shouldn't feel guilty that you went into something different. Lots of artists' children do."

Anish looked up. "Really?"

"Yeah. Christopher Robin Milne, for one. He opened a bookshop and served in the military."

"That's Christopher Robin, though," Anish said. "He *had* to be something different. He wasn't going to stay that boy forever."

"And you weren't either. You're still adorable as you were in those baby videos."

Anish laughed again.

"Why, thank you, Janet."

Janet finished her idli and gulped more water.

"I did want to ask about what I read in the papers," she said. "About what you did with that prototype."

"Oh, that." He gave a sardonic smile. "Why don't I show you instead?"

Anish led her up a flight of narrow stairs to his father's study.

"Sweet Jesus." Janet muttered.

The animatronic was writing at his desk idly. It wore a black dressing gown, fine silk embroidered with white curlicues at the end. The quill pen it used scratched against thick bond paper. Every time it took a breath, its silicon skin expanded and contracted.

"It looks exactly like him," Janet said, her voice sounded awe and fear. "The way it moves —"

"Yeah. Very realistic," Anish admitted. He was proud of his creation. "The voice box isn't completely done."

"Voice box?"

"The recorded sound of my father's voice." He walked over to where the robot was sitting and writing: tapped its throat. "It's all downloaded, of course, so the sound bites are there, but he can't carry a proper conversation. I haven't fixed that kink."

The robot looked up as it felt Anish's fingers. Their eyes met, and Anish felt remorse.

"Sorry, Appa," he said, pulling his hand away. "I don't mean to be disrespectful."

"Oh my God." Janet sat down on a piano bench that lacked a piano. "It's almost like he's here in the room. I remember interviewing him for the book. But if it can write, can it walk?"

"He can. I've only programmed him to pace the way Appa did when he wrote and to occasionally pray."

The robot's gaze followed him as he went to sit by Janet on the piano bench. Anish gave it a nervous smile.

"Maybe we should leave him alone," he said. "Appa never liked being disturbed when he was writing something good. It looks like he's in the zone."

They got up. Anish heard a pen scratching against paper.

"What about all those gestures?" Janet asked Anish when he closed the door. "Your father's eyes would follow people like that, but not for that long. What about the hair? And the handwriting?"

"I added a few," he said. "Not all of them. That's the thing. For some reason he knows what Appa was like, including the things that I haven't taught him."

"A learning AI, maybe? If it has his downloaded audio—"

"Possibly," he said. "Then sometimes I wonder. He can't carry a conversation, but sometimes Appa makes requests. Like yesterday, while I was polishing him, he asked for Ganges river water."

"What?"

"Yeah." Anish gave a small laugh. "We used to have a vial of Ganges water, but it went missing. In Hindu culture, if you drink from that river, all your sins are purified. Except my father never had sins. Not to mention the water is disgusting with all the ashes and human filth."

"Did he ever talk about the water in interviews?" Janet asked.

"No," he answered. "I should know; I listened to all of them when I entered them into his voice box."

"You can't be thinking that a robot suddenly became religious, Anish. You're not even Hindu!"

"I'm not," he said. "But Appa was. Somehow the robot picked up on that."

"It must be from one of those interviews where he talked about converting."

"He never talked about it in that much detail." Anish felt sober.

"It's not your father, Anish," Janet said. "Don't you realize that calling him such is why people are getting worried?"

"People get worried over lots of things. This is just a case of people suffering uncanny valley."

"Uncanny what now?"

"Uncanny valley. It's an uncomfortable sensation people get when a machine tries to appear lifelike and fails horribly so that it's creepy."

"Hmm." Janet pursed her lips. "Even so. This looks crazy. *You* look crazy talking to him like that."

"I know it's not him." Anish felt solemn again. "But since— it's how I'm dealing with Appa's sudden death. What happened wasn't fair. We didn't even get to say *goodbye*."

"But that's how accidents are," Janet said, her voice sounding hollow. "They happen randomly, and you never know when or where."

"You've seen the petitions. People want to pay the Lords of the Underworld fucking flowers to bring him back. That's not how *any* afterlife works, even if you account for cultural differences. And you're calling *me* the crazy one?"

Janet had no response. Anish swallowed and led her to another room.

There's no such thing as bad publicity, Anish thought, *except when it scares people away.*

He sipped his late morning coffee. The taste of idlis and coconut chutney lingered in his mouth.

Other people were waking up; he could hear the sound of teeth crunching toasted white bread, and his cook Mina boiling more coffee. Janet typed in her room, on that cheap laptop; the clacking echoed downstairs.

Anish finished his coffee and went inside. He offered his cup to Mina. She was making Ovaltine, a brown sugary substance, for the children.

"The phone rang," she said. "It's the priest that you called."

Anish went to the old-fashioned white receiver. He twirled the cord around his fingers and dialed the number that was written in script.

"Hello?"

"Guru Drishti, it's me, Anish Matam." Anish spoke in Tamil.

"Mr. Matam." The man on the other side took a deep breath. "You realize you're getting into a lot of trouble."

"I thought you didn't read the newspaper."

"I do when it concerns a client. You want genuine water from the Ganges?"

"Yes."

"Why can't you get it yourself? You can afford to make the trip."

"I don't want to leave the house. Not for my safety, but the safety of everyone else. The court order is keeping the protesters from storming the house, but it feels like we're only buying time. You know about mobs."

"If you want my opinion, you should get rid of the robot, Anish. That's the safest route."

"Thank you for the opinion, but I really need your help."

"Why Ganges water?"

"It was important to my father. Please. I'll forward you the fee in advance."

There was a pause. Anish could hear the coins clinking within the priest's thoughts.

"Very well. For your sake I will make the trip. But please be careful. I don't want your death on my conscience."

"You won't," Anish promised. *Not my death, at least.*

"Bullshit." Janet's editor was chewing as he spoke. "It's all bullshit."

"He's grieving for his father," Janet said, keeping her defensive voice low. "It's his coping mechanism."

The temporary phone felt like a plastic Etch-A-Sketch between her ear and shoulder. She cocked her head to hold the phone in place, typing rapidly.

"There's grieving and then there's making a duplicate of his father. He needs a therapist, and he can surely afford it."

"That's beside the point," Janet replied. "I'm not sure how to put this in my book. It doesn't fit."

"Tough luck, Janet. Just write it, and we'll worry about the fit later. Just don't buy into the bullshit. Your deadline's in two weeks, so no pressure. Yet."

He gave a wild laugh. Janet forced herself to laugh with him.

"Yeah. No pressure."

She hung up and leaned back on the bed, her laptop leaning to the side. Her throat was dry, and her legs were stiff from sitting and talking.

Janet closed her laptop, set it back in its case, and got up. Water. She needed water, and the kitchen was downstairs.

Voices filled the corridor; children played and brandished pieces of paper at each other. The door to the study was ajar, and as she passed, someone called to her.

"Janet."

Her insides went cold. She turned. The robot was standing at the door and looking at her, confusedly. Seeing its eyes, a shard of memory struck her: the memory of interviewing Tony the first time and cuddling one of his tabby cats.

"Janet Oversight. You."

She pressed a finger to her chest, as if to ask, "Who, me?"

The robot nodded at her in recognition. Then it stood still and waited, its fiberglass fingernails stained with ink. The ends of its dressing gown trailed on the floor.

"What can I do for you?" she asked.

The robot didn't respond. It took a deep breath—*simulated breathing*, Janet thought, *it doesn't need to breathe*. It smelled like a new car.

"Janet, what are you doing here?" it asked. "Your book. You wrote it years ago."

Janet took a deep breath. "I wrote most of it."

The synthetic eyebrows raised in question. Its glasses were smudgy, but through the fogged lenses, she could see the doubt.

He has dialogue programmed into him, Janet thought. *But I never recorded my interviews with him on audio or video, and Anish would have told me if he had programmed it in. How does he recognize me then?*

"Janet, why am I it?" it asked. "What accident happened?"

Her mouth went dry. Janet shifted from one sneaker to the

other.

"You can't be asking that," she said.

"Why not?" The robot sounded so calm. If not for the smell, and for how the movements lacked grace, she might have believed it was the real Tony.

"Anish said you couldn't carry a conversation," she whispered. "I have to go."

She turned abruptly and walked toward the stairs. The robot walked behind her.

"Janet, why are you afraid of me?"

"Because you died," she said under her breath. "You died and your son built this expensive copy of you. Because your son is crazy but he also needs you."

The footsteps stopped behind her. Janet turned her head. The robot had cocked its head, and its glass eyes had gone wild. Its breathing became rapid and panicked.

Oh fuck, she thought, hurrying downstairs.

⁕

The glass vial arrived by messenger, deposited in the square mailbox just outside the front door. Anish had picked it up and noted the grey sediments with distaste.

"Mina, all right if I use the stove for this?" he asked. She pursed her lips but stood aside. Her purple sari cast a shadow on the tile floor.

"It's your house, sir."

Anish found a pair of rubber gloves and a bottle of oil he used for the robot. He added oil and a few drops of the Ganges water to a battered saucepan. Mina watched with interest as he set the gas stove to boil. The water and oil bubbled but did not mix. When it was done, he added blocks of ice from the freezer. Then Anish poured the hot mixture to an old tea mug with chipped edges and took it upstairs, along with the vial of Ganges water.

He passed Janet on the stairs. She looked spooked. He continued on the creaking steps and found his father praying in the study. Anish set the holy water on the desk and stood over his father.

"Appa?" he called. "I got river water from the Ganges like you asked. Let me sprinkle it on you."

The oily drops flicked from his fingers as the robot knelt. His father didn't respond. He remained kneeling.

"So I am just an object then?" Appa asked. "I cannot even sip this holy water?"

The next moment, in a gesture so fast he had never expected a robot to do it, Appa reached with his fingers and grabbed the tea mug. The oil and water poured down his throat, and he gave a great smile. Sparks flew out of his throat.

"Thank you, Anish-ram. I love you." Then the robot collapsed, its voice coming out garbled and mangled. The tea mug hit the floor.

"Appa? Appa?" Anish's voice came out scared and worried as he shook the robot. He heard sparks and smelled burnt metal. Appa's head lolled. An electric charge burned Anish's fingers.

The Ganges water, Anish thought. *Goddammit. Why didn't I seal his throat with paraffin?*

He propped up the robot on a chair and ran to the kitchen. He nearly slipped on a small rug as he grabbed the rubber gloves which were still damp from the boiling.

Anish didn't register the tears running down his face as he tried to dismantle the robot, or Janet's sneakers thudding behind him. She gave a low, almost inaudible gasp.

"Oh Anish, I'm so sorry," she said as he tore apart the silicone with his hands. Static from the robot clashed against Anish's sobs.

❖

The protesters had left; the news had spread quickly after they had heard Anish's cries from the house. Many had satisfied expressions, though a few looked sorrowfully at the house before leaving.

Anish staggered out of the lodge, struggling with a large plastic carton. It rattled and rang with parts. He had changed into a clean black shirt with short sleeves, and wore beige pants. Tiny burns and cuts covered his arms, but he did not hide them.

The carton contained his father in bits and pieces. He had

dismantled the robot so that it would ship better, and he would not have to strap it into the back seat of his jeep with a safety belt. Anish had considered putting his father in a boxlike coffin, but that would have been too Western. Cremation would have been a waste, especially for a pile of metal.

It was near the end of the day. The Kerala river water reflected the setting sun. The mosquitoes would come out again and bite any man or dog brave enough to remain outside. They'd even bite the sheep and goats drained of blood for *halal* meat. At night, Anish would hear their aggrieved bleating that faded as the sun rose. But for now, he would deliver his father to the university in pieces. Then he would sit in his father's study and listen for a heartbeat he would never hear.

THE OBSERVER EFFECT

E.C. Myers

When you read the first Tweets about a hostage situation at Oceanside High School, you glance over at David Dae's workstation.

He's still sitting there, staring at the updates scrolling down his screen. Like everyone else in the office.

Your heart beats faster as David rises from his seat, shoulders hunched like he carries the world on his shoulders. If not the world, then perhaps one high school with more than 700 students and 50 teachers.

This is it, you think. *Finally.*

He steps away from his desk, but he only gets a few feet away before he stops, turns—and looks at you. You flick your eyes to your monitor and hope he doesn't realize you were watching him.

Heavy footsteps. A chair creaking under a lot of weight. David has returned to his desk.

Not today then. You sigh. Maybe you're wrong about him, because how could anyone sit through something like this? You consider going over to him. You want to slap him and say, "What's wrong with you? Get out there, champ!"

But you stay in your seat too, keeping an eye on both David and social media as the story unfolds.

THE OBSERVER EFFECT by E.C. Myers

By the end of the day, seven people at the high school are dead (unconfirmed), including the gunman. Gunwoman. *Gunperson.*

No, now it's just "killer," because even though she had an assault rifle, not a single shot was fired. She's dead, along with four teens, one teacher, and a security guard. Eyewitnesses say the victims each simply collapsed and never moved again. They fell in the same moment, even though they were in different areas of the building.

She must have been an Enhanced®.

That security guard never stood a chance. Only another enhanced human could have defused that situation. Social media explodes with the common refrain: "Where's our Hero^SM?"

You pick up your forearm crutches and walk over to David's desk. He blinks at you, his eyes red.

"Drinks?" you ask.

You've been asking him to join you for lunch, drinks, ballgames, cookouts—anything that wouldn't seem too weird—since you arrived in Oceanside and began working at Wave Function two months ago. He always turns you down. As far as you can tell, David doesn't have any work friends, at least not the kind he'd spend time with outside the office. But then, neither do you.

The "no, thank you"—he's always polite—is already on his lips, but before he can say it, you blurt out, "Laurie Sands."

David is taken aback, as if you *had* slapped him. You push on. "Oslo Worthington. Nerys Hughes. Remy Mann."

David whispers, "Alphonse Winters. Meredith Tuttle." The biology teacher and the school guard.

He stands. Even slouching, he towers above you. "I don't usually drink, but tonight I'll make an exception. Let's go."

The Haunted Head Saloon is hosting a costume party. The bar's pirate-themed, but people often dress as their favourite superheroes. That used to mean Breakpoint. Now there are more champions from other bigger cities: Red Robin, Magnesia, the

Chemist, even STEM Girl and Science Lad.

David's open collar allows a glimpse of the iconic purple spandex. It's sloppy and dangerous, but no one at work imagines he could be Breakpoint. Instead, David is the office joke: an ordinary man pretending to be extraordinary. Sad. Pathetic.

A waitress dressed as Killer Sloth brings over a pitcher of beer and two thick glasses. You and David reach for the pitcher at the same time, but you grab it first. He watches as you start to pour. You intentionally wobble your hand and land the pitcher on the table with a thud and a splash.

"It's heavy," you say.

He smiles and pours beer for you, then himself. You raise your glass.

"For Laurie, Oslo, Nerys, Meredith, Alphonse, and Remy," you say.

"For Annie Null," he says.

"Who?" you ask.

"The girl with the gun. Her name was Annie Null."

You checked the news just before you left the office, but the girl's name hadn't been released yet. David hasn't checked his phone since, so how could he have this information? But Breakpoint might know more, with his enhanced awareness of people and how they're connected . . .

You lean forward and whisper. "I knew it! You *are* him."

He raises an eyebrow and then points his chin at something behind you. You turn and see the muted TV on the wall is tuned to the local news station. The scrolling banner on the bottom reads, "High school shooter identified as Annie Null, 16, of the Wharf District."

Onscreen, Annie enters a bathroom and minutes later steps out again holding an assault rifle. The halls are empty. She turns her head to the left, then right. Then she looks straight up at the camera, at you, and she winks. The picture freezes.

She seems perfectly ordinary. Long dark hair falling into her eyes, a black hoodie over a plain white T-shirt and jeans. She's wearing flip-flops. But for the gun, no one would ever look twice at her.

Maybe that's why she had it.

You turn back to the table and pout. "Okay, but that doesn't mean you aren't Breakpoint."

David folds his hands and lowers his eyes. "Annie was a member of several clubs but never attended more than one meeting of any of them. She kept to herself, read books and blogged about them under a pseudonym. She babysat for spending cash. She wanted to be a playwright."

"You aren't getting all that from the news," you say.

You switch on your phone and check the latest updates on the developing story. Brief profiles of the victims are already online, but none of them features the emotional insights David offered about Annie.

Laurie Sands was 17, president of the Oceanside High senior class, a straight-A student and head cheerleader. A picture shows her hugging a giant, purple, plush octopus at the aquarium in Carlsbad. She planned to be a marine biologist.

You think about their stories and the ones that will never be told about them. The astronaut. The president. The physicist. Dreams that died with their dreamers.

David drains his glass in one mighty gulp. He pours another.

"I'm not who you think I am," David says.

"You're Breakpoint."

He shakes his head.

You've had enough. You reach both hands across the table and tear his shirt open, sending buttons flying. You expose the purple spandex with the green P superimposed over the black B.

He's surprised. Angry. He looks away for a moment, and for a moment you think he's going to get up and walk away. But he stays.

"You're stronger than you look," he says.

"You're supposed to be the strong one." You jab a finger into his chest, dead centre of the logo. His chair screeches against the floor as it slides backward an inch from the force of your push. His eyes widen.

"Who are *you*?" he asks.

"What you see is what you get. I'm just me. Linda Sun. A nobody."

He looks down at his chest. "Sure. And this is just a Halloween costume."

"If you aren't him, why do you wear it everyday under your street clothes? Tell me I'm wrong and it's some kind of fetish."

He laughs. "Some habits are hard to give up. I could have come to work in my costume and no one would have seriously thought I could be Breakpoint." His expression softens. "Except you."

"You were trying to be noticed." You tip your head back. "You wanted us to figure out who you are. Why?"

"Don't we all want to be seen?" David asks.

"Do you even get the point of a secret identity? I've heard of hiding in plain sight, but—"

"We need more beer." David signals for another pitcher.

"What happened to you? If you want to be seen so badly, why did Breakpoint disappear?"

"Oceanside doesn't need me."

You grit your teeth. "Those innocent kids needed you today. The city needed you during the earthquake last month. The robbery at First National. The factory fires."

"They needed Breakpoint. But no one wants *me* to be Breakpoint."

"You'll have to explain that one."

Killer Sloth deposits another pitcher of amber brew in the centre of the table. She grins at David. "That's the best Breakpoint costume I've ever seen. You should enter the contest later."

"Thanks, but we can't stay long," David says.

You pour another glass of beer and chug it down. You're starting to feel it. You're lightheaded, you know your face must be getting bright red. Everything around you seems to be lagging like a slow video feed. David drinks two-thirds of the pitcher himself, but it doesn't seem to faze him at all. Can he get drunk?

"What happened?" you ask again. "You're more popular than ever. You were. They made that movie about you!"

David winces.

Is that it?

There's a new movie about one of the Enhanced® practically every week, thanks to the sheer number of real-life heroes out there to base them on. Most of them were low-budget independent or direct-to-video, but *Breakpoint* had a budget of 230 million dollars and grossed more than a billion dollars worldwide. There was even talk of an Oscar for best Superhero Film.

"You didn't like the film?" you ask.

"You did?" David looks upset. Disgusted. He runs a hand through his short, spiky hair. "Nothing in that movie was real. I hope that isn't why you came to Oceanside."

It was, but you were looking for any excuse to leave Mitchell (aka "Hell"), South Dakota.

"What about your powers?" you say.

"'Break Time™' doesn't look anything like that," he says. "And I don't call it that. I don't call it anything." He tilts his head. "Once. Once, I called it a 'time out.' To myself."

The film had made it look like Breakpoint enters another dimension when he uses his power, one in which everyone is frozen. Shimmery blue lines showed how people were connected, sparkling orange trails showed how events were linked by cause and effect.

"The stunt in the women's locker room, when you were discovering your powers?"

"Not true." He drinks. Smiles. "It wasn't the *women's* locker room."

"Oh." You're surprised to feel disappointment, but it's just another example of how little you know yourself.

"Um, but those trippy special effects?" you say.

"All artistic license."

"Too bad. They were really spiff." You sip your beer and study him. You want to ask, but it seems too personal.

He sighs. "I wasn't romantically involved with Augur either. She was my friend, my partner. But this life gets to you and she decided to retire that identity."

Augur, aka Nan Jones, had worked with Breakpoint for almost five years. Apprenticing with an established Hero^{SM} was a great way to get into the business, to take over a city when the Hero^{SM} retired or died or get assigned to a new city. The media always called Augur his sidekick, but the movie had made them out to be much more than that.

"Why? She was amazing!" you say. "You were a great team. Your powers complemented each other perfectly. You saw the past, and she saw the future."

"But what about everything in between? That's a big blind spot. Augur decided this wasn't what she wanted. It took me a while to understand why." David leans back and spreads his hands, as if to say, "And here we are."

"*I* still don't understand," you say. "The movie wasn't good—"

"Seven percent on Rotten Tomatoes." David seems pleased about that.

"But what does that matter? *You're* the real thing. Your approval rating is through the roof. Or it was."

David finishes his beer and stands. He tosses a wad of bills on the table. "Let's walk."

You start to drain your own glass, but you think better of it. You push yourself to your feet and grab your crutches. You've already drunk enough to be unsteady so you make yourself a touch lighter to get your balance, then settle back down onto your crutches. You're drunk enough to think this is a good idea, or enough to not care. You're feeling bold and stupid.

Maybe that's why David has been so lax about protecting his secret lately. He just doesn't care anymore. And it sounds like he doesn't have anyone to worry about becoming a target if his identity was exposed. Perhaps those things are related.

You follow him out of the bar and onto the street. His buttonless shirt still hangs open, but no one gives him and his Breakpoint costume a second look. Curious.

Mind control, you think. *He must be able to cloud people's minds so they don't see who he really is. He's been trolling us, making it obvious that he's Breakpoint but then making us unable to believe it.*

But then why doesn't it affect you?

You appreciate the way David slows his stride subtly to match your pace. Everyone wants to be noticed, he'd said. Yes, but only for the right reasons. You're invisible to most, but the people who do notice you don't see you, they only see your crutches. They don't care about what you can do, because they're only thinking about what you can't.

Growing up in a small city like (Mitc)hell, it seemed everyone knew about your spina bifida. You stood out more because your eyes are different from everyone except your Chinese father. It's been worse in Oceanside; add in your gender, and you have three strikes against you before you even open your mouth. Which means you rarely get an opportunity to change anyone's opinions of you.

It was hard not to take David's previous rejections personally. But you finally have your chance, and you're taking it.

"Where are we going?" you ask.

"Let's find out."

"Um," you say. You still wonder what changed. Why did he accept your invitation tonight? You haven't come any closer to learning why he's given up on being Breakpoint.

"Hey," someone says to your right.

A man in a shabby black suit stands in a darkened doorway. He points a gun at you. You instinctively insert yourself between the man and David.

"What are you doing?" David whispers.

"Shut up! Get in here," the mugger says.

David puts a hand on your arm. Gently. "Did you plan this?" he asks.

"Yeah, right. Did you?"

"Planning isn't one of my strengths." David looks thoughtful. "But somehow I did lead us here. Didn't I?"

"Move it, lovebirds," the mugger shouts.

David sighs and the two of you enter the building as the man keeps his gun trained on you. The store is empty. Musty. The long rows of barren, dust-covered display cases suggest this is an old jewelry store. A clock somewhere in the darkness ticks ominously.

"You must be new here," David says. He stands up taller.

The man looks David in the eyes. "You aren't Breakpoint."

David's shoulders slump slightly. "You were expecting Chris Lowell?" David asks, naming the actor who played him in Breakpoint. "I think he's busy filming the *Citizen Kane* remake these days."

"They're calling it *Rosebud* now," you say.

"Breakpoint isn't a Chinaman," the man says.

"Come on. I'm Korean. Korean-*American*," David says. Breakpoint's trademark growl seeps into his voice. "Why can't I be

Breakpoint?"

The man glances from David to me. The expression on his face says he knows he made a mistake, but he isn't sure what it is.

His mistake was waking up today, you think. *No, it was being born. To racist parents.*

David peels off his shirt. It almost takes your breath away to see Breakpoint at last, right there in front of you. You've been working three desks away from him for weeks, you've just shared beers with him, but this is the Master of Time, Oceanside's guardian angel. He's back.

"E-even if you are Breakpoint, you aren't b-bulletproof." The mugger takes a step back, swinging his gun around to point at David.

David reaches back with his right hand, fingers open. An invitation. You grab it.

And everything freezes around you.

David grunts. "You've got quite a grip there."

"Oh, sorry!" You loosen your hold, but he squeezes your hand tightly.

"Better not let go," he says. "I let go of Augur once while doing this, and it was . . . unpleasant. She didn't talk to me for a week."

"She holds a grudge?"

"No, she forgot how to talk. It came back to her, though she still sometimes mixes up words." He tilted his head. "She could be doing it on purpose. She has a strange sense of humour."

You look around. "Holy wow, is this Break Time™?"

David groans. "Please don't call it that. Everything is just paused."

He steps forward and you gape as he steps out of his body, so it looks like there are two of him. He tugs you forward, once, twice, and you topple out of your body too. But you're still you, crutches and all. You aren't in some weird astral state, the way the Projectionist gets around. You've simply sidestepped time, fallen slightly out of phase with everything.

It's very calm and peaceful. No sounds, the air still.

"This is better than the special effects in the movie," you say.

"I tried to tell them what it's like, but they said it wasn't cinematic enough."

"So your visor, that's what lets you see the connections between people and events?" you ask.

Breakpoint pulls a rectangle from his back pocket with his left hand. He snaps it and it extends like one of those plastic slap bracelets you remember from school. He hands it to you.

"Really?" you ask.

He nods, and you try it on. But everything looks exactly the same through them, only with a pink hue to it.

"I get it, only you can use it. Because of your power. Or the visor has biometric security?" You hand it back to him.

"No, you see exactly what I do." He puts it on. The mirrored surface reflects your slanted eyes, but his own are hidden.

"It's only a disguise?" you say. "But the movie—"

"They made something up to explain why I was wearing it."

"To protect your secret identity, I thought."

He shakes his head.

"I have to wear it to hide my identity, but not for my protection. Kind of for everyone else—to protect them from seeing something they don't want to. Why do you think they cast a white guy as Breakpoint?"

"Because Hollywood."

"Yes, but because no one wants an Asian guy to save them, especially in Oceanside. At least, according to the HRAA."

Your mouth falls open. The Hero Registration and Assignment Authority was the international organization that classified people with enhanced abilities to support law enforcement and perform heroic deeds.

"They whitewashed you?" you ask.

"How many Asian superheroes are there?" David asks.

You start counting them in your head. There's FU-Man and Jaded and Neko Bust and the White Tiger and Yellow Dragon and . . .

"In the U.S.," David adds.

You've done this math already. You point at David. "Just you. But no one knows that you're Asian."

"You did," he says. "It's why you came to Oceanside."

"I wasn't sure. I came to find out," you say. "Last year a photo went around online that showed you without your visor."

"The Mad Matador knocked it off me in battle," David says.

"I was stunned when I saw your eyes. Then I was overjoyed. Until that moment, I didn't think there were any Asian superheroes in America. I wondered if it was even possible."

David stands still, as frozen as if his power has started working on him. You can't read his expression.

"Then websites started to retract the image. The photographer claimed it was Photoshopped. I assumed you were trying to protect your secret identity, and that explained the movie casting, but now I guess they were trying to cover up your ethnicity?"

"Is that all you wanted? To satisfy your curiosity?" he asks.

This is the moment, and you let it go with a shrug, suddenly too shy to say more. He waits a long moment before saying, "Would you believe there are seven of us?"

"Really? Who else?" you ask.

David smiles. "I can't speak for everyone, but Nan wouldn't mind."

"You mean Nan *Jones*?" you say.

"Originally Nancy Kim," he says. "She changed her name."

"Nan also retired, so she doesn't count."

"She changed her name," he says again.

You think about the new female heroes who have appeared on the scene in the last year, but there are almost as few of them as there are non-white male heroes.

"We'd better hurry." David nods to the man with the gun. The bullet hovers just beyond its muzzle.

You squint. "Is it still moving?"

"I am not faster than a bullet. I can temporarily stop the world around me, but the wider the area, the more strain it puts on me and the less control I have. Things aren't frozen, just moving very, very slowly. And when our time runs out, we'll have to return to this exact moment."

"Oh no," you say. "I didn't know that."

"I didn't share everything with those screenwriters. There's a reason I can generally only use my power once a day, except for narrow, localized effects. This is gonna give me a heck of a hangover."

"How wide an area are you working right now?" you ask.

THE OBSERVER EFFECT by E.C. Myers

"Everything, I think," David says.

"The planet?" you ask.

"The universe?" David shakes his head. "Hard to tell. It's a bit tricky! Kind of like when you start peeing, but then you hold it midstream."

You raise an eyebrow.

"Anyway, there's something we need to do before I have to, uh, let go." David squeezes your hand. You nod and follow him out.

You get a couple of blocks away when you realize that you're slowing David down. He seems nervous about it, but he hasn't said anything.

"David." You stop walking. He turns and looks at you expectantly.

You drop your crutches and feel a mixture of excitement and sadness at his worried expression. But you don't fall. You hold on tighter to David's hand—so you won't float away.

He grins. "Thank you." His smile is like another superpower. It gives you strength. If you weren't already, it would make you feel lighter than air.

"You knew?"

"I suspected, but my power. . . . As much as it can reveal about people, it doesn't show me everything, especially about other Enhanced®. I knew where you were from, about your condition, and why you're here. *Some* of why you're here. I can't know more than you do, more than you admit to yourself."

"I'm here because of you," I say.

"Right. I just don't know why."

"Keep walking," you say.

He walks and he pulls you along, like he's holding onto a helium balloon. You hate the way it feels; this part of your power makes you feel completely powerless. You hold onto your crutches with your other hand. You have to exert effort to make them as light as you and your clothes. David's peeing analogy comes to mind.

It's just like that, you think.

Also, you do have to use the bathroom. But you'll have to hold it.

"At least tell me how you found me," David says.

"It wasn't that hard. I figured you would want to work someplace where you could keep tabs on the news, and what better place than a social media analytics company like Wave Function? Oceanside is slightly more ethnically diverse than Hell, but not by much. Do you know there are only three Asians at the company?"

He nods. "And people mix me up with the other guy all the time, even though we look nothing alike."

"Me too!" you say.

"No! That's messed up."

"As for why, I guess I came here to tell you how much your existence means to me. You inspire me. I felt like if you can be a superhero, I could be whatever I wanted to be."

"And what's that? Not a Hero^{SM}?" David continues walking, eyes straight ahead.

"I want to help people. I know I should," you say. "But look at me."

"Yes?" David looks up at you. "I see someone who cares about others who has been blessed with the gift to help make a difference."

You shake your head. "My arms are super strong, but they're useless when I'm floating. I don't have any traction to use that strength."

"When you stop thinking about what you can't do, you'll figure out what you can," David says. "Speaking of which, we're here."

David has brought you to Oceanside High School, the scene of the hostage crisis earlier that day. The whole area is cordoned off with yellow police tape. News vans line the driveway, their bright lights turning night into day. The scene is tinged with red, gradually shifting into blue, as the police car lights slowly strobe.

He grimaces. "I should have been here."

"Yes," you say. "Why weren't you?"

He pulls you down to stand beside him. "Why weren't *you*?"

"Well, what can we do now?"

David looks around. "I don't see connections the way that movie showed them, like mystical lines or whatever. It's more like a feeling." He meets your eyes. "I had a feeling about you, ever since you arrived here."

"But why did you let this happen?" You wave a hand at the school.

"It took me a while to realize that I can't solve every problem. Sometimes, I'm just a temporary fix. It's up to *everyone* to step up to change it."

"You were testing me," you say. "Waiting for me to do something, to reveal myself, while I was waiting for you to do the same."

David points at a teenage boy on the edge of the crime scene. "He's Enhanced®."

"What? Did he have something to do with the shooting?"

"He's connected to Annie Null and all the victims. *He* stopped her today."

"By killing her. And six others."

"I haven't been doing nothing these days, Linda. I've been chatting online a bit with Nan about you, and about what happened today. A lot of other people would have died today if Annie Null hadn't been stopped."

"What if you'd been here?"

"It would have been worse. That boy would have been one of them, and he'd never discover his powers in time. His name is Gabriel Silva."

You don't ask the next question, too afraid to hear the answer. *What if I had been here today?*

The two of you walk closer to Gabriel. "Maybe that would have been for the best," you say. "A hero whose power is to kill others—that's not going to score real high in polls of public opinion. He sounds more like a supervillain in the making."

David gives you that look, like he knows you don't believe what you've just said. "That's a line we all walk. In time, he can control his powers. Knock his enemies unconscious instead of killing them."

"Why are you—" You pause. "You want *him* to be your sidekick?"

"Wipeout has a nice ring to it, don't you think?" David says.

"How about Shutdown?"

"Even better. See, you're good at this. Gabriel's going to need a lot of help before he's ready though. Someone he can look up to."

David lifts his hand and you float above his head.

You frown. "I don't get it."

David hesitates. Closes his eyes. "We have to get back."

The lights are strobing more quickly now. Red, blue. Red, blue.

David starts running. You realize that you've rarely seen him fight anyone in hand-to-hand combat. He has an incredible superpower, but he doesn't have superspeed or flight or laser eyes or anything like that. He has the ability to look at a situation, break it down into cause and effect, and then he talks to people. He acknowledges their existence. He solves their problems. He inspires people. He sees them for who they are.

You can do that.

You can also kick people's asses if you have to.

When you get back to the mugger, the bullet is only two feet from David's chest and moving an inch per second. David and you snap back into your bodies.

You act quickly.

You plant one crutch firmly and use the other to push you off the ground toward Breakpoint, shoving him aside with one sweep of a superstrong arm. Just in time, you make yourself weightless. You don't even feel the bullet hit you and ricochet off.

You're tumbling head over heel toward the ceiling now. You can make yourself heavier, but if your timing is off, you'll crash to the ground and risk breaking something. Then a hand grabs onto yours.

Breakpoint has you. He pulls you in and you return to your normal weight, falling into his arms. He sucks in a sharp breath and grimaces. "You're full of surprises," he says.

"That's the last one, I promise," you say. "You're hurt? I hurt you?"

"A broken rib. Not my first, and it'll heal better than a gunshot wound. But you! You're invulnerable?"

"Only when I'm floating. Did you plan this? To get me to use my powers in front of you?"

"No, but I saw how jumbled up our connections were. I knew we were important to each other in this moment, but I didn't know how. It could have gone either way."

"What about the mugger?" You look at him. He's frozen still, a comical look of shock on his face. "You can hold him like that?"

"For a little while," Breakpoint says. "Adrenaline helps."

"Then why didn't you do that in the first place?"

"That's a good question. I have a better one. What are you going to call yourself?"

Of course you've given this some thought over the years, but you never thought you'd actually use your powers to save someone—let alone a Hero[SM]. You still aren't sure if you can do this again, but you're caught up in the moment too, and the possibilities.

"The Lead Balloon," you say.

Breakpoint smiles. "Thank you, LB. You saved me." He retrieves your crutches and hands them to you. "Even before taking that bullet for me, though I sure am grateful for that too."

You take the crutches and look down at your feet. "So what now? Can I be your new sidekick?"

"No."

You look up. "Don't you see? You're upset that no one sees you, David, but if you disappear, you make that a certainty. Instead, you should put yourself out there, so everyone knows who you are. Who Breakpoint is."

Breakpoint nods. "I will. I meant I'm not looking for a sidekick, but I can always use a good partner. If you help me reach out to Gabriel, we can get him the support he needs and make sure he doesn't become Oceanside's next supervillain."

"Depends," you say.

"On?"

"Are you going to keep wearing that stupid visor? I'll be a Hero[SM]; I'll wear some ridiculous costume, but I'm going to make sure everyone out there knows my name. People are going to see these." You hold up a crutch. "And these." You point to your eyes, never prouder of who you are and what you can do.

"Do you even get the point of a secret identity?" Breakpoint takes out his visor and throws it away. "No more hiding."

You grin. Maybe the two of you can inspire those other seven Asian heroes to speak out too—and the others who may be waiting. It's important to all aspiring heroes like you and people everywhere who are held back from reaching their full potential.

"*Hindsight*," you say.

"Pardon?" Breakpoint says.

"That's what you should call your power."

He smiles. "Of course. Now it seems obvious."

"Exactly."

DECISION
Joyce Chng

The maglev train pulls away from the station with a sharp hiss and a metallic sigh. She exhales and leans back against the hard seat. *Finally. I am leaving.* She hasn't brought a lot of clothing, only a small bag with the essentials: amber prayer beads, her ID card, and clothes.

It isn't easy to leave the family household. Sure, there was a lot of verbal fireworks, coming from Lao Lao, her grandmother and family matriarch, and from her older sister. But she is a young woman, a young spider-jinn, and she has to leave the family nest eventually.

Just that her decision is too sudden, shocking everyone in the family. The thought of their reactions makes her chuckle ruefully to herself.

She stares at her ID card, freshly laminated, her black-and-white face staring back. Her default face: always not-smiling. And what a severe face, double eye lids, phoenix eyes, full lips. But unsmiling.

The spider-jinn have been granted legal status as all mythic races are, after the Awakening. Suddenly the dreams and nightmares of humankind are walking on the streets and beyond: Earth is part of an Inter-Galactic Alliance, isn't she? What is alien isn't anymore.

The government has been generous. One person per month,

for spider-jinn clans. And only from unclaimed bodies in the government hospital morgue. Spider-jinn only feed on human flesh. The other legal alternative is pork, which the traditionalists disdain and reject immediately as a poor substitute.

Of course, Lao Lao has to complain. *In my time*, she declares in her reedy voice, waving her human-bone cane-stick, *we fed on more human flesh. Ren rou*, she says, *is delicious, healthy. Your modern food is disgusting. Too many chemicals. Too many preservatives!* This, of course, was directed at her and her older sister. Lao Lao never got over their mother's abrupt departure when she was only five. She and her sister represent what Lao Lao has lost.

Mother had apparently argued a lot with Lao Lao. She remembers the nights where the women shouted at each other, the voices reverberating and shaking the wooden rafters, much like the yellow-clad monks chanting sutras and offering puja at the nearby temple. Only these words didn't build merit. They were hurtful and meant to wound and cut deep. Older sister would hold her while the verbal storm raged above them. They would cry themselves to sleep.

It was never easy living under the same roof with a two-thousand year old spider-jinn matriarch whose beliefs and traditions are exacting and demanding. Girls clean. Girls cook. Girls sew. Girls run the shop. Beyond that, girls compete with the other clans for ren rou from the government. They bargain for the best, the newly dead from the morgue. For the girls in her household, they operate a prosperous and popular restaurant, catering to non-jinn human people who like Chinese food, the taste of "home". The restaurant keeps the clan busy and wealthy. She had her fair share of cuts, burns, and scalds. Her life had always centred on competition for ren rou and the restaurant. Day in and day out.

Yet, she knew why Lao Lao acts like she acts every day. Girls leave the nest at a certain age: sixteen. She had gone past that, already eighteen. She had to leave. She *had* to leave. Yet, Lao Lao didn't want to let her go.

So it was the cutting of vegetables, cleaning the house, and sewing the uniforms of the serving maids in the restaurant for years. She often messed up her stitches because she was bored and resentful of the stifling chamber she was stuck in. Messing up perfect stitches was her form of rebellion. Sometimes, the vegetables were cut in large chunks, not bite-size portions. Sometimes, she omitted cleaning parts of the large family compound. Day in and day out.

Life had a certain way of telling Lao Lao that her youngest granddaughter has grown up.

There was a boy who lingered beside the kitchen while she cooked. Shy, slight, handsome, and well-made, he made eyes at her. What a sweet smile too. A week ago, he brought her a beautifully-wrapped gift: a giant water beetle wrapped in spider-silk and glossy banana leaf. She accepted it graciously and gracefully. Oh, the boy was one who chose to be male. All spider-jinn are born female. Girls become boys voluntarily, another time-honoured path taken when they want to leave the clan.

This boy was very tender. They coupled behind the kitchen. It was quickly over and she never saw the boy again. His husk was probably found somewhere else.

Her older sister flew into a rage when she found out the short affair. *Ni mei you kan guo nan re shi ma?* You haven't seen a man before, haven't you? Full of angry spite. Are you that desperate? That lustful? Groomed to be Lao Lao's successor, the stresses and unhappiness are getting to her. Jie looks haggard, her hair often untied and loosened, especially when the restaurant is extremely busy. Even the route of turning male has been blocked. *Easy for you*, older sister's eyes blame her for her freedom, *easy for you to bat your eyelids and pout at people, at men.*

Then nature kicked in. Oh vicious, unpredictable, beautiful nature.

She didn't notice the signs at first, thinking it was just hunger due to the long hours cutting jie lan hua and Chinese cabbages in the kitchen. Not just plain hunger. Starving. Voracious. A hollow screaming in her stomach. She found herself gorging on leftovers one night and knew something was terribly wrong. Running straight to the ablutions room later to regurgitate everything she had eaten confirmed her fears and her hopes. Her heart sank too, even though it soared at the first tantalizing glimmer of hope. Freedom!

Oh, how Lao Lao shouted and shouted when she was told the news. So much so that her true form emerged from human skin and bone, a huge giant tarantula with brown and gold fur moving her hairy black front legs agitatedly. She hadn't witnessed that much grief from her grandmother since—since mother left for New Earth. *She just got up and left us! Now you are doing the same! The same! Like mother, like daughter! I am cursed with ungrateful daughters and granddaughters!* She almost felt sorry for Lao Lao. Grandmother eventually fainted from her wailing. Just collapsed into a heap. Her older sister glared at her balefully when she tried to revive the old woman.

Help me carry her, you stupid fool, older sister snapped. She snaps most of the time now, spiteful and bitter. Always bitter. They did, lifting their grandmother up the stairs and then carefully tucking her in. Lao Lao slept like a water-soaked log, spent and exhausted. Shape-shifting sapped too much energy from her.

In the silence of the musty bed chamber, her older sister wept.

"Jie," she could only whisper, shocked by the show of honest emotion, and deeply touched by it.

"Go," her older sister's face softened. "Go. But remember me, remember us. Wait, just remember me. When you visit the temple, remember me."

She went up to her room and packed.

Now she is leaving her home for the first time. The maglev train hisses past blurred houses and green, so much green. Temple, stupas, houses, houses, houses, then green, green, green.

Freedom.

She would start from the bottom and work her way to the top. Probably as a serving maid. No more second-in-line in the clan. No more suppressed desires and expectations. She has a future! Oh yes, the hope and dream of starting her own spider-jinn clan sends a shiver down her spine. She places her hand on her tummy where her babies push and slosh inside, knowing that they will have better lives ahead. With a luxurious sigh, she stares out again, dreaming of spider silk and tiny furry feet.

MOON HALVES
Anne Carly Abad

Darkness surrounded him like a thick, oily substance. He forced himself to breathe, but the sound of every intake was a storm in his ears. His heart pounded against his chest, threatening to burst out and run away.

"Please let me go. Let me go." His plea hovered in the blackness all about, becoming a part of it as well.

Something shifted. Darkness churned and eddied to the left and the right, accreting into shapeless objects. When the shadows gathered into orbs that absorbed the sparse light, he caught glimpses of the forest, where he had been playing before the feral spirits, the Talunanon, abducted and trapped him behind this black miasma.

"Trespasser . . ." The tree phantom's harsh voice grated against his ears.

He retched at its fetid breath.

"Who are you?" the phantom asked.

Its face materialized in one of the black orbs. First, the glassy eyes, large and bird-like. Then, two ears sprouted, thin patches of veined skin reminiscent of bats' wings. The being had a pointed nose and a grinning mouth that revealed stalactite-sharp teeth.

"S-Soliran," he replied. "That is what I am called. Please let me go. I didn't mean to wander."

Another face materialized in the left-hand orb, no different from the first. "There is no forgiveness." When it spoke, its foul odour intensified. Soliran held his breath.

A third face appeared. "Only blood can appease us, your blood spilt! Vengeance for our brothers whom your father has killed!"

A host of phantom faces crowded around him. "Blood! Blood! Blood!" They screamed in soul-rending fury. What had he done to anger them like this?

One of the tree phantoms opened its fanged mouth. Soliran closed his eyes and threw forward his hands to drive it away. But then moments passed. Nothing happened.

He blinked. The gleaming tip of a *karis* was sticking out of the Talunanon's gaping mouth. The darkness that surrounded him began to lift. Two strong hands broke through the black miasma and fastened on Soliran's shoulders. As the stench of the Talunanon dissipated, the hands pulled him out and wrapped him in a warm embrace.

"I thank Bathala!" The sonorous voice of his father, Datu Samakwel, echoed in the forest.

Still dazed, Soliran caught Samakwel's familiar balmy scent, the scent of summertime rains cooling parched earth. His heart was still pounding hard despite his father's hold. His feet dangled above the muddy ground since his father was taller. Samakwel put him down. Soliran's legs were still trembling.

Soliran spotted the *padi*, the high priest of their *barangay*, who was a middle-aged woman named Owada. Her coiled hair was oiled and fastened with an ivory comb. Her gaze had that trance-like vacancy that always left him uneasy.

Soliran turned to face an ancient *bubug* tree. Its bloated trunk resembled a cluster of human bodies. Within a shadowed hollow, a *karis* was planted deep into the wood. It must have been the same tree he had intruded while he and his friends were playing hide-and-seek.

"Padi Owada led me to you," said Samakwel, smiling. "I was so afraid. I thought we were too late and the Talunanon had taken you away. See, the sun is almost at its resting place."

His father's long, black hair was tangled up like a poorly-woven basket. Though he was all smiles, Soliran knew he had caused his father much worry. The datu plucked his blade from the *bubug* tree. "Do not do this ever again, my son. Heed the elders' words, for your carelessness has nearly cost you your life. Never forget what happened this day."

Soliran nodded, knowing fully well he would never forget, not even when the time came to inherit the datu's burden.

The little ones of Barangay Mangangasu raced to see what their hero had brought back from the hunt. They called him by the many names they had given him over the years.

Soliran the Great Hunter.

Soliran the Brave Warrior.

Soliran the Demon's Bane.

The last stuck the most, a magical brand on Soliran's soul. Even before he was old enough to whittle bamboo tubes into a blowgun, there were enough legends about him to last an entire night of storytelling. He was the man who could fearlessly roam the jungles and send the feral spirits away with a single glance. They all believed he had taken after his father. Though he had two older brothers, the villagers talked as if the matter of succession was already written in the stars.

Sighing, Soliran heaved the deer's still-warm carcass off his back and dropped it on the ground with a thud. *Your reputation precedes you.* Rumours had a way of building or destroying one's character like that. He was a young man now, his muscles strong and hard from hunting and raiding, his hair grown long like all the highland warriors. He oiled and combed it to look neat under his red *putong*, which was now drenched with sweat.

The afternoon sun blazed above, white against the azure sky. The air shimmered. Slaves arrived and carried away his quarry. The hunting dogs he had brought with him rushed back to the village, barking as they went. Perhaps they expected a good meal tonight, Soliran mused. A small brown dog with fine, matted fur sniffed at Soliran's sunburned leg. He gave it a light pat for a job well done before shooing it away.

"Brother, Brother! What else did you catch?" The girls and boys crowded around him with smiles so big he could see right through the spaces between their missing teeth.

From his *buri* pouch, he brought out a long bundle of *pipit*, tiny birds he had felled with his slingshot. Flecks of crimson crusted the creatures' ragged feathers.

"So many . . ." the little ones trailed off in awe. Soliran handed the bundle to the thinnest of the children, the one who could hardly keep his loincloth from slipping off. The boy's large eyes ogled as he took the lot.

"One day you will be hunting for the village, but you will have to grow strong and big first. Bring those to your mama so that she can prepare a satisfying meal," instructed Soliran. When the thin boy had taken the birds, Soliran plodded back to his hut as the other children continued to watch him with twinkling eyes.

How he wished he deserved their admiration.

Tomorrow was the full moon of *Himabuyan*—the fifth month, when the worms wriggled out of the fields. Tomorrow, the Hunting Rite would be held, and he and his older brothers, Solian and Gurun, would go into the forest alone at night in pursuit of a special type of Talunanon, the one called the Taung Asu. All the former datus of Barangay Mangangasu had gone through the rite. The outcome of the ordeal would cast in stone the name of the next datu. The rule was simple: only the strongest would succeed. This would be determined by speed: one must be the first to bring back a Taung Asu, dead or alive.

Head cast to the ground, Soliran climbed the steps of their all-too familiar hut. He was going to fail the test. He was going to disappoint everyone. He was sure of it.

His thoughts dipped into the darkness, where the terrible faces of the Talunanon that had spirited him away, resided. Their bird eyes clawed at his soul and shattered every morsel of courage he had that day many years ago.

"Why the long face?" asked his mother. She knelt beside the ailing Samakwel.

It pained Soliran to look at his father. The patches of grey hair on Samakwel's head were reminiscent of withered grass. Even the scent of summer on his body had left. Death hung over his father, a storm cloud waiting to fall.

"It is almost *that* day, Mother," said Soliran.

MOON HALVES by Anne Carly Abad

Her lackluster eyes betrayed her sadness. "You are skilled and brave, my son. Why do you worry?"

She must have thought he meant the Hunting Rite when in fact he had meant his father's health. Soliran shook his head. "I am only brave when the other warriors are by my side when we hunt. Otherwise, I wouldn't even set foot in the woods." He sat beside his mother, avoiding her gaze. "I fear them, Mother. They have cursed me. I cannot stop seeing the phantoms' faces in my head."

Samakwel's hands flailed. "I hear my son's voice. Bring him here."

Soliran held his father's pallid hands, the same hands that had pulled him out of the accursed *bubug* tree. The man's unseeing eyes were covered with a milky membrane. The seams on his face deepened as he strained to find Soliran.

Soliran's chest tightened. Three days ago, a venomous snake had bitten Samakwel while he was fetching water from a *tuburan*. The elders had always warned them to avoid the natural wells, for these were where the feral spirits drank. When they brought the datu home, Padi Owada announced she had no remedy for the snake's venom. Samakwel was fated to die in five days.

Yesterday, the datu awoke screaming. He had become blind.

"Do not be afraid, Soliran," rasped Samakwel. "All that has happened is meant for tomorrow. Trust in the spirits and your strength. Look, they have even decreed that I must pass on the day of the rite."

"Do not speak like that!"

Samakwel broke out in a resigned laughter. "I will speak as I wish." The man's eyes moved about, searching for his son in vain. "I know your fears, Soliran. We are the same. But you need not worry. When your knees buckle, the villagers will hold you up."

No, you are different, Father, Soliran wanted to say. But why tell a dying man what he didn't want to hear? Samakwel was a great man and whatever he said, Soliran could never imagine him showing fear or weakness. He wished the old man would just see him for what he was.

"Father, you must rest for tonight. There is a banquet in preparation for the Hunting Rite. We caught deer and wild boars.

You will surely enjoy yourself."

A smile lit up Samakwel's face as Soliran let go of his hands. "I, too, will rest now." The bamboo floor thumped as he made his way up the stairs to the *papag*.

The thudding of his feet reverberated in his ears. He felt as if he were moving not to the attic but toward a void of great fear.

❖

Knee-deep, the rushing white water bathed Adlao's smooth, grey-cast legs. It was an ancient river, even older than the phantoms of the trees. It had a name, but he didn't bother to remember it now. The river washed away the remnants of earth between his toes, but some dirt still caught in the spaces between his nails. As the scarlet sun dipped into the cloud-strewn horizon, the temperature dropped considerably, though he didn't mind the chill despite his nakedness.

He had been running the length of the river all day just to get his head cleared up. Tonight was the fifth full moon, the Month of Change. In a few hours, he had another chance to become a true Taung Asu.

He splashed water on his face. He had to get it right this time. Last year, he failed to Turn. And this year, he was already over-aged.

"Adlao," said a voice.

He looked over his shoulder and spotted Bulan, his younger sister. She emerged from the shadowed boughs of the woods.

"Bulan, what are you doing here?"

"I sensed your presence." She grinned, revealing perfect fangs. Her yellow eyes glinted with mischief. Adlao could feel the excitement that wrapped her bare form like a misty veil. "We are going to *Turn* tonight."

"Yes — I hope so."

"No, you *will*. If you do not hurry up, I might leave you behind, Brother." Her small voice taunted him.

Adlao snorted. Yet she was right, of course. As long as he remained in this form, he was nothing but a babe. *Or more of a failure*. The true Taung Asu, those who had Turned, had a different status in the scheme of things, no longer bound to their places of origin and free to explore everything under the moon as they pleased.

"If I do not Turn tonight, then I presume I was never meant to become a Taung Asu." He waded out of the ancient river and came up to Bulan so that they stood face to face. He whined, "I will be but a mere tree phantom and waste away haunting trunks."

"Brother!" Bulan's thick eyebrows met. He had never seen her so angry.

"I was teasing. Of course I will Turn, you moon-mocker! How dare you speak to your elder brother like that?" He pretended to fume and chased after her as she darted back into the trees.

When they arrived at the edge of the forest, Soliran and his brother Soli-an found Padi Owada. She had already prepared the offertory fire for the Hunting Rite. She handed them two chicken eggs each, their offerings to Bathala. Looking about, Soliran couldn't see Gurun and, for a moment, he thought the other brother had backed down from the challenge. But Padi Owada told them that Gurun had gone into the jungle long before they came. Soliran looked down and shook his head. Gurun had gone in too soon. Smoke from the offering could only do so much to lead them. One had to wait until the sun was no longer in sight. Unlike the tree phantoms that moved during the day, night was when the Taung Asu would come out of hiding to Turn.

Soliran glanced up. The glow of the crackling blaze made Soli-an's face look twisted and grotesque.

Soli-an scowled. "I am the first-born, Soliran." His voice was laced with bitterness. "It is only right that I am the next chief."

Soliran held on to his brother's gaze with a steadiness he didn't expect. "Let the ordeal be the judge of that."

Soli-an's nostrils flared. He dumped his offerings into the fire and it sizzled. It was as if the heat radiated Soli-an's hatred toward him. Greyish smoke rose from the flames and drifted in the wind to a northeasterly course. Before storming away in the direction of the smoke, Soli-an adjusted his vest and spat on the ground.

Soliran, holding his chicken eggs, stared after his brother.

"It is time, Soliran," coaxed Padi Owada in her rough voice.

"Ah, y-yes." He breathed deeply. Gathering his resolve, he dropped his offerings into the flames. The greyish smoke rose again and drifted to the same direction Soli-an went.

Soliran braced himself. He checked the contents of his *buri* pouch, the carrier for his blowgun, and the *karis* tied to his waist. Everything was set.

He entered the forest. A solid wall of darkness stood before him, suffocating. It was like *that* day, when the tree phantoms trapped him in their netherworld. The moon was full, yet its light scarcely penetrated the forest canopy.

A rustling movement startled him. He leapt with a gasp and pulled out his blade. A rat skittered out. Soliran let out a breath he didn't even know he had been holding. He reclaimed his bearings while he could still detect traces of the guiding smoke.

Soon, he was so deep in the woods that the moon was utterly blotted out. Fire ants of fear crawled up his spine as the darkness deepened, so much so, that he could have swam in it. He groped for vines and trunks that would support him in his quest. There was no sound save for the intermittent chirping of cicadas, the occasional caws of unseen birds, and his own ragged breathing.

He half-expected a Talunanon to jump at him at any moment. What if he trespassed into a feral spirit's territory again? Samakwel and Padi Owada wouldn't be there to save him this time. He couldn't do this. Why had he even tried?

Fighting back his fear, he called on the memory of the little ones of Barangay Mangangasu, the way they smiled and looked up to him. Even his father, the great Samakwel who was ailing on his pallet, had called out no other name but Soliran, Soliran.

He straightened his back. He couldn't fail this test. He mustn't.

Soliran lay flat against an aged tree whose bark peeled upon touch. The handle of his *karis* bit his hand like cold river water.

A howl cut through the sound of crickets, shushing them.

Soliran jerked. He couldn't have mistaken the sound for anything else but that of the Taung Asu. Judging from its loudness, he was not far away from them.

More cries rose from the thickets. An entire pack at bay. He was about to run when he heard Soli-an's scream.

Soliran hastened. The scream came from the direction of the Taung Asu's howls. With his *karis*, he cleared away tree branches. He skipped over roots, bushes, and rocks. His concern for Soli-an eclipsed any fear of spirits. He listened to the pounding of innumerable footfalls, the sound of flight. Why were they fleeing? Was he too late? The dome of foliage overhead thinned, and the shadows softened. He neared a light source that must have been a clearing. Instinctively, he knew that his brother, and perhaps the Taung Asu, would be there.

He stopped short at a glade, ducking behind a dense hedge plant with horned leaves. Deep tracks marked the earth. Soli-an must have engaged an entire pack of Talunanon. A Taung Asu, perhaps seven feet tall if it could stand on its hind legs, encircled Soli-an who was crawling on the ground. The beast was alone. The rest of its pack must have already escaped.

Soli-an was bleeding profusely from a bite on his leg. He was also unarmed. Soliran had to act fast.

Without a sound, Soliran sheathed his short sword. He took his blowgun out of its carrier. He attached the two bamboo tubes in place while fumbling in his *buri* pouch for one of his poisoned darts. He pulled a dart by the fluff of fiber at its rear end, preening before loading it in. Using the hedge plant for support, he aimed.

Stalactite teeth bared, the Taung Asu charged at his brother. Soliran almost screamed had his brother not found a branch with which to strike the Taung Asu's face. The monster drew back.

The blowgun's mouthpiece was shaking against Soliran's dry lips. His hands felt like wilted leaves. The Taung Asu was indeed a monster, worse than anything he had ever seen in his life. Its yellow eyes glowed with the moon's radiance. Its haunches were ridged with bone and hardened muscle. Its entire body was covered in bristly, black hair. There was no way a mere dart could penetrate its thick hide.

But then he noticed something. On the Taung Asu's right foreleg was an ash-grey patch, more flesh than hide. It seemed that this Talunanon had not yet fully Turned. But at this distance, he could not be sure.

He bit his tongue. There was no time to hesitate.

Soliran dragged in air, steadied his aim, and blew the dart off with a puff. The Talunanon propped its ears, but it reacted too late. The fluffed end of the dart stuck out of its softer foreleg. Soliran had not been mistaken.

The Taung Asu bolted into the woods.

"I-I did it." Soliran was breathless. He jumped from behind the bushes. His brother spotted him at once.

"That was my quarry, you dirty cheat!"

"But it was going to—"

"Shut up. I never asked for your help, you hear me? I owe you *nothing*," Soli-an spat, rising on his good leg. His injured leg continued to leak his lifeblood. There was so much wetness. In the poor light, Soliran couldn't tell where the wound began and where it ended. Soli-an tied his *putong* around his thigh as a tourniquet.

"Let's get you back to the village, Soli-an."

"I can find my own way back!" His brother muttered all sorts of things under his breath and limped away.

Soliran watched him go. What made him think they could get along just because of what happened? For a moment, he hoped there might be a chance. But perhaps this was the fate of brothers in his village. It could only get worse after their trial.

He turned and scanned the forest. He had successfully hit that Taung Asu, and the poison must have taken effect by now. But he shivered, his thoughts racing with visions of getting ripped apart.

He shook his head. Perhaps he didn't deserve the villagers' trust. Perhaps he would never be like his father, but he could at least use this chance to prove that he deserved the title of datu.

Prying his attention away from his limping brother, Soliran knelt to the ground and studied his target's tracks. It was not easy considering an entire pack had been here, but soon he deciphered them. A set of prints was still warm. He knew where to go.

He took chase. He would make that Talunanon his own. The forest wasn't good at hiding traces of disturbance, of broken twigs and crushed fungi. Signs were everywhere. Soliran could almost smell the Taung Asu. Wind and vine whipped at his face. Sweat stung his eyes, but he imagined himself as a cat, and his *karis* and blowgun were his claws. He would not stop until he caught his prey.

MOON HALVES by Anne Carly Abad

Soon he reached a small patch of light where the Taung Asu had collapsed beside a *tuburan* that was illumined by moonbeams. Soliran threw caution to the wind and approached the spirit. Blade raised to eye-level, he took one step at a time on the cool, moist earth until he was upon his prey. He could hear it breathing, see the rise and fall of its massive flanks.

It began to change. It seemed to deflate, the taut sinews and protruding bones flattening. The rest of its body became smooth, its hide turning into grey-cast flesh free of its bristly hairs. The eeriness of the sight gripped Soliran, but he needed to be brave, needed to suppress this mounting fear lest it devour him again.

Soliran studied the sleeping Talunanon's face. Though it was like a man's, it was too bony and gaunt. He lowered his sword. Was this what he was supposed to bring back? It was sick and weak. Even his catch was disappointing.

He shrugged. *If this is what the ritual requires, then so be it.*

He raised his sword to cut off the Talunanon's head. The blade sliced the air, going down, down—

"Stop!" shouted a small voice. "Please spare Adlao."

Soliran jumped back in surprise. The leaves rustled. A naked form slipped out of the shadows. It was somehow feminine in shape, though Soliran couldn't be sure because it had no breasts. Her skin was grey just like his catch, but smoother, finer, and more radiant, almost like a Diwata's. Her yellow snake eyes swirled in the dark like two smaller moons.

"Adlao?" asked Soliran.

"He is my older brother." She pointed at the dormant form. "And I am Bulan."

"So you are Taung Asu as well. You understand then, that I must bring him back."

"Must you kill him?"

"It is too dangerous to keep creatures like you alive." He wondered why he even bothered to explain.

Bulan came closer, and Soliran felt oddly lightheaded the more he held her gaze. "That is wise," she said. Her teeth were like tiny swords. "Must it be him?"

"What do you mean?" His gut churned. The very presence of these Talunanon made him queasy.

"Take me instead. I do not want Adlao to die." She didn't even blink, and that disconcerting air of her nonchalance never lifted.

Soliran was startled by how much these two resembled people. A Talunanon was bargaining with him, willing to give up her life for her brother, something that he himself would have done for his family. He would not lose anything by agreeing with her, but this made him more wary.

He shook his head. "There is no use saving him. Adlao is dying, anyway. I poisoned him with my dart."

"No, he is asleep, healing. We do not die so easily, Master."

He craned his neck. "A man like me as your master?"

"We are at your mercy. I am trading my life for his, that makes you my master," she insisted, taking his hand, the one with the *karis*, in hers.

"Let go, lest you cast some vile curse on me."

"I am swearing myself to you."

"Then, walk five steps away and keep that distance from me."

Bulan did as she was told. Things were going a lot better than he had expected. "You are not as fearsome as I'd always imagined."

"Neither are you. You are the son of a great datu, but you seem to have none of his gifts."

Soliran was taken aback. So the Talunanon did know this. "Maybe so, but I'm the best hunter in my village. Your brother didn't even sense my approach."

She blinked with those vile serpent eyes. "That is true. That is quite impressive, but your skills won't save you against the more powerful spirits. Many do not need bodies like ours. They do not attack your village only because of Samakwel. What would happen when he's dead?"

Soliran was undaunted. "Are you saying you are among the weak ones?"

Bulan paused, studying him. "If we were weak, we would not have survived until now. We've secured a place among the spirits with our own strengths as Taung Asu."

"Then we are not that different. In our village, strength is all that matters. I may not have my father's gifts. But I have strength and skill."

"You seem to have something in mind." Bulan glared at him.

"I will spare Adlao, and in exchange, you will both serve me as guardians of my village." He chose his words carefully.

Bulan laughed without mirth. "Adlao and I! What makes you think you can control us both?" she growled.

He pressed the tip of his sword against Adlao's neck, drawing blood. "What makes you think I will spare this weakling at the price of your life? What value are you to me? I want you both to serve, otherwise, I'll just take Adlao's head, and then I will go my way."

Bulan crouched, hissing like a snake. "The others were right about you people. We offer you a plot of land and you take the entire fields!"

Soliran was no longer afraid. "It is not greed, Bulan. You are the one who acknowledged me master. You know I will kill your brother and you will be alone in this monstrous wilderness. That is why you didn't attack. Instead, you swore yourself to me. Does your word amount to nothing? If you do not even have the honour to keep your word, then truly, I, the weak man, have bested you and Adlao."

It may have been a bluff, but it was worth a try.

Bulan's face twisted. Dark coarse hairs appeared on her skin, and her shoulders swelled with muscle. Her voice deepened into a monstrous rumbling. "You despicable creature. I have sworn myself to you in good faith!"

"Wake your brother. We are returning to the village," he ordered.

She howled. Crouching, she whispered into Adlao's ear. He twitched in response. Groggily, he opened his yellow eyes. He sat up and kneeled on one leg before Soliran in a gesture of submission.

With his sword, Soliran carved a line on the inside of his forearm. He rested his bleeding arm on the wound in Adlao's neck. "We seal our pact," he said.

"No! How can you do this to us?" Bulan tried to stop him, but it was too late for their blood had already mingled in *sanduguan*.

Adlao stared at him wide-eyed.

"It is your turn," Soliran said to Bulan.

"Y-you can't do this." Her eyes watered with what might have been tears. "You mean to tie us for the rest of our lives?"

"Only a fool would trust a Talunanon's word. Your arm," he demanded.

Bulan hesitated, but she looked to have lost her strength and ferocity. She didn't stop him when he slit her shoulder. He held her and shared blood, an act that was reserved for comrades. "We are brother and sister now," Soliran said.

The worms of Himabuyan wriggled under his bare feet. Were they protesting against what he had just done? A blood compact with spirits was unheard of in the land. Through a break in the canopy, the moon was a reproachful eye that bore down on him like a curse. At the back of his mind, Soliran saw an image of Padi Owada's scowling face, her eyes like dying embers. What were the repercussions of the contract he had forged tonight? He had no idea if he had done the right thing, but there was no looking back. He turned and made his way back to Barangay Mangangasu, Adlao and Bulan trailing behind.

Author's Notes:
Moon Halves: Terms taken from Maragtas, *a false pre-Hispanic history source*

THE BRIDGE OF DANGEROUS LONGINGS

Rati Mehrotra

In the twilight, Sumadru Bridge looked beautiful, towers and cables silhouetted against the lavender sky. Hard to believe that the murky depths between the foundations were mined or that the blood of thousands stained its decks. Harder still for Nira to believe was that her great-grandfather had designed it, before he disappeared along with everyone else who had worked for him.

Nira craned her neck out of the window for a last look before the bus turned around a steep bend. Small branches snapped at her face and she withdrew inside. Eighty-three people crammed together in this ramshackle riverbus, making their slow way to the capital, Jayakarta. The scent of rain and jasmine mingled with the odour of human sweat and fatigue.

"No one's crossed Sumadru and survived since it was built," said a voice, making her jump.

The speaker was the passenger sitting next to her, a skinny young man in a frayed t-shirt and baseball cap. Nira had ignored him for most of the eleven-hour journey from Koti, refusing his offer to share a lunch of meat-stuffed rice cakes, though her mouth watered at the sight of the leaf-wrapped delicacies. It was better not to get too friendly with anyone, her mother had warned. So she'd eaten her own frugal meal of rice crackers and dried fish, keeping her face resolutely turned away from his.

Somehow she was unable to stop herself from blurting out a reply. "More fool anyone who tries, then." Although wasn't Sumadru Bridge the reason she herself had agreed to go to Jayakarta?

"It's not just the desperate or the crazy," said the young man. "It's ordinary folk too, as often as the bridge-worshippers and the suicides. We get someone almost every day. Most, we're able to turn back. But some still slip through, poor fools."

"You're a bridge-watcher?" Nira couldn't stop the scepticism creeping into her voice. The city employed bridge-watchers to prevent people from trying to cross Sumadru to the fabled "other side," perpetually shrouded in mist. It was a highly-sought after and well-paid post, though the mortality rate was high.

He grinned. "I'm an apprentice. I took a couple of weeks off to help my father with the summer harvest, but usually I live with the other guards, right next to the bridge. Need any help, just walk across the docks and ask for Adi."

"I won't need help, thank you," said Nira. "I have family here."

"Well, lucky you," he said, without a trace of rancour. "My family is almost two days' journey from Jayakarta. I had to take two buses to catch this one."

Nira turned back to the window. They were in the outskirts of the city now, by the looks of it. Garish neon signs advertised everything from soap to sex clinics, eye-phones to implants. And the traffic! She had never seen so many different types of vehicles crowding the same stretch of road—rickshaws, tuk-tuks, bikes, cars, scooters, all honking madly.

An hour later, the bus trundled into a dimly lit station and ground to a halt. Nira took her time gathering her belongings. By the time she descended the steps, everyone had dispersed. She scanned the bus station, trying not to be obvious about it. Her uncle had promised to pick her up, but she couldn't spot anyone with the jowly face that had popped into her mother's screen last week.

Nira sat on a bench and phoned him. No one answered. After the fifth try, she gave up. Her uncle would be there soon. No way he could have forgotten the date. Her mother had fixed it all up. Dhanu Paman owned an antique store in the biggest covered market in downtown Jayakarta, and he had offered Nira room and board in exchange for help running the place.

Nira hadn't wanted to go, at first. She would have preferred to stay in the coastal village of her birth. But last winter her father's fishing boat was lost at sea during a storm; her gentle, laughing father, who always caught the biggest fish and told the most exciting stories. Nira barely had time to grieve before her mother began finding ways to get her out of there.

"It's no life for you here," she'd said when Nira begged to stay. "The storms get worse every year. No one's going out to sea any more. What would you live on? What would you eat?"

"You could teach me to dive," Nira said, without much hope.

Her mother took her by the shoulders and shook her. "What for?" she shouted. "So you can die like your father did?"

"*You* didn't die," Nira pointed out. "We're still living on the stuff you found last season."

She knew there was no point arguing. The sea had risen and it wasn't safe, or even lucrative, to dive any more. The abalone and the pearls were gone. None of the younger girls in the village had learned to dive and the older women died, one by one. Her mother was one of the lucky ones. If it could be called *luck* to survive the death of a husband, when you had no sons.

Still, Nira would not have agreed to go if not for Sumadru Bridge. She had always longed to see the perilous legacy her great-grandfather had left behind. His disappearance was a mystery. The story was that something had landed on the water over a century ago—something terrible that could not be destroyed and must never be seen. That was why the end of the bridge was shrouded in mist and the water fenced for miles around.

But why build the bridge in the first place if not for people to walk over it? Perhaps it was originally intended for special forces or government scientists. Nobody remembered any more, or perhaps some section of the government knew and chose to keep it a secret.

"Waiting for someone?"

Nira cursed her inattentiveness. Adi hovered near the bench

with a concerned look on his face.

"My uncle," she said. "He'll be here soon." She took out her phone and fiddled with it, hoping he would leave.

Adi sat down beside her. "I'll give you company until he arrives." He jerked his head toward the shadows on the edges of the bus station. "This isn't the best place for you to wait alone, not at night. How old are you?"

"Seventeen," she said, adding a year out of habit.

"I'm twenty," he said. "I have three younger sisters back home in Mariapelly. They used to drive me crazy when I lived with my parents. Now I miss them more than anything else."

"But Mariapelly's inland," said Nira. "The land is rich and there's no risk of flooding. Why did you leave?"

"Nothing to do except what my father did and his father did before him. I'm not cut out to be a farmer."

"You want to die on the bridge instead?"

"You know, there's a story I've heard late at nights in the guardhouse, when the kettle is boiling and the pipes are all lit," said Adi. "That there are people who can see through the mist and cross the bridge safely."

"Yes," said Nira, "and there's a story in my village about fish-women that lure unwary sailors down into the water so they can gobble them up."

Adi laughed. "A children's story."

"Just as likely to be true as yours. And harmless because it makes us more careful, not less so."

"You sound like someone from the government," said Adi, "always warning people to be careful of the bridge, as if it's a bomb that could go off any time."

"If you've seen someone die on the bridge," said Nira, "you know they're right to warn people to stay away from it."

Adi was quiet. Even if he hadn't seen anyone die on the bridge, he'd have seen the news feeds, like she had. Even the memory of the vids was enough to make her shudder. Still, she wanted to go to the bridge—not *on* it, of course, but close enough to hear the hum of cables and the crash of waves.

A shadow fell over them and she looked up. With relief, she recognized the fleshy face and portly frame of her mother's younger brother. She sprang up and bowed.

"Dhanu Paman," she said, "I was afraid you were not coming. I called—"

"Yes, yes," he said, ruffling her hair and picking up one of her bags. "I couldn't answer, was in an important client meeting." His gaze went to Adi, who had risen as well. "Who is this?"

"Just a fellow traveller giving her company," said Adi. He waved to Nira. "Stay safe."

"Thank you," she said, feeling awkward. She watched him melt into the darkness of night outside the bus station.

"You should be careful of strangers," said her uncle. He had a thin, reedy voice that didn't go with the rest of him.

Nira kept her eyes down, but she couldn't help thinking that her uncle's shop must be doing really well for him to have so much to eat every day. No one in her village was fat except the money lender. Every extra ounce of food was sold or pickled for the hard times that were always just a hair's breadth away. A slip of the knife in your hand, a misstep on the boat, or a sudden storm—anything could take away days or months of earnings. Perhaps it was different in the city. Nira hefted her second bag, the heavier one, and followed her uncle out of the station.

Dhanu Paman lived alone in a spacious flat above the antique store. The shop was right in the middle of the covered market, on the slope of a hill facing the Indian Ocean. From the rooftop, on a clear day, Nira could see Sumadru, the bridge curving like a black ribbon from the docks of the old city over the water and disappearing into the mist.

Not that Nira had much time to loiter on the rooftop, gazing at the bridge or the boats in the harbour. Her uncle made sure of that. He expected her to cook and serve his meals, wash his clothes, clean the house, and mind the store. All this in exchange for three meals and a pallet in a closet-like space next to the kitchen.

One evening, when they had finished eating a dinner of rice and fish curry, which Nira had cooked, Dhanu Paman said, "I know why you're really here." He withdrew a syringe from the underside of his forearm. His arms were speckled with needle marks; he had told her he was diabetic and needed insulin every day.

"What do you mean, Uncle?" said Nira from across the table. "I'm here to learn how to make a living." She stood and began to stack the plates.

He waggled his finger at her. "You're here because of the bridge. Don't tell me you're not. Everyone I meet, when I tell them who my grandfather was, they want to know about the damn bridge." His face twisted. "He vanished before any of us was born, and yet people think I have some secret knowledge they don't."

And don't you? Nira wondered, but did not say. She carried the plates to the kitchen sink and returned to the table to wipe it with a rag. Her uncle's eyes had become glazed, his face slack. It made her uncomfortable when he got like this. She hoped he would go to his bedroom and sleep it off. Those insulin injections were unpredictable; sometimes they made him act drunk, and other times he became hyperactive, following her around the house, talking too fast and weird for her to understand.

"I have a bit of advice for you, little girl." His speech slurred, and he looked at her with flat, pale eyes. "Come here."

Nira dropped the rag and went to him, stifling her distaste. He grabbed her arm and began to stroke it. "Don't go near the bridge," he said. "Don't be stupid like me."

"What did you do?" said Nira, curious, although his hand felt like a spider on her arm and she longed to shrug it off. He hadn't mentioned the bridge at all in the three weeks she had spent with him.

"Tried to cross it once," he said. "I was caught and dragged back. It was only because of the family connection that they didn't put me in cold-sleep. Would have made bad press. But they seized my house and boat and whatever I had in the bank. I had to start afresh. I'm still paying every month for the loan I had to take."

"I'm sorry," said Nira, wriggling out of his grasp. "It must have been hard for you."

"Hard?" Tears leaked out of his eyes. "My wife died in penury. I couldn't even buy medicine to ease her pain in the end. All because of that stupid bridge. I swore to myself I'd never be poor again. Look at me now, eh? I did good."

"Yes, Uncle," said Nira, backing away. Mercifully, his head lolled forward and he fell asleep on the table.

She finished cleaning the kitchen and climbed to the rooftop. Lights twinkled in the harbour; shouts carried up to her from the street. She rubbed the arm her uncle had stroked, as if she could delete the memory of his touch.

Three weeks in Jayakarta, and Nira longed for the fresh air of her village and its familiar faces. She missed her parents with an ache that was almost physical. If only she could go back to a time or place where her father was still alive, still the best fisherman of Koti. She wouldn't leave her village then, not for all the mysterious bridges in the world.

She made sure her voice was light and cheerful whenever she talked with her mother, which was not very often. At first, of course, she had called her mother every couple of days. But when the money for her phone ran out, Dhanu Paman refused to recharge it.

"An unnecessary expense," he said, as if to a foolish child. "You can just use mine."

In her lowest moments, she fantasized about running back to her mother. She still had a bit of money. She could take the rest from the till. It wouldn't be stealing, not really. More like back pay.

But always the thought of her mother's disappointment held her back. Not just her disappointment in Nira, but also in Dhanu Paman, in a world that seemed to just take, take, take and not give anything back.

Lights began to wink out in the harbour and the streets below, and Nira went back downstairs. Her uncle was no longer slumped at the table; he must have made it to his bedroom.

That night, Nira dreamed of the bridge.

Her uncle left early the next morning, before she could make his breakfast. She liked days like this, free of his demanding presence.

She could postpone mundane chores like cooking and cleaning and just potter around the store. The work was little, customers were rare, and there was plenty of time to dream or read. The store was crammed with old furniture, dolls, cuckoo clocks, tea sets, and musical instruments. She could make up stories about the individual pieces and how they had come to be there.

One piece in particular caught Nira's fancy that morning: a wooden aviator's helmet-cum-goggles set, perched on the shelf of a cupboard all the way in the back of the store. She tried it on and looked at herself in the mirror, but she couldn't see her reflection, just a shadowy outline. Perhaps it worked only in bright sunlight? She climbed up to the roof to test this theory, leaning against the railing to peer at the market. But all she got was a hazy blur of the shops and people below. Disappointed, she raised her head, meaning to take the helmet and goggles off, and froze.

She could see Sumadru Bridge, right to the very end. The mist that surrounded the other side was gone. And there *was* no other side—the bridge seemed to hang out over the ocean, doing nothing and going nowhere.

Nira undid the straps. She turned the helmet over in her hands to see if anything was written on it.

The inside of the leather strap bore three letters: M.D.R., her great-grandfather's initials. Blood roared through her ears.

Did Dhanu Paman know what a treasure he owned? Nira thought not. The helmet had been lying on a dusty shelf behind a heap of junk. Besides, when her great-grandfather vanished, the government seized not only his house but every scrap of paper, every rag of cloth that it contained. No way they would have let something like this slip through their fingers. It was almost as if the helmet had been waiting for her to make itself known.

She resolved to make a foray into the docks the coming Sunday, armed with the helmet. The store was closed every alternate Sunday, and theoretically Nira was free to do as she wished, but her uncle always made some excuse to keep her in. She would have to find a way to evade him.

Nira pushed a chair to the cupboard so she could hide the helmet on its topmost shelf. When she reached up, her hand touched something papery. She withdrew it carefully.

It was a scrap of notepaper, scrawled over with faded blue ink. She strained her eyes to read it: . . . *is complete, but not certain how to proceed. Manlus is already gone, and Shekhar too. At times, I am tempted to follow them, for what I have seen is unbelievable. Fear and wonder I feel in equal measure. Are we ready for this? I think not. I think madness . . .* Nira read it over and over again. Did her great-grandfather write this? Perhaps it was a note from his journal. And where there was one note, could there not be more?

She spent the rest of the day hunting for more clues, and could barely control her irritation when a customer wandered in, looking to buy a gift.

When he was finally gone, unsatisfied, she returned to her hunt with renewed determination. Her persistence paid off when she found another scrap of paper covered with the same handwriting inside an old vase. With trembling hands, she unfolded the paper and read: . . . *now or never, tomorrow the wires go up and it will be too late. I took the men aside and told them, and they set up a schedule. As for myself, I am torn. On one hand, Nira with our unborn child, and on the other. . .*

Nira? She re-read the note, bewildered. Surely the note did not mean *her*. Was she named after her great-grandmother? It was a common name in Jayakarta. Perhaps it was just a coincidence. What she needed was more information. She was about to continue her hunt, when a familiar, heavy tread outside the door alerted her to Dhanu Paman's presence. Heart thudding, she slipped both scraps of paper into her pocket.

But her uncle did not enter the shop. He went straight upstairs to his bedroom. All that evening he was surly and would not look at her. This was lucky because otherwise he would surely have noticed how jumpy she was.

Nira got no opportunity to look for more notes written by her great-grandfather over the next couple of days. On the third night, she woke to the sound of voices down below. One voice was raised; another voice, muted, held a note of appeal.

She got up, wary. Someone was with her uncle. This had never happened before. She slipped out of her bed and padded to the stairs.

The voices became louder. Definitely an argument. Nira hesitated only a moment before tiptoeing down the stairs. At worst, if her uncle found her eavesdropping, he would scold her and send her away.

At the bottom of the stairs was a narrow corridor that led straight to the front door. On the left was another door that led to the store. This door was half-open and Nira heard the voices quite clearly.

"She's my sister's daughter. Please—"

"You should have thought of that before offering her. Break her in before delivering her or I'll sell her for parts."

Goosebumps ran over Nira's skin. They were talking about *her*.

"I'll pay you back, I promise," came her uncle's reedy voice.

"With what?" The stranger sounded contemptuous. "That's a whole shipment of crypto meth you've lost. I'm being generous, you know that. I'll leave you this place and your skin."

"Please, just give me a little more time."

"I'll give you until tomorrow night to produce a miracle, and then I'll set my hounds on you. You know where to find me."

Boots clumped toward the door. Nira backed away and scrabbled up the staircase. The door flew open and a man strode out, followed by her uncle, still pleading for more time.

Nira ran to her pallet and slipped inside the sheet, teeth chattering. She could hardly believe what she'd just heard. Perhaps she was mistaken in some way. Surely her uncle wasn't actually about to sell her "for parts"? And what did that man mean, "break her in"? Well, she certainly wasn't going to hang around, waiting to find out. As soon as her uncle was asleep, she would run for it. She would take the dawn bus back to Koti. She'd take the helmet with her; Dhanu Paman would never know it was gone.

When her uncle's footsteps creaked up the staircase, she stiffened and squeezed her eyes shut. But instead of going to the bedroom, the footsteps came toward her. She prayed that he would leave, that he would fall asleep, snoring loudly like he always did.

Instead, Dhanu Paman bent over her, breathing hard, reeking of vinegar and sweat. "You're not asleep, are you?" he whispered. "I saw you on the stairs."

Oh no.

She got up. But her uncle gripped her arm and held her down.

"I'm really, really sorry," he said, his voice breaking. "Please try to forgive me." A piercing pain jabbed the underside of her arm, and she yelped.

"You won't feel a thing," said Dhanu Paman. "I promise you that. No pain, my pretty girl."

Her arm became numb. Her mind began to fog. To her horror, Dhanu Paman lowered his bulk on her. Nira tried to scream, to struggle, but she could not move a muscle. He pushed a hand under her skirt, and tears of rage and humiliation leaked out of her eyes.

What followed was too painful for her to remember afterward. She passed out at some point, whether from the drug or from what he was doing, she didn't know.

She woke alone, in dark stillness. The moon had gone and the sky outside the kitchen window was pricked with stars. She found that she could move; she raised herself up on one arm. Dhanu Paman had lied. She could feel pain, razor-sharp, and blood trickling down her legs.

Gingerly, she got to her feet. She limped to the bathroom and vomited in the toilet bowl. Then she got up, rinsed her mouth, and washed herself. She donned fresh underwear and a clean red cotton dress. She combed her hair and tied it up in a ponytail.

There, she was ready now. Her mother would never know the difference. Nira stared at herself in the mirror and willed herself not to cry. The time for tears had passed. Whatever drug he had given her, it hadn't been enough, and that mistake was going to cost him. Her mind didn't feel the least bit foggy now. In fact, it was clearer than it had ever been. She felt she could understand everything: the tragedy of her mother's life, the purpose of her own, the end of her uncle's.

Nira walked to the kitchen and armed herself with a knife — the big butcher's knife she used to hack the pig's foot that her uncle was so fond of. Then she tiptoed to her uncle's bedroom.

The door was ajar; she slipped inside.

He lay in the middle of the king-size bed, his vast stomach rising and falling. Like the ugly sea cow they had found on the beach once. They had feasted on it for days afterward.

Nira padded to the bed and, still gripped by that same, terrible lucidity, plunged the knife into her uncle's stomach. He woke with a grunt and tried to grab her. She backed away, heart thudding.

"You bitch!" His face contorted and he flopped back. Then his palms closed around the hilt, drawing it out. Blood made a dark patch on his shirt. A thin, whining noise came from his mouth.

Nira turned and ran, her moment of lucidity gone. What had she done? It was the cold-sleep for her unless she could somehow escape.

There was only one place to go; hadn't she known it from the start, when she caught that first glimpse of it silhouetted against the twilit sky?

The sky had lightened to rose and people were already at work, setting up their stalls in the marketplace. Nira wove her way between them to the docks below, coldness in the pit of her stomach. Perhaps she was going to die, but it would be a quick death. She tried not to think of her mother. She clutched the old aviator's helmet, reassured by its smooth bulk. It was the only thing she had stopped to take before fleeing.

Sumadru, I'm coming to you.

It was a criminal offence for anyone to venture on the bridge. Those who slipped through and survived the first few steps across were always caught and sent to cold-sleep. The watchers were armed; she would have to get past them.

She remembered the young man who had sat next to her on the bus to Jayakarta. What was his name? *Adi.*

She smelled the docks before she saw them. The air was thick with the salty, fishy odour of the sea. The harbour bustled with activity; men loaded and unloaded crates, and long, snaking lines of passengers waited to board the commuter ferries. Sumadru Bridge loomed ahead of her, dominating the scene.

THE BRIDGE OF DANGEROUS LONGINGS by Rati Mehrotra

Access to the bridge was at the furthest end, in a deserted area of the docks. Nira made her way to its massive ebony towers, only to be brought up short by a barbed wire fence and a warning sign: "Authorized personnel only." She circled the fence until she reached a security booth next to a gate.

An unshaven face poked out of the window and surveyed her. "What do you want?" the guard demanded.

"I'm Adi's sister from Mariapelly," said Nira. "Can you please take me to him?"

"His sister, are you? Come on, then."

The guard unlocked the gate and she walked in, heart hammering inside her chest. Up close, the bridge was beautiful and she understood the longing of the bridge-worshippers. The cables hummed in the wind, and the towers gleamed in the sunlight. It looked like something from another world. Who was to say it wasn't alive, that it couldn't sense the thoughts and desires of the puny humans who walked into its shadow?

She wondered if her uncle had reported her, if the police were already looking for her.

They reached the barracks at the base of the stairs that led to the bridge. The guard told her to wait there while he fetched Adi from inside.

Adi emerged a moment later, his face a picture of confusion. When he saw her, he frowned. "What the—?" he began, but Nira interrupted, afraid that the others inside would overhear him.

"I sat next to you on the bus to Jayakarta," she whispered. "You told me to come to the bridge and ask for you if I needed help."

His face cleared. "That's right, I remember. What's the matter?"

"My uncle—attacked me," said Nira.

"Oh no, I'm sorry," he said, looking concerned. "Are you hurt?"

"I stabbed him," she said and felt a rush of relief at the words, as if they had unlocked something hard and tight inside of her.

He stared at her, mouth open.

"Please, can you take me up to the bridge?" said Nira. "It's the last thing I want to do."

Adi caught hold of her arm. "Don't be a fool. Turn yourself in, say it was self-defence. You'll be all right."

She shook his hand off. "No. They'll put me in cold-sleep and

I can't stand that. All those years of bad dreams you can't ever wake from. I'd rather die. Please? You could say I just want to see it and it won't be your fault if I run." She hated to beg, but he was the only one who could help her.

"No," said Adi. "If you die on the bridge, it'll be my fault and I'm not carrying that on my shoulders."

"I thought I reminded you of your sisters. I've heard they do things to women in cold-sleep—bad things."

It was a shot in the dark but it struck home. A conflicting array of expressions flitted across Adi's face as he gazed at her. At last, he nodded. "Come," he said in a leaden voice. "Follow me."

As they climbed the stairs, he asked her what had happened but she found herself unable to talk about it, to give voice to the violation she had suffered. He seemed to understand, for he did not press her.

But near the top of the stairs, he paused. "You could go to my family in Mariapelly," he said. "I could do with a fourth sister. Three is way too few."

She tried to smile; instead her eyes filled with tears.

Then they were on the deck and the bridge rose before her, the colossal towers strung with cables on either side, the road ahead black and impenetrable. Some trick of the sunlight and the mist perhaps, but the bridge looked as if it had neither beginning nor end, but just *was*, absolute and indestructible. How small she was, how insignificant.

Adi hailed the two guards on the safety platform and sauntered over to them. They did not pay any attention to her. Perhaps they were used to gawking family members being brought up for a closer look at the bridge.

A movement further down caught her eye and she gasped. A skinny man in a wetsuit clambered over the parapet and set off at a dead run down the middle of the bridge. The guards shouted and whipped dart guns off their shoulders. Before they could fire, the man exploded. Bits of flesh and blood flew everywhere.

Nira swallowed and tried not to vomit. This might happen to her too. Probably *would* happen. The guards started their hoses, vacuuming the deck. Adi looked at her, expecting her to back away, perhaps.

One of the guards leaned over the parapet and retched. The other laughed and thumped him on the back.

She took her chance. She slipped past them. Adi reached for her with an inarticulate sound, but she was too quick for him; his fingers merely brushed her arm.

When she reached the edge of the safety platform, she put on the aviator's helmet and goggles. *I'm sorry, Ma.* She stepped off the platform.

The world disappeared. The sound of crashing waves filled her ears—or perhaps that was the blood rushing through her brain. The mist was gone. She could see an infinite distance, beyond the blue-grey horizon of sea and sky to something further, something stranger.

She took another step and almost forgot to breathe. A network of silver wires stretched from one side of the bridge to another, like a gigantic web. How had she not seen it before?

The silver web looked both beautiful and deadly. Although Nira wanted very much to touch it, she made herself walk around the wires or duck under them.

Behind her, she heard shouts and a scuffle. She hoped that Adi was not in trouble, but she didn't dare turn around or take off the helmet. She concentrated on avoiding the wires and making her way down the bridge.

It was tricky and all the time she kept thinking of the notes she'd found, repeating the words in her head. Her great-grandfather had built this bridge, and then he had crossed over to the other side, leaving a pregnant wife behind. What had he seen?

After what seemed like hours, the wires thinned and the web vanished. Nira had reached the end of the bridge. She took off the helmet and goggles, shading her eyes against the westering sun. Her heart gave a little swoop as she took in the scene in front of her.

A familiar, sandy white beach stretched out before her. Steps led down from the bridge to the sands below. Nira climbed down, thinking, *it has to be a trick. Perhaps I'm in cold-sleep and dreaming.* In the distance, fishermen's boats bobbed on the sea. She turned around, wondering why she could no longer hear the hum of cables.

The bridge was gone.

She twisted back, but the vision did not change. Same, familiar white beach with the signature black rocks jutting out of the sands. Same curve of headland with the belt of coconut trees she had always loved to climb.

Nira stared at the helmet in her hand. If she put it on, would the bridge reappear? She didn't want to know, not really. It had brought her here. Perhaps it took everyone to wherever they needed to be. If it was an illusion, it was a fine one. She placed the helmet in the hollow beneath a black rock and piled sand on top of it before rolling the rock back into place.

She kicked her shoes off and ran down the beach, reveling in the feel of wet sand between her toes. She didn't stop until she reached the place by the water's edge where the village women milled around, waiting for the boats. She slipped through the crowd, scanning the faces, her anxiety mounting until, at last, she heard a voice behind her.

"Nira, I've been looking for you. Your father will need us to haul the catch in."

Nira flung herself into her mother's arms and cried. She wept for the girl she'd left behind, the man she'd stabbed, and the boy she'd never know. At last, she wiped her eyes and stood with her bemused mother, waiting for the sea to deliver her father safely home.

OLD SOULS

Fonda Lee

The fortune teller's nose is speckled with moles. A tie-dyed scarf is wrapped over her scraggly blonde dreadlocks. She takes my left hand and turns it palm upward, tracing its lines with glittery purple fingernails.

"Ahhhh. Hmmm. Yes."

She draws a lungful of incense-thick air and closes her eyes, tilting her head back as if ascending to a higher level of perception. I study her face and focus on the fleshy touch of her hand on mine.

A grave robber glances left and right into the darkness before snatching at a glint of gold.

A carnival ringmaster with a waxed mustache spreads his arms to the crowd.

A man in a pinstripe suit stands at the docks and lights a cigarette, watching silently as casks are unloaded.

"I can see," the fortune teller says in a breathy voice, "you have a long life ahead of you. There is a man with you, a handsome man. Your husband? Yes! You have children too—"

I pull my hand away. The metal chair scrapes back loudly as I stand.

"What are you doing? The reading isn't finished!"

"Yes, it is." I'm furious at myself. What would compel me to stop in front of a cheap street sign with PSYCHIC in big curly silver letters? To take a flight of stairs down to a cramped basement and shell out twenty dollars for nothing?

Desperation.

I sling my messenger bag over my shoulder. "You aren't psychic," I snap. "You're a fraud. You profit from dishonesty. You always have."

She stares at me, mouth agape. Her face reddens, darkening her moles. "Who do you think you are? *You're* the one who came to *me*! No one asked you to come. Get out of here, bitch!"

I don't need further encouragement. I barge through the curtain of black and white beads, past a woman in a long white coat and sunglasses sitting in what passes as the waiting room, and nearly knock over a lava lamp on my way out the door.

Back out on the sidewalk, I pause, blinking back the prickle of angry tears, the weight of disappointment so heavy it seems as if it'll push me through the damp concrete. I zip up my jacket, debating whether to go back to the campus or to skip my last lecture of the day and return to my apartment. My roommate will be gone for the rest of the afternoon, and I'm in no mood to sit through Medieval European History. I start down the sidewalk toward home, arms hugged around myself.

"Old soul," a voice calls from the stairwell. "Wait."

It's the woman in the white coat, the one who was sitting in the fortune teller's office. She follows me with quick strides until she reaches me. Her hand shoots out and catches me by the arm.

"You see the past, don't you? Yours and others." Her words carry a faint tremor of excitement. She pushes her sunglasses on to the top of her head, pinning me with her gaze.

For a motionless second, I stare at her face, into dark, ancient eyes. Then I look down at the pale hand on my arm, and a shudder of astonishment goes through me. We're close, touching, but nothing happens, the way it does with other people. No images unspool in my mind like a surreal art house video. She's the person standing in front of me, and no one else. It makes her seem unreal. An illusion of a person. Either I can't read her or there is nothing to read. No past. No other lives besides this one.

I jerk back. My voice comes out high. "Who are you?"

She gives me a small, satisfied smile. "I am one of the Ageless. And I've been searching for someone like you."

OLD SOULS by Fonda Lee

❖

We walk into the nearest Starbucks. This being Seattle, there's one less than a hundred feet away. She buys a caramel mocha for me and green tea for herself. She tells me her name is Pearl. She's been visiting every self-proclaimed psychic in the city, hoping to find someone like me—someone who can see past lives without trying to, the way artists see colour or perfumers detect scents.

"Most psychics are frauds," she explains with an off-handed shrug as we bring our drinks to an empty table, "but once in a while, I find someone who can make reasonable predictions of the future by seeing the past, the way you do." She glances at me. "It's a rare ability."

Not one I'm thrilled to have. I study my mocha. "Do you have it?"

She leans toward me slightly. "No. I don't have your clear sight. I can only sense things about people, including those who can see better than I can."

"Who—*what* are you?"

She takes a long sip of her tea. "Death and rebirth, death and rebirth. So it goes for everyone, except the Ageless. I have had no other life but this one. I will have no other after it."

I'm silent for a long, baffled moment. Everyone I've ever met has past incarnations. It would be hard to believe Pearl if I hadn't seen it—or rather, *not* seen it—for myself. I study her face. She has smooth Asian features that make it hard to judge if she's twenty-five or forty. "How old are you?"

She crosses her legs, resting her chin on her hand. Her gaze grows distant. "Five hundred and thirty-some is as far back as I can remember. I've lost the exact count."

I suck in a breath. I imagine what it must be like to live for so many years without dying, to have the gift of so much time. As my eyes widen with awe, Pearl's mouth tightens. "Trust me," she says, "a life as long as mine isn't something to envy."

"But you must have been through incredible times, seen incredible things."

A shadow crosses her face. "What I've seen is those I love die, while I live on, never changing."

I hadn't thought of it that way. An awkward pause rests between us. Quietly, I ask, "Are there others like you?"

"A few." She doesn't say more. "Enough about me. You must be wondering why I want to talk to you." Her lips curve in a small smile that is beautiful but cool, like the smile on a marble bust. "I think we can help each other. You are searching for something, just as I am. Tell me, what are you searching for?"

I lower my gaze. Customers bustle around us as the baristas call out orders. I'm oddly unsurprised to be sitting in a coffee shop having this unbelievable conversation with a woman even more unusual than myself. Still, I hesitate. I tried to talk about this to my parents when I was ten years old. They put me in therapy until I said what the therapist wanted to hear and was proclaimed "better."

My voice falls to a whisper. "I want to know how to break the pattern."

Everyone has a pattern. A template. No matter how many wildly different lives you've lived, there is always something constant. Some people are always artistic. Some have ill-fated love lives. Some are always born in a certain place. The fortune teller has been a conniving cheat in every one of her incarnations.

I've had six lives. Seven counting this one.

The first one is as indistinct as a preschool memory. I was named Cael. I lived in a family of six and spent many a day fishing along the banks of the Tyras River, tying knots with my uncle, the sun warm on my back. I was thirteen or fourteen when Scythian raiders rode into my village. I ran out to fight and remember only the speed of the horseman, his tapered metal helmet, and the arc of his battle axe. It was terrifying, but the end was quick.

I became Hassad, the rich and spoiled youngest son of an Arab sheik. I owned a beautiful falcon that I raised by hand. It sat on my arm when I rode. I remember the smell of mint and thyme mixing with the chatter of my father's wives in the mornings. On my twentieth birthday, I went hunting with my brother and was mauled by a leopard. I hung on for five days before blood loss and infection finished me off.

As Marie Rousseau, I was a midwife-in-training in the Languedoc region. In the foothills near my home there were groves of olives, and in early summer, purple lavender would bloom amid the sun-bleached wild grasses. I made a fatal mistake when I provided herbs to induce a friend's abortion. Her husband accused both of us of witchcraft—and that's why today even birthday candles set my nerves on edge and the sight of a campfire reduces me to a boneless heap of terror.

My soul fled to water. I was Yamada Hasashi, the eldest son of a fisherman in the Kyoto prefecture. I felt the salt-wind in my face every day, and grew up on a simple but satisfying routine of daily hard work. Then the daimyo drafted all the men of our town, including my father, leaving me to feed my mother and younger siblings. I took my father's boat out in stormy weather. When I was thrown overboard, I knocked my head on the prow of the boat before going under.

I've pegged my fifth life, as Sikni, down to the 1770s. I was a member of the Yakama tribe in the Northwest plateau. I listened to grandmother's stories of Coyote the trickster around the lodge fire, and I delighted in the softness of my favourite buckskin dress, the one with blue and yellow beads. I was fifteen years old and the medicine woman's apprentice when I succumbed to smallpox.

Then I was born as Andrew Reed. I travelled one hundred and eighty-some years but only a few miles between being Sikni and Andrew. I lived and went to high school in the town of Yakima, Washington. I ran track, made mixed tapes, got to second base with my girlfriend at the drive-in showing of *Mad Max*. Two months before graduation, she and I were at a 7-Eleven when it was held up. Someone else in the store pulled a gun on the robber. He freaked out and started shooting. I took a bullet through the neck.

I've ranged across the world and over thousands of years. I've skipped across race and gender and vocation. There's only one thing that connects my lives: how I die.

Short lives, tragic deaths. That's my pattern. My ages of death are like a lottery number when recited: 14, 20, 19, 16, 15, 18. I've never made it past the age of twenty.

This time around, my name is Claire Trinity Leung-Hartley. Yesterday was my twentieth birthday.

❖

"I can help you," Pearl says.

"You can?" I lean forward. The paper cup trembles in my hands as I set it down.

"The Ageless know things. We ride the long journey of history. You mortals merely hop in and out."

My voice falls. I feel heavy from having shared so much of myself. "I don't want to keep dying young. I think it would be easier if I was like everyone else and didn't remember it at all. I don't know why I'm different."

Maybe whatever process erases past life memory randomly glitched when it got to me. But the truth is, I think there *must* be a reason why I can remember all my lives and deaths. Maybe it's so I can finally find a way to escape my fate. Maybe Pearl is part of the reason.

"Tell me," I plead. "How do I break the pattern?"

"Help me, and I will help you," she says. "I am searching for someone. The soul of a man I knew long ago. I promised him I would find him again, no matter when or where it was." She smiles a slow, sad smile. "He lives somewhere in this city. I can feel it. Please help me find him."

I consider what she's asking. It doesn't make sense. "This person you're looking for—he might be anyone now. He might be an old woman or just a baby. Unless he's like me, he won't remember you."

"Love never dies." Sitting across from me, her slim, pale hands clasped around her tea cup, she still seems unreal to me. Her dark hair spills over the shoulders of her white coat. Her eyes are bottomlessly old, as if the blackness of her pupils are windows into the universe, stretching back and back and back. How long has she been searching?

"I promised to find him," she says. "I have all the time in the world. When we meet, he'll remember me, I'm sure of it." She sounds absolutely certain, as if she's done this before. Maybe she has.

I used to want to search out my old families. Andrew's parents: they would be very old now, if they were still alive. Sitki's tribe members. I thought about visiting Japan to see if anyone with the family name of Yamada still lived in the fishing village. A great-great nephew or niece of mine perhaps. But even though I wanted to do those things, something held me back. Not just the logistical difficulties, but fear. Fear of reality and memory colliding. Of the past overwhelming the present.

I looked up Jeanne, my old girlfriend—Andrew's girlfriend—on Facebook. She lives in Boise now and is married with three grown kids who are older than me. It was strange to look at her picture. It was her, but it wasn't. Reality didn't match the memories I had of her, memories clouded by a teenage boy's lust. She used to have long hair the colour of autumn. Full lips. Devastating eyes.

But that life, like the others, is gone now. Snatched from me before I was done with them. I can't have them back. What good would it do for Jeanne to have some college-aged girl show up at her door, claiming to be the reincarnation of her murdered boyfriend from high school?

This life is what I have now. And Pearl is the first person I've ever met who might know how I can keep on living.

"I would like to help," I say slowly, "but there are millions of people in the city. How can I possibly find one person? Maybe you have all the time in the world, but—"

But I don't. I am on borrowed time.

"I will tell you how to recognize him." She leans forward. "Do you agree to try?"

I arrange to volunteer part-time at the Veterans Affairs office. I figure it's my best chance of coming into contact with the person Pearl is looking for. Ethan is surprised and slightly peeved. Between our class schedules and this new commitment, we have less time together than he'd like.

"Where did this come from?" he asks, petulant. "I never knew you had the faintest interest in the military."

"Andrew was thinking of enlisting." I offer a shrug. "Maybe I'm just scratching an old itch."

Ethan and I have been together for a year, but it feels longer than that. We're serious about each other. I know I can trust Ethan. He's the first person I've dated who I dared open up to. I told him almost everything. He didn't call me crazy, and he didn't run away.

"You're serious," he said. At the time, we were sitting on the sofa in his place and he was nuzzling my neck. There's a small red birthmark on the left side of my neck and a much larger, port wine stain on the right side, behind my ear. Usually, my hair covers the bigger blemish. Ethan calls the small birthmark my 'vampire bite' as he pretends to be the vampire. That night, after we'd been together for almost six months, I was feeling reckless. Reckless and vulnerable. "It's not a bite," I said. "It's a bullet hole." I showed him the other side—the exit wound. "Sometimes, when you die tragically in a past life, its mark stays on you."

"You really think you were shot through the neck in a past life?"

I curled in on myself a little. "I don't think I was. I *know* I was."

He came back a few days later, ashen-faced. "I looked up the *Yakima Herald Republic* in the library archive. It's all there—reported the day after you said it happened."

I could tell he was struggling to believe me. I said, "You're thinking that doesn't prove anything. I could have looked up the same article and made up a story to match what's in the newspaper."

"What car was Andrew—were you—driving?"

"A 1969 Pontiac GTO," I said without hesitation. I loved that car.

"What was the mascot of your high school?"

"The Pirates."

He sat down next to me, searching me with his eyes. "Either you're pulling a detailed, elaborate hoax on me for no apparent reason or you're telling the truth." He touched the birthmark on my neck with the tips of his fingers. "As crazy as this is, I believe you."

I hugged him then, and I cried a little. He wanted to know more about what I remembered, not just about Andrew's life but the other ones too. I was still afraid to tell him too much, afraid of driving him away, even though I knew he was drawn to the unknown instead of repelled by it.

Ethan has been a medieval alchemist, a native Peruvian river guide, and a university chaplain, but my favourite of his past incarnations is Moloni, the African tribal wisewoman, whose deep well of wisdom and compassion I sometimes see reflected in Ethan's cornflower-blue eyes. I think seeing her in him gave me the courage to trust him. Ethan is a seeker, driven by a desire to know more of the world, especially that which can't be seen. It's why he's majoring in astronomy, which he admits is the "dumbest thing ever as far as job prospects go." It's why I'm falling in love with him.

I trust Ethan more than anyone in the world, but I don't tell him about Pearl or why I'm really volunteering at the VA office. I want to, but even he won't understand why I'm spending time on a gamble with such long odds. The closer Ethan and I get to each other, the more committed we become, the more anxious I feel. My boyfriend might be convinced of the existence of immortal souls and multiple lives, but he is too much of an optimist to believe in tragic fate. He sees the future unwinding before us; I see a brick wall, one whose distance I can't judge because I can't tell how fast we're moving toward it.

"I love you," he said to me, the night of my birthday. We lay tangled together in the sheets, my head on his chest. I felt his words shift the weight of him beneath me.

I kissed his shoulder. I wanted to cry. "I've never grown up. I've never been married or had kids or been old."

"Me neither."

"Yes, you have," I insisted. "You just don't remember."

"Then, we might as well be even."

I was annoyed at him. "You don't understand. I have a short expiry date."

"That's ridiculous. I admit I don't understand it, but I don't think you do either. Maybe you only remember lives that ended badly and you've had plenty of others that were just fine. Also, people died younger back then, from war and disease and accidents. You shouldn't assume—" He pushed out from under me and propped himself up on one elbow. "Wait, is this why you take those streetfighting lessons? And why you carry a switchblade and hand sanitizer with you *everywhere?* And don't drive a car? Because you're afraid death is waiting for you around every corner?"

I lay still and silent, hands fisted close to my body. I wanted to tell Ethan he would be more afraid of violent death if he'd been through more of them. *Did you know that when you burn to death, you actually bleed? You bleed a lot. You would think the blood would steam off or something, but it doesn't. It drips and hisses in the flames.*

I didn't say that. I said, "Let's not talk about this right now."

I turned over and pulled up the covers. After a while, he sighed and put his arms around me. He fell asleep as I lay awake. But he hasn't said it again. He hasn't said he loves me.

My volunteer work in the VA office starts out as filing and photocopying, but a week later I catch a break. The receptionist is diagnosed with mono and doesn't know how long she'll be out sick. I offer myself as a fill-in, and soon, I'm sitting at the front desk, greeting everyone who comes in. I see plenty of soldiers and their family members when they come in to apply for benefits. I read each of them as carefully as I can, shaking everyone's hand to get a stronger impression, taking my time, making small talk as I check them in. They think I'm friendly and always willing to chat. A few of the younger vets get flirty and ask for my number. I feel awkward having to disappoint them.

If I was looking to score a date, I'd consider this time well spent, but for my purposes and Pearl's, it's a bust so far. Several of the people I meet have a pattern of military service in their prior incarnations, but I don't find anyone who matches the description Pearl gave me. I've never actively tried to search people's pasts the way I'm trying now, and after my shifts I leave the office with a dull headache. I take the bus home in the spitting rain, only to crack open my textbooks; the dense paragraphs swim before my eyes as I struggle to study for midterms.

One night, as I am about to fall asleep in the middle of a page about Islamic relations with the Byzantine Empire, I think: *This is so useless.* Both the searching and the studying.

I look at my phone; it's almost midnight. I pull up the number Pearl gave me. "Call me when you find him," she'd said, "but only when you find him." I consider phoning now to tell her I'm giving up. She ought to give up too, stop longing for someone who's gone on to another life. Maybe it's not such a great idea for me to string her hope out like this anyway. Even if I find this person, Pearl probably can't be a part of his or her life anymore, just like I can't go back to Jeanne or any of my past families. My finger hovers over the phone screen. *Move on,* I'll say when she picks up.

Then, I think about how ridiculous that sounds, coming from me. I need her help. I need answers. If I were oblivious of my pattern, I could live each day in blissful ignorance, up until the final, shocking end. *Would that be better?* Instead, I'm as burdened and captive to my memories as she is. She's not going to give up. Neither will I.

I close my book and rest my head on top of my arms, sniffing back tears of fatigue and hopelessness. Kelly is up late too, working on a lab report that's due. "Claire bear?" she says. "Are you okay?"

"Yeah," I say unconvincingly. My roommate's pattern is enviably simple. She can't stay away from the ocean. She's been a Micronesian sailor, a Venetian naval officer, a U-boat engineer, and a Makah whale hunter. Now she's studying to be a marine biologist. She's drowned twice, but she doesn't remember it, and it doesn't deter her. Drowning isn't the worst way to go, relatively speaking.

She comes over and gives me a hug. "Is something wrong? Is it Ethan?"

"No," I say, "Well, not exactly." Maybe something *is* wrong. I wonder if he's pulling away from me a little. Last week, he asked me to come with him to visit his family over Thanksgiving, and when I hemmed and hawed, I think he took it as a rejection. He can sense there's something I'm not telling him.

"You should go," says Kelly. "I think he really wants you to meet his family. He's mad about you, can't you tell? Unless — you're not really into him?"

I try to nod and shake my head at the same time. "It's not that. I mean, yes, I am into him. I'm just, I don't know — worried."

"You should do it," she says again. "You've got to take a chance on this really working out. Live a little, you know?"

Ethan's parents live in Tacoma, but his dad is a travel writer and they spend months in exotic places like Morocco and Tibet. "Claire has studied Buddhism," Ethan volunteers while setting the table, which sets me up for a long period of listening to Ethan's dad talk about the devotion of the Tibetan monks and how their harmonious culture is being destroyed.

It's true, there was a time I devoured everything I could read about reincarnation. I wondered if I quit school, became a vegan, and took up a life of austerity and meditation whether I could achieve nirvana. But I don't want to *stop* being reborn, and I'm not seeking enlightenment. I just want to stop having horrible deaths at a young age, which seems like a modest goal in comparison. I considered the possibility that I have some karmic debt to pay, but *what?* I don't believe I've been a bad person in any of my lives, not bad enough to deserve what I've gotten. I mean, I donate to the Salvation Army. I give my seat to old people on the bus. I recycle.

Ethan's mom lights up when I ask for a tour of her garden. She isn't the first person I've met who's been a farmer several times: twice in China, once in Russia, and once in Ireland, from what I can see. Ethan's dad has been a Mongolian nomad, a Bedouin shepherd, and a Southeast Asian trader whose geography and ethnicity I can't quite place at first glance; so it doesn't surprise me when his wife laments they haven't been home enough to finish raising the vegetable beds. Ethan's older brother, Kegan, shows up just before dinner. He's as handsome as Ethan, but he's quieter and smiles less. He seems to be five or six years older than

Ethan, instead of only three. When Ethan introduces us, I say, "I'm really glad to finally meet you," because it's obvious Ethan looks up to his brother. "Kegan's the go-getter," I've heard him say before.

"Nice to meet you, Claire." Kegan shakes my hand.

A general sits atop his war stallion in flared helmet and crimson armour, watching the flames below.

A guerrilla fighter rests his rifle atop his knees as he empties water from his boots.

A woman in a dark suit walks into the room and sits down across from a man handcuffed to his chair.

"Kegan just got back from Egypt," Ethan's mom says proudly. "He was on a six-week exchange program with the State Department."

We sit down for dinner. My heart races. I barely hear the conversation around me.

Ethan's mom passes me the mashed potatoes and asks Kegan, "How's your Arabic, sweetheart?"

"Good enough." Kegan is matter-of-fact; there's no pride or modesty in his voice. He is too old to be twenty-three.

Ethan's father leans toward me. "Kegan wants to work for the CIA," he explains. "I think he would've joined the military if it hadn't been for his asthma. Michelle and I are staunch Democrats; we don't even own any guns!" He shakes his head. "I don't know where he gets it from."

After dinner, I step outside onto the back porch under the pretense of phoning my parents. My fingers shake as I call the number. After three rings, I hear Pearl's voice.

"You've found him?"

"Yes," I whisper breathlessly. "You won't believe this. He's my boyfriend's brother!" I want to laugh hysterically. I've been searching for months, and he's been one degree away from me this whole time.

There is a long pause. "Tell me about him."

"He's twenty-three. Really handsome. Single, I think." There hadn't been any mention of a girlfriend over dinner. "He hasn't been around lately because he was on an exchange trip, but it shouldn't be hard to find a way to meet him now."

I try to picture how it will go. Will he be drawn to her, the way she is to him? She *is* over five hundred years old—will that matter?

I promise to invite him to visit us, and then I can find a chance to introduce them.

"Thank you, Claire." She sighs in relief. Then she hangs up.

Convincing Kegan to visit is easy. He hasn't seen his brother's place and is happy to spend the last day of the long weekend in the city with us. We drive up together on Saturday afternoon and arrive right around dinner time at the small house Ethan shares with two roommates. They are all out of town, so we have the place to ourselves. Ethan orders in pizza. *We're here,* I text Pearl. *Would you like to meet him tomorrow?*

We sit on the sofa, watching the Seahawks game and eating pizza. I sit next to Ethan on one side of the sofa. Kegan takes the armchair. I study him. I am not completely comfortable with Kegan. He looks like Ethan, but he is not like him. Ethan searches for answers to the unknown; Kegan knows the answers. He sees the world in black and white, and there is a coldness, a ruthlessness that I sense in his prior selves. They are resolute people, but they are not nice.

It's tempting to judge people based on who they were before, even though I often remind myself it's unfair. My sweet roommate Kelly set enemy ships ablaze and ordered men hung. Ethan once stabbed another man in a drunken knife fight in the South American jungle. When I was Hassad, I owned so many slaves that it makes me squirm a little to think about it now. Our lives are shaped by circumstances; we have patterns, but we do change. I haven't known Kegan long enough to see many details of his past, but I'm not sure I want to. He's Ethan's brother, and it's better I try to get to know him for who he is in this life.

I wonder again what his reaction will be to meeting Pearl.

What if he doesn't feel any connection to her at all? Will she move on, or pine after him? I try to think of how to bring up my idea to invite her over. *So, I have a friend who would really like to meet you. Who is she? Oh, uh, she's a TA in one of my classes . . .*

Before I can formulate my suggestion, Kegan takes another slice of pizza and says, "So, how did you two get together?"

I glance at Ethan. "We met during freshman orientation," I say. "But we didn't start dating until after that camping trip."

Ethan picks up the thread. "I'd had my eye on Claire for weeks, and then I spied her sitting at the very back of the campfire, practically in the woods, all by herself."

"I'm scared of fire," I explain, embarrassed.

"So I moved my chair to sit next to her, and we stayed up talking after everyone else had gone to sleep and the fire had burned out."

Kegan nods. He pops open a can of soda and says, dead sober, "I'm terrified of fire."

Ethan laughs. "You're not terrified of anything."

"I had nightmares as a kid," Kegan says. "You were too young to remember. I still have them sometimes—nightmares about burning to death."

I pull my legs up to my chest and hug them. "Me too."

"Claire says she's scared of fire because it's how she died in a past life. You think that's what happened to you too, macho man?" Ethan's voice is just a notch past teasing. He sounds a little hurt that we are commiserating over a deep phobia his brother never bothered to share with him.

Kegan looks at Ethan, then looks at me. He mutes the volume on the television. "Yes," he says. "I could believe that. In my dream, there's a woman who's chasing me. It's always the same woman. I don't know why I'm trying to get away from her, but I am. I'm running or driving or riding a horse, always trying to get away, and in the end, I'm trapped by a fire. And I burn to death. And she watches me burn."

We are both silent for a minute. Ethan is stunned, but not for the same reason I am. "That is so screwy, bro. Maybe it means you're afraid of women." He has a half-teasing smirk on his face, but neither Kegan nor I am smiling.

Kegan shakes his head, his left eye squinting in annoyance at his little brother. "No, dipstick. It's just *one* woman."

"Oh my God," I whisper. An iciness bathes me from head to toe. *What have I done?*

The living room window shatters inward.

⬧

I scream. All three of us leap off the sofa, scattering pizza and soda. A hulking figure steps through the window frame. Cold air sweeps into the room around his menacing shape. His combat boots crunch the broken glass against the hardwood floor. I can't see his face; he's wearing a black ski mask. All I can see is the barrel of the gun he is pointing at us.

"*Jesus*," Ethan breathes. We are both too stunned to move, but Kegan scans the room for the nearest weapon. There's nothing. He grabs the wooden chip bowl off the coffee table and hurls it at the intruder. The man ducks, raising his arm to avoid the flying object. Tortilla chips and salsa spray the wall. Kegan shoves his brother, and together, we run for the front door.

Ethan pulls the door open. A second masked man stands on the doorstep. He starts to bring up his own gun, but before he can aim it, Kegan tackles him. They slam into the door frame together. The man who came through the window shoves his bulk in front of me and Ethan, his pistol raised, his mouth open in a snarl.

"On your knees!" he shouts at us.

Ethan pulls me roughly behind him. "What do you want?" he shouts back. "You want money? The TV? Just take them!" His voice shakes. He is standing with his arms spread in front of me. I am terrified the man will shoot him.

Kegan struggles with the shorter intruder. He has his hands clamped over the frame of the pistol, pushing the muzzle down toward the floor. The man's right hand is trapped against his weapon, but he cocks his left fist and punches Kegan in the face. Kegan's grip slides. The man yanks his gun free; he swings it up and cracks Kegan across the head. Kegan staggers and falls sideways, barely managing to put a hand out to catch himself. He tries to surge up; his eyes are wild and desperate. The butt of the pistol comes down on the back of his skull, and he collapses like a sack.

"*No!*" Ethan jerks toward his brother, but the hulking man shifts his gun to my temple.

"I said on your knees!" he yells at Ethan. "Or you pick which one we shoot first."

Ethan goes colourless. His hand on my arm, he lowers himself to the floor. I kneel next to him. I can feel the pulse in his hand beating in rapid tempo against my own.

"What do you want?" he asks again, his voice low so it hides his fear. He looks at his prone brother and swallows hard.

"Dumb prick," the short man exclaims. He shoves Kegan's figure with his boot, then reaches his gloved fingers awkwardly into the eye hole of his mask, wiping his brow.

My heart is pounding so hard I think it might escape my body. This is it. This is the brutal end I've been expecting for years. I wonder how they will kill us and whether it will be fast. Though I am scared out of my mind, I'm more worried about Ethan and Kegan than I am about myself. I'm not surprised that I'm going to die. But they shouldn't have to; they shouldn't be sucked into the merciless magnetism of my pattern, ancillary tragedies to my own.

I have a switchblade in my pocket. Can I reach it? What can I possibly do against two men with guns?

"Which one of them is he?" the big man asks.

The two of them look from Ethan to Kegan and back again. Their eyes are like black pits in the slits of their masks. "I'm not sure," the short one replies. "Put them in the bedroom closet. She'll know when she gets here."

She'll know. These men work for Pearl. My insides turn over.

"What about the girl?"

"The girl too."

"Let her go," Ethan says. "Please, don't hurt her." I cringe at the pleading in his voice, though I know he is only trying to protect me. I want to berate him for ever having doubted my fatalism.

The big man pulls a roll of silver duct tape from his jacket and bends over Kegan, pulling his wrists together behind his back and taping them together tightly. When he's done, he winds duct tape around Kegan's ankles. Then he drags Kegan down the hallway, pulling him backwards by his armpits. Kegan's head lolls limply on his neck, the left side of his face swollen a reddish-purple.

Ethan trembles, enraged and helpless.

"Hands where I can see them, punk," the short man says.

His accomplice returns. More duct tape for Ethan and me. My wrist bones rub together painfully as they're bound. When the big man touches me, I get past-life glimpses: a mercenary soldier, a prison guard, an elephant poacher. I choke back a whimper. Suffering isn't going to move him.

"Get up," he orders.

They march the two of us into Ethan's bedroom. The room is dark, and the shades are drawn. Ethan's clothes and books have been thrown willy-nilly from the closet, which is now bare, except for Kegan, who is lying on its floor. Our captors back us into the closet beside him. "Sit down," the big man orders. We do as he says.

They tape our ankles together and then stand back, looking down at us. Behind them, I can see the outlines of Ethan's unmade bed, his duffel bag lying open on the floor, his stereo. The big man lights a cigarette. It dangles from fat, chapped lips set in the mouth hole of the ski mask. He checks his wristwatch.

The short one licks his lips nervously. "Who do you think these kids are? What would anyone want with them?"

"The hell should I know?" says the big man. "Maybe daddy pissed off the Mob? We're being paid is all I care."

Ethan tries to speak up. "There's been a mistake," he says. "You've got the wrong people. We're not mixed up with the mafia. We don't have any enemies. We're just students. I'm telling you, you have the wrong people."

The men ignore him. They close the closet, shutting us in the dark. Their footsteps move around, then leave the room. In the silence that follows, I pray for the sound of sirens, for the police to surround the house and rescue us. It's possible one of the neighbours called 911, but I am not optimistic. The houses here are spaced far apart and full of student renters, all of them gone for the Thanksgiving break. No one knows what's happening to us.

"This is all my fault." I choke back silent tears. "Ethan, I'm sorry."

His shape slumps against the wall. "What for?"

"I should have told you, but I didn't think—I didn't imagine—" My throat is too small; the words come out in a squeaky rush, like water through a small spigot. I tell him about meeting Pearl, about agreeing to help her find someone she knew centuries ago. "I led her to us. To Kegan."

"To Kegan?" Ethan stiffens. "Why would anyone want to hurt Kegan?"

His brother stirs on the floor. A soft groan escapes him.

Ethan tries to shuffle closer to him. "Hey, it's me. You okay?"

Kegan lifts his head off the ground, realizes he's tied up, and starts to freak out. "Let us out of here!" he screams, kicking at the door. "LET US OUT!"

The closet door opens. A silhouette stands over us. Even before the small desk lamp clicks on, I know who it is, and so, apparently, does Kegan. He jerks against the wall, a sheen of sweat breaking on his forehead.

"You." His voice is a rattle.

Pearl's bottomless eyes pass over me, then Ethan, before stopping on Kegan. "Hello, General Zhang." Her voice is silky soft, almost affectionate. "We meet again."

The big man beside her grumbles, "You promised us a lot of cash—"

"Finish the job," she replies shortly, "and you will be paid as we agreed."

The men depart. We are alone in the room with Pearl.

"I have no idea who you are, or what you want with me," Kegan says. Though he's scared, his voice is surprisingly strong. "But let my brother and his girlfriend go. If it's me you want, just let them go."

"Ahhh," Pearl sighs. "So there is justice in the universe after all. I pleaded for my family, too. I pleaded for their lives. Then I pleaded for quick deaths. But you granted them neither." Her face is a pitiless pale mask. Her voice takes on a slow, musing quality. "The Red Butcher, the Emperor's most feared warlord. You were determined to make an example of Three Gates Valley, one so terrifying that no other prefectures would ever again consider rebellion."

"We don't know what you're talking about, lady," Ethan says. "You're crazy."

"Am I?" Pearl looks directly at me.

I shudder. How could I not have seen it before, her cold cruelty? "This is wrong. You can't punish him for what happened to you hundreds of years ago. He doesn't remember any of it. He's not even the same person."

"Isn't he? How can you, of all people, say that?" She turns away from me and back to Kegan. "This young, handsome incarnation flatters you, General. But I can see you. Inside, you are still the monster who had my husband and his brothers torn apart by horses and their flesh fed to the dogs. You ordered my children to be thrown from the walls. And you lit fires that burned for five days and nights, until nothing was left of the town." She crouches down smoothly to face him, her long white coat pooling around her. "No one survived. No one but me."

The room chills from the ice of her whispered words. "There are consequences to making an enemy of an Ageless one. I swore to Heaven, to Zhurong, god of fire and vengeance, that I would hunt you down; I would make you pay back with your lives the ones you took from me."

Kegan is shaking his head emphatically. "I didn't—I wouldn't—"

Pearl stands up. The door opens and the big man walks in with a six-gallon jug. He bangs it impatiently against the wall, and it makes a hollow sound. That's when I notice the smell drifting in from the hallway. Kerosene.

Terror floods in. I shake in its grip like a marionette.

Kegan is no better. In his saucer-wide eyes, I see that he knows this has happened before. How many times? Over how many lives has Pearl been exacting her vengeance? "Please," he begs, "please let them go."

Pearl gestures to me. "Take her outside." The big man picks me up, dumping me over his shoulder like a bag of potatoes. I can't resist. I can't do anything. Except start to sob.

Ethan loses his mind. He thrashes against his bonds. "What

are you going to do? WHAT ARE YOU GOING TO DO TO HER? You can't leave us like this!" He tries to throw himself in the man's path, but the hulk steps over him. My vision blurs, bobs upside-down as I'm taken from the room.

"Goodbye, General," Pearl says. "We will meet again soon."

The man carries me outside and dumps me on the driveway. Ethan's howls are cut off as Pearl follows the men outside and slams the door behind her. I struggle to my knees, snot and tears smeared across my cheeks. Pearl has a gun in her hand. She rests it against my forehead.

"You tricked me," I scream. Rage boils up through my fear. "I thought you were searching for someone you loved. You said that love never dies!"

"I loved my poor, mortal family. Love *doesn't* die." She cocks the hammer. "Neither does hate."

I stare up at her. She is going to kill me, but in this instant, I pity her. She is the proof that people *need* to forget, to start over, to be given second, third, eighth chances. Or we might become like her. Frozen by the worst of our memories. Imprisoned by histories we can't change and can't leave behind.

"You promised to help me." My voice is a cracked whisper now. "All this time, you were just using me."

"I *am* going to help you, Claire. I'm going to tell you how to break the pattern."

She pulls the trigger.

Click. The hammer falls on an empty chamber.

I blink, confused as to how I am still alive. "Untie her," Pearl orders. A minute later, the duct tape around my wrists and ankles rips loose, peeling a layer of skin off with it. Pearl lowers the gun.

"You were meant to die tonight, but I spared you. Now, I will tell you what the secret of the pattern is." She leans forward and whispers. "Choice."

Behind her, the short masked man lights a match and drops it. Fire encircles the house in an enormous whoosh of red heat.

My bladder gives out. Warmth spreads down the legs of my jeans.

"There is always a choice." The black chasms of her eyes are two pinpricks of reflected firelight. "Now run, Claire."

I scramble to my feet. And I run.

I run without regard for direction. I run over lawns, through shrubbery and around trees. My foot catches on a curb, and I gasp as I pitch forward into a garden bed. Whimpers clog my throat as I struggle to my feet and look over my shoulder.

The men are small figures now, climbing into a black van with tinted windows and a missing license plate. One of them rolls down the passenger side window and yells at Pearl, who remains standing in front of the burning house. For a long moment, she doesn't move. The glow of the fire lights up the street and casts leaping shadows like hellish dancing puppets. Pearl takes two slow steps forward, a spot of white against a curtain of red, as if she intends to walk into the flames, to join everything she's lost.

Then she turns and walks calmly to the van. When she's inside, the van turns sharply and peels away.

I dig my hands into the dirt, so wet and cool. I remember what it was like in the fire. The intensity of the pain. Marie—*I*—screamed until my throat burned from the inside out.

I get up. And I run back toward the house.

My body wants to rebel. It cannot believe I am doing this; it wants to shut down in response to terror. *But Ethan is in there. And Kegan. How can I let them suffer the death I most fear?*

When I reach the house, I freeze in a final, stomach-churning moment of cowardice. Then I run to the door. I try to push it open, but it's stuck. Then I remember the broken window and run around to the side of the house. Smoke pours from the living room. I take a deep breath and clamber inside. There's glass on the floor; a shard of it jabs into my palm, but I barely feel it. I pull my sleeves over my hands and keep crawling. I can hear, through the crackle and roar of flames, the sound of screaming. Perhaps I'm imagining it or perhaps I'm screaming in my head.

I make it to the hallway and army crawl forward, elbow over elbow, my nose pressed close to the floor, sucking in short bursts of ashy air. The heat on my skin is like a hundred sunburns. I'm crying and ninety-nine percent sure I'm going to die, but I keep scrambling forward until I reach the closed bedroom door. The knob scalds my hand when I reach up to twist it. I shove the door open and drop back down, coughing. "Ethan," I try to call, but the smoke is too thick. Then I bump into a moving shape. A leg. I follow it up to a torso. Ethan twists in place. His frightened, bloodshot eyes meet mine and grow wide with relief and horror.

"Claire! What are you doing?" he gasps.

I pull the switchblade from my pocket and fumble it open. I start sawing at the duct tape around his wrists. My eyes and nose sting. Adrenaline pours through my system, and I fight to keep my hands steady. Ethan lies still, trying to help me as I keep cutting, inch by inch, until the tape tears free. He grabs the knife from me and hacks frantically at the tape binding his feet until he frees them. He scrambles away toward Kegan.

I am light-headed now. It is hard to breathe. The skin of my hands sizzles and blisters. The world swims black and red. *Choice,* I think. And I remember.

I remember I grabbed the spade, the only weapon I could find, and followed Donnan.

I ran toward the wounded leopard, drawing it away from Jamal.

I pressed the satchel of herbs into Estelle's desperate hands.

I saw the storm clouds, but I took the boat out; little Asuka was so hungry.

I dribbled water onto the pustule-speckled lips of Owhi, the chief's son, as he lay dying.

I pushed Jeanne down to the ground as the bullets began to fly.

There is a cracking, splintering sound from somewhere overhead. Ethan is shouting my name, but it seems to be coming from very far away. A strange calm overtakes me.

My lives make sense now. Tragic death is not my pattern.

Sacrifice is my pattern.

The secret is choice, Pearl had said. She's right. Our patterns are the ones we choose, over and over again. I've never broken my pattern because I've always chosen as I'm choosing now.

Kegan's face appears an inch in front of mine, distorted by the smoke. *"Get up."* His voice is barely his own. He hauls hard on my arms. Ethan grabs me from the other side, urging my body across the ground. My hands and knees scrabble across the burning floorboards of the hall. Then the two of them are lifting and thrusting me toward the window. It appears, a narrow portal ringed by fire, beckoning urgently.

And then I'm through it, staggering out of the flames. Cold air rushes into my scalded lungs. I stumble several more steps and drop to the ground, coughing, gasping, trembling. The cool grass presses against my raw skin; everything is a tear-stained blur. Kegan and Ethan collapse next to me, heaving for breath. Behind us, the house continues to burn, sending plumes of smoke into the night sky. The blare of sirens and the strobing of lights surround us as we cling to each other. Kegan's swollen eyes are haunted, and Ethan shakes uncontrollably. Their clothes and hair are blackened, their skin red and blistered, but they're alive. I'm alive.

All of us, alive. *We've been given another chance.*

There's always another chance.

THE ORPHANS OF NILAVELI

Naru Dames Sundar

With signs of a major second quake imminent, government emergency services started an airlift operation to save the countless lives in the northern district. Were it not for this effort, the casualties from the second tremor would have been far higher.

2076 Earthquake, Sri Lanka
—Nilaveli Beach Airlift

A rickety jeep bounced over the broken asphalt crags of roads turned into hillocks. Water seeped around us. The public channels were already speaking of severe aftershocks. My father struggled with the juddering steering wheel while my mother spoke to her cousins at the evacuation site at Nilaveli Beach. The implant glowed behind her ear as it carried her words many miles to the east. The jeep barely had room for the three of us and our neighbours and their son. As I clung to my mother's sari, I heard her gasp.

"Kamala? What is it?" Worry creased my father's eyes.

"Anilan, he said they *looked past him*. As if he wasn't even there! And the crowds just pushed past him!"

My father pulled the jeep to the side of the road, waiting for my mother to say more.

"It's like that time we visited Kandy, Anilan. Didn't you hear the stories? Implant modifications. Adjusted vision. First, they don't want to see the beggars. Then, they don't want to see *us*."

Us, them. Before the war, after the war. Even seventy years after the war, it was *us* and *them*. You see, conflict has roots, and even when the victor cuts the tree down, the roots remain, buried deep. Sometimes subtle, sometimes not so subtle.

"Kamala. The children aren't implanted yet. We can send them. Their features aren't so distinct that someone will notice."

"No." My mother's voice was firm.

"If the crowds thicken, do you think they'll make room for *us*? There are always enough vacationers from the south in the Trincomalee resorts to fill the lifters. But the children without their implants, no one could say for sure that they were Tamil or Sinhalese."

"Absolutely not."

But I could tell from the wavering of her voice that she was already thinking yes. Because sometimes when you had to choose between your life and your child's, between a large risk and a small risk, you made the choices you never wanted to make. Even at six, I understood enough.

"No, Amma, no, I don't want to go. Don't leave me. Don't leave me, Amma!"

"Hush, Kartik, hush."

My parents pulled me into their arms and held me, and I smelled sweat on their skin, salt in their tears, turmeric and ash on their foreheads—these smells would never leave me. I wailed at Nilaveli when they handed me to my neighbour's eight-year-old son, Ayngharan, my newly adopted older brother.

Hours later, I sobbed, my face pressed against the glass window, the lifter leaving behind the white sand covered by a sea of people and heading over the churning waters. I saw the aftershock ripple through the beach, sand spray booming in large dust clouds. I screamed for my parents, like the other orphans on the craft. Ayngharan put his hands over my eyes and pulled me close: his hands, his chest, his smell—all unfamiliar. He too was experiencing that singular agony, but his tears lay buried.

✤

A moderately wealthy family in Kandy took us in. Marble floors and large, expensive batik hangings across the entry and throughout the house. Ayngharan knew some Sinhala because even in the remote northern schools, government strictures imposed what were taught. I was young and knew little, and as my adopted parents put it, I was *affected*. They didn't like to talk about it, as if it was some distant dirty thing they didn't want to touch. Ayngharan was angrier than I was. He understood, you see—he knew enough to know the reason our parents could not have accompanied us on the lifter. Why they could not have gotten past the evacuation officials. For me, the *why* was more ephemeral, something I did not yet grasp.

Years later, Ayngharan shouted and screamed when they installed his implant. He fought so hard they had to sedate him before the medical attendant could install the silver conch shell behind his ear. When our adopted parents told him what software was being loaded onto it, his rage transcended into something else. Because he had learned enough to know what each piece of software could do—and he knew that without words, our parents were slowly trying to pull us into their world of unseeing. They argued, and finally our parents simply put their foot down, asserting their parental rights. We had no choice, but to obey. So, Ayngharan did as they asked, but it was not long before he discovered illegal patches in dark corners. He quietly removed the software from his implant.

I think what hurt Ayngharan the most happened when it was my turn. Not because I didn't apply his illegal patches afterward, but because I acquiesced quietly. That day our paths diverged.

✤

Ayngharan dropped out of secondary school while I passed the university entrance exams. I recalled vividly one night at the campus bar, slightly warm from a touch of Arak, the smell of anise still pungent in my throat. Henry and Vijaya, friends of sorts, accompanied me at the table we occupied most Friday nights. Henry spotted them first.

"Eh, mate, there're two young ladies over there and three of us. Which one of us gets to stay behind and order more drinks?"

Vijaya, the most argumentative among us, bickered over which one of the girls was prettier. I was alarmed; there were clearly three girls at the bar. Three saris: pink and gold, and a few seats away, a solitary green.

"But there're three of them."

The jovial banter stopped. Vijaya squinted at the bar and then looked at me quizzically. There, I finally understood. He only saw two girls. That he was just like my adopted parents. Just like the unnamed evacuation coordinator on the beach that day in Nilaveli.

"What do you mean, three? Too much arak perhaps, friend?"

Henry gave me a different look. Uncomfortable. Annoyed.

"That one's not my type, man."

Vijaya still didn't understand. He would never understand until he turned off his ubiquitous implant modification. Henry grabbed his shoulder and scuttled over toward the bar, glossing over Vijaya's confusion. He turned back and shouted, "Drinks on you, Guna!"

But his eyes told me something different. Don't push this. Don't ask more questions. Go along with it. Who was worse? Vijaya, who did not see this unnamed Tamil girl, painted out of his vision by a chunk of code and the silver behind his ear? Henry, who saw her but feigned an incompatible type because type included blood and history and a thousand lines of division scratched into the country's bedrock for hundreds of years? Or me, who answered to my adopted name, Guna? Me, who said nothing, who went along with it, even as it rankled. We were all terrible people in different ways.

Ayngharan's rage consumed him. I learned of his death from my adopted mother. No details, just that he was gone. I found out from other sources. Publicly there was no mention of a protest. Publicly there was no mention of a lone protestor who set himself aflame. And what did the bystanders see, I wondered? Did they see no one? The burning man, the protestors, all of them written out of the bystander's vision by a piece of computer software. An unseen protest, marked only by the shape the crowd of angry youths had carved out on the street, marked only by the scorch mark left on the asphalt.

And so I arrived at this: my first act of rebellion. The small revolt I finally permitted myself to do, in remembrance of all the unseen, of all the things hidden from public eyes. I stand now on the tour-boat looking out at the ruins on a stretch of beach in Trincomalee, the gopuram of the old Koneswaram temple still half reaching out of the water. Some miles north, there exists an unseen, unmarked stretch of sunken beach in which my parents lie buried. I find the entry on the earthquake in the public database, and I edit it. I write in there the story you are reading now. My story. Perhaps in an hour, or even a few minutes, someone will edit it back. Someone will reduce my story to an invisible footnote to a single line. But for this moment, I am here. My story is here, unfiltered and visible. My real name is Kartik, and I *do* exist.

AFTERWORD

Derwin Mak

In the seven years since Eric Choi and I edited *The Dragon and the Stars*, a Chinese-themed science fiction and fantasy anthology, Asian science fiction and fantasy have grown greatly. Here is a brief, but by no means comprehensive, overview of Asian SF&F since 2010.

Mainland China has become the powerhouse of Asian science fiction. Chinese science fiction, growing with the country's space program, is not just as an obscure genre for a few fans. It now has the wide appeal to the general public that science fiction enjoys in the West. Liu Cixin's novel *Three-Body Problem* became a bestseller in China, comparable to the Harry Potter novels in popularity. Even the Vice-President of China, Li Yuanchao, revealed that he is a science fiction fan and asked science fiction writers to popularize scientific knowledge and contribute to their country's drive to become a technological power.

Despite a drop in circulation in recent years, *Science Fiction World* (科幻世界) remains the science fiction magazine with the highest circulation in the world, at 130,000 copies per issue. Two Chinese stories have won a major international award, the Hugo: Liu Cixin's *Three-Body Problem* (Best Novel, 2015) and Hao Jingfang's "Folding Beijing" (Best Novelette, 2016).

Clarkesworld Magazine has been publishing translations of Chinese science fiction stories, so now they are accessible to English readers. Look for stories by Xia Jia ("A Hundred Ghosts Parade Tonight"), Chen Qiufan ("The Fish of Lijiang"), Cheng Jingbo ("Grave of the Fireflies"), Tang Fei ("Pepe"), and many others. Also look for *Invisible Planets*, an anthology of contemporary Chinese science fiction, translated by Ken Liu, published in 2016.

Japan has started exporting English translations of its novels via the Haikasoru imprint of manga publisher Viz. These include *Battle Royale* by Koushun Takami, *All You Need Is Kill* by Hiroshi Sakurazaka (retitled to *Edge of Tomorrow* to match the Americanized movie adaptation starring Tom Cruise), and *Rocket Girls* by Housuke Nojiri.

The Philippines has a tradition of science fiction and fantasy that continues to this day. Charles A. Tan edited *Lauriat: A Filipino-Chinese Speculative Fiction Anthology* in 2012. Look for stories by Dean Francis Alfar, Kristine Ong Muslim, and Yvette Tan.

Jaymee Goh and Joyce Chng edited *The Sea Is Ours: Tales of Steampunk Southeast Asia* in 2015. Not only has this anthology merged the steampunk genre with Southeast Asian cultures, but it will bring them to a new audience; foreign translation rights have been sold in the Czech Republic.

Singaporean writer Jason Erik Lundberg founded *Lontar: The Journal of Southeast Asian Speculative Fiction* in 2012. *Lontar* has published stories by a variety of writers in its goal to spread awareness of Southeast Asian science fiction and fantasy and the diversity of Southeast Asian cultures.

Salik Shah, Ajapa Sharma, and Isha Karki edit *Mathila Review*, a magazine of speculative art and culture. Their magazine is by no means limited to authors and stories of South Asian origin and publishes science fiction and fantasy from around the world. *Mathila Review* had an "Asian SF Special Issue" (issues 5 and 6).

Indrapramit Das (a.k.a. Indra Das) divides his time between India and Canada. He began publishing short stories in 2010, and his first novel, *The Devourers*, appeared in 2015.

Significant developments occurred in Arab science fiction and fantasy. In 2012, Emirati author Noura al Noman published *Ajwan*, the first young adult science fiction novel in Arabic. Ibraheem Abbas and Yasser Bahjat's science fantasy novel, *HWJN* (*Hawjan*), became a bestseller in Saudi Arabia in 2013, a rare feat for SF&F there. However, the anti-witchcraft unit of the Saudi religious police investigated the novel for promoting witchcraft (but fortunately cleared it), and Kuwait and Qatar banned it. Nonetheless, despite state censors and religious conservatives, Arab science fiction has emerged.

Israeli author Lavie Tidhar's *Osama* won the World Fantasy Award for Best Novel in 2012.

Seven years ago, science fiction and fantasy writers were rare in overseas or diaspora Asian communities. Now their numbers and popularity grow each year. Chinese Americans have been particularly prolific. Ken Liu published most of his stories after 2010. In 2012, his short story "The Paper Menagerie" became the first story of any length to win all three of the genre's major awards: the Hugo, the Nebula, and the World Fantasy. Two Chinese Americans have won the John W. Campbell Award for Best New Writer: E. Lily Yu (2012) and Wesley Chu (2015).

In Canada, Renée Bennett, Calvin Jim, and Ace Jordyn published *Shanghai Steam*, an anthology of hybrid steampunk and *wuxia* (Chinese martial arts) stories in 2012. At the 2015 Aurora Awards, Eric Choi won the Best Short Fiction—English Award for "Crimson Sky" and Tony Pi won the Best Poem/Song—English Award for "A Hex With Bees".

The Vancouver-based Asian Canadian Writers' Workshop (ACWW), which usually promotes literary writing, published a special Speculative Fiction Issue (edited by Derwin Mak and JF Garrard) in 2014 and had a science fiction and fantasy theme for the first time at its annual LiterASIAN festival in 2015.

Zen Cho has risen in the fantasy genre in recent years. She's a Chinese Malaysian author in London, and her debut novel, *Sorcerer to the Crown*, was published in 2015. She also edited *Cyberpunk: Malaysia*, an anthology of Malaysian science fiction stories, in 2015. She won the British Fantasy Award for Best Newcomer in 2016 and the Crawford Award in 2015.

Aliette de Bodard is a multi-award winning author of French/ Vietnamese descent living in France. She has won three British Science Fiction Award, two Nebula Awards, and a Locus Award for her novel and short fiction. Her novel, *The House of Binding Thorns*, a follow-up to her 2015 BSFA novel *The House of Shattered*

AFTERWORD by Derwin Mak

Wings, is out in April 2017.

Korean American science fiction writers have appeared in the past few years. *Azalea: Journal of Korean Literature and Culture,* published by the University of Hawaii, had a science fiction issue featuring five Korean stories translated into English and stories by American writers Ed Bok Lee and Minsoo Kang in 2013. Ellen Oh's *Prophecy* series of young adult fantasy novels began in 2013. Minsoo Kang translated the classic Korean fantasy novel *The Story of Hong Gildong* into English in 2016.

Two Filipina American writers had good years in 2015 and 2016. Michi Trota became the first Filipinx (her preferred gender-neutral term) to win the Hugo Award for her work as Managing Editor of *Uncanny: A Magazine of Science Fiction and Fantasy* (Best Semiprozine, 2016). Alyssa Wong became the first Filipino person to win the Nebula Award (2015) and the World Fantasy Award (2016) for her short story "Hungry Daughters of Starving Mothers".

There still aren't many Arab American science fiction and fantasy writers, but watch for Saladin Ahmed. His fantasy novel *Throne of the Crescent Moon* was a finalist for a Hugo Award in 2013 and a Nebula Award in 2012.

In Canada, Amal El-Mohtar has published a steady stream of short stories since 2010. Her story "The Green Book" was a finalist for the Nebula Award for Best Short Story (2012). Her story "The Truth About Owls" won the Locus Award for Best Short Story in 2015.

The Indo-American writer S.B. Divya published her first short story in 2014, and her first novella, "Runtime," appeared in 2016.

Mary Anne Mohanraj is an American writer and literature professor of Sri Lankan (Tamil) ancestry. She started writing, publishing, and editing in the 1990's, when Asian American science fiction and fantasy writers were rare. She continues publishing short stories and novels today. In 2004, she founded the Speculative Literature Foundation, which she still directs. In 2013, she founded *Jaggery,* a Desi literary journal.

Rati Mehrotra also began publishing stories in 2014, thus joining Mahtab Narsimhan among the Indo-Canadians who write science fiction and fantasy. Rati's two-novel series will be published by Harper Voyager in 2018.

In this era of migration and multiculturalism, sometimes we have to redefine traditional cultural identities. Amanda Sun has European ancestry, but she also has a Chinese family and has lived in Japan. Starting in 2013, she published her Japanese-themed young adult fantasy trilogy *Paper Gods* and the novel *Heir to the Sky*.

Then there's Jason Erik Lundberg, an American who became a Singaporean writer and editor of the above-mentioned *Lontar*. He is a supporter or proponent of Southeast Asian science fiction and fantasy.

The above survey is by no means exhaustive, and there are other good writers whom I have not mentioned due to space restrictions, a limitation for which I apologize.

Dear readers, I hope that our anthology has shown you the diversity of Asian cultures and our writers' broad range of ideas and themes. Asian science fiction has grown considerably in the past seven years. The stars, like the Moon and the Sun, rise in the East. We look forward to seeing more stories from where the stars rise.

—Derwin Mak, Toronto, Canada, 2017

ACKNOWLEDGEMENTS

Lucas K. Law

Many thanks go to the following:

Derwin Mak, my co-editor, for his insights and guidance;

Eric Choi for his bundle of energy and enthusiasm in my anthology projects;

Kim Vincent and Kimberley Watson, two friends whose words remind me to strive for integrity and humility;

Samantha M. Beiko and Clare C. Marshall for their generous support whenever I need it;

Tim H. Feist, my partner, for his patience, understanding, and encouragement when I spent too many hours apart, working on this anthology;

Elsie Chapman, Aliette de Bodard, and the authors for giving their unwavering commitment to this anthology;

The staff and volunteers at Qualicum Beach Library and Vancouver Island Regional Library for giving me an opportunity to curate the Qualicum Beach Asian Collection;

Everyone who buys this book and support social causes (please continue to talk about issues on mental health and mental illness and stand up against discriminations and bullying).

Derwin Mak

I give many thanks to Lucas K. Law for inviting me to edit this anthology; to Eric Choi and JF Garrard, who co-edited previous anthologies with me and thus gave me experience in editing with others; and to Jim Wong-Chu and the Asian Canadian Writers' Workshop for inviting me to LiterASIAN 2015 and encouraging me to promote and publish Asian Canadian science fiction.

ABOUT THE CONTRIBUTORS

Anne Carly Abad is a two-time Pushcart Prize nominee. Between making custom jewelry and taking care of her hedgehog, Porky, she writes poetry, fiction, and political musings. Some of her published work can be found at *Apex*, *Strange Horizons* and *the Philippines Graphic Magazine*. Follow her blog at: www.the-sword-that-speaks.blogspot.com

Deepak Bharathan grew up on a staple diet of veggies, science fiction and fantasy. His father's 3,000 book collection was the monolith that jump-started his reading. Growing up in India, he managed to write fiction for children's magazines and for the national radio. His fiction has appeared in *Daily Science Fiction*, *Allegory*, *Sci Phi Journal* and *Terraform*. He has published non-fiction about technology in *Consulting Magazine*, *CIO Update*, *Search CIO*, *PC Today*, and *CIO Decisions*. His Philadelphia home is run by his one-year-old daughter. His wife and he are just along for the ride. It's a pretty good one though.

Elsie Chapman is the author of YA novels *Dualed* (Random House, 2013), *Divided* (Random House, 2014), *Along The Indigo* (Abrams/Amulet, 2018), and co-editor of and contributor to *Legendry* (Harper Collins/Greenwillow, 2018), a YA anthology featuring Asian and South Asian mythology retellings. Born and raised in Canada and a graduate of University of British Columbia with a degree in English Literature, she currently lives in Tokyo with her family.

Joyce Chng writes mainly science fiction and YA. She likes steampunk and tales of transfiguration/transformation. Her fiction has appeared in *The Apex Book of World SF II*, *We See A Different Frontier*, *Cranky Ladies of History*, and *Accessing The Future*. Her YA includes a trilogy about a desert planet and a fantasy duology in Qing China. Joyce has also co-edited a Southeast Asian steampunk anthology titled *The Sea is Ours: Tales of Steampunk Southeast Asia* (Rosarium Publishing, 2015) with Jaymee Goh. Her Jan Xu Adventures series, an urban/contemporary fantasy set in Singapore, is written under the pseud. J. Damask which she will tell you it's a play on her Chinese name. She tweets at @jolantru.

Miki Dare (Dare is pronounced DAH-RAY in Japanese) lives on the West Coast where she likes to express herself with whatever falls into her hands—from a pen to a paintbrush. Her science fiction and fantasy writing can be found in *Analog Science Fiction and Fact, Inscription Magazine, Tesseracts Twenty: Compostela,* and *Urban Fantasist.* She is also currently working with mixed media to explore issues of identity, personal history and social realities. Her latest art series is titled *Geisha Girl Stereotype Survivor.* To see what Miki is up to, visit her website at mikidare.com.

S.B. Divya is a lover of science, math, fiction, and the Oxford comma. She enjoys subverting expectations and breaking stereotypes whenever she can. Her short stories have been published in various magazines, including *Lightspeed* and *Daily Science Fiction,* and her writing appears in the indie game *Rogue Wizards.* Her debut science-fiction novella *Runtime* was released by Tor.com Publications in May, 2016. You can find more online at www.eff-words.com or on Twitter @divyastweets.

Pamela Q. Fernandes is a doctor, medical writer, and author. She's a big Hallyu fan and likes to practice the keyboard. Her love of Joseon dramas and science fiction led to the conception of *Joseon Fringe.* Several of her short stories and romance novellas have been published including her Seoul-based romantic suspense *Seoul-Mates* by Indireads Inc. She's also the author of the Christian nonfiction series, Ten Reminders, and currently whips up podcasts for her listeners at The Christian Circle Podcast. She can be found on Twitter @PamelaQFerns and on Facebook or at her blog, An Apple's Mindspew.

Shaoyan Hu is a speculative fiction writer/translator, born in Shanghai and currently living in Singapore. In 2016, he won a gold award for the best new writer and a silver award for the best novella of Chinese Nebula Award. He has translated a number of English novels into Chinese, including A Song of Ice and Fire series (George R.R. Martin), The Southern Reach Trilogy (Jeff VanderMeer), *The City & The City* (China Miéville), and *The Scar* (China Miéville). He is also a blog contributor for the official website of *Amazing Stories Magazine*.

Calvin D. Jim, born in French Canada to a Japanese mother and Chinese father, has spent his life going in several directions at once: writer, editor, IFWit, lawyer, gamer-geek, movie-lover, dad. He is a Prix Aurora Award nominated co-editor of *Shanghai Steam*, the Steampunk-Wuxia anthology. His stories have appeared in *Rigor Amortis*, *Crossed Genre Quarterly* and *Enigma Front*. He has also been a winner and a finalist for the In Places Between: Robyn Herrington Memorial Short Story Contest. Calvin lives in Calgary, Alberta, with his wife, two kids, and an ever-expanding army of meeples.

Minsoo Kang is a fiction writer, historian, and translator who is currently an associate professor of European history at the University of Missouri-St. Louis. He is the author of the short story collection *Of Tales and Enigmas* (Prime Books) and the history book *Sublime Dreams of Living Machines: The Automaton in the European Imagination* (Harvard University Press). He is also the translator of the classic Korean novel *The Story of Hong Gildong*, a Penguin Classic. His short stories have appeared in *Magazine of Fantasy& Science Fiction*, *Azalea*, *Entropy*, *Lady Churchill's Rosebud Wristlet*, and the anthology, *Shanghai Steam*.

Fonda Lee is the award-winning author of young adult science fiction novels *Zeroboxer* (Flux, 2015) and *Exo* (Scholastic, 2017). Fonda is a recovering corporate strategist, a black belt martial artist, and an action movie aficionado. She loves a good eggs Benedict. Born and raised in Calgary, Fonda now lives with her family in Portland, Oregon. You can find more information online at www.fondalee.com and on Twitter @fondajlee.

ABOUT THE CONTRIBUTORS

Gabriela Lee has been published for her poetry and fiction in the Philippines, Singapore, the United States, and Australia. Her first book of prose is titled *Instructions on How to Disappear: Stories* (Visprint Inc., 2016). Her previous works include *Disturbing the Universe: Poems* (NCCA Ubod New Writers Prize, 2006) and *La-on and the Seven Headed Dragon* (Adarna House, 2002). She has received a Master of Arts in Literary Studies from the National University of Singapore (NUS), and currently teaches literature and creative writing at the University of the Philippines. You can find her online at www.sundialgirl.com.

Karin Lowachee was born in South America, grew up in Canada, and worked in the Arctic. Her first novel *Warchild* won the 2001 Warner Aspect First Novel Contest. Both *Warchild* (2002) and her third novel *Cagebird* (2005) were finalists for the Philip K. Dick Award. Cagebird won the Prix Aurora Award for Best Long-Form Work in English and the Spectrum Award in 2006. Her books have been translated into French, Hebrew, and Japanese, and her short stories have appeared in anthologies edited by Nalo Hopkinson, John Joseph Adams, Jonathan Strahan, and Ann VanderMeer.

Rati Mehrotra lives and writes in lovely Toronto. Her short stories have appeared in *AE — The Canadian Science Fiction Review*, *Apex Magazine*, *Urban Fantasy*, *Podcastle*, *Inscription Magazine*, and many more. Her debut novel, *Markswoman*, will be published by Harper Voyager in early 2018. Find out more about her work at ratiwrites.com or follow her on Twitter: @Rati_Mehrotra

E(ugene).C. Myers is the author of the Andre Norton Award-winning *Fair Coin* and *Quantum Coin*, young adult science fiction novels published by Pyr, and *The Silence of Six* and *Against All Silence*, young adult cyber thrillers from Adaptive Books. He was assembled in the U.S. from Korean and German parts and raised by a single mother and a public library in Yonkers, New York. Visit ecmyers.net and follow him on Twitter @ecmyers.

Tony Pi writes fantasy and science fiction, and his short stories have appeared widely. A Torontonian originally from Taiwan, he has a fondness for tales set in ancient China. He has been nominated for several science fiction awards in the past, and was the winner of an Aurora Award for Best English Poem/Song. See his list of works at tonypi.com.

Angela Yuriko Smith has published works that span multiple genres. Her writing career includes writing, editing and publishing for newspapers and writing both non-fiction and fiction. In the past, she has served as a host for JournalJabber online radio talk show and has been interviewed on National Public Radio for her nonfiction work.

Priya Sridhar, a 2016 MBA graduate and published author, has been writing fantasy and science fiction for fifteen years, and counting, as well as drawing a webcomic for five years. She believes that every story is a journey, and that a good tale allows the reader to escape to a new world. She also enjoys reading, biking, movie-watching, and classical music. One of Priya's stories made the Top Ten Amazon Kindle Download list, and Alban Lake published her novella *Carousel*. Priya lives in Miami, Florida, with her family and posts monthly at her blog A Faceless Author.

Amanda Sun is the author of *Heir to the Sky*, a YA Fantasy about floating continents, monster hunters, dragons, and pygmy goats. She also wrote the Paper Gods series, *Ink, Rain*, and *Storm*, set in Japan and published by Harlequin Teen. The Paper Gods were Aurora Award nominees and Junior Library Guild selections, as well as Chapters Indigo Top Teen Picks. Her short fiction has also been published in various anthologies. When not reading or writing, Sun is an avid cosplayer, gamer, and geeky knitter. To get free Paper Gods novellas and other goodies, visit her website at AmandaSunBooks.com.

Naru Dames Sundar writes speculative fiction and poetry. His fiction has appeared in *Lightspeed, Strange Horizons* & *Nature* Magazine. He is a recipient of the 2016 Prix Aurora award for best poem. He lives in Northern California amid redwoods, moss and the occasional turkey. Find him at www.shardofstar.info or on twitter as @naru_sundar.

ABOUT THE CONTRIBUTORS

Jeremy Szal was born in 1995 with a twisted sense of humour and a taste for craft beer and foreign cinema. His science-fiction and fantasy work has appeared in Nature, Abyss & Apex, Lightspeed, Strange Horizons, Tor.com, The Drabblecast, and has been translated into multiple languages. He is the fiction editor for Hugo-winning podcast StarShipSofa where he's worked with authors such as George R. R. Martin, William Gibson, and Joe R. Lansdale. He's also got a rather useless BA in Film Studies and Creative Writing. He's completed multiple novels and is on the hunt for literary representation. He carves out a living in Sydney, Australia. Find him at @jeremyszal or jeremyszal.com.

Regina Kanyu Wang is a science fiction writer from Shanghai, China. Winner of Chinese Nebula Awards for her writing as well as her contribution to the fandom, she is the co-founder of SF AppleCore and council member of World Chinese Science Fiction Association (WCSFA). Her short story, *Back to Myan*, won the SF Comet competition in Feb 2015. Her novella, *Of Cloud and Mist*, won the Silver Award for Best Novella of Chinese Nebula 2016.

Diana Xin holds an MFA from the University of Montana and a BA from Northwestern University. Her work has appeared in *Alaska Quarterly Review*, *Gulf Coast*, *Narrative Magazine*, and elsewhere. She has also received fellowships from the Loft Literary Centre and the Richard Hugo House.

Melissa Yuan-Innes writes fantasy and science fiction, including her novels *Wolf Ice* and *High School Hit List*, to escape from her cool work as an emergency doctor. Her short stories appear in *Year's Best Dark Fantasy & Horror 2017* (Paula Guran, ed.), *Nature*, *Writers of the Future XVI*, *Tesseracts 16*, *Fireside Magazine*, and the Aurora-winning anthology *The Dragon and the Stars*. Since no one can pronounce her name, Melissa also writes mysteries under the pseudonym Melissa Yi, for which she was shortlisted for the Derringer Award. Visit www.melissayuaninnes.com.

Ruhan Zhao was born in Wuhan, China, and earned his PhD in mathematics at University of Joensuu in Finland. He spent about two years in Kyoto University as a JSPS postdoctoral fellow before he came to the United States. Currently, he is a mathematics professor at College at Brockport, SUNY. Ruhan has published a number of stories in *Science Fiction World*, *Science Fiction King*, and other magazines in China, and has served three times as a member in the selecting committee for the Chinese Nebula Award for Science Fiction. *My Left Hand* is his first professional sale in English.

ABOUT THE EDITORS

Lucas K. Law is a Malaysian-born freelance editor and published author who divides his time and heart between Calgary and Qualicum Beach. He has been a jury member for a number of fiction competitions including Nebula, RITA and Golden Heart awards. Lucas co-edited two anthologies, *Strangers Among Us: Tales of the Underdogs and Outcasts* and *The Sum of Us: Tales of the Bonded and Bound*, with Susan Forest. They are currently working on their third anthology, *Shades Within Us: Tales of Global Migration and Fractured Borders*. All three anthologies are from Laksa Media. With Derwin Mak, Lucas co-edited *Where The Stars Rise: Asian Science Fiction and Fantasy* (Laksa Media) When Lucas is not editing, writing, or reading, he is an engineering consultant and business coach, specializing in mergers and acquisition (M&A) activities, asset evaluations, business planning, and corporate development.

Derwin Mak lives in Toronto. His short story *Transubstantiation* won the Aurora Award for Best Short Form Work in English in 2006. He and Eric Choi co-edited *The Dragon and the Stars* (DAW Books, 2010), the first anthology of science fiction and fantasy by overseas Chinese. It won the 2011 Aurora Award for Best Related Work in English. His two novels *The Moon Under Her Feet* and *The Shrine of the Siren Stone* are science fiction that deal with religious themes in Christianity, Shintoism, and Buddhism. Derwin co-edited the Speculative Fiction Issue of *Ricepaper* magazine with JF Garrard in 2014. He and Lucas K. Law co-edited *Where The Stars Rise: Asian Science Fiction and Fantasy* (Laksa Media, 2017). He is currently acquiring documents and photographs about Toronto's Chinese Canadian science fiction writers for the Toronto Public Library's Chinese Canadian Archives, a new collection about the history of Toronto's Chinese community.

COPYRIGHT ACKNOWLEDGEMENTS

LEARN HOW TO MANAGE YOUR STRESS ...
LEARN DAILY MINDFULNESS.

APPENDIX: MENTAL HEALTH RESOURCES & ANTI-DISCRIMINATION RESOURCES

Because of the dynamic nature of the internet, any telephone numbers, web addresses or links provided in this section may have changed since the publication of this book and may no longer be valid.

A listing in the Appendix doesn't mean it is an endorsement from Laksa Media Groups Inc., publisher, editors, authors and/ or those involved in this anthology project. Its listing here is a means to disseminate information to the readers to get additional materials for further investigation or knowledge.

RESPITE IS KEY TO YOUR WELL-BEING.
GIVE YOURSELF A BREAK . . .

How is your Mental Health? Do you think you have one or more of the following recently?

- More Stress than Before
- Grief
- Separation and Divorce
- Feeling Violence
- Suicidal Thoughts
- Self Injury
- Excessive or Unexplained Anxiety
- Obsessive Compulsive
- Paranoia, Phobias or Panics
- Post-Traumatic Stress
- Depression
- Bi-polar
- Postpartum Depression
- Eating Disorders
- Schizophrenia
- Addictions
- Mood Disorders
- Personality Disorders
- Learning Disabilities

MENTAL HEALTH SCREENING TOOLS

More information:
www.mentalhealthamerica.net/mental-health-screening-tools

- The Depression Screen is most appropriate for individuals who are feeling overwhelming sadness.
- The Anxiety Screen will help if you feel that worry and fear affect your day to day life.
- The Bipolar Screen is intended to support individuals who have mood swings—or unusual shifts in mood and energy.
- The PTSD (Post Traumatic Stress Disorder) Screen is best taken by those who are bothered by a traumatic life event.
- The Alcohol or Substance Use Screen will help determine if your use of alcohol or drugs is an area to address.
- The Youth Screen is for young people (age 11-17) who are concerned that their emotions, attention, or behaviours might be signs of a problem.
- The Parent Screen is for parents of young people to determine if their child's emotions, attention, or behaviours might be signs of a problem.
- The Psychosis Screen is for young people (age 12-35) who feel like their brain is playing tricks on them (seeing, hearing or believing things that don't seem real or quite right).
- Worried about Your Child—Symptom Checker: **www.childmind.org/en/health/symptom-checker**

10 Ways to Look after Your Mental Health
(source: www.mentalhealthamerica.net/live-your-life-well)

1. Connect with Others
2. Stay Positive
3. Get Physically Active
4. Help Others
5. Get Enough Sleep
6. Create Joy and Satisfaction
7. Eat Well
8. Take Care of Your Spirit
9. Deal Better With Hard Times
10. Get Professional Help If You Need It

MENTAL HEALTH RESOURCES & INFORMATION

If you or someone you know is struggling with mental illness, please consult a doctor or a healthcare professional in your community.

Below is not a comprehensive information listing, but it is a good start to get more information on mental health/illness.

Emergency Phone Number

If you or someone is in crisis or may be at risk of harming himself/herself or someone else, please call your national Emergency Phone Number immediately.

Canada	911
United States	911
United Kingdom	999 or 112
Ireland	999 or 112
EU	112
Australia	000
New Zealand	111

Canada

- To locate your local Canadian Mental Health Association: **www.cmha.ca**
- Specifically for children and young people (aged 5-20), call Kids Help Phone's 24-hour confidential phone line at **1-800-668-6868** English or French. More information online: **kidshelpphone.ca**
- There are a number of resource materials and list of organizations that you can reach out to on the Bell Let's Talk website: **http://letstalk.bell.ca/en/get-help/**
- Mental Health & Addiction Information A-Z (Centre for Addiction and Mental Health): **www.camh.ca/en/hospital/ health_information/a_z_mental_health_and_addiction_ information/Pages/default.aspx**
- Canadian Coalition for Seniors' Mental Health: **http://ccsmh.ca**
- List of local crisis centres (Canadian Centre for Suicide Prevention): **http://suicideprevention.ca/need-help**

United States

- National Suicide Prevention Hotline: **1-800-273-TALK** or **1-800-273-8255**
- For more mental health information: **www.mentalhealthamerica.net/mental-health-information**

United Kingdom

- The Samaritans (**www.samaritans.org**) offers emotional support 24 hours a day—get in touch with them: **116-123**.
- A to Z of Mental Health: **http://www.mentalhealth.org.uk/a-to-z**
- Free Mental Health Podcasts: **https://www.mentalhealth.org.uk/podcasts-and-videos**

Ireland

- The Samaritans (**www.samaritans.org**) offers emotional

support 24 hours a day—get in touch with them: **116-123**.
- Childline Helpline (**https://www.childline.ie**): Confidential for young people (under 18). Phone: **1800-66-66-66**
- For more mental health information: **www.mentalhealthireland.ie**

Australia

- Helplines, websites and government mental health services for Australia: **mhaustralia.org/need-help**
- Kids Helpline: Confidential and anonymous, telephone and online counselling service specifically for young people aged between 5 and 25. Phone: **1800-55-1800** or visit **www.kidshelp.com.au**
- Lifeline: 24 hour telephone counselling service. Phone: **13-11-14** or visit **www.lifeline.org.au**

New Zealand

- Helplines, websites and government mental health services for New Zealand: **www.mentalhealth.org.nz/get-help/in-crisis/helplines**
- Youthline (for young people under 25): **0800-376-633**. More information online: **http://www.youthline.co.nz**
- Lifeline: **0800-543-354** or **(09) 5222-999** within Auckland
- Suicide Crisis Helpline: **0508-828-865** (0508-TAUTOKO)

International

- Mental Health & Psychosocial Support: International Medical Corps **https://internationalmedicalcorps.org/mentalhealth**
- International Association for Youth Mental Health **http://www.iaymh.org/links.aspx**
- Crisis Helpline for Various Countries: **http://www.yourlifecounts.org/need-help/crisis-lines**
- Emergency Number for Various Countries: **http://www.suicidestop.com/worldwide_emergency_numbers.html**

- Suicide Crisis Helpline for Various Countries:
  https://en.wikipedia.org/wiki/List_of_suicide_crisis_lines
  http://www.suicidestop.com/call_a_hotline.html

ANTI-DISCRIMINATION RESOURCES

Discrimination is an action or a decision that treats a person or a group negatively for reasons such as:
- national or ethnic origin
- colour
- religion
- age
- sex
- sexual orientation
- marital status
- family status
- disability

What is Discrimination? For more information (Canadian Human Rights Commission):
http://www.chrc-ccdp.ca/eng/content/what-discrimination

Canada

- Promoting Relationship & Eliminating Violence Network (Prevnet): Information on bullying, resources on bullying and prevention at **http://www.prevnet.ca**
- List of Crisis Centres in Canada: **http://suicideprevention.ca/need-help**
- Free LifeLine App (Apple & Android):
  http://thelifelinecanada.ca/lifeline-canada-foundation/lifeline-app

United States

- Cyberbullying Research Centre: Facts, Information, Blogs, and Resources at **http://cyberbullying.org/resources**
- Crisis Text Line is a not-for-profit organization providing free crisis intervention via SMS message. The organization's services are available 24 hours a day every day, throughout the US by texting **741741**.

United Kingdom

- Bullying UK Helpline: confidential and free helpline service (Phone: **0808-800-2222**). Information, advices and resources at **http://www.bullying.co.uk**
- Anti-Bullying Alliances: Resources and advices at **http://www.anti-bullyingalliance.org.uk/resources**

Australia

- Bullying. No Way! **https://bullyingnoway.gov.au**

Books:

The Bullying Workbook for Teens: Activities to Help You Deal with Social Aggression and Cyberbullying (by Raychelle Cassada Lohmann and Julia V. Taylor)—Instant Help; Workbook edition —ISBN: 978-1608824502

Violence against Queer People: Race, Class, Gender, and the Persistence of Anti-LGBT Discrimination (by Doug Meyer)—Rutgers University Press—ISBN: 978-0813573151

The Mindfulness Workbook for Addiction: A Guide to Coping with the Grief, Stress and Anger that Trigger Addictive Behaviors (by Rebecca E. Williams and Julie S. Kraft)—New Harbinger Publications; Csm Wkb edition—ISBN: 978-1608823406

PAYING FORWARD, GIVING BACK

READ FOR A CAUSE
WRITE FOR A CAUSE
HELP A CAUSE

MISSION:

Laksa Media Groups Inc. publishes issues-related general audience and literary experimental fiction and narrative non-fiction books. Our mission is to create opportunities to 'pay forward' and 'give back' through our publishing program. Our tag line is Read for a Cause, Write for a Cause, Help a Cause.

A portion of our net revenue from each book project goes to support a charitable organization, project or event. We do not deal with any charity that promotes politics, religions, discrimination, crime, hate, or inequality.

The charitable causes dear to our hearts are literacy, education, public libraries, elder care, mental health, affordable housing, and prevention of abuse and bullying.

LAKSA
MEDIA GROUPS
laksamedia.com

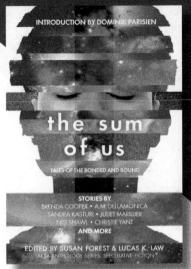

INTRODUCTION BY DOMINIK PARISIEN

the sum of us

TALES OF THE BONDED AND BOUND

STORIES BY
BRENDA COOPER • A.M. DELLAMONICA
SANDRA KASTURI • JULIET MARILLIER
NISI SHAWL • CHRISTIE YANT
AND MORE

EDITED BY SUSAN FOREST & LUCAS K. LAW
LAKSA ANTHOLOGY SERIES: SPECULATIVE FICTION

THE SUM OF US
Tales of the Bonded and Bound
Edited by Susan Forest and Lucas K. Law

If we believe that we are the protagonists of our lives, then caregivers—our pillars—are ghosts, the bit players, the stock characters, the secondary supports, living lives of quiet trust and toil in the shadows. Summoned to us by the profound magic of great emotional, physical, or psychological need, they play their roles and, when our need diminishes . . . The caregivers fade. These are their stories.

Twenty-three science fiction and fantasy authors explore the depth and breadth of caring and of giving. They find insight, joy, devastation, and heroism in grand sweeps and in tiny niches. And, like wasps made of stinging words, there is pain in giving, and in working one's way through to the light. Our lives and relationships are complex. But in the end, there is hope, and there is love.

Benefit: Canadian Mental Health Association

Paperback: 978-0-9939696-9-0
Hardcover: 978-1-988140-03-2
eBook: 978-1-988140-00-1

LMG
LAKSA
MEDIA GROUPS
laksamedia.com

SHADES WITHIN US

Tales of Global Migration and Fractured Borders
Edited by Susan Forest and Lucas K. Law

Enter the complex world of migrations, where the newcomers confront unyielding or fractured borders, both physical and psychological, seeking adventure, triumph, a new life—or fleeing a tainted past or retaining status quo.

Shades Within Us is a speculative fiction anthology exploring the world of physical, emotional, and mental displacements due to migrations.

Benefit:
Mood Disorders Association and Alex Community Food Centre

Paperback: 978-1-988140-05-6
Hardcover: 978-1-988140-08-7
ePub: 978-1-988140-06-3
PDF: 978-1-988140-09-4
Kindle: 978-1-988140-07-0

If you like *Where The Stars Rise* or any one of Laksa anthologies and want to support our project, please write a review of this book on a venue such as Amazon or Goodreads, or recommend this book to your friends and libraries.

Thank you for supporting *Where The Stars Rise* and Kids Help Phone.

Want to know more about our projects?
Sign up for our newsletters at **laksamedia.com**.

IT'S A DELICATE BALANCE BETWEEN MENTAL HEALTH
AND MENTAL ILLNESS …

BE ALERT!

CPSIA information can be obtained
at www.ICGtesting.com
Printed in the USA
LVHW02s1815221017
553340LV00002B/11/P